BAEN BOOKS by TIM AKERS

KNIGHT WATCH
Knight Watch
Valhellions
The Eccentrics

THE SPIRITBINDER SAGA
Wraithbound

THE ECCENTRICS

TIM AKERS

The Eccentrics

A Baen Books Original

Baen Publishing Enterprises
P.O. Box 1403
Riverdale, NY 10471
www.baen.com

ISBN: 978-1-9821-9339-3

Cover art by Todd Lockwood

First printing, May 2024

Distributed by Simon & Schuster
1230 Avenue of the Americas
New York, NY 10020

Library of Congress Cataloging-in-Publication Data

Names: Akers, Tim, 1972- author.
Title: The eccentrics / Tim Akers.
Description: Riverdale, NY : Baen Publishing Enterprises, 2024. | Series:
   Knight Watch ; 3
Identifiers: LCCN 2023055198 (print) | LCCN 2023055199 (ebook) | ISBN
   9781982193393 (trade paperback) | ISBN 9781625799630 (e-book)
Subjects: LCGFT: Science fiction. | Fantasy fiction. | Novels.
Classification: LCC PS3601.K48 E33 2024 (print) | LCC PS3601.K48 (ebook)
   | DDC 813/.6—dc23/eng/20231208
LC record available at https://lccn.loc.gov/2023055198
LC ebook record available at https://lccn.loc.gov/2023055199

Printed in the United States of America

10 9 8 7 6 5 4 3 2 1

DEDICATION

To the boys and girls at Grognard.
Roll for initiative!

CHAPTER ONE

I have never been so happy to smell raw foot cheese. Our mode of transportation, the Naglfr, was a flying Viking longship made entirely from the clipped nails of dead warriors, worthy of Valhalla but also desperately in need of a pedicure and perhaps a change of socks. The sunbaked deck of the Naglfr shimmered with waves of pure, rancid stench. The cold winds cutting through my armor and into my bones did little to alleviate the stink. Not even Sir Gregory d'Haute, despite being drenched in perfume and hair oil, was immune to the cloud of filth wafting off the surface of the grotesque, flying longship. Our noble paladin huddled close to the side of the ship, his face pale and eyes watering. A particularly foul odor wafted off the deck, and Gregory lunged for the gunwale. The very satisfying sound of Greg losing his lunch followed. I leaned back on my plank and closed my eyes, basking in the morning light and the reek of toenails.

Now this was traveling in luxury.

"Why are you smiling, John?" Chesa asked. She huddled opposite me, nose and mouth wrapped in a perfumed stole, eyes watering. "I swear, you're almost enjoying this!"

"Think how much worse it could be," I said. "We could be in the stomach of a whale. Or falling through a rainbow. Or in the backseat of a taxi the morning after Mardi Gras. This isn't so bad."

"The business with the rainbow wasn't terrible," Tembo said demurely. "At least when you are falling out of heaven, the view is quite nice."

"Was it? I didn't notice, seeing as how I was screaming in terror," I answered. "Here we have the view, and only a little bit of smell."

1

"You're the one who complained endlessly about the stink," Chesa pointed out.

"Let's just say I've seen the advantages of having a flying longship to carry you around, even if it kind of smells."

"Kind of smells?" Gregory groused. "My lungs are burning. Like, actually burning." He coughed violently, then spat something black and viscous over the side of the ship. "We should have brought the Saint."

"Matthew had other business. God business," Tembo said. "We'll be fine."

"I get the feeling God business looks a lot like sleeping in," Gregory said.

"Not ours to judge." I stood up and stretched, feeling the wind buffet my face. This wasn't so bad. And it certainly beat the alternative. Which, given the restrictions of our magical powers and the laws concerning horses on the highway, usually meant walking.

For a brief while, the Naglfr had been taken from us by the valkyries, back when they thought we were responsible for the theft of a very important and dangerous sword called the tatertot. Or something like that. Tater . . . thot? Anyway. They gave it back after we uncovered the true thief, who, of course, turned out to be one of their own, thereby saving the world. All part of the job.

"It's good to see you settling into the team, Sir John," Tembo said. The bald mage sat comfortably in the front of the ship, wreathed in a cloud of swirling mist. It was some kind of reverse Stinking Cloud spell that protected him from the worst of the Naglfr's distinct aroma. "There were doubts about you, you know. You seemed awfully attached to the Mundane."

"That's not my fault," I said, poking a finger at him. "You guys need to work on your onboarding process. There has to be a better way to recruit members than trawling through Ren faires waiting for the world to fall apart."

"It was a bit of a shock for us, too," Tembo said. "You and your car were not exactly what we were expecting."

I had gotten onto the Knight Watch team by killing a dragon that popped up in the middle of a Ren faire last year. It wasn't a glorious battle, more a matter of driving my mom's station wagon through the beast's skull, which isn't supposed to work. The creatures of the

Unreal are supposed to be immune to modern weapons like guns, grenades, and the engine blocks of Volvo station wagons. That started a whole chain of events that ended with my friend Eric trying to destroy Knight Watch so he could live out his dream of being a wizard. Typical stuff, if you think about it.

"I'm just happy to be a hero." I leaned against the side of the ship and stretched my back. Actual armor was so much heavier than the Ren faire stuff I was once used to. I was gaining new muscle just by wearing it around, not to mention the bulk gained in practicing with Gregory. Slowly, I was becoming the kind of knight I had dreamed of being. Very slowly.

I looked over at Chesa. She rolled her eyes.

"What?" I asked.

"You're flexing. Or trying to, but there's armor in the way, so it just looks like you're trying to fart without anyone noticing."

"I can take the armor off, if you'd like."

"Whatever," she said, looking away. I smiled. Chesa was the ex-girlfriend I will always regret leaving. It was a special irony that we ended up in Knight Watch together. Not that I really thought we had a chance of getting back together. Chesa lived in a realm of shirtless, oiled elven men with abs like knuckledusters. Difficult to compete with that. Not to mention Gregory d'Haute, our newest recruit, and every straight woman's dream of gallantry, jawline, and butt muscle.

"Better leave the armor on for now, John," Tembo said from the prow. "We're getting close to the anomaly."

"Thank the light," Gregory muttered.

"Right, so, what's the plan?" I asked as the longship began to descend. Whatever powers controlled the vessel, they rarely took into account the comfort of the passengers. I clung to the oar rail and tried to maintain my composure as we dropped out of the sky.

"According to the Anomaly Actuator, there's a major incursion of the Unreal in this stripping center—"

"I believe you mean strip mall," I interrupted. Our job was keeping the mythic world from interfering with reality. It mostly involved rounding up gangs of gnomes who had discovered spreadsheets, or rogue air elementals hiding in the ductwork of abandoned malls. Today, we were dispatched to a strip mall in exurbia. Or, as Tembo liked to say . . .

"Stripping mall, yes." Tembo gathered his robes and peered over the side of the longship. "Esther thinks it could be an accidental intrusion into the Mundane, but there's something else interfering with the signal. Better safe than sorry."

"If she wanted safe, she should have sent the healer," I said. Saint Matthew was already on assignment, along with our rogue, Bethany. I hated when the healer was absent. Bad things always happened. Usually to me.

"Just don't get hurt," Gregory answered, sliding his massive zweihander across his lap and caressing the hilt. "Kill them before they kill you. Simple enough."

"Great advice, Haute. Keep it coming." I gripped the oarlock and tried to lean casually, despite the Naglfr's perilous descent. "If a troll is trying to bite me, do I let it? Or should I avoid that?"

"Depends on the troll," he said with a smirk. My eyebrows shot up.

"Wait, are there sexy trolls?" I asked. "Is that a thing?"

"Gods, John, you're terrible," Chesa said, covering her face with both hands.

"I'm just asking. Is it?" Gregory and Chesa exchanged a look and chuckled. Fortunately, the rapidly approaching ground saved me from further ridicule.

"Here we are," Tembo said.

The Naglfr crunched down in the middle of a parking lot, skidding to a halt next to a light pole. The mage leapt smoothly from the ship, followed by Chesa, graceful in her elven leather and glimmering scale-mail armor. Gregory and I clambered awkwardly down the ladder, our steel boots clanging as we hit the pavement.

The strip mall looked abandoned. Weeds filled the cracked parking lot, and the half dozen businesses stood dark, their lights extinguished and doors shut. This happened sometimes, when the Unreal intruded on the Mundane: things got spooky, driving away the usual crowds. It was reality's way of protecting the fragile illusion of normalcy. It's easier to pretend there aren't dragons when there aren't any witnesses.

"Looks creepy enough," Chesa said. "Might just be abandoned. Where should we start?"

I scanned the store fronts. Vape store, laundromat, vape store, Cash 4 Gold, nail salon . . . there it was. Used bookstore. I pointed.

"Dog-eared Discount Books," I said. "If we don't find a bunch of gnolls in that place, I'll eat my hat."

"Your hat is forge-welded steel, Sir John," Tembo noted. "Quite a meal."

"You know what I mean," I said, taking the helm off my belt and pulling it onto my head. The cheekguards pressed tight against my face. I left the visor up for now, then drew my sword and unslung my shield. The shield was new, a gift given to me by the valkyries for saving Valhalla from certain doom. They called it Svalinn, the shield that protected the earth from the sun's heat. Its frosty steel stung the knuckles of my hand through the iron grip of my gauntlet. I smiled and pointed at the bookstore. "Let's make trouble."

"We are here to prevent trouble—"

"Will everyone please stop analyzing my cool dialogue!" I stomped across the parking lot, approaching the storefront. The team, at least one of them giggling into her hand, fell in behind me.

The front window display of Dog-eared Discount Books depicted an alchemist's lab, complete with bubbling cauldron, tended by a cloak-draped figure wearing a medieval plague mask. Oddly, the figure was surrounded by leprechauns, and the misty depths of the cauldron glimmered with false gold. I paused to consider the situation.

"Are leprechauns part of our jurisdiction?" I asked.

"Only if they find their way into the banking system." Tembo waved his arm at the display, casting a beam of light across the green-clad munchkins. "Those are just dolls. Not what we're here for."

"Okay then." I put my shoulder into the front door, half expecting it to be locked or, worse, barricaded. But the door swung open, ringing a quiet bell. We swept inside.

Silent rows of bookcases stretched the length of the building, obscuring sight lines while filling the air with the heady aroma of moldering pulp and dusty cardboard. A wave of nostalgia hit me, for days spent in libraries and nights tucked into the bookcase nook in my childhood home, filling my head with stories of knights and dragons and ladies fair. I remembered heavy tomes crushing my lap, and the bleary shock of looking up to realize it was night, and dinner had been missed, and homework forgotten, along with all the troubles of my waking life. Reading had been like a dream I never wanted to wake up from. If I hadn't become a knight, I think it would have been a good fate to become a monk, hidden away in some monastery's library, surrounded by histories and the conversations with the dead that came with them.

"Man, this place stinks," Chesa said, snapping me out of my reverie. She shouldered her way past me, casting a distasteful eye over the display tables and stained carpets. "Haunted by a mildew sprite, if you ask me."

"We just got off a boat made of toenails, and you're complaining about musty books?" I asked. "Have you no respect for the written word?"

"I was more of a gamer girl. And every time I showed any kind of interest in books, Eric would drop one of his stories in my lap and stand there until I'd read it."

"Ah, yes. 'Zenith Hammer, Legend of the Inchoate Blade of Ebon Vengeance'. Both a blade, and a hammer, but also inchoate vengeance. How could I forget?" Eric, my friend who once tried to destroy Knight Watch, was also a writer in addition to being a self-made wizard and former villain. Mostly a writer of adjectives, but not even good adjectives like *quickly* or *clearly*. Eric was more of an *effulgently* kind of guy. He had once written a first-person flashback in second-person imperfect. The mind boggles. Eric and his torrent of literature had nearly beaten the joy of words out of me, and I didn't have a lot of other stuff going on in those days to distract me.

"Enough chatter," Gregory said. He drew the wavy blade of his zweihander and took up position at the head of the stacks. "There are monsters to vanquish and mundanity to restore!"

"Hooray. Mundanity." I snapped my visor closed and headed for the aisles.

Stacks of violently read and discarded books rose around us. The deeper into the store we got, the higher those shelves rose, until it felt like we were in a cathedral of abandoned literature. We were deep in the Unreal, as the bookstore transformed around us into a labyrinth of musty tomes. What had once been the information desk was now a babbling fountain with a statue of an owl in the center. Water poured down the intricately carved feathers to splash into a pool at its feet. The bottom of the pool was filled with glittering coins, apparently tossed by hopeful patrons looking for the latest Grisham novel. We paused at the water's edge.

"What are we thinking? Is there some kind of library spirit we need to know about, Tem? A particular kind of faerie that frequents used bookstores?" I asked.

"There are many pathways into the Unreal, but most of them start with books." The mage ran a hand over the dark dome of his forehead, mopping up sweat with the hem of his robes. "We're as likely to meet dragons as halflings, though both are usually content to sit in their respective holes and let the world pass them by. We must be ready for anything." He took another pass at his head, then adjusted the collar of his robes. "Is anyone else . . . hot?"

"Now that you mention it." A trickle of sweat ran across my face, joining a salty stream dripping down my chest. "I figured it was just the armor."

"I'm not wearing a third of what you are, and I'm about to croak," Chesa said. Her tan face glistened majestically in the fading fluorescent lights, beads of sweat quivering on her supple lips. A flush broke out across her ample—

"We must be in the romance section," I said quickly. "Let's keep moving."

"Wait." Gregory threw an arm in front of Chesa, pushing her back. "Do you hear that? Is it . . . ?"

"Chittering," I said. The sound rose from all directions, the rattling chirrup of a thousand pointy mouths. It drew closer. "Positions, everyone!"

We formed a defensive front, Gregory and I slightly in front, Chesa between us with her bow drawn, Tembo at the back, already drawing skeins of swirling light into his staff. Red eyes, low to the ground and glowing with malevolence, appeared in the growing shadows. One pair at first, then a dozen, then hundreds.

"This feels bad," I said.

"Maybe it's just rats." Chesa pulled an arrow to her cheek and sent it into the shadows. The darkness shrieked. Drums joined the chittering chorus. "Or not."

"Goblins," Tembo said. "More than I've ever seen in my life."

"Well, there's about to be fewer of them," Gregory answered with a smile. I really wish that idiot would wear a helm. Not because I cared for his safety. I just got tired of looking at his smug face, and the spray of oiled curls that somehow always looked like he'd just stepped from the fountain of eternal beauty. "Come, friends, let us face them with bravery, that we might win glory and honor for—"

The goblins didn't wait for Gregory's speech. They rushed out of the shadows in a horde, wave after wave of greasy, scaly, hairy bodies, wearing mismatched armor and carrying rusty swords and crooked spears.

Rats would have been better.

CHAPTER TWO

This goblin had been on my head for the better part of two minutes, trying to pry open my visor so it could scoop out my eyeballs and puke in the bloody sockets. I know this because it kept telling me, in very specific detail, its plans for my bloody eye holes. Fortunately for me, and my eyes, the goblin was about as strong as it was smart, and it was very, very not smart.

"Give 'em to us!" it shrieked, banging on my helm with a rusty spoon, its claws scrabbling across my faceplate. I batted at it with my sword, but with each swing it slithered to the other side of my head and clung there, reedy breath hissing in my ear. "Give us your peepers!"

"We've discussed this! I will not be giving you my eyes!"

"Eye holes, then?" The goblin pressed its triangular face against the eye slit of my helm. Its breath smelled like rancid meat and boiled peanuts. "For puking?"

"None of this is up for negotiation!" I shouted, brushing at the foul beast with the edge of my shield. It scrambled out of the way, banging that cursed spoon off the shield's metal rim as it retreated.

"You doing okay there, John?" Chesa called. She stood on top of the owl statue at the center of the fountain that used to be the help desk counter. She had her bow in hand and a pile of dead goblins bobbed in the bloody waters at her feet. "You've got a little something on your forehead. Looks like it's trying to kill you."

"I'm handling it!"

"Are you, though?"

"Yes! Yes I am!" I pointed the tip of my sword at my forehead and jabbed at the goblin, but each time I thrust, the beast cackled and swung to the side. "Will you hold still so I can kill you?"

"You stab you instead?" the goblin suggested.

Finally, I gave up on killing it with my sword, plunging the blade into the mossy carpet and reaching for the goblin with my bare hand. I wrapped my fingers around its scrawny, scaly back. It shrieked in distress and banged away on my gauntlet with its spoon. With some effort I was able to disentangle it from my helm. The scrawny beast wrapped thorn-tipped limbs around my arm, scraping at my wrist through the chain mail and generally making a nuisance of itself. When I tried to throw it to the ground, it clung to my hand like a sticky diaper. I shook it a couple times, but only succeeded in loosening my gauntlet. The goblin dropped its spoon and sunk needle-sharp teeth into the meat of my exposed thumb. I screamed, dropped my shield, and punched the creature with all my might. It flew across the room and landed with a thump on the rows and rows of books lining the wall.

"Good job, John! You're doing great!" Chesa said, before sending an arrow whistling toward the goblin, pinning it to a moldering copy of *Bullfinch's Mythology*. "Got that situation totally in hand."

"You don't have to be a jerk about it, Ches," I said, collecting my weapons before stomping over to the twitching goblin and impaling it on my sword. I held it up to my face. The dead goblin looked like a cross between an oversized rat, an iguana, and a sock puppet that had been dipped in tar and fish scales. I grimaced at the smell wafting off its body. "I don't know what I was expecting a goblin to look like, but this is way worse."

"These are really closer to boggies than goblins, in the traditional sense," Tembo said. I could just see his bald head over a row of bookcases. There was a flash of light that traveled from his hands down the aisle, then the sound of sizzling flesh and tiny, popping lungs. "Though when you burn them they smell more like kobolds, don't they?"

"I wouldn't know," I said, shaking the dead goblin off my sword. Pain shot through my hand. The quarter-sized bite mark on my wrist burned. "Man, I wish Matthew were here. This better not get infected."

"That's just a scratch, Sir John." Gregory rounded the corner from the Mystery section. His armor gleamed in the flickering lights, though his sword was smeared in the blood of his foes. "Maybe you'll get lucky and get a scar out of it. Women like scars."

"Some scars," Chesa clarified. "Honestly, I wouldn't count on it improving your situation, John. It would take a lot of scars to make you attractive."

"You do remember that we used to date, right? That I'm the one who dumped you?"

"Something I try to forget," she said. "Every. Day."

"It is good that Fate has bound the two of you together." Tembo joined us at the information desk, smoke wafting off the tip of his staff. "Otherwise these missions would be downright dull."

"Hmph," Chesa and I said in unison. We glared at each other, to the great amusement of both Tembo and Gregory. "Hmph," we repeated. I turned back to my gear, slinging my shield over my shoulder before digging out a kerchief to clean my sword.

The ground surrounding the fountain was covered in a carpet of dead goblins, and the bookstore was slowly melting back into the Mundane. I didn't like to imagine what the staff would find when they showed up for work today. Rats, or whatever it was these things pretended to be when they were trying to pass in the real world. A pack of feral Chihuahuas, maybe. Either way, it wasn't going to be our problem for much longer.

"Okay, folks. Let's wrap this up." No one had put me in charge, but no one had explicitly forbidden me from being in charge, and I was feeling pretty good today. "Tembo, we're going to need to put all these bodies somewhere, without damaging the store. Gregory, see if you can do something about the smell. Sprinkle around some of that hair oil. And Chesa—"

"Don't," she said.

"Right. I was just going to say, you know, follow your true self. Express your intention. Whatever." I rinsed my sword off in the rapidly shrinking pool. "Good job today, everyone. Really great—"

"Um. Guys?" Chesa was squinting over my shoulder in the direction of the front of the store. "Is everyone else seeing this?"

Sunbeams broke through the cluttered windows that lined the storefront, cutting through the dusty air like a light show. We'd done some damage to the bookstore in our fight with the goblins. Toppled shelves and avalanches of deteriorating paperbacks littered the aisles, while mounds of broken spines (book, not skeletal) rose to the ceiling. Frankly, I didn't remember wrecking the store that badly. But that wasn't what really caught my attention.

On one of those mounds of broken books stood a goblin. Unlike the lot we'd just massacred, this goblin was dressed in a neat vest, complete with tiny pocket watch. It was also wearing a bowler pressed low over its beady little eyes. The goblin slung a clockwork contraption over its shoulder and started messing with the buttons on the side.

"Huh," I said. "That looks like . . . some kind of handgun?"

"Where does a goblin get a pistol?" Chesa asked.

"Hardly matters. Modern technology can't hurt us while we're in mythic mode. That thing's as dangerous as a warm breeze." I strolled toward the goblin. "Hey buddy, why don't you put that thing down before you hurt yourself? We've got—"

There was a loud bang, followed by a heavy thud in my left shoulder. I looked down to see a puckered hole in my armor, quickly filling with blood. The pain followed a moment later. My shield hit the floor with a clang.

The goblin chittered joyfully and started working on the shoulder-mounted pistol, cycling the chamber and working a series of complicated levers with its feet. A thin trail of smoke rose lazily from the barrel. The sharp sound of the discharge rang in my ears.

Chesa ran to my side, putting herself in front of the rapidly reloading goblin. I tried to push her out of the way, but she kept pulling at my armor and yelling. My ears were ringing and the pain in my shoulder hammered through my skull. I realized I was waving my sword around, endangering both Chesa and Tembo, who was trying to get a look at the wound. With a great deal of effort, I sheathed the sword.

"I'm fine!" I yelled. "Do something about the gun!"

The goblin must have heard us, because it chittered loudly, then sighted down the barrel, aiming at me for a second shot. I shoved Chesa to the ground and lurched in front of the goblin, shielding her from the attack. Tembo was weaving a spell in the air, creating a shield of purple light.

Gregory's zweihander went straight through the goblin and his infernal weapon, slicing through meat and bone and steel, to bury the blade three inches deep in moldering paperbacks. The pistol, which looked like a cross between a flintlock, a ray gun, and a portable vacuum cleaner, slid harmlessly down the mountain of books.

"Get off me," Chesa grunted, pushing me aside. I had practically been lying on top of her, and in my armor, that's a lot of weight. I rolled over onto one knee. She got up and dusted herself off, grimacing at the blood that had leaked out of me and onto her elvish battle dress. "That was hardly necessary."

"I was trying to save your life," I said. "You know, from the gun."

"Whatever. I was fine. You're the one who got shot."

"Oh yeah," I said, peering at the wound in my shoulder. I sat down abruptly. "Going to have to do something about that."

Tembo knelt beside me, pulling off the pauldron and making low, comforting noises under his breath. He wasn't a healer, but the big mage knew enough about human physiology to perform basic maintenance. In this case, that meant plugging the hole in my shoulder with a wad of cloth and patting me on the head.

"Barely grazed you," he said. "Your armor will need some maintenance, but otherwise you'll be fine."

"All the blood . . ."

"The human body contains well over a gallon of blood. This is barely"—he glanced over my chest and the spray of crimson decorating Chesa's corset—"eight tablespoons."

"What I want to know is how a goblin got a gun," Gregory said, prodding the overly complicated firearm with his toe. "And why it worked at all? Should have gone off like a wet paper bag, especially with Rast around."

"I just want to be clear: I'm not getting any more sympathy for being shot?" I asked. "No warm embrace, no promises of vengeance sworn against my mortal enemies?"

"Nope," Chesa answered.

"Doesn't seem necessary," Gregory said.

"You are better than that, Sir Rast," Tembo said, patting my head a second time.

"Okay, fine." I worked my way to my feet, flexing my arm back and forth, feeling the wound pull at the bandage. It hurt, but I'd live.

"Then let's bag that gun and drop a Tell on Esther. She should see this. In fact—"

An entire bookcase next to the entrance toppled over with a thunderous crash, spilling its contents in our direction and filling the air with dust. Gregory and I exchanged a meaningful glance, the kind of glance heroes give one another at critical moments. He swung his sword down from his shoulder, taking it in both hands with a look of unabashed zeal. I scooped up my shield, wincing in discomfort as I slung the enarme straps around my arm, then lowered my visor. My flourish was much less dramatic and flashy than Gregory and his two-handed sword. I really needed to come up with something a little more eye-catching. A battle cry, or something. Or I could—

"John! Stop daydreaming and get over there!" Chesa shouted.

"Right, right!" I mumbled, then hurried forward. Gregory formed up next to me, with Chesa covering the rear and Tembo at the center.

As the dust cleared, I saw a figure creeping away from the toppled shelves. I could just make out glowing green eyes the size of teacups, and a hooked nose like a raven. The figure skittered, insect-like, to the next stack over.

"Over there!" I shouted, pointing. Chesa drew and fired, sending an arrow whickering into the shadows. Something yelped, but when we rushed in that direction, there was no sign of a body.

"Musta nicked him," Chesa said. "Flush him out, and I'll skewer the bastard."

"Whatever that was, it was no goblin." I kicked aside a crumbling tower of hardcovers, clearing the way to the front door. "Maybe we pull out and call for assistance?"

"Let's solve this. Now," Gregory said. "Better to report our glory than request aid."

"Better aid than a stretcher," I muttered. But I pressed on toward the shadows in the corner where Chesa's arrow had flown.

"There it is!" Chesa shouted. Her arrow thumped into a figure on the ground, but rather than drawing blood, the wound belched dark smoke. Billowing clouds of thick mist rolled out, quickly wrapping around us and cloaking the light.

"Close ranks! Back to back!" I shouted. Gregory growled, but took up position opposite me, with Chesa and Tembo between us. We whirled around, watching the roiling shadows. The sound of chittering feet and scything jaws echoed from the darkness. I braced for the inevitable attack.

A stroke of lightning flashed near the door, lingering silently before expanding into a circular portal, through which stepped three figures. The first two were a study in contrast. An impeccably dressed woman in riding pants and knee-high boots, with a long silk tie and shiny red vest under a black thigh-length duster, rested both hands on a long-barreled six-shooter cross-slung at her hip. Her right arm was made of brass and steel, the delicate engines of its workings fully exposed, like the inside of a clock. She wore her jet-black hair in a bun, held in place by wicked looking silver pins. She scanned the room, barely sparing a glance for the heavily armed and armored strangers directly in front of her.

Her companion was a large black man who looked like he'd just stepped out of a bar fight, and had gotten the worst of the exchange. He wore dull gray overalls over a bloodstained white shirt, the cuffs rolled up to bulky elbows, and a misshapen cap over his close-cropped hair. He cracked his knuckles, a sharp popping noise that was followed by the unexpected sound of a metallic sigh and the exhalation of steam from his elbows. Both of the new arrivals scanned the room, then parted to let the third figure step through the portal.

"I think that's quite enough drama, my dear doctor." The man's voice was precise, with enunciation that crackled like breaking glass. He was dressed like a shopkeeper in a Wild West flick, except for the bright steel-and-brass contraption strapped to his back. The device had a pair of whirring antennae, like giant egg beaters, spinning dangerously close to the man's head. Sparks of electricity danced between them. The man was thin and slightly awkward looking, with a head too large for his shoulders, and legs that made up too much of his frame. With a flick of his hand, the egg beaters cycled down and the lightning portal sizzled shut.

Immediately, the shadows dispersed. The plague doctor from the window display hobbled out from between the shelves, knobbly hands working the dials on a device that looked like a cross between a gramophone and a flamethrower. Fetid smoke boiled out of the object's mouth, but as we watched it slowly retracted, as though the noxious cloud was a fishing line that could be hauled back inside. The doctor bowed to us briefly, before turning his full attention to the object in his hands.

Knight Watch formed into a skirmish line. I stood with my sword and shield up, left shoulder still throbbing from the gunshot wound as I squared off with the impeccably dressed woman. She looked at me and curled her lip in a sneer.

The man with the complicated backpack stepped forward, clasping his hands at his belt. He swept a calculating gaze over each of us in turn, lingering on Tembo, and then me.

"Well, that took long enough. You lot are bloody hard to find." He brushed imaginary lint off his sleeves, then extended his hand in greeting. "You think it would be easier, what with the oppressive body odor and outlandish costumes. I take it you're members of Knight Watch?" When we didn't answer right away, he took a step forward, thrusting his hand in my face. "My name is Nikola Tesla. I'm in desperate need of your help."

"Uh . . ." I looked at my compatriots. "We're going to need to call someone."

CHAPTER THREE

Esther, summoned by a distant-thought spell courtesy of Tembo, arrived ten minutes later in the middle of a caravan of screeching black SUVs driven by Mundane Actual operatives. The members of Knight Watch stood in a loose semicircle in front of the store. Tesla and his weirdos were still inside. There are procedures in place to deal with all sorts of strangeness in the Unreal. And when encountering strange men claiming to be famous dead inventors, the SOP is to call the boss.

"That was fast," I said as Esther disembarked. "I thought we were supposed to be the magic ones around here."

"You'd be amazed what Gabby can do with five hundred horsepower and an air raid siren," Esther answered. She was wearing her Knight Watch fatigues, a mix of olive drab coveralls and high-tech metal armor, short sword on one hip and 9mm on the other. The MA operatives who followed her were dressed similarly, with an emphasis on traditional firearms and terse commands. MA's job was to keep us safe from mundane interference, be that curious journalists or angry criminals whose Unreal boss just got ganked by a kid in plate armor. Gabrielle Rodriguez was with them. She was technically my minder, personally assigned to watching over my parents. I think my mom believed we were dating, though why she thought a military-grade black woman with a shaved head would be interested in a sap like me was a complete mystery. Maternal optimism is endless. Esther shouldered her way through the Knight Watch team and stared nervously at the storefront. "Your Tell said something about a major anomalous incursion into the Unreal. What are we looking at? Ogres at a CrossFit? Succubi massage parlor?"

"Goblins in top hats," Chesa said. "With guns."

"Uh . . . what?"

"We were clearing out a hive of goblins in that used bookstore over there. Everything was going fine, until one of the goblins crawled out of the rubble in fancy dress with some kind of shoulder-mounted derringer." I tapped the hole in my shoulder. "I thought firearms weren't supposed to be able to pierce the Unreal. I feel pretty darn pierced."

"Well, you're a never-ending conundrum, Rast," Esther said, looking over my shoulder at the bookstore. "Might be a one-shot adventure gone rogue. Any of you break protocols recently? Secretly eating processed foods or shaving with alternating current?"

"Everyone is within protocols, Esther," Tembo said. "I did a scan before we deployed. We're securely medieval."

"Huh. Well, did you at least clear out the goblins?" she asked.

"Yeah, but then these other guys showed up. They seemed to know who we were. Guy inside claims to be Nikola Tesla," I said. "Looks like he might have stolen the dangerous bits off an electric generator and strapped them to his back."

"Oh, gods, no. Not the Society." Esther winced and glanced over my shoulder, like she was dodging a clingy ex. "Did they bring that stupid train?"

"Train? No. But three of them walked through a door made of lightning."

"Yeah, that's Nik, alright. Explains the top hats. Who else is with him? That creepy chick with the mechanical spiders in her hair? Or Reverend Dynamo?"

"I didn't get anyone else's name," I said. "They insulted our lack of hygiene, then asked for our help. We pulled back and dropped you a Tell." Short for psychic telegram, a trick Tembo picked up some time back. Only to be used in emergencies, since it apparently disrupted cell service, along with turning all the water in its path into chicken broth. "So you know this guy?"

"Unfortunately." Esther folded her arms and nodded to the door. "Looks like they're coming out."

The doors to Dog-eared Discount Books opened, and Tesla emerged, flanked by the gunslinger and her bulky friend. The plague doctor scuttled along behind, head twitching back and forth like a curious insect's. Tesla threw his arms wide and smiled.

"Esther MacRae! So glad I've finally found you. The Watch is incredibly difficult to get a hold of. Have you given any thought to installing that telegraph device I proposed?" When he reached us, he embraced our commanding officer. I was too shocked to react. The concept of hugging Esther MacRae was too much to consider. Esther stood stiff as a board as the thin man's arms wrapped around her head. "Ah, you smell like burnt strawberries."

"And you smell like lightning and old tweed." Esther squirmed out of the embrace. "What's your team doing on the wrong side of the border? We were on a routine patrol when things started going all clockwork and top hats in there. Sounds like you've got some explaining to do."

"It's a matter of some delicacy, Esther. We need to employ the services of Knight Watch. It's quite urgent. My entire team is spread out, searching for you, trying to make contact. I have agents in every county fair and knife shop this side of the Gray Havens. The Good Doctor was the first to report a promising encounter." Tesla tipped his head at the plague doctor. "We employed the electro-port immediately."

"Well, pull 'em out. I can't imagine what sort of havoc your team is causing in my world. What are you thinking, risking the Unreal like that? The timelines are isolated. That's the whole point of this operation." The MA operatives were spreading out in a military cordon, encircling our position. The gunslinger flanking Tesla tapped her bulky companion on the shoulder, and two of them shifted slightly, as though they were preparing to fight. I wondered if we were about to get into a tussle with the nineteenth century. Esther seemed oblivious to the escalation. "We shouldn't even be having this conversation. There are protocols in place."

"I am well aware of your precious protocols, Esther. I helped form them," Nik said sharply. At his side, the gunslinger loosened the revolver at her hip. "If it weren't for me, we'd have another Henry Ford incident."

"Oh, you love bringing up Ford and his damned séances!" Esther spat. "Well, how about Zeppelin and his love affair with that djinn, eh? What about that?"

"You know, as much as I enjoy watching the two of you stand in a parking lot yelling at one another, I think we're all due an explanation," I said, cutting between them. "I have no idea what's going on, or why you're both on the verge of violence, but it's obvious that you know each other. So maybe you could clue the rest of us in? You know, before someone else gets shot."

Both Esther and Tesla grimaced at me, before turning their energy back to scowling at one another. I sighed and extended my hand to the lanky electromage.

"I'll start. Hi, I'm John Rast. I'm the tank. This is Chesa, Gregory, and Tembo." My hand hung in the air between us, un-shook. I turned away from Tesla and presented myself to the gun-toting riverboat gambler. "I take it you're the DPS? Or do you do things differently on your team?"

"Very differently," she said, looking me up and down. "We take showers, for a start."

"You know, the hygiene jokes are getting a little old. At least I have some history behind me. Where'd you get your costume? Fall into a vat of glue and roll around the inside of a grandfather clock for a while?"

"Careful, child." The woman bristled. "You're wearing a lot of metal to be insulting a friend of Nikola Tesla."

"I just think we're all being equally weird, here, and there's no reason weird people shouldn't get along," I said. "The real world sucks enough without geeks going for each other's throats all the time."

"At least we're in agreement on that," Tesla said, smiling grimly. He put a hand on the gunslinger's shoulder. "As well as how important the protocols are that isolate us from one another. I hope that makes clear how dire our situation has become."

"Fine. If something has spooked you badly enough to seek us out, it must be serious," Esther said. "I have some forms for everyone to fill out."

Tesla smiled stiffly at Esther. "Good to see you're still as daintily truculent as ever. How is Clarence?"

"Retired. Along with everyone else you knew. Whole new team." Esther relaxed. "What about you? Josiah still driving you insane?"

"Alas, dear Josiah has passed from this world. He's set up shop on Venus, last time I checked. And Cleopatra broke her promise to Anansi. It wasn't pretty. How about—"

"We're not here to reminisce about old names, Nik. In fact, the last time we talked, I think you threatened to drop a bomb on Mundane Actual if I ever screwed with your timeline again. So." Esther cocked her head, looking down her oft-broken nose at Tesla, which was quite a feat considering how much taller he was. "What brings you to the Unreal?"

"It's best we discuss it in private, if possible. There are certain aspects that are, um, sensitive." Tesla cast a disapproving eye over the Knight Watch team. "If possible, we should adjourn to the Silverhawk. Talk about old times."

"Old times are over, Nik," Esther said.

"Not for us, they're not. I think that's the point, isn't it?"

For a long moment, it seemed like Esther would turn him away. Then she let out a long, exasperated sigh. "The *Silverhawk*, then. Safer than bringing the rest of you into Mundane Actual."

"What the hell's a silver hawk?" I asked.

"It is better to show than to tell. Don't the bibliomancers say that?" Tesla swept his arms toward the sky and gestured to a gray smudge, descending from the clouds.

The gray smudge resolved into a flat tube against the low-lying clouds. As it drew closer, I could make out the sleek prow of a vessel, its sides reflecting the sunlight in shades of brass and silver and gold. The overall shape of the vessel was like a humpback whale, down to fins that paddled the air. A series of smokestacks bristled down its dorsal spine, though whatever exhaust they released was invisible at this distance. Glass observation decks hung from sponson terraces above the fins, and a much larger glass dome crowned the top of the ship, about one-third of the way down the length. My first impression was of tremendous size, but as it settled onto the grass next to Naglfr, I realized it wasn't much larger than a really nice yacht, maybe thirty or forty yards in length, though it was easily ten yards tall.

The airship didn't land so much as hover a few feet off the ground, wafting back and forth like a balloon on a string. Several figures watched us from the sponson deck on this side of the vessel (port? Starside? I'm not a water person), but the first sign of movement came from the front of the ship. A hidden port irised open and a set of ornate stairs rolled down, each step articulated by a set of hissing pistons that flexed to keep it level, even as the ship rose and fell slightly in the breeze.

"Oh, cool. You have a zeppelin!" I exclaimed.

"It is *not* a bloody zeppelin!" Tesla said sharply. "Kids these days, calling everything that flies a bloody zeppelin. You'd think the *Hindenburg* was a mild sunburn." He stomped aggressively up the stairs, followed by the rest of his team. Esther shot me a warning look.

"He's sensitive about the nomenclature," she said. "Whatever you do, don't talk about alternating current or lightbulbs."

"Seems like an odd trigger, but okay."

"Gabbie, make sure no one gets near that longship," Esther called over her shoulder. "Maybe deploy some tactical deodorant to mask the smell. We don't want to draw the attention of the EPA."

"Aye, Chief," Gabriella said, turning to bark orders at her troops. The rest of us followed Esther up into the belly of the flying clockwork whale.

CHAPTER FOUR

The interior of the airship looked like a cross between a clock with all the parts on the outside, and the set of a Victorian-era murder mystery, complete with suspicious characters lurking in the shadows. Bloodred carpet lined the corridors, with wood paneling on the walls and stained-glass wall sconces every few yards. But these ornate surroundings were interrupted by steel bulkheads, rows of brass pipes that burrowed through the dark wood paneling, and the steady thrum of engines underfoot. Crew members in pinstripe suits scurried through the halls, all of them wearing top hats and goggles. Curiously, they all had bushy mustaches as well. Even the women.

"It can be a bit cramped, especially when we're all on duty, but I think it's homey enough. Certainly more comfortable than Eiffel's ridiculous meditation chamber." Tesla gestured down one passageway as he led us to a set of wrought iron spiral stairs. "Control room is that way, crew quarters downstairs. But the real gem is up here."

"I still say you should establish something more secure," Esther muttered as we wound our way up the stairs. "What happens if this thing goes down?"

"Counterpoint, Ms. MacRae: What happens if one of your sword-toothed nasties finds its way into your hole in the ground? I imagine a dracolich could do a lot of damage in the halls of Mundane Actual. If we're attacked, we can just fly away. You, on the other hand, must stand and fight."

"That would never happen," Esther said. I bit my tongue, because that's precisely what had happened when my friend Eric tricked his way into Mundane Actual and nearly destroyed our base of operations. "Besides, you can't run forever. You have to fight sometime."

"We're more than capable," the gunslinger said. She trailed behind us, one hand eternally resting on the handle of her complicated revolver. "Anything that finds its way aboard the *Silverhawk* would have a hard time getting back off alive."

"Lady speaks truth," her companion said quietly. His voice was surprisingly gentle, though it carried a whistling mechanical quality that was slightly unnerving. "We're more than capable."

"Here we are!" Tesla said as we reached the top of the stairs. The stairs led to a circular observation deck on the top of the airship, encased in a dome of iron latticework and glass. The deck itself looked like a formal drawing room, with leather chairs and low tables lined with felt. The air smelled like cigar smoke and spilled brandy. "It's more impressive in flight, of course, but you can use your imagination. Adelaide spends a lot of time up here, brooding and writing poetry. Don't you, my dear?"

The gun-toting countess sniffed dismissively. "Poetry. It's what he calls my requisition forms."

"So you have a name!" I said with a smile. "Adelaide, you said?"

"Yes. Not really a countess, obviously, any more than you're a member of the peerage, Sir John. It's part of the illusion." Tesla sat in one of the room's expansive chairs, folding his lanky legs. "We're all pretending to be someone else."

"What about you?" Chesa asked. "Are you the real Nikola Tesla?"

"Ah, so we have a historian. It was much easier when no one knew..." Tesla waved his lanky fingers. "The man you know as Nikola Tesla is long dead. I am the eighth manifestation of the true saint of electricity. Locked in endless conflict with Edison's vile spawn, doomed to a life of obscure genius. It's all quite epic."

"Eighth manifestation? Like a reincarnation?" I asked.

"Close enough. Turns out, being at the forefront of electrical innovation offers plenty of opportunities to die. In fact, by the time Tesla was famous, he was already on his third manifestation."

"Huh. And the rest of you?" I gestured around the room. "The ghosts of famous people?"

"Just common folks, with uncommon imaginations, and the will to make their dreams reality." Tesla nodded to the stairs as the plague doctor scuttled into view. "You've already met The Good Doctor. He can be a touch unsettling. But mostly harmless, and quite a hand in battle. I think some formal introductions are in order. Cassius?"

The enormous black man with the literal brass knuckles emerged from the staircase. Now that I had a better look, I could see that pistons and valves ran the length of his forearms just below the skin, sprouting into exhaust pipes at the elbow and wrist. Similar machinery was also evident in his neck and along his jaw. A bulge between his shoulders huffed quietly, expelling a cloud of steam that hung around his shoulders like a cloak. When he flexed his fingers, puffs of steam wreathed his hands.

"Cassius Jones," he said quietly. "I stay between the boss here and danger."

"Then you and I have a lot in common," I said.

Cassius snorted. "This crew don't look that dangerous. I could take 'em."

"No doubt you could, if the fight were fair. Then again, you're not really a fair fighter, are you?" Tesla asked. He placed a hand on Cassius's arm, pulling him back. "There's no need for that. We're all friends here."

"They don't smell like friends. They smell like street urchins." The speaker followed Cassius up the stairs. He was a smartly dressed man, his clothes almost like a uniform, with too many buttons and a dramatically open vest under a bandolier of shotgun shells. He wore a leather airman's cap, complete with complicated goggles and silk scarf. "They're leaving a funk on the carpet. I'm going to have to fumigate."

"That would be the Naglfr," I said. "Our ship. It's . . . uh . . . made of toenails."

"How horrendous!" the man said. "But it flies, you say? I wonder how. Is there some kind of airfoil in the sails? What's the torsion rating of the human toenail? A fascinating thought. I'd love to take a ride on it sometime."

"Be fair, Captain. We're not all blessed with the cutting-edge science of the nineteenth century." Tesla gestured to the man. "This is Captain Honorius Skyhook. The *Silverhawk* is his bird. He's very protective of her. Will Ida be joining us?"

"She's fighting with a disruption in the condensers. Probably something to do with these vagrants." Skyhook loped across the room, poured a glass of whiskey, then set the glass aside and took the cut-glass bottle to a chair and sat down. "I'm sure she'll be along eventually."

"Ida keeps this bird running," Tesla explained. "Not so good with people, though. If you see a pile of brown hair and engine grease watching you from the ducts, try to not panic too much."

"So you're basically Victorian Knight Watch, huh?" I asked as I settled onto a crushed velvet divan. My armor dimpled the fabric and set the legs groaning. "What's that make you? Steam Patrol? Clock Watch? Seems like that'd get kind of confusing."

The top hat crowd visibly shuddered. Tesla took a moment to calm himself, picking a piece of lint off his lapel before addressing me in a terse, even voice.

"Sir, we are not some kind of joke organization, with a gimmicky name that looks good on a badge. We take our role in the preservation of reality very seriously. It is an honorable tradition stretching back—"

"Yeah, yeah, I get it. But you have a name, right?" Tesla glared at me. "Right?"

"For purposes of the founding charter, we are the Eccentric Society of Curious Adventurers, Extravagant Explorers, and Philosophers of Scientific Renown."

"Now that's a mouthful," I said, leaning back. "I think we're just going to call you the Eccentrics."

Nikola Tesla stared at me, blinking like a man who has just been asked to eat a bug in the service of his country. After a moment's stunned silence, he began to burble.

"That is . . . it's preposterous! It's inappropriate! We are men and women of science! Of adventure! You cannot merely shorten our illustrious Society to something as . . . as . . ."

"I like it," Adelaide said simply. "It has panache."

"Hmm," Cassius rumbled, which I took as approval. Tesla continued opening and closing his mouth at a rapid pace. Skyhook smiled into his drink.

"We . . . we have a charter!" Tesla exclaimed. "A long history of service! A pedigree!"

"You have an awkward name, and a problem with branding," I said. "Listen, I'm sure this is very traumatic. You can hold a vote or something. Have you invented voting yet?" I tapped my chest. "We're still working our way through the divine right of kings and militant Catholicism. Makes it a lot easier to pick what we're having for dinner."

"I vote aye!" Captain Skyhook raised his hand. Cassius nodded, joined by Addie and the others. Only Tesla remained unmoved.

"So it's settled," I said. "The Eccentrics. I'm sure Esther can whip you up a badge and a company song in no time. You must have some instruments around here somewhere. A Victrola or something like that. Right?"

"Let's spare them the company song," Chesa muttered. "I'm still recovering from the psychic damage."

"Do you have your own version of Mundane Actual? Not the place, obviously, but the team?" I jerked my thumb downstairs. "Tactical boys and girls tasked with protecting you from the mundane world?"

"The Pinkertons. You saw a few of them when you boarded," Skyhook said. "They serve as crew, as well as forming landing parties to patrol the Mundane for signs of trouble. They run interference for us with the more everyday elements, the kinds of things it's easy to lose track of while you're fighting giant mechanical spiders and the like. Tax collectors and that sort of thing."

"Ah, yes. Taxes. The scourge that corrupts all timelines," Gregory said.

"I'm beginning to regret inviting you aboard," Tesla said, squirming uncomfortably in his chair. "It's only a matter of time before you start upsetting the Gestalt."

"And what's the Gestalt?" I asked. "Sounds like something to do with indigestion."

"The spirit of the age." Tesla stood up, strolled to the bar that lined the back of the room and poured himself an extremely small glass of brandy. "You would call it the Unreal, or the Mythic. Knight Watch deals with the mythical past, the remnants of the stories our ancestors told, and the legends that lie at the foundation of the mundane world. The Eccentric Society is responsible for the future that was imagined, but never came to pass."

"So, like, science fiction?" I asked.

"The Gernsback Continuum is beyond our grasp. Think Verne, or Shelley. Steam-powered computers, luxurious submarines, airships that run on aether and a firm upper lip. There has been a great resurgence of our Gestalt in the popular imagination lately."

"Oh . . . steampunks." I nodded. "Yeah, okay, this is all starting to make sense now."

"We came to realize the need for a second team shortly after the war," Esther said. "Certain anomalies were occurring that we couldn't detect, not even with the Actuator. Cleo was the first member of the group that eventually became the Eccentrics. We thought she was a spider goddess. Turns out—"

"She was an archeology student who somehow captured the soul of an Egyptian god in a mechanical hairpin," Tesla continued. "Could have gone either way with her. I think she chose the Gestalt because we've invented indoor plumbing and hygiene."

"Are we going to have to sit through another lecture on soap?" I asked.

Tesla ignored me, pressing on. "We found Reverend Dynamo after his church nativity scene drained the power from half of Yonkers, and transformed the other half into clockwork angels. Took the better part of a week getting them back to their boring, suburban forms. Josiah felt terrible, but turned out to be a master of transmutation. Pity what happened to him." He paused for a long moment, frowning into his tiny brandy. "After that, the team filled out pretty handily. Which is fortunate, because the threats to the Gestalt just kept mounting. And there was nothing Esther and her sword-swingers could do about most of them."

"We handled those goblins well enough," Gregory said. "If that was the kind of thing you deal with, I don't see what the big deal is."

"A goblin with a derringer is nothing," Adelaide said. "I'd like to see how you pretty boys stand up to a sixty-foot-tall clockwork automaton with piston jaws and a rotary cannon."

"You think I'm pretty?" I bubbled. "Aw, that's—"

"Not the point, John," Chesa snapped. "These geniuses think mecha-gorillas are dangerous. Sweetcheeks, we've faced off against gods—big, hairy, shirtless gods!"

"There's no need to be explicit," I said. "Their shirtlessness was hardly relevant."

"The interference between timelines can be unmanageable," Esther said "Dragons are one thing. Dragons who have figured out how to operate machine guns are another matter entirely."

"The feeling is mutual," Tesla said, gesturing at Cassius. "How do you think our friend feels when his inner workings start turning into sawdust and cotton?"

I was familiar with this problem, going back to before I joined Knight Watch. Technology seemed to break around me, from cars to televisions, but when my cell phone magically transformed into a deck of Tarot cards, I knew things were getting out of hand.

"Does that happen?" I asked. "All this technology can just ... poof? Fall apart?"

"It's happening right now, you ruddy bastard," Honorius said cheerfully. "Main drive is slowly turning into some kind of pipe organ. Only a matter of time before it comes apart completely. Absolute disaster!" His tone did not match his words. I suspected the brandy.

"Should we ... go?" Chesa asked. Her brows pinched together in concern.

"The point is that our timelines don't mix well," Esther cut in. "Dragons and clockwork knights create a lot of instability in the mundane world. As long as they stay in their own lanes, it's a lot easier for us to manage. Our magic works better, their magic works better ... everyone is happy. After the Society of Eccentrics was established and Nik was given command, we had to separate to keep each timeline intact. Too much intermingling and the results can be quite dangerous." She glared at Tesla from across the room. "Which brings us to the question of why you're looking for us in the first place."

"Cassius and The Good Doctor were on a mission when they ran into some trouble," Tesla said. "I'll let them tell the tale."

Seeing as how The Good Doctor didn't seem like the talkative type, we all turned to Cassius.

"So what happened? You were mucking through the vents of some steampunk monstrosity when you were attacked?"

"Patisserie," Cassius answered.

"You ... ate too many éclairs?" Esther raised her eyebrows. "That hardly seems possible."

"No, it was the patisserie itself. My favorite. The Doc and I always go there whenever we can." Cassius rubbed one giant thumb across his nose, a little embarrassed. "They make the most decadent mille-feuille I've ever tasted. The place closed in the eighties, but"—he gestured to the other Eccentrics—"we still have access to it."

"Because of the Gestalt. So it's not a real place," I said.

"It's as real as your castle, or monastery, or wherever it is you call home," Cassius snarled at me. "Just because they don't serve everything with a side of scurvy and genocide doesn't mean it's not real."

"Whoa, whoa, there's no need to get nasty," Esther said, standing and stepping between us. "Let's just stick to the story. So this bakery, it's part of the Eccentrics' Gestalt?"

"Yeah, I suppose. Anyway. Doc and I, we headed down there as soon as we landed. Except it was gone."

"Precious madeleines," The Good Doctor whispered. "No more."

"Gone? Like, the door was missing? The whole bakery?" I asked.

"The *patisserie* was still there. It just wasn't the same. Older, and the pastries were . . . awful." Cassius glanced in my direction with open contempt. "They were serving pancakes. As though they were . . . dessert!"

"Downright medieval," Esther said thoughtfully.

"Right. So we left, except we were no longer in the Gestalt. The street had turned to mud, and there was a heavy fog." His eyes lost focus, and I thought I saw a shudder go through his shoulders. "That's all I remember. When I came to, I was back in the *Silverhawk*."

"Fog. Some kind of gas attack?" Esther asked. "What was that guy's name? Dr. Pestilence?"

"Pestilence is cooling his heels in an Anachronism Containment Unit, off the coast of the Isle of Mann. Besides, if it was a gas attack, The Good Doctor would have been immune." The masked healer chittered loudly, drawing a nod from Tesla. "It was something supernatural. A spell, he says."

"There are such things in the Unreal." Tembo leaned back on the couch, steepling his fingers together. "Mists that cling to the mind, to befuddle the victim. Swamp hags are especially fond of that sort of trick. Neither of you woke with the taste of mud in your mouth?"

Cassius and The Good Doctor shook their heads. "Hms. Still, could have been something similar."

"He nearly died," Tesla said. "Which takes some doing, as I'm sure you can imagine."

"What got him? Surely not some kind of bread golem?" I asked.

"That's where it gets complicated," Tesla said. "You're not going to like this, Esther."

"I don't like anything about this," she answered. "Stop stalling and get to the details."

The Good Doctor shrugged, then nodded to Cassuis. The big man grimaced, but he unbuttoned his shirt and revealed a scar on his neck. Two puncture wounds.

"Oh, hey, vampire! That's exciting," I said. "I haven't dealt with a vampire before."

"That's because there aren't any more vampires," Tesla said. "They were too dangerous, too predatory. That was one of the first things we did, Knight Watch and the Eccentric Society, working together. We tracked them, found them, hunted them down..."

"And killed every last vampire in the world," Esther said. She was visibly shaken. "Okay, we're in. Whatever you need from us, you've got it."

CHAPTER FIVE

"Wait. You killed all the vampires? All of them?" I nearly fell out of my chair. "That doesn't seem like a very Knight Watch thing to do."

"That's because when you think of vampires, you think of sexually amorous gothic ladies in bustiers and brooding poets in capes," Esther said. "Vampires are monsters. Pure vermin, the likes of which you have never seen. They refused to follow the accords, and they faced the consequences."

"If you say so," I said, uncertainly. "Still sounds pretty extreme to me."

"You weren't there," Tesla said quietly. "You don't know what it was like."

"The point is that if there are vampires hunting the world again, it is very much our business," Esther said. "I'm surprised the Anomaly Actuator didn't pick them up."

"Our theory is that the fiend is somehow hiding in our Gestalt while maintaining a very localized bubble of the Unreal," Tesla said. "We can't get at him without compromising our timeline. Which is why we need your assistance."

"That would mean sending members of Knight Watch into the Gestalt. Which means no magical powers," Esther said.

"I don't like the sound of that." Gregory frowned. "If we top off in our domains before we head out, shouldn't we be at full power?"

"Not exactly." Esther stepped in before Tesla could answer. "Both the Unreal and the Gestalt are mythic realms, but they have their own internally consistent magic systems. In the Unreal we have mages and rogues and priests. In the Gestalt, it's"—she gestured at Adelaide and Cassius—"whatever this is."

33

"Science," Tesla said tersely. "The very cutting edge of steam power and bio-automatic—"

"A different kind of magic," I said. "It doesn't have to make sense, as long as it makes sense to them."

"Right. But they can't cross-pollinate," Tesla said. "Which is why guns don't work on us, at least not while we're in the Unreal. And in the Gestalt, fireballs and holy healing is just snake oil."

"The point is that mixing the timelines screws things up for everyone—members of Knight Watch who are exposed to the Gestalt are compromised, and vice versa." Esther gestured around us. "Just being in here is probably degrading our powers, while also causing all sorts of problems for Skyhook and his crew."

"We're already dealing with significant anachronism buildup in the engines. Ida's been keeping a lid on it for now, but if something breaks in mid-flight, well . . ." Skyhook shrugged. "It's a great airship, but a terrible submarine."

"Well, then how are we going to be of any use to them?" I asked. "How are we supposed to help track down this vampire if we can't use our powers?"

"Isolation," Tembo said. "Strip out of our magical gear, empty our mythic reserves, travel as close to the mundane as possible."

"Any chance Matthew could come with us?" I asked. "No offense, Nik, but I'd rather have our own healer. Your guy creeps me out."

The Good Doctor glared at me. Or, I assume he glared at me. It was impossible to tell what was happening beneath those goggles.

"We'd have to round him up. And Bethany, while we're at it." Esther slapped her knees and stood. "We better get to it. What's your schedule look like, Nik? Do we have time to head back to MA to collect the rest of our team?"

"We're running tight. This all happened two days ago. We've been searching for you ever since," he said. "We really don't have time to fly back to your base."

"Tembo, get a portal going. The rest of you start emptying your reserves."

"I'm still not clear on how we're supposed to be of any use if we don't have our powers," I said. "Without the healing and magic armor, I'm just a witty guy in fancy armor."

"Only kinda witty," Chesa muttered.

I glared at her.

"Don't underestimate the power of a sword in the right hands," Esther said. "You've trained to fight, you're in the best armor money can buy, and that shield was forged in Valhalla. It carries its own magic. You are all more capable than you imagine."

"With Bright Vengeance in my hands, and the lovely Chesa at my side, there is nothing I fear," Sir Gregory announced, certainly louder than the confines of the observation deck required. He stood at stiff attention, clasping the sheathed zweihander to his chest. "Knight Watch will vanquish this evil, you have my word!"

"Gods, you've named your sword?" I rolled my eyes so hard I was staring at yesterday. "Can we all agree that's a bit extra?"

"She has named herself. Revealed to me in a dream, where the spirit of the blade, clad only in finest silk and the glory of her bosom, drew me into the sky and laid me on a bed of clouds. There, we—"

"Okay, I've heard enough," I said, standing suddenly. "Swords and shields and armor are all well and good, but you can't really expect us to go into battle against a vampire with mundane weapons."

"We could open new portals into our domains once we find the anomaly," Tembo said. "We did that during the Florida Event."

"The whole idea is for them to be submerged in Tesla's Gestalt. If you open a portal from Steampunk World, you risk contamination of the domains, and vice versa," Esther said. "Next thing you know, John has clockwork teeth and Chesa's wearing a corset."

"I think she'd look good in a corset," I said. Out loud. Like an idiot.

Chesa stood up, sweeping her battle-skirts aside to reach for her quiver. Somehow, a stray beam of sunlight mingled with her obsidian-black hair, throwing light across the liquid-smooth links of chain, catching the elven runes that declared her queen of the fae. Quick as lightning, she had an arrow nocked and drawn, muscles of her arm bunching as she pulled the fletching back to her cheek. Her eyes, the color of emeralds—if emeralds were fire—sparkled at me. The tip of the arrow hovered three inches from my forehead.

"You think I don't look good in battle armor, John?" she whispered.

"Um . . . no, not . . . that's not what I was . . . I mean . . ."

"She'll do nicely," Countess Adelaide said with a laugh. "And we have to bring her boyfriend along, just for the awkward conversations."

"He is *not* my boyfriend." Chesa held the bow drawn for a long moment, then released the tension, both in the string and my heart.

"We, uh . . . broke up," I said, my face flushed. "It was a mistake."

"You have a history of mistakes," Chesa said angrily before stomping to the sandwich tray and loading up.

"If the lovers have resolved their quarrel, I have an idea," Tembo said. "Amulets. If everyone gives me access, I can create an amulet that will link them to their domains. Invoking the amulet's power won't have the same effect as a full session of rest, but it will provide a slow recharge. Think of it like getting a trickle of water, rather than bathing in the depths of your domain."

"How did you know about the baths?" Gregory asked. "They are sacred, and not to be shared with just any—"

"It's a metaphor, you clod," I said. "That sounds workable. As long as it gives us some power, I'd be willing to try it."

"That might work," Esther said thoughtfully. "You'd need to be more careful about how much power you used, because it's going to take a lot longer to restore yourself. On the plus side, you'd never be cut off from the Unreal completely. Might provide some protection from corruption by the Gestalt."

"No clockwork teeth!" I said. "What do you need from us, Tembo?"

"Onetime passes to your domains, and some privacy. I can deliver the amulets before we leave."

"Do it," Esther said. "The rest of you—"

She was interrupted by a deep thrumming sound that reverberated through the floor. There were several loud bangs, then a vent in the wall blew open, followed by a tidal wave of cold, sludgy water. The wave washed through the observatory, upsetting the tea cart and floating the furniture closest to the shattered vent. I jumped to my feet, only to be swept off them immediately by the flood. I fell onto the soggy couch, my weight sinking into the embroidered cushions and sending another wave through the room. The rest of the team was in a similar predicament. Cassius was trying to rescue the plate of crumpets that had fallen into the drink. Tesla, Esther, and the rest of Knight Watch fought to keep upright, as the flow of water was creating a strong current down the stairs and into the rest of the ship. On the bridge below, the Pinkertons ran around chuffing in alarm.

A large slimy black shape slipped through the open vent and

landed, flopping, in the middle of the observation deck. It looked like a cross between a harbor seal and a shark, with sleek, spotted fur and dextrous fins, but also a mouth full of cruel teeth and the eyes of a murderer. It twisted its head back and forth, chomping loudly at the air and howling.

"What the hell is that?" I shouted, struggling to my feet as I drew my sword.

"Selkie!" Esther yelled back. She pulled her Colt and sent three shots into the beast, but between the water and the stifling interference of the Unreal, the gun just burped loudly before coming apart in her hands. "Do something!"

Fighting to stay upright, I waded through the churning flood of cold water to face off with the selkie. Water continued to pour in from the vent, and despite the growing current down the stairs, the observation deck was becoming deluged. By the time I reached the beast, the water was up to my waist. The water pouring into my steel pants made it difficult to move and harder to think straight.

"I don't know how you got here, but you've got to go," I said, waving my sword to get the selkie's attention. I really wished I had my shield, especially as the beast turned its attention to me. Those jaws creaked open, revealing row after row of wickedly sharp teeth.

"Got your back, Rast!" Gregory splashed past me, swinging his massive zweihander overhead, throwing up a wake that nearly toppled me once again. He smashed the blade into the observation deck's glass dome, shattering several panes and denting the lead frames that held them in place. The selkie snapped at him, catching him by the shoulder and crumpling his armor. He dropped the sword and wheeled away, slapping at the creature with his gauntlet. "Oh crap, never mind!"

I lunged forward, plunging my sword into the blubbery skin of the beast, both hands wrapped around the hilt and my full weight in the thrust. The selkie howled, discarded Gregory like a rag doll, then turned its full attention to me.

"Really wish I had that shield..." I muttered as the selkie reared back, its nightmare eyes glistening with cold hatred.

The deluge of water from the vent sputtered, and a second shape erupted into the room. This figure was much smaller, a thin girl with a mop of brown curls that clung to her shoulders like a shawl. She wore twelve shades of brown, made darker by the water drenching through them, a hodgepodge of leather apron, work belts, workman's pants, and sturdy boots with enough grip to climb walls. Screaming, she hurtled across the room, landing on the selkie's back. With a shout, the girl lifted a giant wrench over her head.

"Back to the taps with you, you slimy bastard!" She dropped the wrench on the selkie's skull with a satisfying crack.

The selkie bucked upward, crashing into the glass dome of the observation deck, shattering glass and sending sharp splinters throughout the room. The girl hung on, swinging her wrench again and again. Something gave way in the selkie's skull, and the beast flopped forward, sending a final wave across the room. The torrent of water from the vent immediately cut out. Water drained down the stairs and through a dozen other gaps in the walls. From belowdecks, I heard the strangely proper swearing of the Pinkertons, and the creaking of metal and steam.

"Are you okay?" I asked. The girl slid off the dead monster, landing in the receding waters with a splash. When I reached out to help her to her feet, she stared daggers at my hand.

"Get your medieval ass off. My. AIRSHIP!" she shouted. "Now!"

"Now, now, we spoke about this," Tesla said. He was tugging his sodden cuffs back into place, as though nothing spectacular had just happened. "These are our guests."

"I don't care if they're the King and Queen of La La Land. They're turning the *Silverhawk* into a waterpark. I've already fished three of these things out of the pipes. If this goes on much longer, we should just install a slide and start charging admission."

"I have complete faith in your ability to handle the situation," Nik said. "What are problems but—"

"Stuff it, Nik! I have complete faith in your ability to wreck my airship!" The girl stormed past us, somehow shouldering each member of Knight Watch aside before stepping awkwardly past Tesla and storming down the waterfall on the stairs. Down below, I could hear her voice booming. "I'm going to need a mop!"

"Yes, well," Tesla said demurely. "And that was Ida. But I think you might understand our problem a bit more clearly, yes?"

"Yeah," I said, kicking the dead selkie. Water and blood sloshed out of its barbed jaws. "I think it's clear as mud."

CHAPTER SIX

Chesa, Gregory, and I stood in the parking lot, shivering in our era-appropriate underwear, wrapped in equally medieval blankets that were about as comfortable as barbed wire, except damp and cold. Our clothes were drying over a campfire that crackled fiercely in the brisk morning breeze that blew across the asphalt. My body was coming up with new parts to go numb, and Chesa's teeth chattered like glassware in an earthquake. Gregory suffered stoically, which somehow only made the whole experience worse. Turns out it takes quite some time for chain mail to dry. Tembo had ported back to MA to set up the magic faucet thingie and to fetch the rest of the team, while Esther argued with Tesla up in the *Silverhawk* over who would cover the dry cleaning.

"This is not a great start to an adventure," Chesa muttered.

"We're setting a baseline for misery," I said. "No matter how bad things get from here on out, we can look back at this and think, well, at least we have dry pants."

"Don't tempt fate, Rast," Gregory said.

"Just saying. It could be worse. It might be kind of cool to explore a new world. Think of it as a side quest. We're rerolling into steampunk world."

"I didn't join Knight Watch to cosplay as a clock," Gregory said stiffly.

"At least we're getting out from under Esther's thumb for a while," I answered.

"Do you think this Tesla guy is any better? Seems pretty crazy," Gregory said.

"Anyone willing to strap a generator onto his back has something wrong with his head," Chesa said. "And the doctor? I don't trust him."

"Have you met *our* guy? I love the Saint, but man, he could outchill a yeti. When I'm bleeding out from a spear to the gut, I'd like the healer to be a little more . . . attentive." I pulled my blanket tighter and shot a glance up at the airship. "Look, we can make the best of this, or we can complain."

"Sorry, John," Gregory said with a smirk. "From here on out we'll leave the complaining to the expert."

"Thanks. Wait, I—"

Gabbie strolled over and dropped six backpacks at our feet. They looked unnecessarily heavy. "What's this?" I asked.

"Esther asked me to prep an Adventurer's Kit for you guys," she said. "And a change of clothes. I don't think the Eccentrics are going to let you on board with your wonderoos hanging out."

"I don't think we'll need kit." I hefted one of the packs and nearly pulled my shoulder out of the socket. "What's in there, bricks? Are we planning on rebuilding Hadrian's Wall by hand or something?"

"That's probably the jerky. We keep a whole stockpile of timeline-appropriate supplies in the trucks, in case we have to mobilize suddenly," she said. "The basic package is a bedroll, fifty feet of rope, a bag of caltrops, three flasks of weapon oil, pitons, hammer, tinderbox, and enough hard rations to give you constipation for a month. You're going to have to eat something while you're in the Gestalt."

"Something like croissants? Éclairs? Caviar?" Chesa asked. "You know—good stuff?"

"All of which will interfere with your mythic abilities. Esther said you're going to be running on fumes, so timeline discipline is paramount." Gabbie slapped the top of the pack. "That means iron rations. Jerky and biscuits, no gravy."

"What am I going to do with pitons?" I asked.

"I'm sure you'll think of something," Gabbie said. "Now get changed. Unless you want to complain to the boss?"

Esther emerged from the *Silverhawk* with a frustrated look on her face and a sheaf of papers tucked under her arm. She marched down the stairs and made straight for the vans. I knew better than to disturb the boss when she was on the warpath like that. Gregory, on the other hand, seemed impervious to Esther's body language.

"My lady!" he said, stepping directly in her path. Esther skidded to a halt and stared daggers at him. "My lady Esther, we are nearly ready to depart. Would you honor us with a favor before—"

"Land of Goshen, Haute, if you don't get out of my way I swear I'm going to fill your helm with sawdust and solder it shut!" When Gregory didn't immediately get out of her way, she thumped him with the sheaf of papers. "I have real work to do: expense reports, bills of lading, dry cleaner estimates, even a bloody schematic of the main deck, so they can replace the furniture! This is going to put us back months on our credit cards."

I never had been clear how Knight Watch financed itself. I suppose I always imagined musty vaults full of dwarven gold and the buried treasures of forgotten civilizations. But given the fact that the real world didn't exactly recognize the myths for what they were, I suppose those vaults would look like a hoarder's basement and stacks of moldering magazines. Now didn't seem like the best time to ask. Instead, I stepped between Esther and Gregory, drawing the boss's attention, just like a good tank.

"Couple questions about the operation," I said. Esther's gaze fell on me like a thunderbolt. I hurried forward before she could set in. "What happens if we get separated from the Eccentrics? I don't want to get stranded in some abandoned amusement park somewhere, with nothing but a longsword and a story about secret dragons. Cops tend to frown at that stuff. If worse comes to worst, will we be able to reenter the Gestalt on our own?"

"No chance. The Gestalt is a freestanding delusion, typically inaccessible to members of Knight Watch. Tesla will get you inside, and you can't leave until you solve whatever the hell is going on with their timeline. If you do drop out, somehow, you'll have to find your way back from the Victorian era."

"Any advice on how we do that?"

"Yeah. Don't. Just don't screw up and you'll be fine," she said. "Aren't you supposed to be getting dressed?"

I took the escape route, dragging Gregory along with me. The provided uniforms were very basic. Gregory and I had gambesons with leather belts, leggings, and boots. For Chesa they had a simple jerkin with underdress and long boots. We didn't have the kit necessary for hanging scabbards, quivers, and daggers.

"What about our gear?" I asked. "Sword and shield, at the very least."

"Tesla's provided us with a containment device for anything that's even vaguely magical. That includes all of your weapons, the shield, Chesa's quiver. You'll need to stow your gear once you're on the *Silverhawk*." Esther nodded to our armor and weapons, still drying by the fire. "The Pinkertons seem reluctant to touch anything, so you'll have to ruck the armor in yourselves."

"I don't love traveling unarmed or armored. Are you sure we can trust this Tesla guy?" I asked.

"I would trust him with your lives," Esther answered, smiling tightly. "For whatever that's worth."

"And you're sure there's no way we can leave Rast behind?" Chesa asked, pulling her jerkin tight and fastening a silver belt around her waist. "Screwing up is kind of his modus operandi."

"If it weren't for him, we'd all be drinking warm beer in Valhalla. And not the good version of Valhalla, with the beefcakes and volleyball. I'm talking about an angry, bitter Valhalla." Esther glanced up at the *Silverhawk*. A couple of the Pinkertons had followed her down and were now loading our still-drying armor, gear, and the backpacks Gabbie had provided into the isolation chest. "Much as it pains me to say, John's shaping up into something of a hero."

"Gosh, boss, that's the nicest thing you've ever said to me. I mean, it's the only nice thing you've ever said, but I'll take it."

"Don't get a big head, Rast. You still need to fit into that helm."

Our conversation was interrupted by the arrival of Tembo in a flash of ochre light. Saint Matthew and Bethany followed him through the glowing portal. Matthew was already wearing the mundane version of his outfit, various shades of white stained with spilled beer and other substances. Even Bethany, typically armed to the teeth, looked fairly innocuous in leggings and silk. They both had backpacks on their shoulders, and weapons in their hands.

"What sort of nonsense have you gotten us into this time, Rast?" Bee asked as she stared up at the *Silverhawk*. "Something about goths wearing brown?"

"Why is everyone blaming me?" I complained. Chesa rolled her eyes, and Gregory shrugged.

"They'll give you the full briefing on the flight," Esther said. "Turn anything magical over to the Pinkertons for stowage. You need to go in as close to mundane as you can manage."

"Sounds great. Just what I signed up for," Bethany said. Tembo cleared his throat to draw our attention.

"I have done what I can with the amulets. It is not a perfect solution, but I think they will suffice." The big mage held out his broad hand, over which were draped six amulets, dangling from silver chains. He presented them to Esther. "They are ready."

"Excellent," she said, setting her sheaf of papers on the damp grass before taking the pendants from Tembo. "Do you think this will work?"

"In principle, yes. In practice"—he shrugged—"I have never tried anything like this before."

"Principle will have to do. Chesa, this is yours. And Gregory. John." She handed me one of the amulets. A small silver shield hung on a length of sturdy silver chain. It was cold to the touch. I confirmed that each pendant matched the wearer's role in Knight Watch: a sword for Sir Gregory, bundled arrows for Chesa. She distributed the rest of the amulets. "Wear it close to your skin."

"What's the principle?" I asked as I looped the chain around my neck and dropped it down the front of my shirt. As it settled over my heart, I felt a blossom of light go through my skin. "Kind of a portable door to the domain?"

"Think of it like a water tap that's been left on a trickle," Tembo said. "It will send a very small amount of energy into your soul. Like a cup under a leaky faucet, you will fill up eventually. But if you empty the cup, it will take quite a while to replenish your power."

"These don't need to be in the isolation chest?" Chesa asked.

"They don't exude magic of any kind until you activate them," Tembo said. "So don't do that in-flight. No telling what might happen to the *Silverhawk*."

"Can we take some of that magic juice? The potion thing?" I asked. One time we had been forced to drink condensed magical energy. It was like replacing your blood with sunlight. Sounds neat, but the sunburn was unbearable.

"That stuff's for emergencies only. Terrible for your teeth." Esther cast a furtive glance toward the *Silverhawk*, then drew us closer. "Shut up for a second and listen close. There's something I have to tell you, and I don't want anyone in the Eccentrics to know about it. It's a little complicated."

"Were you and Tesla secret lovers? Are we going to have to deal with some kind of centuries-old high school drama?" Chesa asked, leaning closer. "Please say yes."

Esther pointedly ignored the question.

"This thing you're looking for, it isn't a vampire. Whatever did that to Cassius, it wasn't a vampire." Esther hesitated.

"Because you killed them all," I filled in. "So it must be something else. A chimera, or perhaps—"

"No, you misunderstand." Esther clenched her jaw, refusing to look at the *Silverhawk*. "We ... didn't actually kill all the vampires."

"What do you mean?" Gregory asked.

"Nik thinks they're all dead, but we ... Okay, I decided. It was an executive decision." She squared her shoulders. "And I'll take the credit and the blame. *I* decided it wasn't right. There were a few troublemakers who had to go, but the rest are safely tucked away into the Unreal. They would never risk detection. Especially by the Eccentrics."

"Oh, so, this is the complicated part, isn't it?" I asked. "You need us to find out what's doing this without letting Tesla know you lied to him."

"And without exposing the vampires that still live in the Gestalt. If it looks like Tesla might have a lead on some of the nightbreed, you'll have to misdirect them." Esther wiped her forehead, leaving a long smudge of ink over her eyebrows. "Look, I know it's a difficult ask, but you have to solve one mystery while maintaining a different mystery."

"Wait, in the Gestalt? You said they were in the Unreal." I looked at the rest of the team. "Am I missing something here?"

"No. Because we did exactly what Nik guessed: created a pocket of the Unreal deep in the Gestalt," Esther said. "They're effectively isolated from both timelines."

"Or, and hear me out, they really are killing people again," I said. "Those scars on Cassius looked pretty convincing to me!"

"Sir John has a compelling point, Lady MacRae," Tembo said, leaning closer. "It sounds to me like we should start our investigation with these hidden vampires."

"No. No chance. I made a promise." Esther stared us down.

I sighed and relented. "Fine. We'll run interference. But how will we know if we're getting too close to the real deal? I've only been to a couple steampunk gatherings, but pale ladies in lace with bloody lips aren't exactly going to stand out."

"I'll give you some contact information," Esther said. "Only use it as a last resort, okay? We really can't afford for the Society to find out about this."

"Deal," I said.

Esther produced a small leather jewelry box from under her stack of papers and handed it to me. It creaked when I opened it. Inside was a silver talisman on a bed of red velvet. The talisman looked like a leering gargoyle's face, complete with serpentine tongue, sharp teeth, and glittering rubies for eyes. There was a silver plaque on the inside of the lid. 1066 Rue de Mort.

"Well," I said. "That's creepy as hell."

"That road only exists in the Unreal," Esther said. "That's how we've kept them safe, right under Nik's nose. No way to get there from the Gestalt unless you're channeling Unreal energy."

"Couldn't just be a vacation, could it?" Chesa mumbled.

"Nothing ever is," I said, snapping the case shut. "Don't worry, boss. We're on the job."

"This is what I'm worried about," Esther said. "Just . . . try not to screw it up too badly, will you?" She nodded at us curtly, then made for the door. "Let's get moving. Tesla's probably wondering what's keeping us so long."

CHAPTER SEVEN

The crew accommodations aboard the *Silverhawk* were extravagant. I know this, not from personal experience, but because I was able to peer into them as Tesla led us through the ship. Crystal chandeliers, expansive davenports, plush Turkish carpets, I even saw what looked like an espresso machine combined with a locomotive engine, chuffing out the delectable aroma of coffee. Bookcases filled every available nook and cranny of the airship, bursting with gold-embossed leather-bound tomes on every subject imaginable. Though cramped, every square foot of the *Silverhawk* was dedicated to the life of the mind and the comfort of the body.

Our rooms, on the other hand, were . . . less than luxurious.

Rather than being led up to the top observation deck, Tesla took us through one of the sponson decks that jutted out from the hull of the *Silverhawk*. The room was a semicircle, dominated by floor-to-ceiling windows along the curved outer wall that offered a grand view of the surrounding landscape. Most of the rest of the room was occupied with padded benches that faced the window, backed up by shelf after shelf of books. I ran a finger along one of the shelves.

"That's an extensive library," I said. "I could spend a lot of time in here."

"More extensive than you know," Tesla said. "There's a built-in printing press, and a babbage engine capable of three thousand words per minute. We can produce any book ever written, as long as it's stored in the babbage's memory valves."

"See, that feels an awful lot like magic." I pulled a book and

47

flipped through it. Something about a clockwork angel and a mathematical church. "Are you sure you guys aren't part of the Unreal?"

"The things you will see in the Gestalt may feel like magic, but I assure you, they are part of something grander. Something forward looking, not stuck in the past, like your Mythos. We are men and women of Science!"

"I hate to break it to you, but airships and steam engines went out of style almost a hundred years ago." I snapped the book shut and put it back on the shelf. "Flipping a switch to make it go, instead of chanting a spell, doesn't mean it's any less fantastical."

"Dear boy, just because you've chosen to live in a musty castle and eat boiled meat doesn't mean you have to be bitter. That was your destiny. And this"—he gestured broadly at the airship—"this is mine. But you make a point. Both timelines are magic when compared to the mundane."

"There's probably someone flying around on a rocket, wondering why we're content with such primitive lives," I said. After a moment's hesitation, I added, "I'll admit, sometimes I miss the internet."

"Unless that's some kind of intergalactic fishing device, I don't want to know about it," Tesla said. "I've seen the whales that trawl the currents south of Mars. Those are treacherous waters, my friend."

"Man of science," Bethany said with a snort. She vaulted over the back of one of the leather chairs, dangling one leg over the arm as she settled back. "Yeah, this'll do."

"Um. This is not your room," Tesla said uncomfortably. "And I believe you're getting the Middle Ages onto my aniline leather."

Bethany grimaced, looking under her leg at the streak of mud and grime on the chair. She rubbed at it with her open palm.

"The Saint and I were doing a necromancer thing. It's probably just graveyard mud." The streak got bigger and thinner, until it covered most of the chair's arm. "Little bit of corpse juice in there, too. Gonna need some holy water to get that out."

"Corpse . . ." Tesla's face purpled. "I will speak to The Good Doctor. Now, if you will please . . ." He gestured desperately toward the hallway. "Vacate the chair and my library. At once!"

"Come, Bethany. We are needed elsewhere," Tembo said patiently. The rogue danced out of the chair, landing with a pirouette.

"Sheesh. If I'd known they were going to be so picky, I'd have worn my fancy leathers," she said as we exited the library.

After twisting through narrow passageways, we ended up in a cargo bay, complete with wide doors in the back and industrial-scale bulkheads all around. And by "our rooms" I really mean one room separated by sheets. The floor was covered in hay, and the smell of must and mildew choked the air. Tesla entered the room with a flourish, like a carnival barker revealing the three-eyed woman. We stood in the doorway, staring.

"Never mind about the fancy leathers," Bethany said under her breath.

"What the hell is this?" I kicked my way through the hay to one of the partitions and pulled it aside. A cot, a ceramic bedpan, and a low table with a jug of water. "Steerage? You're putting us in steerage?"

"Esther said it was important to keep you in your particular milieu," Tesla said. "This is as medieval as we can manage on short notice. The Good Doctor was able to provide a selection of fleas and bedbugs from his personal collection, but—"

"Buddy, do I *look* like a fleas-and-bedbugs kind of girl?" Chesa asked, flipping her leaf-woven hair over her shoulder. "You better get someone to make it all Rivendell up in this place, or you and I are going to have WORDS."

"As much as I admire the professor's work, we simply don't have any other option." Tesla crossed his arms. "You will have free range of the *Silverhawk*, of course, providing you maintain certain . . . standards of hygiene. But if any anachronisms arise we will be forced to confine you to quarters."

"What sort of anachronisms?" Gregory asked, looming forward. "Pirate attacks? Marauding bandits?"

"Gremlins."

We all turned to see where the voice had come from. The doorway was empty, and the twin bay doors in the back of the room were closed tight. I started to whisk away curtains when a wrench fell next to my foot. I looked up.

A shock of brown hair held in place by thick goggles had sprouted from one of the conduit pipes overhead. It grew into a grease-smudged tan face with a button nose and a mouth drawn into a tiny, thin line. A familiar face blinked at me.

"Hello again, Ida," I said.

"Sorry," she said, then produced an arm and reached for the wayward wrench. "I dropped that. Please. Thank you."

Bemused, I fetched the wrench and returned it to the pipe-apparition. She tucked her arm back into the conduit, then slowly started to disappear into the open grate.

"Wait, what was that about gremlins?" I shouted.

"Concentrated protomundanity, to be precise. Not really gremlins. High levels of nonconforming anachronistic probability fields centered on the presence of certain…individuals…." She said all this without looking away from me, though I got the feeling her attention was akin to a deer slowly backing away from an oncoming truck rather than anything romantic. She blinked again, eyes darting to Tesla, then back to me. "Things get weird around you. I mentioned this earlier."

"Yes, well, Skyhook thinks we'll be able to get us into the Gestalt without any issues, as long as we follow the appropriate protocols."

"Skyhook thinks whiskey tastes good. Tastes like burned wood and carpet tacks. Okay, bye now." She disappeared as quickly as she had arrived, though I could make out a steady progression of thumps and muttered curses in the conduits as she retreated.

"She looks less intimidating when she's not braining a selkie with a giant wrench," I said.

"She is quite pleasant, as long as you aren't messing with her ship," Tesla said with a sigh. "But Ida is correct. The last time Knight Watch and the Society crossed paths, we mistakenly inserted a Trickster spirit into the stock market, leading to some irregularities in the investment portfolios of half the world. Can't risk that again." He gestured to a large trunk in the corner of the room. "That's the isolation chamber. If you'd be so kind as to deposit any magical items inside and seal it before we depart."

The isolation chamber looked like a steamer trunk that had been dipped in glue and thrown through the front window of a clock repair shop. Pipes wrapped around the outside of the trunk, liberally sprinkled with gears and pistons and clockwork mechanisms that seemed to serve no purpose other than clicking or hissing or spinning about. Steam leaked from the lid, and when Tesla threw it open, a pillar of noxious mist rolled across the floor, illuminated by a pale green light from the interior of the box.

"There's no way I'm putting my armor in there," Chesa said. "It smells like motor oil and sweaty leather."

"I think that last part is just Rast." Gregory looped his scabbard over his head, then kissed the hilt of his sword and lay it in the trunk, with the same care one might treat the baby Moses and his basket of reeds. "We must be apart, but only for a moment. I shall return to you. Sleep well."

"Okay, creeper," I said, shouldering Gregory aside to lay my shield in the trunk. "I'm sure our toys will be perfectly fine in the magic box."

"Actually, if there's too much interference, I will happily jettison the entire lot like so much ballast," Tesla said. "But I'm sure that won't happen. Feel free to wander the cabins, chat with the rest of the team."

"Jettison? You can't jettison our gear. That shield was forged in Valhalla! And...look, I don't want to get personal, but I think Gregory's in a relationship with that sword."

"I'm sure it won't come to that. Please enjoy the voyage." Tesla clapped his hands together, again reminding me of sharp thunder. "If you need anything, I'm sure someone will be able to help you. Just...not Ida. Be sure to seal up that chest before we take off."

He left us among the hay and bedbugs. Reluctantly, Chesa stowed her bow and the crescent-bladed daggers, while Bethany had a brief, loudly whispered conversation with each of the MANY daggers she set inside. Even Tembo, the well-rounded and generally stable elder statesman of our party, patted his staff as he lay it in the chest. Our armor went on racks that lined one wall. Once everything was secured, we stood in a loose circle in the middle of the room.

"We're sure about the amulets?" Chesa asked. "We don't need to stow those as well?"

"They are magically inert until we turn them on," Tembo said. "Given all the talk of jettisoning and interference, I would rather hang on to them. Just in case."

"I agree," Gregory said. "Even if we lose all our gear, we're not helpless as long as we can access our domains."

"Sounds good to me." Chesa braided her amulet into her hair, letting it dangle down her neck. "I don't like this. I haven't felt this normie since...well, since we joined the Watch."

"I know what you mean. I'm sure everything will be fine, once we sort this anomaly out," I said. The floor rumbled under our feet. "That sounds like takeoff. Better seal up the magic box."

The trunk hissed closed, and a bright light shimmered down the length of the lid while the collection of gears and pistons along the side whirred and hummed. Finally, the whole contraption clenched like a fist.

"So . . . if I kept one knife back, just in case something needed cutting . . ." Bethany said shyly. We all glared at her. "I'm not saying I did! Just, if I did. Is that okay?"

"I suppose we'll find out soon enough," I said. "If the airship crashes, for example."

"It's just a dagger. Not even magical," she said. "Simply sharp."

Tembo sighed dramatically. "I'm sure that's fine, Bethany."

"Great! Oh, dibs on the corner suite!" Bethany disappeared behind the wall of sheets. "Just need to make a couple adjustments . . ."

"Hey, did you guys know they have a bar out here?" Saint Matthew appeared in the doorway. He was carrying a wide mouthed silver goblet, half full of bright green liquid. "And I think maybe we're flying?"

"Matt! Do you have any magic stuff on you?" I asked. "It's all supposed to be in the isolation chest before we take off."

"Nah, man. Magic isn't real." He took a deep drink, then smiled. "Miracles, on the other hand . . ."

"Look. We're not currently crashing. I say we just count ourselves lucky and see how it goes," Gregory said. "Saint, get in here and close the door. We're slumming."

"Cool, man. Like camping. Or homelessness." He strolled across the hay-strewn floor before dropping onto one of the cots and passing out. After an awkward moment, I cleared my throat.

"Alright, well. I'll take the dingy cubicle by the front door. The rest of you can . . ." I turned around to find myself alone in the room. "Sure. Great. Wander off." Under my feet, the engine roared to life, and the whole room tipped to one side. Loose hay and unsecured cots slid across the floor. I clung to the wall as the invisible hand of acceleration pressed against me. "Say what you will about the Naglfr, at least the ride is smooth."

Fortunately, the flight evened out once we were in the air. I returned the cots to their original positions, then left Matthew snoring in his cubby and set out to tour the *Silverhawk*. I found the rest of the team in the library. Gregory and Chesa huddled in the corner over something small and unimportant, laughing loudly into their hands. Tembo sat in one of the chairs with a thick tome in his lap. Bethany had found the liquor cabinet and was working her way through various shades of brown alcohol. None of them seemed interested in conversation, so I doubled back and made my way through the engine decks before emerging in familiar corridors that led to the upper observation deck.

The rest of the crew had sequestered themselves in their cabins for the time being, and I had the deck to myself. The bar had been locked down for takeoff, along with what remained of the sandwiches. I did a lap of the room, examining all the tiny cabinets and profusion of potted plants, before stopping at the grand glass dome. Pressing my face against the glass, I tried to relax and enjoy the scenery. Not that there was much to see. We were still in the clouds.

"Don't lean against that." Adelaide rose from the staircase, startling me. "Ida will have your head."

"Sorry, I just . . ." I leaned away from the window, leaving a John-shaped smear behind. Using the sleeve of my gambeson, I tried to clean it away, but managed only to smear it into a non-John blur. "That's better."

"I heard your cabins leave something to be desired," she said. Instead of her typical fifteen-gun holster vest and tactical dress suit, Adelaide was wearing gray slacks and a button-down shirt, with her hair woven into a ponytail that almost reached her waist. "You can't blame Nik for taking precautions. Last thing we want is this hunk of cogs going down in the middle of Lake Michigan."

"Well, if that happens, I know a guy. A whale, actually." I tried to find something to lean against casually, like cool dudes do, but the only leaning surface was the glass, which I had already thoroughly besmirched with my presence. I settled for crossing my arms and smirking. "So is this place really your domain? Like, you don't have your own enchanted fairy-tale land to get away from it all?"

"Not sure how it works for you guys, but this is home for the Society." Addie strode to the bar, slipped the lock off, and started mixing something complicated. "Ida keeps it running. Tesla finds our targets and manages deployment. The rest of us recharge in the library, or the shuffleboard courts, or in the lab. Depends on our powers. I've got a whole gunsmithy down in steerage. Can I make you something?" she asked, holding up a glass of ice and shaking it.

"Pretty sure cocktails weren't a thing in medieval Europe."

"That's got to be rough. They ever let you out of the museum? Give you a weekend on the riverboat or something?"

"Sounds like a great way to spend my vacation, accidentally summoning voodoo spirits and drinking mai-tais." I gave up my leaning smirk and sat down on one of the couches. "Anyway. The trade-off is worth it. Magic should have a price, right?"

"If you insist. Though from where I'm sitting, your magic is a right pain in the ass." She stowed the bottles and sat across from me, balancing a tall glass of something clear and effervescent on her crossed legs. "What are your powers, anyway? Special sword magic? Cutting torsos in twain? That kind of thing?"

"Magic shield. And apparently I can take a punch pretty well." She raised her brows at me. "Oh, and I'm good at pissing people off."

"That seems like it comes naturally."

"Maybe. So what about you? What's your superpower?"

She answered by flicking her right arm, as though she was tossing an invisible frisbee. A pistol appeared out of her cuff, with a mother-of-pearl handle, twin engraved barrels, and a hammer in the shape of a lion's head. With the drink still balanced on her knee, Addie flipped the little pistol around in her hand, cracking open the breach and removing a few parts. With a twirl of her fingers those parts changed, and in seconds she was reassembling the pistol into something else, something larger. A moment later she held a full-sized revolver in her hands. Spinning the cylinder, Addie took a long pull from her drink, then set the glass aside and stood up. Once again she stripped the weapon, tucking barrels and guide rods into her belt, replacing them with other glistening parts, faster than my eyes could follow. The cylinder stopped spinning, and she slapped it closed, revealing a shotgun with a revolver-style magazine and stacked barrels. She broke the breach across her knee, spun the stock back, swapped out the barrel, and then worked the charging handle. The derringer turned revolver turned shotgun was now a lever-action long rifle, complete with heavy bolt and shiny brass scope. I let out a low whistle.

"Now *that*'s magic," I said.

"Call it what you will, it's damned useful in a fight." With a snap of her wrist, the whole weapon collapsed down to the derringer once again, before disappearing into the lacy sleeve of her shirt. "Long as the Gestalt holds, I never run out of bullets. Or guns."

"It doesn't seem like you'd need our help," I said.

"No," she said, a little stiffly. "It doesn't. Yet here we are."

Acutely aware that she didn't think much of me or my magic shield, I decided to change the direction of the conversation. It's never too early to research the enemy.

"What do you know about the vampire? Or whatever it was that attacked Cassius?"

"I know nothing puts Cass down without a fight, and a hell of a fight at that. Nik was right spooked by that." Addie settled back onto the couch, stretching her legs out, like a cheetah lounging on her prey. "The Good Doctor didn't have much to say about it. You buy this whole vampire genocide thing?"

"If Esther says it, I believe it," I said. "Why? You have reason to doubt?"

"Just the way Tesla talks about it. I've known him to do some shady stuff in the past, but wiping out an entire species of monsters, just because a few of them went feral?" She shook her head slowly. "Seems out of character. Whatever happened, seems like at least one escaped."

"And where there's one, there's bound to be more. Vampires, zombies, car salesmen . . . they spread like spilled milk." I stared out the windows. The clouds were clearing, and the first stars glimmered through the misty veil. "So where are we going, exactly?"

"The Convaclation, where Cassius's special bakery is located. Kind of a permanent steampunk festival in the middle of nowhere. We should get there tomorrow," she said. "Part of the *Silverhawk*'s special trick. We leave at night, and we're always at our destination in the morning, no matter how far it is—Paris, Mumbai, Olympus Mons." Throwing her head back, Addie drained her glass, then crunched a cube of ice in her teeth. "Might as well enjoy the view. We'll be in the thick of it soon enough."

CHAPTER EIGHT

The clouds parted like silk sliced open by a razor blade, and the *Silverhawk* plunged out of the sky. We held onto the railing that ran the length of the library, staring down at the glory of... well, frankly it was just a field outside of Toledo, Ohio. But you'd never know it. This field was filled with a jigsaw puzzle of Victorian buildings, cobblestone streets, and glittering glass domes. An overly complicated train, with stacked pairs of coupling rods driving wheels taller than the entire engine, and a boiler tank of gleaming brass, chuffed around the perimeter of the encampment, while other modes of transportation lurched, loped, and pinwheeled between buildings. Parts of the impromptu city looked like they had been cut out of Paris and dropped out of the sky, while others resembled something out of Jules Verne's worst fever dreams. There were even canals in the loamy midwestern earth, spanned by bridges and plied by various watercraft, some resembling Venetian gondolas, others more like brass spheres, rolling through the water.

The far end of the Convaclation consisted of a standing pool, perforated by gaudy fountains, with an artificial island constructed from stained glass and optimism smack-dab in the middle. The near side of the encampment was dominated by a manicured garden, punctuated by glittering greenhouses and hedgerow paths that twisted like mitochondria through stately orchards. The opposite border contained an airfield, flanked by iron trestle zeppelin docks from which dangled smooth-sided airships, floating like helium balloons in the breeze. The whole field gave the impression of one of those puzzle picture books, with a million tiny details boggling the mind. I stared in wonder.

"That's impressive," I said. "I didn't know steampunks did this kind of thing."

"Looks like a midwestern knockoff Burning Man," Bethany grumbled. "A good Ren faire should have a castle, at the very least."

"This is more than castles and jousting grounds," Tesla said. He, Addie, and Captain Skyhook stood nearby. "The Convaclation is a meeting of the minds. We gather to show off our latest inventions, and wonder at the discoveries of our most intrepid explorers. Here you will find rocks from the surface of Mars, crystal specimens harvested from the heart of the Earth, and everything in between."

"Plus we have indoor plumbing," Addie said. "So, hey, no crapping in a bucket!"

"The elves of Rith'ralin do not crap in buckets," Chesa muttered.

"Not even during the magical bucket-crapping festival?" I asked. She answered with a glare that could cut throats. "Well, point in your favor. I do miss indoor plumbing."

"But the air show is the real star of the Convaclation!" Tesla brushed aside Addie's snark, gesturing grandly to the makeshift city below. "Aviators from across the Gestalt gather to race, to break records, and to generally show off their latest aerodynamics!"

"Well, there's not a lot of that going on at the moment," Matthew said. He seemed unaffected by whatever concoction had knocked him out the night before. Unlike Bethany, who was turning three shades of green as we plunged out of the skies. "You think they called off the races?"

"Look closer," Tesla said, then pointed. "There."

Just then, an aircraft took flight at the edge of the village. The flying machine looked like a pipe organ attached to a pair of diaphanous wings that flapped much too slowly to propel such a large and awkward vehicle. The plane circled the zeppelin tower once before wobbling unsteadily back toward the landing field, where it disappeared behind the tree line. Now that I was looking for them, I could see other airships, none larger than a bus, strung out across the sky like beads on a string. Nik sighed.

"During the Convaclation, the skies should be filled with the most magnificent flying machines you've ever imagined," he said. "Not a simple geargoyle looking for a place to nest. The dream of the Gestalt was born in the sky, nurtured in airships and barnstormers and zeppelins of ingenious design. This is just . . . sad."

"I imagine Jules Verne would have something to say about that," Tembo said. "Are there submarines in your Gestalt? We could have used one of those."

"Of course. But it's so dark down there." Nik shivered. He strolled to the window, shaking his head in disappointment. "I much prefer the skies."

"Well, maybe it will make it easier to find a parking spot," I said. I folded my arms and turned to Nik. "The bakery's down there somewhere?"

"I'm sure Esther's overreacting with this whole vampire thing. But I agree that the bakery would be a good place to start," Nik said, nodding. "I will arrange an escort for you. You should change back into your fancy dress costumes while we finish our descent."

"What about our magic items?" I asked. "Can we unseal the steampunk trunk?"

"Heavens no! Not until we're safely on terra firma. Landing is the dangerous bit, after all." Tesla signaled to a passing Pinkerton agent. "Have the Watch's baggage prepared for disembarkment." The agent nodded her bushy mustache and scurried down the stairs. "Honorius, a gentle landing, if you would. As close to the bakery as you can manage."

"Aye, mate. I'll be glad to get her down, before this lot breaks something serious." Skyhook pushed off the door and clambered back to the cockpit, situated somewhere near the front of the 'ship. I had tried to get a tour last night, but the captain was adamant that we stay away from the complicated bits. *Don't want the gears turning to hamster wheels, do we?*

We gave the rapidly approaching cityscape a final look, then trudged back to our flea-ridden holding sty in the back of the plane. Once inside, Nik closed the door behind us, invoking some kind of electromagnetic seal. A band of light lined the bulkhead before settling down into a barrier of glowing runes.

"That's obviously just a warding spell." I sat down on my cot, wincing as it threatened to collapse. "All this science talk is nothing more than magic with some fake math attached to it."

"Maybe that's just what it looks like to us, because we're in the

Unreal," Chesa said as she disappeared behind her curtain to change.

"Then why doesn't the *Silverhawk* look like a dragon?" I asked.

"Why do you care so much, Rast?" Gregory leaned against the bulkhead. "We're flying on something that doesn't smell like foot cheese. And they have coffee. You should be happy."

"You shouldn't be drinking the coffee, or eating the food, or anything that might interfere with your powers." I pulled my amulet out from under my gambeson and held it in my palm. "We're already limited in our ability to recover. We can't afford to be careless."

"I swear, John, you're such a spoilsport," Gregory said. "Relax. We're on assignment, without Esther poking her head in every time we violate protocols. Let's enjoy it a little, can't we?"

"For once in my life, I'm with the paladin," Bethany said. The floor lurched as Skyhook took us down, causing the green-faced rogue to sit heavily on her cot. "Though maybe less of the bourbon would be wise. You know, because of the protocols."

"Scotch dates back to the fifteenth century," Tembo said. "Don't blame your illness on a violation of the Unreal."

"Right, right, okay. I'm just going to lie still for a moment." Bethany lay back, covering her face with one arm and moaning. "Are we crashing? It feels like we're crashing."

"Do you think they have grilled cheese here?" Chesa asked as she emerged from her cubicle, ready for adventure. "I haven't had a decent grilled cheese in over a year. You'd think elves could manage hot butter and bread, but it's somehow off-limits. Bloody elves."

"I'm curious about this bakery. There could be donuts to go with the coffee." Gregory stretched his arms wide, as though taking in the sights. Then, unsubtly, he lay one arm across Chesa's shoulders. "You should come with me, Chesa. We could take in the sights, have a light breakfast—"

"No one's going on breakfast dates, or grilling cheese, or hitting up the saloon!" I stood up abruptly. "Not unless our investigation leads us there. We're not tourists. We're Knight Watch, and we're here to kill a monster."

"The dreaded Good-Time Monster," Chesa muttered, turning back to her cot. "Typical for you, John. You'd think after all this time you'd learn how to have a little fun."

"Sir John is correct," Tembo said. "We can have fun once this vampire thing is solved. Not before."

Gregory was staring darts at me, probably for upsetting his plans for my ex, but maybe just as a general matter of policy. I didn't care. If anything, pissing off Gregory was half the fun.

"You heard the mage, Greg."

"Yes, yes," Gregory waved his hand dismissively. "We will defeat this creature, as we have defeated every threat we have ever faced. Have faith, Sir John. You are in good company."

"I'll try to keep that in mind when it's chewing through my shield. Speaking of which." I yanked my helm off the stand along the wall. "Guess we better start gearing up."

Bethany grunted, standing just long enough to draw the curtain closed over her cubicle. Gregory and I started changing into our battle gear, which was made all the more difficult by the shifting floor of the descending airship. Matthew and Tembo disappeared to do whatever it was spellcasters did before battle. Crosswords, I assumed.

"Do you think we can trust these guys?" Chesa called over the sheet separating us. "I don't know how I feel about having an escort everywhere we go."

"If we need to shake them, it'll be easy enough. They can't follow us into the Unreal," I said, shrugging into my gambeson. The padded jacket smelled of dried sweat and beer, left over from our battles in Valhalla. "In the meantime, this is their territory. We're just visitors here."

"Whatever," Gregory grunted as he struggled into his chest plate, pulling it tight to his shoulders. "Chesa, could you give me a hand?"

"I'm standing right here," I said, stepping up to clasp his armor in place. Gregory rolled his eyes. "Try to keep the mind-searing charisma in check, Greg? At least until—"

Everything got quiet. It's not the kind of thing that's usually noteworthy, unless you're on an airship that, in the background, is incredibly noisy. In that situation, the sudden lack of loud engines and creaking boilers is very, very noteworthy.

In her cubicle, Bethany let out a long and rattling snore.

"That seems bad," Chesa said, her head poking over the top of the curtain.

"I'm more concerned by the lack of seat belts in here," I said. "These cots were not made for a crash landing."

"Maybe this is intentional? Maybe they glide the last—"

We hit the ground. Hard. Metal squealed and glass shattered, then we bounced, were briefly airborne, before hitting a second time and slewing to the side. By now, we were flat on our backs, sliding through the hay in a jumble of arms and ignominy. The *Silverhawk* shuddered for a long, long time. Then it gave a final shake and came to a stop. I sat up and looked around.

All the hay, the broken cots, the metal tubing used for partitioning off our room, and The Good Doctor's menagerie of bedbugs had slid to the front of the room. I was lying in the remains of my backpack, which somewhere along the way had split open, spilling all fifty-eight pounds of jerky to the floor. A mound of hay next to me groaned, shook itself, and resolved into Gregory d'Haute.

"I'm going to go with a 'no' on the intentional question, Greg."

"I think we crashed," he said.

"Good call. Is everyone else alright?" I stood up, then staggered against the wall. The *Silverhawk* was tilted just far enough to the side to make balance difficult. "Chesa! Matthew? Tembo?"

"I'm fine!" Bethany sat up in the middle of a pile of tarps and loose cots. "No need to ask about me, John. Doing great!"

"That left a great deal to be desired in terms of comfort." Tembo clambered out of the wreckage of his cubicle. "The Bifrost isn't looking so bad now, is it, Sir John?"

"Reminded me of a roller coaster," Matthew said. He was lying in a pile of hay, and didn't seem in a hurry to get up. "Though no one's thrown up yet."

"Gimme a minute," Bethany said quietly, still sitting among the detritus of the crash. "And a bucket."

"Chesa? Are you okay?" When there was no answer, I started to panic. "Ches!"

"No need to yell, Rast. I'm fine." Chesa swung down from the rafters, landing gracefully at the edge of the pile of hay. "You guys look like you've been dragged through the messy end of a pigsty."

"It's going to take forever to get this out of my hair," Gregory said.

"Moan about it later. First thing we need to do is find our way out of here." I kicked my way through the refuse to the door. The glowing amber light that had sealed us in was gone, but when I yanked on the handle, nothing happened. "I think the door's jammed."

"Nonsense. You just need to put some muscle into it." Gregory shouldered me aside, wrapped both meaty fists around the handle, and heaved. The handle pulled out of the door like a rotten branch falling off a tree, roots and all. Wires and a jangling assortment of cogwork dangled from the severed handle. Gregory stared at it, dumbfounded.

"Probably too much muscle," Chesa said.

"Hello!" I shouted through the broken door. "We're stuck in here! A little help?"

"They can't hear you!" Ida shouted. Which wasn't necessary, because she was hanging from the ceiling directly overhead. We all flinched, except for Bee, who proceeded to vomit noisily in the corner. Ida watched her with distaste. "Oh. Sorry. Did I do that?"

"Bourbon did that," Matthew said. He pointed at the frizzy-haired mechanic hanging upside down from some of the conduit. I seriously hoped she hadn't been in the pipes when we landed. "Who is this?"

"Oh, right, you weren't here at the start. Saint Matthew, Bethany, meet Ida. The mechanic, as I understand it."

"Aeromancer," Ida said. "Part-time clockwork goddess. Not just a mechanic."

"Oh, right. Sorry. So, uh . . . what happened to the airship?" I asked. "It felt like we just fell out of the air."

"That's precisely what happened. Good news, though, we were already close to the ground. If this had happened over the ocean, we'd still be falling. Well." She wrestled an arm free of the conduit, then unzipped a pocket in her coverall. A small avalanche of nuts, bolts, washers, a pipe, and three used matchsticks fell to the ground. She fished out a watch and squinted at it. "No. We would have hit by now."

"The door's stuck," Chesa said.

"Yes. That's why I'm here."

"To fix the door?"

"Oh, no. To lead you through the pipes." With a grunt, Ida slid out of view, disappearing into an opening not much larger than my shoulders. A second later, she reappeared, blinking slowly. "Are you coming?"

"Might have wanted to hold off on putting on the armor, eh?" I sighed, then cupped my hands. "After you, Greg. I'll give you a boost."

CHAPTER NINE

We emerged from the labyrinth of pipes and conduits in a room that looked like it was trying to eat us alive. Cogwork teeth gnashed, pistons hammered, and shafts cammed all around us. At the heart of the room was a rumbling boiler, hissing with steam. I dropped to the floor in a jumble, afraid to move on the off chance something might suck me into the machinery and turn me into knight paste. The air carried the distinct smell of boiled chicken and broth.

"What are you doing? You can't bring them in here!" Captain Skyhook appeared in the door of the room. "They'll gum up the whole works!"

"I got lost," Ida mumbled. "And the skinny one was starting to panic."

"I was not panicking," I said. "I was just pointing out the very valid reasons that we were probably all going to die. Perfectly reasonable."

"Just . . . get them out. Put them somewhere safe," Skyhook said, shoving us toward the open door. "Preferably on the ground, far from my precious ship."

"In good time, my dear captain," Nik said, appearing from one of the many doors that lined this hallway. The rest appeared to be the crew quarters, judging by the name placards above each doorway.

"So what happened?" I asked as we stumbled into the hallway. "Why'd we drop out of the sky, and why wouldn't our door open?"

"The seals reversed polarity," Nik said. "I almost had it fixed. And then we ran into . . . other problems."

"What sort of problems?" Chesa, freshly deposited in the hall by a disheveled Skyhook, asked curiously.

"The bloody engines went out. I had to bring us down in the middle of the park, like an amateur." Skyhook closed and sealed the engine room, then shoved past us. "I have to see to the ballast, if you don't mind. Try to get us back in the sky before someone notices and writes an article in that bloody newspaper."

"Oh, right. Newspapers. I guess that's still a thing in your world," I mused. "Have they invented the comics page, yet? I miss comics."

"Will you focus, Rast?" Gregory snapped. His marvelous hair had been mussed by our passage through the bowels of the *Silverhawk*, and his face was flushed with sweat. His mirror-bright armor was smeared with oil and scuff marks from our trip through the tubes. "Mr. Tesla, we need to start our investigation as soon as possible. How far is it to the patisserie where Cassius was attacked?"

"Not as close as I'd like. You'll have to walk from here. It's longer than I'd like to have you exposed to the Gestalt, but we're going to be here for a while." Nik flinched as a loud thud rang through the *Silverhawk*'s steel hull, followed by a string of profanity. "I'll get Addie and The Good Doctor to lead the way."

"I think we'd be better off on our own," I said.

"Just give us a map," Bethany said. "We're good with maps."

"I'm afraid I can't allow that. At the very least, there are threats in the Gestalt that you would be ill-equipped to face, and I can't go back to Esther and ask for replacements because I lost you to the Dire Automata, or the Metropolython, or Lord Scatter and his Seven Sinisters. No, that wouldn't do at all."

"Did you hear that, Rast?" Gregory asked. "They have their own monsters here. A whole new bestiary for you to be scared of."

"Stuff it, Greg. Get stuffed. Go stuff yourself."

"Manners, manners," he said with a smile.

With little ceremony and a great deal of haste, Tesla escorted us through the crew quarters and to the upper decks. I caught glimpses of the rest of the ship as we went. For an airship, the *Silverhawk* was crowded with strange little cubbies and weird rooms that hosted everything from gardens to libraries to an aquarium made up mostly of glass tubes and pressurized tanks. It looked like a scaled-down version of some robber baron's wet dream of a mansion.

Just before Tesla kicked us off the airship, Addie and The Good Doctor appeared, armed for bear. Or whatever the Gestalt equivalent might be.

"You're looking properly medieval," Addie said.

"We try to put on a good show," I answered.

She rolled her eyes. "I didn't mean it as a compliment." She banged open the hatch, and gave the folding stairs a solid kick. The stairs unfolded like a vine, snaking its way to the ground. "After you."

"Well, that was unnecessarily dramatic," I said, squinting into the sudden light. A crowd of park-goers had gathered to watch us, dressed in their best La Grande Jatte finery. I had to admit, I felt a little out of place in cuirass and chausieres, even with my silk tabard. Of all of us, only Chesa didn't look out of place, like some Arcadian dream of the warrior princess.

"We warned you about the kind of interference that can happen when we mix timelines," Addie said as we ambled to the bottom of the stairs. She waved to the gathering crowd. "If you end up breaking the *Silverhawk*, you're probably better off walking home. Ida might 'mistakenly' kick you out the door midair."

"If we break it badly enough, there won't be any midair to drop us out of," I said.

"Well, we're down and in one piece, so I suppose that's something." Gregory planted his hands on his hips and smiled brightly at a pair of young women in hoop skirts and corsets, who appeared to be taking pictures with an enormous camera. Tembo frowned at them, and the women scattered, much to Gregory's displeasure.

"Tesla said our gear would be out in a minute," the big mage said.

"Ah, yes. He mentioned that." Addie squinted up at the *Silverhawk*. "Here we go."

A port opened in the side of the airship, followed shortly by what looked like a blunt barreled cannon. Which is exactly what it was. With a loud thump and a pillar of smoke, the chest containing our gear was violently expelled from the *Silverhawk*. It flew in a high arc over the park, to land in the middle of a fountain.

"Bright Vengeance!" Gregory yelped as he ran to the fountain. "No!"

"Don't worry. The pneumatic expulsorator is quite gentle. For a cannon," Addie said, as she strolled after us. "I'm sure your gear is perfectly fine."

She was mostly right. The isolation trunk had taken the brunt of the impact, along with the fountain and what remained of a decorative topiary that surrounded the pool. By the time we got there, Gregory had already dragged the trunk to dry land and thrown it open. My shield and Chesa's armor and bow lay in a pile on the ground, along with a scattering of Bee's knife collection. Tembo's staff stuck out of a nearby shrub. Our rogue hopped around the garden, scooping up daggers and disappearing them, while Saint Matthew fished a handful of coins out of his pocket and tossed them, one at a time, into the fountain as he hummed to himself. Finally extracting his precious blade, Gregory lifted it to the sky.

"Never again shall I let you out of my sight, until death itself closes my eyes! Even then, my firm grip shall remain on your supple steel, lest time and memory cleave us—"

"Okay, okay, we get it." I extracted my shield from the muddy ground and shook it off. Chesa's arrows lay scattered about like a game of pickup sticks, and her bow dangled from a nearby bush. "This is a bloody disaster."

"What was that you said, Rast? A baseline for misery?" Chesa plucked her arrows one at a time from the mud, grimacing as she rinsed them off in the broken fountain. "I think we're making downward progress."

"I would recommend opening the tap in your amulets, so we have time to accumulate a modicum of power before we reach our destination," Tembo said. He gestured with his hand, and a flower of amber light blossomed from his chest. With a deep sigh, he smiled to himself. "Yes. That is much better."

He activated each of our amulets in turn, walking us through the hand gestures and mental commands necessary. I hadn't realized how drably mundane I was getting until a trickle of mythic power washed through my flesh. I breathed deeply of its energy.

"Where's this stupid bakery supposed to be?" I asked. The Good Doctor chirruped and pointed the way. "Then let's get going, before something else happens."

The roads were crowded with vehicles of all shapes, sizes, and improbabilities. There were traditional carriages with ornate filigree and stained-glass windows, drawn by clockwork horses that huffed steam as they clattered down the cobblestone streets. The carriages looked like giant Fabergé eggs, and most had moving parts on the outside that seemed to serve no particular purpose. Right beside them were smaller carts that could have been cars, if Rube Goldberg had designed them. A variety of engines sputtered and hissed and clacked, their drives powered by boilers or complicated windmills; one car even looked like a motorized pipe organ, controlled by the frenetic playing of its driver.

Interspersed throughout this stream of cacophonous vehicles were smaller, single-passenger conveyances that ran the gamut from steampowered mono-wheels to bicycles tall enough to give a weather forecast, and wheelbarrow-sized carts propelled by a jet of hissing steam. The crowd was universally dissimilar, each vehicle the invention of its pilot, as unique and perilous as could be imagined.

"I feel like we're being followed," Chesa said, glancing behind us.

I turned to look. Sure enough, there was a small crowd of picnickers and bicyclists trailing in our wake.

"You're a curiosity," Addie said. "The five of you stick out like broken teeth."

"Well, that's rude," I said. "The Good Doctor looks like a bloody crow, and no one seems to care about him!"

"They know the Doctor, and the Society in general. We saved them from the Rat Kingdom, and made quite a splash when the Dire Automata wrestled itself free from the distributed memechine and went on a rampage through the streets." Addie nodded to a group of gentlemen in top hats. They quickly turned away, talking among themselves in quiet voices. "If you were taking this walk alone, there's no telling what might happen."

"I'm not worried about guys in fancy hats," Chesa said.

"You've just described wizards," Bethany pointed out.

"There's a great deal more to it than hats," Tembo harrumphed. "I don't even wear a hat. They're wildly overblown in the recruiting literature."

"In this case, she's right. Those three are members of the Brotherhood of the Prescient Light. As close to wizards as the Gestalt will allow," Addie said. "We keep an eye on them, but they mostly do card tricks and chat with horny ghosts."

"Still describing wizards," I said. Addie laughed at that, and I felt a warm glow in my chest. "So what kind of thing should we worry about? You know, if we lose our escort at some point."

"You're not going to lose me, nor I you. The Gestalt is populated with all manner of monsters, from failed science experiments to roguish air pirates. And thanks to the Victorians' fascination with myth, we have a persistent problem with the Unseelie Court. They have to follow certain protocols when they visit, but that doesn't make them any less dangerous." Addie resettled her revolver in its holster, probably to emphasize how quickly she could draw it. "Between Verne, Lovecraft, and Miéville, the Gestalt has plenty of horrors haunting it."

"And here I thought it was all tea parties and airships," Chesa said.

"I'll take the lumbering steamwork zombies over tea parties any day of the week," Addie said. "Those social clubs are downright brutal. Last Christmas, the Holly Heralds got into a row with the Divine Knitting Circle over bake-sale rights. Roaming gangs of armed carolers invoking the forgotten names of angels fighting in the streets with surprisingly well-armed spider-women. We had to break it up, eventually. Plus all the cookies got burned."

"The true victims," The Good Doctor whispered. "Sweet macaroons, black as coal."

"He was quite upset," Addie said. "Point is, there's plenty of dangerous stuff out there. So don't wander away, and if you get lost, try to find a landmark you recognize and stick close to it. We'll come find you. And speaking of macaroons..." She sniffed the air, then smiled. "We're nearly there."

CHAPTER TEN

The Gestalt was strange to me. The parts of the Unreal I usually visited were on the brink of chaos most times, in large part because the mythic citizens of that realm were straining against the constraints of mundane reality. But if you took away the clockwork engines and predominant use of bowlers as a fashion accessory, these folks wouldn't be much out of place walking down the street. Fancier clothes, with clockwork sticking out all over the place, but otherwise normal-looking folks.

There were obvious exceptions. The Good Doctor would have drawn attention wherever he went, and the crowd that trailed behind us included a deep-sea-diving suit that looked like it was full of water and fish, at least one impeccably dressed man-sized raven in a top hat, and three clockwork figures exchanging gears like children trading baseball cards.

"This is all so strange," I said. "An entire town, living in an alternate timeline. I don't think the Unreal has anything like this. Mostly it's just covens of rat-witches running laundromats, or the court of a fallen king setting up shop in the condominium's HOA."

"There are ways in which the Gestalt is superior to the Unreal," Addie said. "We are closer to the real world than you, in ways that make it easier to pass undetected among the Mundanes. After all, bowlers and corsets aren't *that* far out of fashion."

"It's the goggles and gearwork that sticks out," I said. "Though not as much as a zweihander. I see your point. I imagine the food's better."

"Much better. As our visit to the bakery will doubtlessly prove. Assuming it's back to normal. It's not all cheese and bread."

71

"Hey, I *like* cheese and bread," I said.

"That's because you haven't supped at the court of the elven queen, and tasted the finest lembas, or sipped the delicate wine of the elden grape," Chesa said. "It's all very polite and proper."

"Still doesn't hold a candle to French cooking," Addie said. "You should see what they can do with butter."

"Precious madeleines," The Good Doctor chirped mournfully.

"Yes, we're making him hungry," Addie said. "Enough chatting. We're almost there. Prepare yourselves."

To the curious fascination of those Gestalt citizens strolling past us, I drew my sword and settled my shield firmly in place. I'd left my helmet back on the *Silverhawk*. Gregory never wore a helmet, due to his lustrous hair and his tendency to wink and smile and generally make a fool of himself. I thought maybe I'd try winking and smiling to see if it did me any good. But when he unsheathed that massive zweihander, the interested pedestrians got a lot less interested and a lot more concerned, gathering in their little clockwork children and hurrying down the street. As Greg and I spread out, the rest of the team fell in behind us.

It wasn't long before we had the street to ourselves. It might have been because our pointy swords and general violent mien scared off the casual observer, but it also felt like our surroundings were changing in some fundamental way. It was the middle of the day, but a heavy murk rose out of the sewers, blotting out the sun. The buildings around us grew dark, and the gas streetlamps that stood at every corner flickered to life.

"Should that be happening?" I asked, pointing to the hissing flames of the lamps.

"Not on its own," Addie said. For the first time since we'd met, the gun princess looked nervous. "Someone's determined to set the mood."

The Good Doctor chittered unhappily.

Adelaide nodded. "He's right. This is what it felt like when we tried to enter the patisserie following the attack on Cassius. Whatever is going on, it's spreading," she said. "Usually the aetheric dampeners take care of this. They must be failing. Tesla will want to know about that."

"Arthur dampening?" I asked. "Sounds a little kinky."

"Aetheric dampener," Adelaide said firmly. "They help stabilize the

Gestalt. Part of our job is maintaining and protecting the network of dampeners. There are three of them in the Convaclation. Once we're done here, we'll need to swing by the closest one and check it out."

"This feels very much like the Unreal," Tembo said.

"Yeah, unless the Convaclation thing has a themed bubonic plague district," Bethany said. "I'm going to scout ahead. Try not to draw too much attention."

"Bee, wait, we should—" But she had already shadowstepped forward, disappearing in a swirl of inky black smoke. "...stick together," I finished.

"So is this a rescue operation now?" Addie asked.

"She's pretty good about taking care of herself," I said. "Usually."

Around the corner and another block, and we came to the haunted patisserie. It was situated right at the corner of two streets, its facade all windows and wood paneling, with the words Boulangerie and Patisserie painted in golden script across the picture windows. Display cases filled the windows, and a pair of wide, brass-faced doors stood at the center of the storefront. Like most things in this version of Paris, it probably wouldn't have been out of place in the modern world. There were no lights on inside and, like the rest of this part of the street, appeared to be abandoned.

"You're sure this is the place? Doesn't look particularly dangerous," Gregory said.

"Madeleines," The Good Doctor whispered.

"Alright, then. I'll go in first, Gregory right behind. Chesa, Tembo, you and Addie hang near the door for support, and to keep Doc from eating whatever we find inside. And the Saint..." I looked around. "Where's the Saint?"

There was no sign of Saint Matthew. I let out a sigh.

"Bloody healers. Just... the rest of you try to not wander off. Are we ready?"

"Let's do this, Rast," Gregory said enthusiastically.

"On you, Sir John," Tembo answered.

"I'm anxious to see what you guys do," Addie said. "Please proceed."

I went to flip my visor down, remembered I didn't have my helm with me, and turned the motion into an awkward nose scratch. "Let's go!"

As we approached the building, I noticed something unusual. The display cases, which I assumed were usually filled with various tarts and cakes and such, looked to be filled with stacks of pancakes. An impractical number of pancakes. They leaned precariously off cake pedestals, lay in soggy columns across lace doilies, and drooped out of bread trays. Some of the pancakes were pretending to be other things: rolled into the shape of éclairs, or cut and stacked like mille-feuille. The deception was futile, and strange.

Just before we reached the doors, I noticed a furtive shape scurrying into the shadows. I pointed, but it was already gone.

"There's someone inside," I said.

"Your rogue friend?" Addie asked.

"Maybe. Don't take a shot until we've confirmed the target," I said, then shouldered the door open and swept into the bakery.

The air smelled like fresh bread and powdered sugar, but undercut by the damp, soggy smell of raw dough. The interior of the building was tiled, and the fixtures looked straight out of the props department Victorian-era drama: polished wood and brass, with sweeping glass display cases on all sides, and a tall mirror behind the counter, flanked by two paintings of nude women apparently fainting in the presence of cakes and bread. There were more display cases beneath the mirror, and a pair of doors that I assumed led to the kitchen. The weak light from the streetlamps outside made it difficult to see much beyond that.

"This is usually when we ask the Saint to shed a little light on the situation, but he seems to have gone walkabout," I said, glancing at The Good Doctor. "Don't suppose you have a similar trick?"

"He does, but it involves way more fire than you want to deal with," Addie said. She took a pair of opera glasses from her vest pocket and unfolded them, then somehow strapped them onto the brim of her hat and started fiddling with the lenses. A second later, her eyes began glowing green. "There. Looks pretty much as I remember. Except for the pancakes."

"Well, that does us zero good," Chesa said. She changed arrows, said something lyrical and heartbreaking, then shot her bow straight up. When the arrow smacked into the ceiling, it burst into brilliant light. Addie swore and played with her goggles some more. "Wow," Chesa said, staring at the ceiling. "That's amazing."

"It's just a flarrow, Ches. You've done that . . . Oh," I said, finally looking up. I had to squint around the glare of the arrow. The ceiling was a dome of plaster, filled with cherubs who were heralding a woman in robes, holding a laurel over her head. She was standing on a marble platform, which was in turn crushing a pile of skeletons. It was all a bit macabre, especially for a bakery.

"No offense to His Majesty Timothy of House Horton, but *this* is how you decorate a bakery," Gregory said quietly.

"The ceiling was gifted by the third Duke of Camwellington, on the occasion of the presentation of a particularly good donut," Addie said. "It was used to negotiate a peace between the Duke and his archrival, the Clockwork Earl of Boiling Green."

"Must have been a hell of a donut," I said.

"Not really. The Duke and the Earl were secretly in love, and just needed an excuse to stop the fighting and run away to the countryside together."

"It's a little much," Bethany said, appearing out of nowhere. "And now you've screwed up my shadows, so I guess I'm back."

I jumped at her sudden appearance, then tried to cover it up by whirling around in the other direction. Once I'd cleared my throat a couple times, I asked if she'd found anything interesting.

"I think there's only one of them. Doesn't look dangerous. Little guy, chef's hat. Very concerned about his pancakes." Bethany pushed her hood off her head, revealing a face covered in flour. "Which, I have to say, are pretty terrible. Even for pancakes."

"Huh. Okay. Well, it doesn't look like we're going to be coming back with any pastries," I said. Now that the lights were on, I could see that the display cases were stuffed with pancakes, just like in the window. The Good Doctor had pressed his beaked mask against the glass, tapping sadly at a stack of dry wheat pancakes, dusted with sawdust. "What's with all the flapjacks?"

"Pancakes were a delicacy in the long ago," Chesa said. "They didn't even have syrup. Just . . . pancakes."

"Well, that's a tragedy," I said. "Personally, I would have invented syrup first, then figured out something to put it on."

"Is he always like this?" Addie asked, turning to Chesa. "Random? Irrelevant?"

"Yup."

"That's hardly fair," I protested. "I say some very relevant—"

Something clattered loudly in the kitchen. The whole team froze in place. Addie drew her pistol, then nodded to the door. Gregory and I bumped shoulders in our rush past the counter to the swinging door that led into the kitchen. The only light in that room was a horizontal slit of flickering, orange light coming from the ovens that lined the back wall.

"Ovens are going," I said. "Someone's in there."

"Be careful. If it's the thing that overpowered Cassius…" Addie let the words hang.

"I'm telling you, I saw the guy. Little fellow. Hardly worth our time," Bethany said.

"I've heard that said about rabbits," I warned. "Stay close, Greg. I don't want to have to drag your heavy ass all the way back to the airship."

He smirked. "You just try to keep up. Gregory L'Haute isn't going to die in some bakery."

He kicked the door open and rushed in, zweihander gripped at his hip, wicked tip pointed forward like a spear. I had a brief glimpse of something scurrying across the oven's light before I followed him in. Gregory must have seen it, too, because he let out a monumental bellow and lifted his sword overhead, charging forward. The creature yelped and ran for the back of the shop. I was already there, barreling into it with my shield.

The monster went down with a flop, squealing as it rolled under a heavy wooden table. In the dim light of the kitchen, it was difficult to tell what we were facing. I put one boot against the table and shoved it aside, towering over the squirming figure.

"Alright, beast. It's time to face justice!" I shouted, lifting my sword over my head.

"Non, attendez! Je vous en pleine, attendez!"

"Wait! Wait one second!" Addie's voice cut through the confusion. Her goggles gleamed bright green in the shadows. "Pierre?"

"Oui, madam? Madam Adelaide!" The miserable figure at my feet scrambled to his feet, blinking in the light streaming in from the front room. I noticed that the few windows in this room had been sealed over with parchment paper. The man standing before me was dressed in baker's linens, the white of his coat stained almost black with dried blood. The stink of turned earth and rotten meat rose above the heady smell of fresh pancakes. I took a step back.

"Can we get some light in here?" I called behind me.

"Coming up." Chesa switched arrows and was about to launch a flarrow into the ceiling when Pierre screamed.

"Non, monsieur, s'il vous plaît, non!" He threw his arms over his face. "The light, she burns!"

I motioned for Chesa to hold her fire, then bent close to the tortured baker. His wrinkled face pulled away from my hand, but slowly I was able to lift his head and get a good look at his throat. Two smooth puncture wounds lay just above his clavicle. His skin was cold to the touch.

"What's that, on his neck?" Gregory asked, bending closer. The baker pulled away from me, but as he turned, I saw what Gregory was talking about. A small mechanical insect, like a scarab, clung to the base of the man's skull. Brass pincers sunk into the baker's flesh. Two glass vials made up the scarab's back.

"I think I've found our problem," I said, releasing the poor man. He returned to his shivering squat. "Little doubt what we're facing. Doc, do you think—" I turned around to face Addie, and presumably The Good Doctor and Bee, both of whom had lingered in the front room while we chased shadows.

What I saw was Addie standing casually just inside the door, hands looped over the handle of her pistol like an old western cowboy, with considerably more class. Behind her, emerging from behind the shadows of the door, was a shape. Tall and blocky, with a pair of piercing red eyes.

Its mouth gaped open, revealing steel-bright fangs.

CHAPTER ELEVEN

The first thing that happened was that I screamed. I like to think it was something useful, like "Look out!" or "Vampire!" but in reality I belted out an incoherent shriek while waving my sword at Addie. Being the finely-tuned killing machine that she was, Addie drew her revolver and spun around to face the vampire in a single, smooth motion. The creature caught her wrist in his massive hand and twisted the barrel away from his body. Addie fired desperately, just as the vampire wrenched the pistol from her hand. All of this happened in a heartbeat.

The muzzle flash burned a hole in the darkness, turning the kitchen as bright as daylight. Chesa screamed and Gregory flinched back at the sharp, deafening sound.

In that brief flash of light, I saw everything: Pierre the Undead Baker huddled on the floor, flour dusting the pale flesh of his hands, mixing with the blood smeared across his chest. Gregory, half-turning toward the new threat. Chesa, standing next to Addie, vaulting away from the monster that had just lunged out of the darkness. Tembo, starting to weave a spell around his staff, the amber light dim in the sudden brightness of the flash. And Lady Adelaide, crumpling to the ground as the beast's claws came down on her shoulders. The broken revolver tumbled out of her limp fingers.

Behind her, a vampire. Unmistakable. He was tall, dressed in the blood-spattered tunic of a baker, with glowing red eyes and a tumble of curly black locks. His veins stood out, black on his pale face, and claws burst out of the flesh of his fingers. There was something peering over his shoulder. The creature lifted Addie to its mouth and bore down, closing its jaws around her throat.

The muzzle flash passed, leaving us in total darkness. There was a wet, sloppy, wrenching noise. Addie screamed in pain.

"Chesa, gimme that light!" I shouted, already stumbling blindly forward.

Chesa still had the flarrow on her string, but instead of sending it into the ceiling, she took a blind shot at the creature gripping Addie. Her flight went barely wide, cracking into dazzling sunlight over the vampire's shoulder. Pierre shrieked and scrambled deeper into the shadows, while Gregory and I squinted at the silhouette of the monster before us. It held Addie in its massive hands, claws drawing pinpricks of blood from her shoulder and arm. Her head flopped to one side. Two fresh puncture wounds in her neck sputtered blood, and fresh gore dripped down the vampire's chin. It stared at us with those piercing red eyes, grinning fiercely.

"I guess that settles the vampire question," I said, then lowered my shield and charged the monster.

Tossing Addie to the side like a broken doll, the vampire met my charge head-on. Its fist glanced off my shield, but the force of the blow was still enough to stagger me. I recovered enough to take a swing at its leading leg, but when my blade bit into its calf, it bounced off. The shock of that impact numbed my hand. It felt like striking cold mud. Before I could react, the vampire lowered its shoulder and slammed into my shield, driving me halfway across the room with little effort. I slid to a stop. Gregory stared at me.

"Thick skin, and strong," I said, catching my breath. The vampire watched us carefully, his fanged mouth hanging open. The creature had a very feral appearance, stooped over like a bear, arms dangling. I gave Gregory a nod. "It's going to take both of us."

"This spawn of darkness will not stand against Bright Vengeance!" Gregory shouted, bringing his massive sword into a guard position. "Face me, fiend, and know the meaning of—"

A blur of pale skin and blood-spotted clothes barreled into Gregory, knocking him off his feet and sending him sprawling in a tangle of armored limbs and clanging steel. The vampire loomed over him. Gregory scrambled back, zweihander held awkwardly between them. The vampire moved faster than either of us could react.

"He's too fast!" I shouted. "Tembo, you got anything for this?"

"A moment, Sir John," he replied. His hands wove a complex

pattern around his staff, plucking strands of light out of the air. "Keep him occupied for a moment."

"Occupied, eh? Easy enough."

I rushed in, taking a backswing at the vampire's exposed spine; the blow slid off its thick skin. Apparently that was enough to distract it, though, because the beast twisted to face me, letting Gregory escape to the cover of a long wooden table that ran the length of the room. The vampire took a swipe at my shield, then skittered deeper into the shadows. Gregory clambered to his feet on the other side of the table. As it fled, I got a good look at the device on its back. Similar to the scarab on Pierre's skull, but much larger, with brass arms that sunk deep into its skin. Pistons squirmed across the body of the machine, pumping some foul liquid into the vampire's body.

"Holy crap, Rast, he's fast!" Gregory shouted.

"Yeah, and that skin is tough. So when I say it's going to take both of us, I mean both. Like, at the same time. Okay?"

"Yeah, okay." For once, Gregory looked unsettled. His hair hung in damp loops down his forehead, and his armor already had several dents in it. "Say the word."

"The word is violence." I was regretting my lack of helm, but at least I had a gorget covering my neck. "Let me distract him. You hit him from the other side."

"You guys want me to do anything, or should I just sit around looking pretty?" Chesa asked. She had taken up position near the ovens, balanced on a bread rack that reached the ceiling.

"See if you can find a weak spot," I said. "Hitting him felt like digging a trench in clay. But it's gotta be soft somewhere. Maybe focus on that device on his back."

"One undead pincushion, coming up." Chesa drew an arrow to her cheek, then nodded us forward.

With a flick of my wrist, I changed the configuration of my shield, making it bigger and heavier, with a thick steel rim that I could use for punching. That transformation sapped my magical reserves. I could feel the energy leaving my body. "Reminder to everyone that we're on starvation rations," I said. "Use your powers sparingly."

"Noted," Gregory said. Despite that, he triggered his sword's magical power. A wreath of flame ran up the surface of the wavy blade, bathing the darkened room in heat and flickering light. The vampire flinched away from the sudden flames. "Let's see if steampunk vampires can burn!"

Gregory and I charged in, him swinging Bright Vengeance in great, sweeping arcs, me holding my bulwark high and threatening with my sword. The vampire backed up, feinting first toward me, then doubling back on Gregory when I threw up my shield. Bright Vengeance passed in a burning line over the vampire's head, and then the beast rushed in, crowding Gregory's chest. Fortunately, I was expecting this, and was already moving.

Another tap of magical power, and my massive shield collapsed into a fist-sized buckler, giving me more range of motion and speed. With the vampire close to Gregory, I punched my shield into the beast's lower back, following up with a strong slice with my sword, running from hilt to tip. The blade bit into the beast's stubborn flesh, parting it at the base of the spine. Steel thrummed against bone, throwing sparks. Instead of blood, a thick black liquid smeared across the steel. It smelled like creosote, and bubbled like burning tar.

Not what I was expecting, to say the least.

"Something's wrong," I said, just as the vampire swung around and backhanded me. I got my shield up, but it was still in its smaller configuration, and the bulk of the blow went into my forearm and elbow. I spun around like a top, continuing the movement to face the vampire again. It opened its mouth to bite down on my shoulder. The flames of Gregory's blade flickered across its steel bright fangs.

Steel fangs. Metal arms. Glowing eyes. Strength and speed beyond any flesh-and-blood creature I had ever seen. This wasn't a vampire.

It was a machine.

Just as the vampire lunged at me, an arrow whistled through the air and thunked into its cheek. Another followed close behind, landing with a satisfying smack into its exposed neck, and a third thudded into the creature's eye. The vampire flinched back, swatting at the protruding shafts with its steel claws. The wood snapped like kindling, but the heads remained buried deep in its flesh.

"Nice shot, Ches!" Gregory bellowed.

"Not enough!" I called. "Tembo?"

"Nearly there!" the big mage answered. A tapestry of light hung around him, growing in complexity with each pass of his nimble fingers.

"Fine." I tossed my shield like a sling, holding on to the enarme straps and willing the shield face into a longer shape. It settled into a kite shield, but with a front edge that was as sharp as a razor. If I was going to beat a machine, I was literally going to have to beat the machine. "Hey, Count Mechula! Come get it!"

Ignoring the trio of arrow shafts sticking out of its face, the vampire came at me, swinging both hooked claws like threshers. I deflected the first swing with my sword, letting the claw travel down the length of the blade before catching it at the hilt. The flesh of the vampire's wrist tore open, but the creature seemed undeterred. The same black ichor splashed down my weapon. When its fist reached the hilt, it curled thick fingers around the quillions, wrestling for control of the weapon.

"That's mine, you grim bastard," I said through gritted teeth. Up close, I could smell the sharp tang of hot metal, and hear the lurch and rumble of machinery. The vampire stared at me blankly, then opened its gaping jaws and snapped at my face.

I punched with the sharp edge of my shield, driving it twice into its open jaws. Eventually its mouth clapped shut. I disengaged, then thrust the bottom point of the shield into the creature's thigh and leaned my whole weight on it. There was enough force in the blow to twist the vampire to the side. I disentangled my sword from the creature's grasping claws, drew back, and smashed the pommel directly into its forehead. Once. Twice. A third time, each strike ringing like a bell. The beast's face began to deform like a mask melting in the fire. I drew back to strike a fourth and, hopefully, final time.

Before I could land the fateful blow, the vampire seized my shield in both hands and lifted it high into the air. I was still attached to the shield in question. My legs dangled off the ground, kicking ineffectively at the vampire's chest. With no leverage, my sword arm hung limp at my side. I tried cutting at the creature's fingers, but my blade simply banged off the hardened flesh of its hand.

"Guys! Figure something out!" I shouted.

"Incoming!" Gregory roared forward, Bright Vengeance overhead. He chopped down, connecting with the vampire's shoulder with all his might. The burning blade sliced deeply into the beast's shoulder. Meat sizzled and cloth burned, sending up plumes of acrid smoke. The blow was enough to release me. I dropped to the ground and rolled out from under the vampire's shadow, coming to my feet against one of the baker's tables. I whirled around to see what damage Gregory had managed.

The vampire's arm dangled lifeless from the socket. The edge of the wound was jagged and twitching with mechanical life. I watched in horror as the dead meat of his shoulder knitted back together, zippering closed like a pair of trousers. The thick black ichor pouring down its side landed in squirming clumps on the floor of the bakery. The engine between its shoulder blades clattered loudly.

"It's the machine! That's what's keeping him alive," I shouted. "Hit the thing on its back!"

The monster responded by catching Gregory's next swing with its bare hand and throwing him across the room. The paladin yelped as he vaulted over the baker's table, to land in a heap at the base of the ovens. Then the creature turned to me and roared.

"Okay, just you and me. That's fine." I could feel my magical reserves running out, but I figured I had enough for one last trick. Hopefully it would be enough.

My shield, Svalinn, was a gift from the valkyries for heading off Ragnarok. In legend, it was the shield that protected the earth from the sun, and had various cold powers associated with it. I rarely used them, because legendary powers absorbed a lot of my mojo, but it seemed the time had come to call on the winter of the Viking armageddon. I gritted my teeth and delved deep into my mythic self, pulling every last scrap of magical power to the fore, then pushed it all into the shield. It returned to its natural form, a Viking round shield, then began to glow.

The surface of my shield swam with pale blue light, and a vortex of snowflakes and freezing mist swirled across the leather face. The air turned as cold as a Wisconsin sunrise in February, the chill traveling down my arm and into my lungs. The limited well of my magical power leaked away, like water through a sieve. Whatever I was going to do, I had to do it fast. I suppressed a shiver, then squared off against the vampire.

Big and Bitey didn't seem to notice the change in temperature, or just didn't care. Distracted by its severed arm, perhaps. It lumbered closer, taking a swipe at my head with its remaining claw. I ducked, then punched my shield forward to strike the elbow of the swinging arm. That didn't have an immediate impact, but when he wound up again I noticed that its arm was a little slow to respond. This time I took its attack full on the face of the shield. My feet slid back as it pushed me along, but when I pulled away it took a second for claws to peel back from the shield.

I've tried to start my car in the middle of January often enough to know what cold weather does to machines. Maybe this monster couldn't feel pain, or fear, but nothing was immune to freezing temperatures and frostbite. Especially if its clockwork depended on oil to function properly.

Frost covered the monster's face, spreading like cobwebs across the steely surface of its skin. Before it could attack again, I shuffled to the side and swung down with my sword. Sparks flew, but this time they were joined by broken cogs and sundered springs. The oil leaking from its wound was as black and slow as tar. The vampire lumbered around to face me, but its joints shrieked in protest as it turned, and its feet dragged along the floor. I bashed the vampire across the face with the boss of the shield, and was rewarded with a spray of cogs and the sound of torquing metal.

Just then, my magical reserves emptied out. The polar vortex snuffed out, along with some of the passive defensive abilities of my mythos. Aches and pains sprang up across my body, as the pain-dampening and resilience powers switched off abruptly. I let out an involuntary moan, but kept moving.

The vampire grabbed at my neck with its outstretched hand. Its fingers closed around my gorget, and I heard the wrinkling metal just as pressure grew around my collar. I really regretted leaving my helm back at the ship. Last time I'd let vanity guide my battle prep. The beast drew me close, its jaws gaping as it pulled me into its embrace. I stuck my knee into its chest, struggling to keep it away from my neck, then I released my shield, letting it swing on its straps around my elbow, and took my sword in both hands. Arrows whistled overhead as Chesa tried to split the difference between hitting the vampire and skewering me. There was no sign of Gregory, or The Good Doctor. Typical healers and heroes, disappearing when things got tough.

Grasping my sword in both hands, I placed the forte of the blade against the vampire's wrist, then worked it back and forth until I found a joint. I might not be able to cut the beast's flesh, but I could wreak havoc with a ball joint, given enough leverage and the will to live. The vampire glanced down at my blade and smiled through gore-stained lips. Its fingers pressed tighter and tighter against my neck.

"Boo!" The shadows overhead coalesced into the falling form of Bethany the Rogue. She dropped onto the vampire's shoulders, one dagger in each hand, and went to work. The sound of punctured skin and breaking metal filled the air, along with a haze of black ichor that flew up in plumes from the dozens of puncture wounds inflicted on the creature's back.

The vampire dropped me and grabbed at Bee, but she was too fast. Somersaulting off the beast, she danced across the flour-dusted table, pirouetting in a blur of steel and skin and sparks. It lurched after her, slowed down by the frost clinging to its flesh, but also by the accumulation of sliced tendons and ruptured muscles. I hopped to my feet.

"The engine!" I croaked. "Break the engine!"

Bethany heard and responded. With each vaulting leap, she came down behind the vampire, striking a dozen times at the machine perched on its shoulders, then dancing away when it whirled to face her. Finally, with one scything blow, the machine came loose.

It dropped to the floor with a slithering whir. A half dozen snaking tendrils ripped free from the vampire's flesh with a meaty schlup. The brass pincers that had held it in place, still slick with blood, twitched as the scarab-like engine clattered on its back. The vampire stood dumbstruck, weaving back and forth on its feet.

"That's enough of that," I said, lifting my shield overhead. The engine smashed into a hundred pieces, carapace and body shattering with a very satisfying crunch.

The vampire leaned forward and slowly, like a tower collapsing in on itself, crashed to the ground.

"Ready!" Tembo called. He balanced a spinning ball of light on the point of his staff. "Just point me to . . . Oh."

"Sorry, Tem. Already killed it," I said. "Better luck next time."

"Hey, have you guys seen all these pancakes?" Matthew asked as he strolled into the kitchen. "They're not bad. Oh, hey. Kind of a mess in here."

I mean . . . healers, right?

CHAPTER TWELVE

I rolled the twice dead vampire onto its back. The angry red light in its eyes slowly dimmed, until only a faint pinprick of crimson remained. I looked at Bethany.

"Took you long enough," I said.

"A rogue is never late. She backstabs precisely when she means to backstab."

"Well, next time, maybe let us know when you're going to disappear on us."

"What's the fun in that, John?" she said with a laugh.

"Will the two of you stop joking around!" Chesa yelled. "Our escort's in pretty bad shape."

All eyes pivoted to where Adelaide had fallen. She lay in a heap just inside the door to the kitchens. I used the vampire's tunic to wipe the black gunk off my sword, then sheathed it and shouldered my shield on my way to the fallen gunslinger. Chesa got there first. She rolled Addie over on her back. The gunslinger's arm flopped lifelessly across her chest.

"She's lost a lot of blood. Addie, can you hear me?" Chesa bent over her. "Don't just stand there, Rast. Get the doc!"

"Didn't we bring a healer?" I asked, then turned to Saint Matthew. "You wanna lay some hands on, big guy?"

"Oh, yeah. Sure." He dropped the featureless ceramic mask that he always wore on adventures over his face, then knelt beside Adelaide. "Might wanna cover up."

There was a brilliance to Matthew's work. Like, literal brilliance. When he was topped up, his skin glowed and his eyes burned with holy fire. I turned away, squinting to protect my eyes and holding one arm over my face. Didn't want a holy sunburn, after all.

Seconds passed. Nearly a minute. I cleared my throat.

"How's that healing going, Saint?" I asked.

"Uh. Yeah. Not great." I looked back. Matthew was massaging the bite wound. His fingers were tipped with blood, but the wound didn't seem to be improving. "Can't get any traction on it. Might want to call the doctor, before we lose her."

I bolted for the door.

The Good Doctor sat behind the counter in the main room, his hands sticky with mashed-up pancakes, which he was feeding through a hole in his mask and humming quietly to himself. Not what I expect of a healer in the middle of battle. I stormed into the room and gesticulated wildly with my sword.

"What do you think you're doing?" I shouted. He looked up at me, the smooth glass eyes of his mask utterly expressionless. "We've had a vampire incident!"

To his credit, The Good Doctor hopped to his feet, shaking pancake off his fingers as he waddled past me. He croaked an apology.

"That's more like it." I escorted him into the back room, which in the glaring light of Chesa's flare looked like a cross between a bakery and an operating theater. Flour mixed with splattered blood from Addie and the thick, viscous oil that had erupted from the vampire, creating a Pollock-like spatter pattern across the floor. Addie lay in the middle of the room, surrounded by a pool of her own blood. Bethany and Chesa sat over by the ovens, tending a nasty wound on Gregory's head. Saint Matthew continued his ineffective ministrations on the fallen gunslinger.

The Good Doctor went to one knee beside Adelaide, peeling open her lips and peering at her gums, then sticking his fingers into her ears and wiggling her head around. Not the sort of medical examination I was used to. He chittered at Matthew, who sat up.

"I didn't try that," Matthew said. "Whatever's wrong with her, it ain't magic."

"Forty percent dead. Everything fine," The Good Doctor chirped. He rummaged around in one of his pockets and produced an empty syringe, which he inserted into Addie's neck, next to the wound.

When he pulled the plunger, the syringe filled up with a thick, viscous fluid the color of radioactive mucous. Addie took a deep, sudden breath, and her eyes flew open. Coughing, she pushed The Good Doctor away.

"I'm fine," Addie said between jagged gasps. "What happened to the vampire?"

"Bee ganked it," Gregory said. He clambered to his feet, pushing away Chesa, who tried to dab delicately at the blood on his forehead. "Enough. I have faced graver injuries than this."

"Yes, but your face is . . ." Chesa fumbled to a halt. "It might scar."

"I mean, hopefully," Bethany said. "You could use a little grimdark in your life."

"Once I return to the Chapel of Eternal Vigilance, the waters of the Shimmering Pool will cleanse my flesh of all impurity," he said confidently, standing over the brass engine that had fallen off the vampire's back. "Now. What is this work of devilry?"

"Looks like some kind of bug," Bethany said. "One of those Egyptian things."

"A scarab." I turned the device over. The arms clattered loudly against the floor. Bethany was right. The twin vials on the back of the device looked like folded wings, and the overall shape definitely looked like the scarab statues I had seen in many museums. "Weird thing to find on a vampire."

"The scarab was a symbol of rebirth and resurrection in ancient Egypt," Tembo said. "And the Victorians were obsessed with Egyptology."

"The thing was burrowed into its body," I said. "As soon as Bee knocked it off, the vampire dropped like a stone."

"Very odd." Tembo glanced back at the dead vampire, and his eyebrows shot up. "And look, the beast is changing."

The former vampire was melting away. The stark black veins in its face disappeared, and its pale flesh regained the rosy bloom of youth. Its once red eyes were now baby blue, staring sightlessly at the ceiling. Blood blossomed from the dozen cuts Gregory and I had given it, though without a beating heart, they did little more than spot its tunic. The bright steel of its jaws crumbled to dust.

"So we're looking at some kind of ersatz vampire?" Gregory asked.

"Such a thing has happened before," Addie said. "We have Jekylls hiding all over the Gestalt. Mad scientists trying to improve themselves, with horrific results."

"This looks more like something that was done to him," I said. "The short guy had one, too. Where'd he go?"

We found the other baker hiding beneath an empty rack, hands over his head, sniffling. Chesa coaxed him out, and Saint Matthew comforted him. He didn't have the metal jaws or glowing eyes, but the device at the base of his skull certainly looked similar. We led him into the light, but he shied away from the vampire's corpse. By now, the effects of the scarab engine had faded completely. The corpse, though pale, looked like a child.

"Not a monster at all," I said. "He's so young. Barely even a man."

"He was a beautiful young man. Such delicate fingers," Pierre said. Reluctantly, he knelt beside the corpse. "All he wanted to do was bake beautiful bread. He had a gift for the croissant."

The Good Doctor chittered sadly. Matthew put a hand on Pierre's shoulder, but the baker flinched, as though the Saint's touch was painful.

"Hey, Pierre. Can you tell us what happened?" I asked. The small baker sniffed and looked around, his eyes glassy. "What do you remember?"

"Souviens pas," the tiny man said. "Je faisais du pain pour le matin, et—"

"Um." I held up a hand, dredging my memory for my high school French. "Je . . . je puh parl un petite poo day . . .'"

"I beg you, sir, this has been a difficult day." Pierre pressed his face into his hands. "Do not torture me further with that sorry excuse for French."

"I was just trying to be nice. Geez." I squatted next to him. "Try it again. English, so neither of us have to live through tenth grade again, ok?"

"I have no memory. I was making bread. I went to put the morning's loaves in the front, and noticed it was brumeux . . . eh . . . foggy? More than usual. When I came back to the ovens, the back door was open. I went to check, and . . ." He gestured hopelessly. "Next thing I remember, you were beating me very rudely sur la tête with your stupid sword."

"So is he a vampire now?" Bethany asked. "Do we need to . . . ?" She mimed staking him in the heart, much to Pierre's distress.

"Let's see if we can get this thing off him first." I turned Pierre's head to the side. The brass scarab glittered brightly in the light of Chesa's flarrow. "Doc, you wanna take a crack at this thing?"

The Good Doctor and Matthew hummed and tutted at the device for a few minutes. Doc tapped at it with various syringes, until finally Matthew cupped his hands over it and hummed the theme song to an obscure '80s sitcom. The beetle clattered to the ground.

"That seems to have done it." I lifted the baker's chin. His skin was warm to the touch, and the twin puncture wounds in his neck had healed almost completely. "How are you feeling?"

"What is that smell?" Pierre wrinkled his nose, looking around. "Where is all my bread?"

"You seem to have gone through a pancake phase," Matthew said.

"Pan . . . cakes? Oh, non, pas les crêpes!" He rushed out of the kitchen. From the other room, we heard several loud exclamations in tortured French, then the wholesale evacuation of damp dough from the shelves.

"So we've got nothing. Pierre doesn't know who attacked him and the vampire is just a weird beetle thing." Chesa sighed and looked out the window. "At least the fog is lifting. Looks like the Gestalt is back in place."

"We have the devices," Gregory said. "Maybe Tesla will be able to make some sense of them."

"Good thought. Let's get those bagged up," I said. "Hopefully Pierre is on his way to recovery. What should we do with the body?"

"We can figure that out later. For now, we need to get back to the *Silverhawk*." Addie sat up a little more. The color drained from her face, and she tottered back and forth. The Good Doctor grabbed at her elbow, but she pushed him aside. "Where's my gun?"

"About that. Um . . ." I looked around awkwardly. "Before you freak out, this is how we found it."

"What? What do you mean? What'd you do to my gun?"

I produced the weapon. Or, at least, the pieces of the weapon I'd been able to find, collected in a muffin tray according to size. Addie snarled at me and snatched the tray out of my hands, then started sorting out the pieces, discarding about half of them with disdain.

"I told you we have a negative effect on modern technology. Be glad that most of those pieces at least resemble your pistol."

"This is a spoon! And a thimble! And these are . . . dice? Why are all my bullets dice?"

"Ooo, d12s. Big damage." I took the dice and rolled them around in my hand. They were a mix of lead and brass, and clunked together in a very satisfying manner. "If you can't get them back to their original form, I'd be happy to take these off your hands. Left most of mine back home, and my mom threw—"

Addie snatched the dice from me and tucked them into her pocket. "This is the kind of thing Nik was talking about. Our magic systems interfere with each other. Most of the time everything will work as you expect it to then, suddenly, bang, your longsword is a grandfather clock and my revolver turns into nerd jewelry." She shuffled the broken pistol around on the table for a second before sighing heavily. "I'd like to get out of this magical backwater before something else breaks."

"Sure thing. Soon as the doc is done with you."

The Good Doctor hummed happily, producing another syringe, this one the size of his forearm. She tried to push him away, but her weakened protests amounted to little more than the flapping of hands and a long string of precise profanity. He shoved the needle into her arm and lowered the plunger. Addie turned green.

"You know, I'm starting to appreciate the Saint," I muttered to Gregory. "A couple cookies, a joke about missing sheep, and you're healed." I glanced over at him. He was staring at the needle, and had turned about the same shade of green as Addie. I quickly backtracked. "Hey, I'm sure he'll have something other than a needle for that head. A poultice or something."

Turns out needles were The Good Doctor's thing—needles, gasses, and glass vials filled with various chemicals that smelled like a collection of urine samples. He used all of these things in healing Gregory of his wounds. I retreated to the front room, happy that I had escaped with minimal scrapes, deciding to not point out the cut on my wrist. Not that I'm scared of needles. I just have a healthy mistrust of them, bordering on fear.

Pierre had managed to clear out the display cases. He retreated back to the kitchens with an armload of flour and a determined look on his face. It wasn't long before the smell of baking bread wafted through the air. I glanced up at the ceiling.

Instead of cherubs and laureled women, the scene was a pastoral setting that seemed to focus once again on scantily-clothed women and the stunning appearance of baked goods. The center of the ceiling was the sky of gilt gold. Chesa's flarrow stuck in the middle of the sun, and was glittering brilliantly off the gold leaf.

"Huh. That's weird. I wonder—"

I heard the footsteps a moment too late. Assuming it was Chesa coming to taunt me, or Bethany practicing her stealth rolls, I glanced over my shoulder, ready to make a joke.

A vampire stood in the middle of the room. Not a baker dressed as a vampire, but an actual vampire—black cloak, bloodred eyes, gray skin, dressed like a Bauhaus song come to life. Pearly white fangs puckered the edge of black, cracked lips.

"What the—" I started to turn toward him. He hissed, then leapt at me, claws extended.

I fumbled my shield off my shoulder, barely getting it between us before he barreled into it. Falling backward, I grabbed at his outstretched arm. Razor-sharp claws scraped across my vambraces before slicing into my cheek. I let out a startled yelp and hit the ground, banging my head off the floor. Dazed, I rolled over onto my belly, putting the shield between us. The vampire stood in the doorframe, backlit by the diffuse light from outside, glaring down at me.

"He is coming for you, mortal. The Iron Lich will be content with nothing less than the destruction of the Gestalt," the vampire purred. Then he swept his cloak over his head and bolted outside. "Be warned!"

A tinny bell sounded as the vampire bolted through the door, disappearing into the foggy street beyond. I stared numbly after him.

"Who the hell is the Iron Lich?" I muttered.

CHAPTER THIRTEEN

"John, what the heck are you doing out here?" Chesa appeared from the kitchen. Her eyes shot up when I turned around. "What happened to your face?"

Blood streamed down my cheek. I rolled to my feet, peering out into the fog. There was no sign of the vampire. Chesa grabbed me by the shoulder.

"You're bleeding all over the place!"

"Vampire. There was a vampire," I stuttered. "Vampire."

"Yes, we know, John. We were all there," Chesa said. "Did you trip and hit your head or something?"

"No, listen, there was a vampire. A real one. It . . ." I pointed outside. "Well, he's gone now." I described the encounter as quickly as possible, while the Eccentrics were out of earshot. Chesa furrowed her brow.

"Well, we're going to need to tell Tesla about this. Maybe the name means something to him," she said.

"We can't. Not until we know what's going on. They can't know about the vampires."

Chesa looked over her shoulder uncertainly. Finally, she shook her head. "Fine. But we keep an eye out."

"Agreed. And thanks for trusting me," I said.

"Oh, I don't trust you. At least not very much," Chesa said.

Just then, Gregory came out of the kitchens. "What are you guys doing out here?" he asked. "John! Your face!"

"Yeah, yeah." I put one hand to my cheek. It came away bloody. "Just a scratch."

"Hey, Doc?" Gregory called over his shoulder. "Looks like we've got one more patient!"

The Good Doctor shuffled into the room, his fingers still sticky with pancake batter. When he saw me, his glassy eyes lit up.

"Hey, I'm perfectly fine. Just a scratch," I said, backing away. "Honest. There's no need—"

The needle he produced from his belt was as thick as a number-two pencil, protruding from a plunger as long and round as my arm. The glass vial bubbled with noxious orange liquid.

"Ah, crap," I mumbled, as Gregory and Chesa gleefully grabbed my arms and held me down for the healing.

My arm felt like a water balloon that someone had filled with hot, pulsing magma. Every time I tried to move my hand, spears of pain shot through my shoulder and cradled my spine in misery. Every heartbeat was throbbing anguish. I had to pry my gauntlet off to keep my fingers from bursting through the chain link, and my fingernails had turned the most amazing shade of purple. The twin puncture wounds on my wrist had boiled with pus and black bile before sealing closed, leaving a pair of shiny scars.

"Next time, get me a priest," I said, wiping the remnants of the vampire-pus from my armor with a pancake. "Or a shot of whiskey."

The Good Doctor chirped dismissively, measuring my arm with his calipers before stowing the syringe in a holster inside his coat. "Aether stabilizing. Take two cocaine tablets and message me tomorrow."

"Is there a reason you didn't step in to help, Matt?" I asked. The Saint lounged just outside the kitchen, admiring the gilt ceiling and chewing thoughtfully on a rolled-up pancake. "I would have much preferred the Brilliance."

"Gotta conserve our energy, man. These amulets are a real slow drip." He tapped his chest. "Long as The Good Doctor's methods work, why not use 'em?"

"I have a list of reasons. I'll start with the syringes. Then the smell. Then the excruciating pain." I stood up. "Oh, hey. Dizziness! Add that to the list."

The Good Doctor made a dismissive gesture, then packed up his gladstone bag and retreated to the kitchens to check on Pierre and Adelaide. As soon as he was gone, I pulled the rest of Knight Watch close.

"Listen, keep the vampire thing quiet. Because I'll bet you dollars to donuts that it wasn't one of these mechanical scarab things." I pointed down the street, where the vampire had run. "That was the real thing."

"If that's the case, shouldn't we warn the Eccentrics?" Chesa asked. "If there's a real vampire running around the Gestalt, they should know."

"Not without clearance from Esther. And unless one of you has a magic telephone, we're pretty much on our own." I glanced over Greg's shoulder at Tembo, who was just emerging from the kitchens. "Let's keep this to the five of us for now. Okay?"

"Sounds like a terrible idea," Bethany said. "I'm in."

"I do not like the idea of providing succor to the foul spawn of the night, but in this I must agree," Gregory said. "The lady Esther has spoken. I have given my word to follow her commands, though the very gates of Hell—"

"Right, okay, you're in. Chesa?" I asked.

"What are we talking about?" Tembo asked, strolling up.

"John saw a third vampire. Maybe a real one," Chesa said. "He doesn't want us to tell the Eccentrics."

"Hm. Well, for now, I agree. Until we know who or what is behind this," Tembo said, placing one broad hand on my shoulder. "I am with you."

"Fine," Chesa tossed her hair over one shoulder. "I'll keep quiet. But if this gets someone killed..."

"If what gets someone killed?" Adelaide stepped out of the kitchens. She was still nursing her right hand, which under The Good Doctor's care had swollen up like a pincushion.

"We were talking about taking Pierre in for an interview," I said. "But I think he's been through enough."

Adelaide looked from me to the rest of the group, then shrugged.

"Sure, whatever. I'm just anxious to get back to the *Silverhawk*, and a shower." She strolled past us. "They're these clever things, Rast. Like rain, only inside, and warm. Oh, and someone needs to bag up the scarabs. Tesla will want to see those."

"Yes, ma'am. I'll get right on that, ma'am," I grumped. "One bag of dead vampire beetle parts, coming right up."

"You really missed your calling, John. You'd have killed it in retail," Chesa said.

✤ ✤ ✤

Tesla stared at the sack in my hand with baffled distaste. Oil and blood dripped through the burlap to pool on the intricate pattern of the parquet floor. The team of Pinkertons who had escorted us into the *Silverhawk* stood in a loose circle behind us, ready to pounce with janitorial supplies and a bucket of lye. We were on the flight deck, a place I'd never seen before. It looked like a cross between the bridge of a submarine and a gentleman's drawing room. Wooden floors, brass railings, and cushy chairs contrasted with pipe-encrusted low ceilings, beeping display cabinets, and an array of controls that boggled the mind. Three bubble-like windows gave a commanding view of the outside, with a fourth window built into the floor and crossed by catwalks. The three command chairs, where we stood, were centered on a parquet wooden floor that wouldn't have been out of place in the finest dance halls in the country. Fortunately, we were still on the ground, or I would have been dealing with significant vertigo issues.

"And what am I supposed to do with this?" Tesla asked delicately.

"I don't know, I figured you'd want to see the body. Isn't that how this works? We kill the monsters, you do science stuff to their corpses." I shrugged. "I did the sword stuff. You're the science guy. Science it."

"It's a wonder you lot ever accomplish anything meaningful." Tesla pressed his knuckles into his brow. "Let's go back a step. Who is this, that you have chopped up and brought to me in a burlap sack?"

"Oh, it's not actually the body. He was way too big for this," I said, lifting the sack. The burlap swung back and forth pendulously, spattering drops of black ichor around the control room. The mob of Pinkertons ebbed and flowed, eager to clean but reluctant to get close to me. "But both he and the other baker had one of these on their backs. Seemed important."

"So you slaughtered a couple of bakers—"

"Just one of them. And he wasn't just a baker," I said.

"Someone or something had turned him into a vampire, boss," Addie called over my shoulder. "Or at least a simulacrum of a vampire. Put up a hell of a fight, too."

"He wasn't too tough," Bethany said with a sniff. "Dropped like a stone once I showed up. Probably scared."

"Well, the rest of us were struggling while you lounged in the rafters," Gregory said.

"Yeah, you're welcome for that," Bethany said.

"Welcome? You're welcome?" Gregory asked with a gulp. His face turned four shades of bright red, none of them cheerful. "What exactly are we welcome for?"

"The rescue? Sheesh, you save some people and they can't even show a little appreciation. Maybe next time I'll just—"

"Okay, enough. Let's at least pretend we're professional heroes," I said sternly. "The point is that both Pierre and his assistant appeared to be vampires, they both had these devices on their backs, and once we took them off, they both changed back."

"Unfortunately, we didn't figure that out until we'd already killed the kid," Addie said. "Or maybe the machine had already killed him, and was just keeping him undead."

The Good Doctor chittered sadly, then slowly fed a croissant into his mouth flap. Pierre wouldn't let us leave until he had provided a basket of warm bread, most of which had already disappeared into the Doc's mask.

"Well that sounds very serious. A device, you say? So we're looking for some kind of engineer, or a toy maker," Tesla mused. "That doesn't do much to narrow down the list of suspects. Well, let's get a look at these things." Tesla gestured to the back of the room. "Put it over there, on the workbench. I'll take a look at it."

I did as asked, dumping the bag's contents out onto the metal workbench in the corner. The latent bilious substance from the glass vials on the scarabs, along with the sticky remnants of blood from the various tubes, hooks, and talons that had burrowed through the dead baker's body put out quite a stench. Tesla produced a pair of articulated telescoping goggles from a cupboard, strapped them on, then set about examining the shattered remnants of the scarab.

"There's something very strange about this," he said, laying the parts out and then slowly fitting them back together. "It follows none of the paradigms I'm familiar with. The psycho-diesel chicanery of House Ford could be involved, but it lacks the hallmark crude lines. No, it's much too elegant of a machine for that fumbler."

"Someday you're going to have to get over that," Addie said quietly.

"Hank has had every opportunity to apologize. So." Tesla rotated the main body of the scarab. "There are familiar aspects to this device, but overall, it is a mystery. And you say both vampires were wearing one?"

"Pierre's was smaller." Addie poked through the parts and recovered the tiny scarab. It wasn't much bigger than her hand. "And he seemed more in control. Didn't attack us, beyond some frightened slapping. He lacked the boy's strength and speed."

"Different scarabs for different purposes? Or perhaps they harvest something from the host as they grow. Very curious," Tesla said. His goggles buzzed and whirred. A pair of tiny arms produced progressively more powerful lenses as he bent to examine the device. "And the Egyptian symbolism is not lost on me. Not uncommon in the Gestalt."

"So this might be someone on your side of things, trying to . . . what? Recreate vampires from scratch?" I asked.

"There is a history of vampire affinity in the Gestalt. Lost souls drawn to macabre and melodramatic," Tesla said.

"So . . . goths?" Bethany asked.

"Goths who have discovered brown," Tesla said. "And electricity. But more precisely, this device does not seem to function on the principle of hematological transmutation."

We stared at him blankly.

"Blood transfer. I'm not an expert on the subject, but my understanding is that vampires of your . . . uh . . . milieu consume blood from living victims and transform it into life energy. Or death energy, depending on your views on the polydynamic nature of good and evil as it relates to—"

"Wait, this thing doesn't suck blood?" I asked. "I'm pretty sure it sucked at least a little blood out of Addie."

"A by-product of the transference process," Nik said. "Resulting from the method of procurement. The, uh . . . the holes it pokes through your skin. Might be a legacy feature, but I suspect it's more a matter of evoking the original format."

"So what is it sucking?" I asked, more than a little uncomfortable about having the baker's teeth in my veins. Not that I was particularly comfortable with the idea in the first place. "Please don't say souls."

"Certainly not souls. Souls are a foolish superstition concocted by religious fanatics to explain away the afterlife," Nik said dismissively. "However, it could be siphoning off the ectoplasmic life identity of its victims, resulting in mimeographic eradication."

"So . . . souls," Chesa said.

"I suppose, for purposes of this discussion, we can agree on that nomenclature," Tesla said with a patient sigh. "Perhaps there is residue."

He reached into the device and unscrewed one of the glass vials mounted in the scarab's wings. He sniffed at the unsealed opening, then wrinkled his nose. "Well, whatever it is, it smells like rotten grapefruit and gasoline, strained through a sweaty stocking."

"Sounds like Malort," I said.

"What kind of monster deals with the undead here in the Gestalt?" Gregory asked. "The Unreal has plenty of options: necromancers, liches, other vampires . . ."

"We have necromancers of a sort," Addie said. "Though they fashion themselves as mediums and spiritualists. Liches aren't a steampunk thing, as far as I know. And as we've previously discussed, all the vampires are supposed to be dead."

"Supposed to be," Chesa said quietly.

"Perhaps there's something inherent in the vampiric archetype that makes the soul transfer work better. Or perhaps they're trying to send some kind of message." Nik set the tank down, drumming his fingers on its green surface. "Our pogrom of the undead was never very popular in the Gestalt. If we're the target, they might be trying to hold us accountable for our past actions.

"I will need to spend more time with these. Perhaps we were wrong to involve Knight Watch. These are clearly Gestalt contraptions, though how they are replicating the Unreal is still a mystery." Tesla stood and pushed the goggles up onto his expansive forehead. "Either way, it's a good thing that you got them off the street."

"Two of them," Addie said. "The third got past Sir John before we could subdue him."

"Third?" Tesla's eyebrows shot up. "There was a third undead baker?"

All eyes turned to me. I really wished I had kept that secret from the rest of the team, at least until I'd had a chance to talk it over with

Esther. If that final vampire was part of the cabal Knight Watch had hidden, it wouldn't do to add them to the mix.

Reluctantly, I explained what I had seen, downplaying the archetypical appearance of the vampire. Tesla rubbed his face and looked thoughtful.

"Well, that certainly complicates matters. If there is a vampire loose in the Gestalt, we must make haste to ensure its corruption does not spread. I assume it had one of these devices on its back?" he asked.

"It all happened too quickly. I didn't notice," I said with a shrug.

"That's John. All bravado, no perception," Chesa said.

"Then we must assume it was behind the attack. A true vampire, or a member of the Gestalt trying to invoke the beast." Tesla tapped thoughtfully on the scarab's glass back. "If it was merely someone acting the part, they wouldn't be able to transfer the infection in the traditional manner, which might explain these devices."

"We don't know it wasn't one of your steampunks, fallen victim to a scarab. The baker had the glowing eyes and pale skin as well," I said, trying to deflect attention away from the possible existence of real vampires. "We shouldn't jump to conclusions."

"But I do know someone we could ask," Addie said. "The vampires certainly had some enemies."

Nik looked up, interested. "Oh, yes . . . yes they did. Do you think she would talk to us?" he asked.

"That depends. Are you ready to apologize?" Addie asked.

Tesla made a face, his fingers still drumming loudly on the glass vial. Addie snorted. "Perhaps best if I stay here," he said. "But she always liked you."

"Who are we talking about?" I asked. "Some kind of vampire hunter?"

"An old friend," Tesla said, ignoring Addie's laughter. "Evelyn Lumiere. No one in the Gestalt knows more about the undead than she does. And no one hates them more. If someone is experimenting with the bloodsucker's powers, she'll know how to counter it."

"So what's the problem? Why didn't we start there?" Chesa asked.

"Nik still owes her an apology," Addie said. "And a new arm."

CHAPTER FOURTEEN

Tesla sent us back to our quarters for the short flight to our next destination, a rendezvous with the mysterious Evelyn Lumiere. Ida emerged from the ductwork long enough to seal us in. She and Adelaide waited for us to return our magic items to the containment chest, then busied themselves securing it while the rest of us tried to get comfortable in the cots and hay. This time, I kept my armor on. After a few moments, the engines whined to life and we tipped up into the sky.

"So why are we meeting this woman?" I asked as we settled into the lice and hay of the fourteenth century. Chesa, Tembo, and the Saint perched uncomfortably on their cots, while Addie and Bethany lingered near the door. Ida sat on the containment chest, swinging her legs and fiddling with the world's most complicated wrench. "Shouldn't we be tracking down whoever built the vampire scarab things?"

"Evelyn Lumiere knows more about the vampires of the Gestalt than any living human. Perhaps more than the vampires themselves," Addie said. "She was a central figure in the vampiric pogrom. And the bloodsuckers' first victim. At least on this side of the border."

"Which border is this?" Chesa asked. "Another part of the Gestalt?"

"Nah. Your side of things." Ida unrolled a leather sleeve full of tools and started disassembling the lock on the isolation chest. "The bastards came through from your world."

"Should she be screwing with that?" I asked. "It seems... unwise?"

"Ida knows what she's doing," Addie said, peering at the young mechanic. "Hopefully. The point is, Evelyn and her family were innocent."

"Not entirely innocent," Ida called over her shoulder. "Can't blame the primitives for that one."

"Primitives? Does she mean us?" Chesa sat up on her cot, poking one sharp finger at Ida. "In my domain, there's no filthy, greasy-fingered—"

"What do you mean that her family wasn't entirely innocent?" I cut in, before Chesa could get us all in trouble. "What part did they play in the war?"

"Evelyn's parents, Claude and Cecilia Lumiere, were pillars of the Gestalt community," Addie explained. "Claude was a brilliant scientist, and the founder of the Fraternity of Curious Minds. Sort of a social club for nerds. He was partially responsible, along with Tesla and a few others, for creating a lot of the technology that sustains us."

"He built the aetheric dampeners, as well as the gravitic dispersion coils that keep the *Silverhawk* afloat," Ida said. There was a shower of sparks from the chest. She continued, unfazed. "Kind of genius."

"Weren't we supposed to go check one of those out?" I asked. "The vampire attack at the bakery kind of threw us off our game."

"I completely forgot about that," Addie said. She turned to Ida. "On our way to the patisserie, we noticed that the corruption of the Gestalt had spread for several blocks. Might want to check out the local dampener."

"I will add it to the list," Ida said. "The extensive, extensive list."

"What exactly do these dampeners do?" Tembo asked.

"Lower the activation energy of Gestalt reality. It probably takes a lot of effort for you guys to get into the Unreal, yeah?" Ida glanced up at me. "Strict rules about diet, those domain things, terrible hygiene. Well, with the dampeners, we can maintain the Gestalt full time."

"Fascinating. I have been wondering how you manage such a long-lived anomaly."

"Just like we manage everything else," Ida said. "Science."

"Don't think real-world science would think much of something called a gravitic dispersion coil," Chesa said.

"That's a failure of imagination, not science," Addie said. "Either way, it works for us. And the Lumiere family made a fortune on it."

"So they're rich?" I asked.

"At one time. Evelyn poured her family's wealth into her crusade against the undead. She financed the *Silverhawk*, and half the gear we still use."

"So why doesn't Tesla want to talk to her?" Gregory asked. He was still flat on his back on his cot, but somehow still managed to look like a Greek god, lounging in Olympus. "Sounds like they have a lot in common."

Adelaide snorted. "Bad blood keeps a different ledger. And there's a lot of bad blood between those two."

"A misunderstanding." Ida shrugged. "Cost her an arm."

"Ah. Yeah, that'll do it," I said. "You mentioned both her parents were important to the Gestalt. So what did her mother do?"

"Spooky stuff." Ida dropped a gear, which rolled under the cot and disappeared into the hay. She ignored it. "Ghosts. Creeped me out."

"Creeped *you* out?" Chesa asked, aghast.

"Cecilia was a medium, and a spiritualist. She conducted séances, dowsed the leylines of the Gestalt, talked to the restless dead. The Order of the Prescient Light owe her a lot. So did Claude, to be honest. Her map of the leylines served as the foundation for aetheric dampeners."

"Still trying to call that science?" Chesa asked. Addie shrugged.

"You're awfully cynical for a girl in a princess costume," Adelaide said. Chesa clenched her fist, but the moment passed quickly. Addie continued. "Anyway, that's really what caused all our trouble. One of the bloodsuckers latched onto Cecilia Lumiere, while she was holding a séance." Addie's eyes got distant. "The Lumieres were holding a ball. Cecilia liked to put on a show for the guests, summon famous ghosts, that sort of thing. But this time, she hooked into something that . . . wasn't really dead."

"She dug too far, and too deep?" I asked.

"Don't bring the professor into this. The leeches came through the aether like mad dogs," Addie said. She looked at me and showed her teeth. "Tore right through the house, killing and feeding. It was a bloodbath. We got called in, but the mix of Unreal and Gestalt was too much. By the time we had it under control, the Lumieres were dead, along with some of the brightest minds of the Gestalt."

I swallowed and looked to Chesa. She was pointedly looking elsewhere.

Addie broke the awkward silence. "Evelyn was one of the only survivors. Both her parents died trying to contain the incursion. Her father was torn to pieces right in front of her. Her mother..." Another pause. "They turned her into a thrall. We had to hunt her down, along with many of our former friends and allies."

"Evelyn staked Lady Lumiere herself," Ida said quietly. She finished whatever she was doing with the isolation chest, then sat cross-legged in front of it and leaned back. "Before my time, but I've heard the stories."

"She wouldn't let anyone else do it. We tried to spare her that, but . . . she was determined."

"Gods. It's no wonder she hates the vampires," I said.

"Yes, well, Madam Lumiere is accustomed to grudges," Addie said. "As I'm sure you shall soon find out."

Skyhook brought us down beside a dusty gravel road that cut through gently rolling cornfields, somewhere outside of Chicago. At this range, honestly, everything was somewhere outside of Chicago. I squinted into the setting sun as Addie, Ida, and the rest of Knight Watch descended the *Silverhawk*'s staircase.

"Steampunk cornfields?" I asked.

"We're still in the Mundane," Tesla said. He and Skyhook stayed at the top of the stairs, waving like beauty queens to see us off. "Madam Lumiere maintains her realm separate from the influence of the dampeners. You'll have to hike your way in."

"You couldn't land us any closer?" Gregory asked. His curls were already starting to collapse in the humidity.

"We suffer from the same limitations as Knight Watch, Sir Gregory. Evelyn's bubble of the Mundane prevents us from getting any closer. We can't do too much to upset the balance, can we?" Tesla checked his pocket watch. "Better get going, if you want to be there before nightfall."

"Didn't you people invent cars or something?" I asked Adelaide as we set off down the road.

"Nik refuses to use them. More of that Henry Ford nonsense," she said. "I've never asked."

As Tesla predicted, we were still walking when the sun set. A chorus of insects rose from the surrounding fields, accompanied by the distant yipping of coyotes. It wasn't quite full dark when we spotted a gate by the side of the road.

"This is it," Addie said. Even she looked exhausted. "Remember. Best behavior."

The Lumiere Estate stood proud in the center of a cornfield, a remnant of a more glorious age, but also a product of this new age of industry and science. The main house was surrounded by a wrought iron fence topped with razor-sharp fleurs-de-lis, the bars worked into the shape of clinging vines. The main gate featured an elaborate coat of arms covered in gold leaf filigree. Through the bars, we could see the main house at the end of a long driveway that terminated in a roundabout, complete with a water fountain, though no water was flowing. The house itself was white marble with broad windows and copper gables. If the Queen of England had answered the bell when we rang, I would not have been surprised. I pressed my face between the bars and squinted at the distant estate.

"I thought you said she emptied the family's coffers?" I asked, gesturing to the coat of arms. "This feels pretty swanky."

"She retains the house and grounds, and enough wealth to see to their care." Addie hooked her thumbs on her belt and frowned up at the gate. "And, frankly, I don't think anyone else would be willing to live in the shadow of such horror."

"Kept the sigil at least. I wish I had a decent sigil." The shield was quartered in gold and black, with a set of three gears in the upper quadrant, and a pentagram in the bottom right. It was flanked by a clockwork lion on the right, and a dragon on the left. I cocked my head at Ida. "Have I mentioned I killed a—"

"No one cares, John," Chesa cut in.

"Doesn't look like anyone's home," Gregory said. The windows were dark, and while the property was immaculately kept, it felt oddly abandoned. "Is she expecting us?"

"If we warned her ahead of time, I guarantee Evelyn would be out of town," Addie said. "Don't worry. She's home."

"How can you tell?" Chesa asked doubtfully.

"Dogs haven't found us yet," Ida said. She stepped up on the lowest rung of the gate and stuck her head between the bars. The great mop of her hair tangled with the fleurs-de-lis. "She only keeps them kenneled when she's in residence."

"The rest of the time they roam the grounds, eating anything that slips through the gate." Addie reached through the bars and pulled the velvet cord hanging next to the empty guardhouse. Distantly, a clarion call jangled. "All I ask is that you let me do the talking."

"What kind of dogs?" I asked.

"Big boys," Ida said enthusiastically, then nodded toward the house.

"Oh dear," Tembo said, as the creatures came into view.

The large oak door creaked open, and three black shapes launched silently into the yard. They shot toward the front gate; the only sound they made was their nails clattering on the cobblestones of the driveway. Muscles rippled under black hides as they bounded closer, their chests as wide as wine barrels, with sleek flanks that reflected the moonlight like lightning on an oil slick. Blunt faces bristling with teeth watched us intently. Ida hopped off the gate as they approached.

"Put that away, Rast," Addie said, leaning against the side of the gate. "This is a social call, not a raid."

Without realizing it, I had backed away from the gate and drawn my sword. Abashed at my reaction, I sheathed the blade and tried to act casual as the dogs reached the gate. They pulled up just short of the iron bars, claws skidding on the stones. Their snuffling breath stank of raw meat and violence.

"G . . . good boy. Good puppies," I whispered. "I have a dog, too."

"I doubt your dog is anything like these," Ida said. "They were a final gift from Evelyn's mother. Hellhounds, trained to guard her precious daughter."

"My dog has a little hellhound in him," I said. Truth was, the World Dog contained every pupper, legendary or otherwise, from Pomeranians to Fenrir himself.

Well. Fenrir got away. But the rest of them are still in there.

The dogs growled at us as they paced the length of the gate, bodies quivering with the promise of imminent violence. The smell of sulfur and blood wafted off their flanks.

"My lady Adelaide. What an unfortunate surprise. And Ida. Come to repair that leaky faucet you took apart last time you were here?" I looked up to see a middle-aged woman strolling casually down the driveway. Her black hair was pulled back into a bun, and she walked with the imperious nonchalance of a woman who was accustomed to wealth. She wore a dark red dress, accented with black lace and white silk. Her eyes were piercing gray. She looked at each of us in turn, barely flickering her gaze over Addie and Ida before considering the members of Knight Watch, then whistled once. The hounds slunk back to her heel, flanking her like guards. It wasn't until she got closer that I realized the sleeve of her right arm was empty and pinned to her shoulder. She had a very faint French accent. "You have brought guests. Does Nikola have the two of you working as a chauffeur?"

"Hiya, Evie," Adelaide said. "Long time."

"I could look at that faucet if you want," Ida volunteered. At Evelyn's icy glare, she shrank away. "Or not. Up to you."

"Yes. I'm sorry that I haven't been more social, Lady Adelaide," Evelyn said stiffly. "Time slips away from me, sometimes."

"We're more of an escort, to make sure they don't get lost, and to keep them from breaking anything." Addie gestured to us. "Evelyn, may I introduce Sir John, the lady Chesa, Sir Gregory, Tembo the mage, Bethany of many knives, and Matthew. Apparently he's a saint. They are the current members of Knight Watch."

That brought her up short. The hounds raised their hackles and let out a low rumble, deep in their chests. She pinned a sterile smile on her face.

"Joys upon joys," she said. "Is that bitch Esther dead yet?"

"No, ma'am. She's still the boss," I said.

"A pity. Well, I don't imagine I have much to say to members of Knight Watch." She nodded to Addie. "Do give Nik my regards. And remind him of his outstanding debt." She began to turn away.

"We need your help, Evelyn," Adelaide said.

"I imagine you do. You're not fool enough to bring these charlatans to my door without good reason. Sorry to disappoint. Adelaide, come around sometime when you aren't trailing these Mort d'Arthur pretenders. We can have tea." She turned and started toward the house. The dogs lingered for a minute, as though they desperately wanted to leap through the bars and tear our throats out. "Good evening."

"There's been a vampire attack," Addie said calmly. Evelyn froze in her tracks. The dogs started barking, the sound loud enough to shake my rib cage. When she turned around, Addie continued. "Nik didn't want to worry you, but it's happening again."

"No," Evelyn said, glancing sternly at the hellhounds. "It is not. We saw to that. Tesla, and I, and"—her piercing gray eyes darted in my direction—"and the rest of you. You must be mistaken."

"Evelyn." Addie loosened the collar of her blouse and pulled her raven-black hair aside. The two puckered scars on her neck glistened in the lamplight. "I'm not mistaken."

For a heartbeat, Evelyn's face changed. She almost looked like a little girl, hiding in her closet, gripping a teddy bear tight to her chest. One of the hellhounds whimpered as the fingers of her left hand twisted in his hackles. But then it was gone, and the iron-hard lady in red was back.

"I hope you're wrong," she said. At a signal, the gate opened on silent hinges. The dogs lunged out, circling close to our legs, snuffling at us. I kept very still. Evelyn whistled, and the dogs bounded off for the manor. "For all our sakes."

CHAPTER FIFTEEN

The interior of the house was just as grand as the exterior, though perhaps more stark than I was expecting. Marble floors swept clean of dust wound through hallways where, judging by the shadows on the walls, portraits had once hung. A seemingly random array of furniture sprinkled otherwise empty rooms. Madam Lumiere led us briskly through the foyer, past an immaculately appointed sitting room complete with grand piano and porcelain statues, but no other furniture, then through the kitchen, and to a glass-paned solarium off the back of the house. There she sat, at a small table barely larger than the teacup it held, in a wicker chair that had seen better days. There were no other chairs. An orange tabby cat watched us from the safety of a potted fern hanging on the far side of the room. The hellhounds circled the chair once, then slumped onto the tile floor flanking Evelyn. They yawned mightily, then fell fast asleep. Madam Lumiere took a sip of tea, then peered at us impatiently.

"Well," she said. "Explain yourselves."

"Right, I guess that's . . ." I gestured to Addie. "Do you want to start? Should I?"

"Cassius and The Good Doctor were attacked at the Convaclation Patisserie. Pierre's place. Doc was able to get the big guy out, but he looked like he had been drained, and had the requisite puncture wounds. We tried to deal with it, but when we went in, our technology fell apart. That's when Nik decided we needed to call in the cavalry. Literally." Addie jerked her head at us. "Took us a couple days, but we tracked them down."

"This is dangerous business," Evelyn said quickly. "Mixing the timelines does not go well. You're risking the entire Gestalt by having them here."

"We're taking precautions. Isolation chambers. And they've been drained of their magic," Addie said. "Right now they're little more than kids in fancy costumes."

"Hey, whoa. Kids in *very* fancy costumes, with sharps," I said. "And the skill to use them."

"You're not going to scare me with knives, boy," Evelyn said. "Not after what I've seen. So if they have no magic, what good are they to you?"

"Conduits," Tembo said, holding his amulet up. "We can draw a small amount of power without disturbing the Gestalt."

"So far, it's been a matter of the Eccentrics—" Addie paused when Evelyn snorted. "Yeah, Nik doesn't like that. Anyway, it's been a matter of us getting them to the fight, then standing back and letting them do their jobs."

"So far, two vampires down," I said proudly. "The bakery is open for business."

"I appreciate the visit, really I do." Evelyn set her teacup down and folded her hands into her lap. "But get to the part with the vampires, before I lose my patience."

"The point is that we took Team Middle Ages back to the bakery, and we found a vampire. Something had turned Pierre. He showed all the classic signs—light sensitivity, pale skin—but he'd also gone full medieval." Addie glanced at us, then dropped her voice. "He'd filled the place with pancakes."

"That's not how vampires work," Evelyn said. "They're monsters. There would be bloodlust, an insatiable hunger. It would be an absolute massacre. Not a breakfast buffet."

"Which brings us to our next problem. Because there *was* a vampire. It attacked us. Fortunately for Adelaide, Knight Watch was there." I produced the small scarab that had been on Pierre's back and set it on the table next to Evelyn's teacup. "They each had one of these on their back. This is Pierre's, who showed the signs of turning, but wasn't aggressive. The other baker—whose name I never caught, actually—the scarab on his back was much bigger."

"And where is that device?" Evelyn asked, peering at the scarab through a pair of opera glasses.

"In pieces, back on the *Silverhawk*," Bethany interjected. "I broke it with my might."

"When she knocked it off the vampire, he collapsed. Once we pried these things off, they turned back to their mortal selves. Unfortunately, the big guy was already dead," I said.

Evelyn sniffed, picking up the scarab with bony fingers and turning it over in her palm. She sighed, and looked up at us.

"Henri," she said. When I didn't respond, she continued. "The other baker. The boy had a gift for madeleines. A bloody shame."

"We think someone is trying to spawn a new generation of vampires. Or, at least, they've created one," Addie said. "What we don't know is who is doing it, or why."

"Ridiculous. No machine of science could create a vampire. Their magic is in the blood, a legacy of the condemnation of their first sire," she said. Her voice rose precipitously. Her hand shook as she held the runed cog. "They are a damned breed. A scourge upon the face of the earth. And they! Are! Dead!"

Suddenly, the previously composed Madam Lumiere broke. Tears rolled down her cheeks, and the gear tumbled from her hand onto the floor. The hellhounds were on full alert now, searching for whatever had caused their mistress such distress. Chesa took a step forward, but Adelaide bowled past her, kneeling at Evelyn's feet and taking her hand delicately.

"I'm sorry, Evie. I'm so sorry." She patted her softly. "If we had left Pierre to rot in his damned bakery, perhaps none of this would have happened."

Evelyn laughed through her tears, then pushed Addie back. She took a lace kerchief from her sleeve and dabbed at her eyes.

"Well. He does make a quite exquisite éclair, does he not?" She smiled sadly, then let out a deep sigh. "I am sorry, friends. This is all a bit much for an old lady. But I should have known it would happen someday. Come. Bring your terrible clockwork. We will see what my father has to say about it."

"Your father? But . . ." I trailed off as she rose and led us back through the kitchen. I gave Addie a questioning look. "I thought her father was dead?" I whispered.

"She kept his lab, his notes, his journals. Maybe there's something in them about such a device. He was very interested in mythical creatures." She waited until Evelyn was out of the room before plucking the cog off the floor. "Some in the Gestalt blame him for what happened with the vampires. Not me, of course. But some."

The hellhounds followed us, loping heavily in our midst, weaving up and down the column like drill sergeants inspecting their wards. Every time their heavy flanks bumped into me, I caught a whiff of sulfur.

We followed Evelyn through the kitchen and down a shadowed hallway. The lamps here were extinguished, and the floors were marked by dust and disuse. We passed an arched doorway that had been chained shut. I arched an eyebrow at Addie.

"Cecilia's Spiritorium. Still haunted, if you're to believe the lore."

"I can hear you, Lady Adelaide," Evelyn called from the front of our little column. "The only thing lingering in my mother's den are memories. Unpleasant ones. Come, it is just down here."

The hallway terminated in a door fashioned to look like a bookcase that swung aside at Evelyn's touch, revealing a hidden staircase. We descended into the basement. It looked like the storage room for the props department of every mad scientist horror movie in history, except nothing looked fake and the air smelled like static electricity and chemicals that shouldn't have been mixed. As we entered the room, Ida let out a tiny squeal of ecstasy.

"So . . . many . . . things to take apart," she squeaked.

"Behave yourself," Addie whispered. "You're a guest in this house."

"There's a box of broken clockworks in the corner, if you need something to distract yourself," Evelyn said, pointing.

Ida zoomed to the treasure trove and set to work.

Other than the sheet-covered tables, racks of jars, half-assembled engines, and all manner of scientific equipment splayed out across the room, there were also shelf after shelf of books and journals, crowding the walls. They added a musty smell to the space. In one corner, far from the chemicals, stood a cozy reading chair with its own dedicated Tiffany-style lamp, and a library trolley of journals, some of them open. Evelyn went to the chair and lovingly closed the one on top of the trolley, hugging it to her chest.

"I come down here sometimes, to be with him. This may all look like dry scientific text, but I hear these words in my father's voice, and smell him in the ink." She smiled, just a little bit. "It's like he's still here, giving me a tour of his laboratory, explaining some new invention or exciting discovery he's just made."

"He was a good man, Evelyn," Addie said, standing awkwardly beside the chair.

"Bah, you never met him. You're just being kind." She set the journal back on the trolley, then looked around the room. "Now, let's see. I think the books about mythical creatures are in this section, behind the hydraulic modulation compressor."

Under Evelyn's direction, we cleared off one of the workbenches and started laying out journals. We didn't get very far before I realized a fundamental problem with our system. I raised my hand.

"Uh, these are in French."

"Yes, of course. Do you write your diaries in another language? No. You write them in your native tongue. Englishmen, thinking everyone should speak English. BAH!"

"We have a lexigramophone back on the *Silverhawk*," Addie said. "Would it be possible for us to borrow some of these?"

"Clearly not. They do not leave this room. Father would not allow it." Evelyn ran a finger down one of the open pages. "It does not matter. I speak both languages quite well. As though I were an educated person with a brain. Imagine that."

"Okay, okay, we get it. You're smart," I muttered. "So anything in there about vampires?"

"Yes, so much. But it will take time to digest everything." She pointed at the scarab, which I had placed in the middle of the bench. "I take it Nikola has had a turn with that?"

"He did. Couldn't make heads nor tails of it," Addie said. "It's part of the Gestalt, but also part of the Unreal."

"A brilliant man, our Nikola. But not good at seeing the value in other people's work. Here, let me take a look." Evelyn abandoned the journal and bent over the scarab, examining it through a jeweler's loupe that she produced from her hair bun. "My eyes are not what they were. But it reminds me of something. Ida, if I can pull you away from your toys for a second, would you fetch me those schematics? Right over there, above the workbench."

Reluctantly, Ida abandoned her work and gathered the requested papers. While she was doing that, I looked over the journals. My French wasn't quite up to par, but I knew enough to recognize some of it. The elder Lumiere certainly had a thing for creatures of legend. There were entries on dragons, centaurs, even the elusive werewolves that Knight Watch insisted didn't exist. All were accompanied by drawings, some surrounded by formulae of varying complexity. Nothing in the book referenced vampires, though. I closed the book and moved on to another.

"This looks promising," I said. "*Histoire de la Nuit*. 'Story of the Night,' right?"

"Very good," Evelyn answered, sarcasm dripping from her lips. "Bon travail."

I cracked open the book and flipped through. No pictures, but words like Blood, Immortal, Monster, and Death popped out at me. "What's the French for vampire?"

"Vampire," Evelyn said.

"Ah. Okay." Scanning the pages, I didn't see that, though there was more than one reference to Une Cage Dame. "The caged lady? Is that what this says?"

"That seems unlikely," Chesa said, looking over my shoulder. "Unless her dad was into some kinky stuff."

"You've disparaged my father quite enough, thank you." Evelyn came over and closed the book, sliding it back onto the shelf. "That book has nothing to do with vampires, I assure you."

Eventually, Ida dumped the rolled pages of the schematics on the bench. Evelyn unfurled them, anchoring the curled corners with various books and vials.

"Yes, see the similarity?" she said. "Here, the aether pump, and this is a hacked-together reversal of the dispersion mechanism. And this tank must serve as some kind of reserve. One of them was wearing this?"

"Yeah, Pierre. Though Henri had a larger version." Addie squinted at the faded ink of the drawings. "So what is this a schematic for?"

"Father's aetheric dampeners. The very devices responsible for preserving the Gestalt," Evelyn said. "I think what you have here is some kind of energy vampire. An engine built for drawing out aether, rather than blood."

"They must have somehow hooked into the mythic ideal of vampirism to make it work. Explains why the attack didn't kill Cassius or Addie," I said. "Only Henri, and he was the host."

"But for what purpose? The aether is everywhere. Why try to steal it?" Addie asked.

"I do not know. But if they interfere with the dampeners, then the whole Gestalt is in danger."

"We haven't detected any fluctuations in the timeline," Addie said. "But maybe we're looking in the wrong places. Why would they attack Pierre? There's no dampener in his bakery."

"Whatever their reason, we need to figure out our next steps," I said. "Where are these dampeners? Can we do something to protect them?"

"They're all over the world. The Convaclation has several, but the network is spread throughout the Gestalt. There's no way for us to cover all the dampeners," Addie said. "Simply too many sites."

"Then we focus on the dampener closest to the attack. You said there were several at the Convaclation. How many, exactly?" I asked.

"Three. One at the airfield, another in the exposition center, and a final one in the gardens of the dead."

"Gardens of the dead?" I asked. "Yikes!"

"So, what, we split up? Two members of Knight Watch to each location, with Eccentric backup?" Chesa asked. Tembo nodded sagely.

"I think that would be best," he said. "I will note, we only have two healers."

"Just a risk we'll have to take," I said.

"I am glad you are willing to volunteer, Sir John," Tembo said. "It speaks well of your character."

"What? No, I—"

"Agreed. It's dangerous. But I think it's our best chance." Addie turned to Evelyn. "Madam Lumiere, we need to make sure you're safe, as well. I suggest you collect the necessary research from the lab and relocate to the *Silverhawk*. We may have need of your expertise."

"Can we revisit this No Healer thing?" I asked. "See, I tend to get hurt. Especially when there aren't any healers."

"We'll send Ida with you," Addie said. "She has a mind for engines."

"Wonderful. She'll be very helpful, should I randomly turn into an engine."

"Not as rare as you might think in the Gestalt," Addie said. She clapped her hands together, causing the hellhounds to snap to attention. "Let's move out, people!"

CHAPTER SIXTEEN

With the help of Ida and Gregory, Evelyn Lumiere collected an array of books, instruments, and mechanical doodads to bring with her. Tembo browsed the shelves, tutting contentedly to himself, while Adelaide went upstairs to try to get a signal to the *Silverhawk*. Evelyn made it abundantly clear that she wasn't going to walk halfway across the world just because Tesla was afraid someone might see his flying whale. "There's no one out here!" she said. "Why do you think I live here?"

Once we'd helped haul an enormous volume of supplies out into the courtyard, Gregory and I took a rest. Night had fallen, and an incredibly clear sky stretched from horizon to horizon. There were so many stars, it looked like God had littered the sky with diamonds, bright enough to drown out the moon. The songs of crickets echoed back and forth through the surrounding cornfields, accompanied by the distant hooting of owls, or the yipping of wolves. Despite the fact that we were completely in the mundane world, it was hard not to feel bathed in magic. Greg and I leaned against the boxes, to gaze up at the heavens and listen to the night run riot.

"So what do you think of our new friend?" Gregory asked after a few minutes.

"Evelyn? It's hard to get a bead on her." I adjusted myself on the pile of crates. There was so much strange stuff in there. "She sincerely seems to hate the vampires. But she doesn't exactly love anyone else."

"Her parents, maybe. I can respect that."

"Maybe. I don't know. Trauma does strange things to people." I saw Chesa come out and glare at us. "Hey, Ches. Check out this sky."

"The others are looking for you. Needed inside," she said. "I told 'em you were probably lying down on the job."

"A knight must take his leisure when he can," Gregory said, clambering upright. "Bereft of the holy waters of my sanctuary, I am weary and worn."

"Whereas I'm just lazy," I said with a grin.

Chesa rolled her eyes, then jabbed her thumb toward the front door. "They want you on guard duty. Just in case."

"Just in case of what?" I asked.

"They didn't say." She shrugged. I gave Gregory a meaningful look, then collected my sword and shield, which I had laid aside while hauling boxes, and headed inside.

The rest of the party was waiting for us by the shackled doors of the main ballroom. Evelyn waited patiently, a delicate silver key in hand.

"What's up, folks?" I asked. "Something needs guarding?"

"A foolish precaution," Evelyn said. "I assured your mage friend that everything is perfectly safe. I just need to collect one last thing."

"There is a dark presence in this room," Tembo answered sternly.

"Well, we're familiar with dark presences." I pulled my helm down over my sweaty bangs, leaving the visor up, then shouldered my shield and drew my sword. "After you, my lady."

Evelyn sighed patiently. The tiny key seemed much too small for such a large lock, but as she turned it, the latch popped open and the chains fell away. That alone felt magical. She held one bony hand against the door for a long moment, as though gathering herself, then turned to us.

"Be kind to her," she said. "She's hardly herself these days."

The once grand ballroom had fallen into disrepair. A thick layer of dust covered the scattered furniture, and the floorboards were warped and twisted with age and neglect. Addie had been right about the bloodstains, as well. Dark shapes covered the floors and splattered the walls. Tears in the fabric wall coverings and upholstery spoke of great violence, and greater rage. The far wall was all window, but had long since been boarded over. A path led through the dusty carpet.

In the center of the room, surrounded by broken chairs and the shattered remnants of a table, was a cube of translucent light. It was slightly taller than me, and about eight feet wide on all sides. On closer inspection, I could tell that I was seeing a sheet draped over something, and the ghostly light was coming from inside.

"So, when you say we're deep in the Mundane, what exactly do you mean?" I whispered as we crept closer. "Because this doesn't meet my expectations."

"I said we were isolated from the Gestalt, and far from the Unreal. I didn't say we were in the Mundane." Evelyn brushed past me, one of the hellhounds close to her heel. "I never cared much for spiritualism. That was my mother's world, and perhaps my mother's downfall. Still. It's hard to throw away old things."

She wrapped the glowing cloth in the fingers of her left hand, then jerked it back, like a magician revealing a trick. There was no dust on the drape nor, I noticed, on the floor surrounding the cube. The covering came away with a whoosh. I stepped back, shield up, ready for whatever came at us.

What lay beneath the sheet was an iron cage of meticulous design. Its curving bars and filigreed walls resembled a giant birdcage, inlaid with silver runes and more esoteric symbols. The floor of the cage incorporated intricate machinery, like the open face of a clock, escapements and gear trains ticking silently forward. Even to my medieval imagination, it was clearly a work of both science and magic. But that's not what really caught my attention.

Floating in the middle of the cage was a ghost. The insubstantial form spun to face us, as though it had been examining something on the other side of its enclosure. The spirit wore diaphanous clothes that faded into nothing at the edges, but resembled the straight lines and low neck of a flapper dress. The woman turned her glowing features toward us. She was beautiful, even in death.

"Hello, Cecilia," Adelaide said quietly. "Death certainly becomes you, doesn't it?"

The glowing phantasm drifted closer to us. As could be expected, the ghost of Cecilia Lumiere bore a striking resemblance to her daughter, though the specter looked younger than Evelyn, and somehow more alive, despite her obviously deceased nature. Cecilia looked us over one at a time, spending extra time on Gregory, as could be expected.

"Mon Dieu, cherie, what have you brought us? A woodland spirit?

Some kind of squire? And a knight in shining armor?" Cecilia asked, putting an insubstantial hand to her throat and batting her eyes. "If I had known the party was fancy dress, I would have worn my angel wings."

"Stop flirting with the help, Mother." Evelyn folded the sheet primly and set it aside. "We're going on a bit of an adventure. Do you like the sound of that?"

"This is quite the setup," I said quietly. "Did you make this?"

"Oh, this old thing?" Cecilia flattened her dress against her bosom. "Just some tat I had lying around. Do you like it?"

"Not the dress, Mother. And I suspect he was talking to me," Evelyn said. "The foundation of it was Father's design, though he never saw it through. She's been haunting me . . . well, ever since."

"Ever since you killed me, dear," the ghost said, her face placid as the fathomless deeps, and just as dark. "I don't think you can blame me for that."

"No. So, rather than leave her trapped between worlds, I offered her a way back. A way home." Evelyn smiled sadly. "A second chance to get to know her daughter."

"My dear little Evie," Cecilia whispered. "So sweet to her mother. So kind."

"Your dad designed this?" I asked. "Seems a little weird for a man of science."

"He was very open-minded. Very curious." Evelyn picked up a leather satchel that had been sitting on the broken remnants of a plush chaise longue. "What say you, Mother? A little trip?"

"You know best, dear." Cecilia drifted closer to the bars, folding both hands under her chin as she gazed dreamily at Gregory. "My little girl is so serious. Always in her father's books. I do wish she would get out more. Meet a nice man. Or a not so nice one," she said with a wink.

"My lady!" Gregory shouldered me aside, clutching the hilt of his zweihander to his heart as he tossed his luscious curls over his shoulder. "The foul evil that has doomed you to this pale existence must be defeated! Be assured that I will not rest until it is vanquished! This I swear by the holy waters of the Everfont, which surges unending from the depths—"

"Now this is how you greet a lady," Cecilia purred. The apparition floated closer still to the bars of her cage. "Tell me more about these surging waters, good sir."

Just then, her hand drifted too close to the cage. A snap of electrical discharge shot out from the arcane runes worked into the metal. Cecilia's hand dissolved, and her entire form flickered, like mist caught in a sudden wind. She swore elaborately and retreated to the center of the enclosure. After a moment, her body returned, though the edges of her figure were frayed.

"Mon Dieu, that hurts." The ghost stared at her fingers, which were only now reforming. "It is like having all of your teeth out at once, without the lovely ether frolic beforehand."

"What have we said about touching the bars, Mother?" Evelyn asked.

"La mort doit mourir," the ghost whispered. "Et toi aussi."

"Be nice," Evelyn said. She opened the leather satchel and produced a small device, about the size of a loaf of bread, covered in dials and gauges with a metal door on one end. "We can talk about this later. Time is of the essence."

The ghost sighed, then batted her eyes at Gregory. "If you get lonely later, my dear boy, you know where to find me."

Evelyn fitted the device to a panel on the side of the runic cage, then fiddled with the dials until the machine began to hum. Cecilia closed her eyes, then placed her hand next to the panel. The machine hoovered her up like so much glitter on a dance floor.

"That seems kind of extreme," Chesa said. "You keep your mother in a box?"

"I do not expect you to understand." Evelyn shut the device down, then secured it back in the satchel and closed the latch. "After all that she and I have been through, I can't very well leave her behind, can I?"

Without another word, Evelyn slipped out of the room. With her mother's ghost gone, the dining room fell into darkness, the only illumination coming from the open door. I cleared my throat.

"That was downright weird," I said.

"What did her mom say? You speak French, don't you Rast?" Gregory asked.

"Something about death and dying. It sounded like a threat."

"Every family has their problems," Adelaide said. "Let's not judge."

"Maybe," I said. "But not every family keeps their dead mother in a magic cage in the dining room."

"Again, not as uncommon as you might think," Addie said. She jerked her head toward the door. "Let's get going. Nik's going to wonder where we've been."

CHAPTER SEVENTEEN

The *Silverhawk* settled into the clearing like a fat bird landing on an icy pond. Watching from the library sponson, I braced myself as clods of turf and several startled rabbits thumped against the windows. By the time we stopped, the *Silverhawk* had dug a trench twenty feet wide and three times as long. I shot Adelaide a questioning look.

"Skyhook's still nervous about having you guys on board. Really lays it on the ground before we crash."

"That still felt like crashing," I said.

She shrugged. "You get used to it. So." She turned the rest of the team. We were all gathered in the library for team assignments. "Tembo, you and Gregory go with The Good Doctor to check out the airfield. Bethany, you're with me and the Saint. We'll look at the expo. That leaves John and Chesa—"

"No!" Chesa barked. Adelaide rolled right through her protest.

"—with Ida at the graveyard. Cassius is still recovering, and will be guarding the airship."

"I'm fit to go," Cassius growled. "Just need to stretch my legs."

"Honestly, I'm more concerned about these vampire things attacking the ship. Stay here, watch out for creepies. You're going to see plenty of action once we find whoever's behind these attacks," Addie said.

The big man sulked, which resulted in a cloud of steam wreathing his shoulders, but he didn't protest.

"I'd much rather go to the airfield," Ida said. "Can we switch?"

"We know you'd rather go to the airfield, Ida. And we all remember what happened the last time you were there." Adelaide leaned down to peer into the curly-headed engineer's eyes. "Don't we?"

"Yes, ma'am."

"Okay, so that's assignments settled. Any questions?"

"What am I supposed to do? Sip tea on this atrocious flying pigsty?" Evelyn asked.

"I thought you'd coordinate with Nik," Adelaide said. "Stay back and gather intel."

"Poppycock. You didn't drag me out of my house to simply sit around and wait for someone else to do something interesting." She had changed out of her formal dress and was wearing safari gear, complete with pith helmet and requisite baggy jodhpur pants. Her hellhounds did not apparently enjoy flying, and huddled at her feet like a pair of frightened kittens. "You can send me with the mouthy one. He could use some matronly guidance."

"That's me, isn't it?" I asked. "I'm the mouthy one."

"I mean . . ." Chesa rolled her eyes. "We'd be glad for your assistance, Lady Lumiere."

"Bloody right you are," she said, hopping to her feet. The hounds startled awake, starting to growl. "Enough talking. Let's be on our way."

Unfortunately, there were detours.

Ida's legs protruded from beneath the steam carriage, like some steampunk version of the Wicked Witch of the East, crushed under a flying house. Only in this case, the flying house was a broken down multipede, and Ida was much more gremlin than witch. The owner of the stranded vehicle stood to the side. He apparently couldn't decide if he was more nervous about the hellhounds pacing around his contraption, the heavily armed medieval peasants glowering at the delay, or the mechanic currently "fixing" his mode of transportation. The vehicle looked like a propane silo tipped over on its side, with about a hundred miniature legs on both sides, driven from an umbrella-shrouded howdah on top. We had tried to keep Ida from interfering, but not even the collective disapproval of Chesa and Evelyn could dissuade her. It was like she was impervious to human interaction of any kind. Evelyn stood to one side, impatiently tapping her foot.

"So that's why you don't want to use artisanal water for your pre-boiler injection array. Locally sourced, especially. Way too much silt. Folks think . . ." A puff of smoke erupted from the engine, rolling out from under the multipede and triggering a cough fit from all five of us. The hellhounds started barking wildly, a sound that startled more passersby than the near explosion of the boiler. When she continued, Ida sounded a little abashed. "Didn't see that coupling. Probably should have tied it off before I released the primary drive. My bad!"

"Can you make it work?" the driver asked, drumming his steepled fingers together. He was dressed like a cross between an arctic explorer and a test pilot, complete with silk scarf, seal skin jacket, and bulbous mirror goggles. His adventurous costume stood in stark contrast to his portly frame, and the fact that he seemed terrified of the machine he was piloting. Or had been piloting, until it rumbled to a halt in front of us. "I have a most important tea—"

"Work? Of course I can make it work. It already works. I'm just trying to make it work better." Something rattled under the carriage, a sound that traveled through the multipede like a marble shooting through pipes. It erupted from one of the dozen exhaust vents on the walker's spine. Ida pulled herself out from under the vehicle, wiping greasy hands on an equally greasy kerchief. "There you go. Should get another couple kilos per hour, if you watch your pressure levels and don't try to turn."

"You made it . . . faster?" The gentleman looked nervously from Ida to the velocipede. "What's this about not trying to turn?"

"You're welcome." Ida extended her dingy hand. The pilot peered at it distastefully.

"Can you . . . unfix it?"

"But . . . I . . ." Ida blinked in confusion.

I stepped in. "The lady said you're welcome." I clapped the man on his shoulder, letting my steel gauntlet come down a little harder than was necessary. "Right?"

"Um, yes. Of course. Thank you." He bowed stiffly, then slowly climbed the ladder up to the howdah. Once his goggles were firmly in place, the man said a little prayer, then started the rumbling engine.

The multipede lurched to life. The whole contraption rattled and shook like a rocket lifting off from the pad. Jets of steam whistled out of the vents, and the clockwork legs twitched in anticipation. With a final look to the heavens, the man released the brake. I stepped back, prepared to shield us both should something erupt.

Whatever the multipede was, it was not fast. The two rows of legs stepped in uneven succession, given the vehicle a rolling gait that made it look like a giant, slightly drunk corgi. The pilot hung on for dear life as his ride ambled slowly down the boulevard.

"That's faster?" I asked.

"Oh, yes. That thing is a piece of trash. Should be scrapped for parts. But we don't build for efficiency around here. We build for style." She holstered the multitool she'd been spinning in one hand, then looked both ways down the street. "Now . . . what were we doing?"

"Looking for the aetheric dampener," Chesa said. "Because of vampires? Remember?"

"Ah, right. Sorry. Got distracted."

"I'll say. That's the eighth time we've stopped to repair something." The first had been a pair of telescoping boots that were stuck in the up position, followed by a personal zeppelin that had sprung a leak. After that, it all blurred together. "The others are going to be done with their rounds before we even start."

"My bad. I just can't stand to see broken machines." She stuck her hands in her pockets and strolled back the way we'd come from. I hooked her shoulder and turned her around. She didn't seem to even notice the interception. Chesa and I shrugged at one another before following. "It's kinda sad how some folks treat their machines. Oh, hey, I think that guy's spinwheel is misaligned! I'll just—"

"Nope," I said, heading her off. "Dampeners. Vampires. Hero stuff."

"I guess." She kicked at a stone, but made no further attempt to align anything that didn't belong to her.

"Lady Lumiere, do you need me to carry your bag?" I asked. Of all the gear she had excavated from her house, Evelyn had only brought the leather bag containing her mother's ghost. It seemed heavy. But when I reached for it, she hugged it to her chest.

"Non. She is my burden to bear," Evelyn said. "And I would not want you scuffing up the bag with your clumsy metal hands."

"She has a point," Ida said, trying to wipe grease off her nose and smearing it liberally across her cheek. "You're kind of a klutz."

"He's good in a fight," Chesa said. When I stared at her, she shrugged. "You are. Own it. There's no reason to always take other people's abuse."

"I . . . uh. Okay."

Ida was watching us with bemusement. Evelyn looked like she was stifling a laugh.

I gave my attention to the mechanic. "So, do you get many field assignments?" I asked.

"Never. They keep me in the pipes. Even when the ship's docked, I stay onboard. Too much sunlight." She glared up at the sky. "And, you know, the engine is there. Gotta keep it humming."

"You were able to repair her, after Skyhook's emergency landing?"

"The crash? Yeah. Chunks of chicken soup in the main boiler. But that was your fault, so I don't feel too bad. Had to flush the whole system." She snorted. "I thought Honor was going to have a fit when Tesla brought you aboard. Insisted we were going to crash and die. Which, I mean, he was half right."

"Not my fault you don't believe in magic. You'd have probably made a pretty good rogue, all that climbing around in pipes and picking locks. If you ever get tired of the Gestalt—"

"I will never get tired of the Gestalt," Ida insisted. "Besides, our food is better."

"Yeah, you've got me there. But we get dragons."

"I can make a dragon, if I want," Ida said.

"Well, then you'd need someone to slay it. Either way, you need us."

"If the two of you will stop chattering, we have arrived," Evelyn declared. She had stopped about ten feet behind us, beside a wrought iron gate. The hellhounds were sitting at her side, wagging their scaled tails back and forth. Sparks flew from the concrete with each pass. We strolled back.

"Garden of the Dead," I read. "Y'all really know how to name stuff."

"It's a cemetery," Evelyn said. "We try to wrap such things in artifice."

"You can get buried in the Gestalt? If we tried that, our corpses would end up rotting in a Ren faire somewhere," Chesa said. "Neat trick."

"It's all thanks to the aetheric dampener," Evelyn said proudly. "Even the dead can dream."

The Garden of the Dead was a quiet, tree-lined plot of land. Grass lanes led between closely set stone memorials, most of them decorated with statues, plaques, and other memorials. Even while on the hunt for vampires, it was a pleasant place to stroll. Except we were here on business.

"Map says the crematorium is near the back of the cemetery," I said, nodding. Despite the odd looks from the other passersby, I drew my sword and shield. "This is prime vampire territory, so be careful."

"But it's the middle of the day," Ida pointed out. "Don't vampires come out at night?"

"We don't know the rules for these guys," I said. "They're not real vampires. Maybe daylight doesn't stop them."

"Or maybe you just like walking around with your sword out," Chesa said.

"I'm just . . . I'm careful! Never mind. It's this way."

"You know, if you added some hydraulics to that sword"—Ida pulled my sword arm to the side, examining the forte and hilt of my blade—"it could really—"

"I don't need hydraulics!" I yelled, storming off. "What I need is for you to stop trying to fix everything!"

"Touchy," Evelyn said before I was out of earshot.

The columbarium sat slightly higher than the rest of the cemetery, a white marble neoclassical building with a golden dome that would have looked perfectly comfortable masquerading as a personal estate in the countryside, surrounded by formal gardens and stables and more money than you could overthrow a king for. Two wings led off the main building, with hallways open to the elements. The walls were lined with small doors for urns. Each door had a shelf in front of it, where mourners could leave flowers and other mementos. Most of the plaques had some kind of memorial by them.

"Kind of a strange place for a scientific device," I said.

"The aether follows the spirit of the age," Evelyn answered. "This place is a cornerstone of the Gestalt—figuratively speaking. The dampener's downstairs."

"Of course it is," I said. "So it's a dungeon crawl?"

"They're crypts," Ida said. "Not the same thing at all."

A terraced staircase led to a second set of hallways, and more walls containing urns. The air here was damp, almost fetid, and the walls were draped in vines that tumbled over the terrace like a green, glistening waterfall. Evelyn walked at our fore with purpose, but my attention was drawn by the memorials. The dates were all over the board. 1887. 1482. 2058. 58 BC.

"Okay, wait a second. BC? 2058? How are these even possible?" I asked.

"We get some time travelers. The Wellsian types. Nik thinks they're creating their own Gestalts, maybe, or just alternate versions of ours," Ida said, pausing to examine the plaques. "A couple go back to your timeline."

"I'm starting to see the appeal of the Gestalt," Chesa muttered.

"Hey, don't abandon me with Greg," I said.

"Wouldn't dream of it," she said with a smile that was actually a smile and not a bitten-off retort. She patted me on the arm, then hurried to catch up with Evelyn, who was marching with the determination of an army general.

I took a second longer to peruse the plaques. All these names, all these people, had lived and died and were buried inside the Gestalt. I shook my head.

"That's so weird." Despite my numerous brushes with death, I hadn't given a lot of thought to where I would be buried. Part of me assumed I'd go back home, to be mourned by my confused parents and planted by the presbytery. Could I be buried in my domain? Or would the World Dog just dig me up? I didn't relish the idea of my skull being a chew toy for all eternity.

"It's over here. The old section," Evelyn called over her shoulder, pointing to the far side of the hall. An arched doorway engraved with gothic-style carvings led to an underground chamber. Ida and Chesa were right behind her. I strolled toward them, my sword mostly forgotten at my side.

"You know, I think I've figured out one difference between us," I said.

"Besides hygiene?" Evelyn asked icily.

"Your citizens are mostly normal people who have entered the Gestalt. You have very few native denizens. But the Unreal is entirely mythic, with the exception of Knight Watch and our allies."

"I hadn't thought of that, but you're right," Chesa said. "The Gestalt is created by folks like Nik and Evelyn's dad. When you meet someone in here, they're just regular people dreaming out loud. But in the Unreal, dragons really are dragons, and valkyries really are valkyries."

"Don't sound so proud of that," Ida said. "It's a sticking point for Tesla. He doesn't agree with the way Esther restricts access to your timeline. Thinks it's too authoritarian. Here, anyone can be what they dream."

"We could probably have used a little more restriction," Evelyn said quietly. She craned her neck up at the entrance to a hallway. "Here we are. Come."

"It also means anyone could be the villain," I said. "You don't have demons and angels. Just people. And people can be bloody terrible." We reached the archway. I looked up, my gaze tracing the gargoyles that hunched overhead. There was a plaque at the center of the archway. "Creepy."

"This was a family crypt before the columbarium was built," Ida said, ignoring the archway. "Family's long gone, so it was the perfect place for the dampener."

"Enough history. We need to check on the dampener," Evelyn snapped.

"Yes, yes. Cool your boilers," Ida said. She got a few steps into the room before fishing around in her tool belt and producing an extremely complicated-looking torch. The thing apparently ran on butane and friction, because it took her a couple pulls on a cord to get it lit, and when she succeeded it blossomed into a cloud of blue flame before she was able to tamp it down to a simple light source. Once that was sorted, she motioned us forward. Evelyn was already charging into the darkness, one hand resting comfortably on her accompanying hellhound.

But I was still staring at the archway. Because in that brief blast of forge-hot light, I had seen the words on the plaque embedded into the peak of the entrance. Not a family, nor a place name. It was an address.

La Rue de Mort.

CHAPTER EIGHTEEN

I fumbled the leather box out of my satchel and squinted at it in the light of Ida's receding torch. The grimacing gargoyle on the front of the box glinted in the light. Below it, the silver plaque: 1066 Rue de Mort. The hidden home of the vampires.

"Damn it," I muttered. "Damn it, damn it, damn it all to hell."

"What's the matter, John? Scared of the dark?" Chesa called over her shoulder.

"Ches, come here for a second." I answered. When she furrowed her brows at me, I waved her back furiously. "I'm serious!"

While Chesa ambled back, I took a second look around. This chamber certainly looked like the kind of place you'd meet a vampire. Spiderwebs draped gothic statues guarding crypts that were straight out of the darkest part of the Dark Ages. Tall, imperious-looking warriors stared down at me, pointing stone swords in accusation, as if they knew the secret I was about to reveal. Even with Ida's torch, the shadows here were ink-dark, clinging to every surface.

"Seriously, John, I don't want to get too far behind. What's your deal?" Chesa asked.

"This. This is my deal." I produced the box, tapping the plaque before pointing at the inscription over the door. "We're heading right to Esther's hidden cabal."

"Ah." She scanned the space in front of us, seeing it in a new light. "Yeah, I think you're right. You did see that vampire at the bakery. Maybe the bloodsuckers really are behind all this."

"Feels weird. Why would they use a machine to turn the bakers? Why not just . . ." I mimed biting a neck. "You know?"

"Covering their tracks? Looking for a new way to harvest human flesh?" She shrugged. "What am I supposed to know about the motivations of thousand-year-old undead bloodsuckers?"

"Why would they want to draw attention to themselves, though? I can believe they might be looking for another way—"

"Are the two of you done flirting?" Evelyn reappeared at the mouth of the tunnel, hellhounds at her side. The beasts' glowing eyes were bright red pinpricks of light in the gloom. "We have vampires to kill!"

"Sorry! Just arguing about, um . . ." I stumbled into silence.

"Take your pick," Chesa said. "Plenty to argue about with Rast."

"Well, get a move on," Evelyn said, then turned back and disappeared into the tunnel. Ida's light was a distant glimmer.

"So what do we do?" Chesa asked, whispering.

"I'm not sure yet. Maybe it's just bad luck that the dampener is near their refuge," I said. "Just keep your eyes peeled. We may have to improvise."

"Sounds terrible," Chesa said. We hurried to catch up with the other two.

Ida and Evelyn had gotten ahead of us. Ida was sticking her head into every nook and cranny with no consideration for the distinct possibility that the shadows may conceal all manner of vile creatures, while Evelyn strolled placidly down the middle of the chamber, one hellhound on either side, examining the surrounding tombs like a tourist. I sheathed my sword and slung my shield over my shoulder, then pulled Ida out from behind a dusty monument. She yelped and dropped her torch, leaving it sizzling in the dust of the stone floor. Once we were in the middle of the room, Ida just stood there, staring at my hand around her wrist for a few moments, then looked around curiously.

"Is there something over here that I'm supposed to be looking at? Because I don't think the dampener is here, in the middle of the room," she asked.

"I'm just trying to watch out for you," I said. "There's no telling what's lurking in here."

"Dead people. Obviously," Evelyn said. "Dead for a very long time."

"John's just the nervous type," Chesa said. She gave me a stern look. "Aren't you?"

"Well, you still can't be too careful," I said, grimacing at the darkness. "Dead doesn't mean not dangerous."

"My father liked to hide things," Evelyn said. "We are going to need to poke around a little if we're going to find it."

"Yeah. So do you want to help, or would you rather stare meaningfully at the shadows while I do all the work?" Ida asked.

"I'm . . . I'm guarding."

"Great. You continue guarding." Ida slipped her wrist free of my grasp, shaking her fingers out. "Odds are you'd break the dampener if you looked at it funny, anyway."

I gave Chesa a nervous look. She shrugged, and started walking around the perimeter of the room, right at the edge of the light thrown by Ida's torch. Evelyn simply stood imperiously in the middle of the room, regarding the whole operation with amused disdain. The hounds lay at her feet.

"This does look familiar," Evelyn said. "I believe I saw that statue in my father's notes."

"Hold this," Ida said, shoving the torch at me. I sheathed my sword and took the torch. Even through my gauntlets, the device was hot to the touch, especially around the coupling that spouted blue flame. I held it away from my face. Ida unfolded her tool kit at the base of the tomb that Evelyn had indicated. That girl carried more tools than a dwarven rogue. "This is going to take a minute."

The statue was of a beheaded knight, carrying its own head in its hands. The moment of decapitation was still captured in the horrified features of the statue's face. I suppressed a shiver. The mechanical torch flickered and dimmed.

"Maybe not the best idea for me to be holding this," I said. "Complicated stuff tends to break in my hands."

"Not just in your hands. My car used to stall every time I drove past you," Chesa said. "You thought I was flirting."

"You *were* flirting. That's how we ended up dating, remember? Your car died, and I walked you home." I sniffed indignantly. "In the rain, I might add."

"I should have seen the signs," Chesa muttered. "If only I'd kept driving . . ."

"Will the two of you shut up for a minute?" Ida asked. She had some sort of device, which she was slapping enthusiastically into the palm of her hand.

"Hm. My pneumohydralizer isn't working. And the readings on

the aetheratic are flat." She looked around curiously. "It's like my technology doesn't work here."

"The Unreal," Evelyn whispered. "The two of you must carry it with you. Fascinating."

"This happened at the bakery as well," I said. "The vampire thing was spreading the Unreal like a fog bank. Be careful."

"Well, I'm going to have to do this the old-fashioned way." Ida produced a screwdriver as long as her arm and started tapping at the base of the statue. "Surely there's an access panel around here somewhere."

After a few moments, Ida found what she was looking for and began to tinker. From the other side of the statue, all I could see was her face light up with a green glow.

"Huh," she said. "That's weird."

We huddled behind her, Chesa and I directly over Ida's shoulders, Evelyn behind us. The statue had a panel built into its base. What I at first took for the glow of a circuit board turned out to be something much more in line with the Gestalt. A long glass cylinder ran horizontally in the space beneath the statue, its ends capped with whirling metal arms that supported brass orbs. Thick glass windows in the cylinder revealed a sloshing reservoir of glowing blue liquid. Pistons and gauges regulated the cylinder, while a series of valves hooked up to automated bellows huffed and hummed at the base of the device. But that's not what caught my attention.

The aetheric dampener was crawling with beetles. Dime-sized scarabs clung in thick clumps to the cylinder, or scrabbled over the spinning arms of the generator caps. They had chewed holes in the bellows, and were swarming in and out of the cylinder like angry bees. And at the center of the dampener sat the largest scarab I had seen yet. Its abdomen was swollen and shiny, and its carapace glistened with ethereal light. The lesser beetles nestled beneath its thorax.

"Well. I think we found the problem," I said softly. "Do you think we should—"

"Destroy it!" Evelyn shouted. She shouldered us aside and struck the beetle with the haft of her surveying rod. The metal tip went through the scarab's body with a loud crunch. She ground the base back and forth, cracking off limbs and shattering metallic wings. The beetle burst, sending out a shimmering wave of iridescent baby beetles.

They flowed over the dampener, out of the compartment, and washed over us in a wave of clicking, scuttling shadows. Chesa shrieked, Ida gasped, and I let out a manly yelp. We all hopped back, all except for Evelyn, who continued to smash the mother scarab to pieces with her stick. The wave of beetles spread out into the darkness, scuttling into cracks in the wall or disappearing into the shadows.

Once they were gone, I composed myself and held the sputtering torch closer to the beetle's corpse. All that was left were broken cogs, fragments of iridescent carapace, and a smear of green-and-black liquid.

Ida sighed. "I was really hoping to examine that," she said. "I could learn a lot by studying it. But you guys keep breaking them."

"Well, this is probably for the better," I said, straightening. "Wouldn't want those baby beetles loose on the *Silverhawk*, anyway. Imagine the trouble they could—"

One of the shadows moved in the corner of the room. I caught a glimpse of red eyes and a dark cloak, crouching on top of a broken pillar at the other end of the corridor. As soon as I saw it, the figure leapt into the air, disappearing behind a crypt with a flutter of black cloth.

I dropped the torch, which hit the stone floor with a crack, and drew my sword. A violent hissing sound erupted from the device. Ida swore and grabbed at it, yelping in pain before cranking the flame into a bare flicker. Chesa and Evelyn spun to face me, and the hellhounds leapt to their feet and started to growl.

"What was the point of that?" Ida yelled. "You've compromised the seal. We're lucky it didn't blow up!"

"I need more light!" I answered. With my light source practically gone, I couldn't see beyond the tip of my sword. Chesa and Evelyn were bare outlines in the gloom, and the hellhounds' glowing eyes disappeared completely. Stones scraped together nearby, then something clanked against the ceiling to my right. I whirled in that direction, only to be drawn back to my left by clattering pebbles. "Chesa! Light!"

"Stop yelling. Geez, you'd think—"

The creature came out of the shadows, barreling into my shield at full speed. It knocked me back into Ida, and we both went into the stone coffin. Whatever had run into me swiped at the shield a couple times, its claws throwing sparks off the steel face. Ida screamed directly into my ear.

"Who's yelling now?" I spat, then braced my shoulder against the tomb and pushed back at the beast. It rolled off my shield and onto the ground, coming up in a swirl of fabric. The torch had fallen once again. Ida lunged for it, then cranked it to full power. A tongue of blue flame erupted from the end, turning the dark chamber as bright as day.

The creature standing in front of us was a hulking monstrosity. Broad shoulders strained against the blood-spattered fabric of a white linen shirt, with a neck like a mountain range erupting out of the frayed collar. He was as bald as a bowling ball, with pale white skin, and enormous bloodred eyes. The rest of its body was out of proportion: hips and legs too small to realistically support those shoulders, and dainty feet in patent leather buckle shoes. When the torch burst into life, the vampire threw an arm over its face, backing away reflexively.

"That's right, bitey-boy!" Ida marched forward, holding up the sputtering torch. "Fear the power of sci—"

The beast lunged at her, striking the torch and sending it spinning into the darkness. The light clattered behind some statues and faded into a dim glow. Ida screamed in pain. I punched at the vampire with my shield, barely deflecting the second strike from its claws with the bright steel of the buckler. Ida crumpled to the ground, nursing her hand. The vampire growled at me as I put myself between it and the injured mechanic.

"Are you okay?" I shouted, keeping my eyes on the monster.

"I've had worse from a blown compressor," Ida said, but her voice was strained. "Oh, I think I can see bone. That's cool."

"Trust me, that is very not cool. Especially when we don't have a healer around. Next time, leave the fighting to the guy with the sword." I slid warily to the side. "Ches? You out there?"

Chesa's answer was an arrow out of the darkness that thumped into the vampire's meaty shoulder. The creature howled, then vaulted into the darkness. I heard Chesa gasp, followed by a frantic scramble of boots and claws on stone. In the dim light, all I could see were shadows leaping from statue to tomb to ceiling then floor, too fast to follow.

"Ches?" I shouted in panic.

"Do something, John!"

"Stay here," I ordered Ida. "And see if you can do something about those lights." Then I charged into the darkness.

The whistle of flying arrows clattering off stone gave me some clue where to go. I skidded to a halt beside a large statue, pressing my back against the wall. Something vaulted over me. I got my shield up just in time for a heavy foot to land square in the middle, crushing me to the ground. Apparently whatever had stepped on me didn't expect their foothold to collapse, because there was a strangled gurgle and crashing stone to my right. In the dimness I caught a glimpse of bloodred eyes, each the size of the palm of my hand. I rolled to my feet and swung at it. My blade glanced off something heavy.

The vampire lunged at me, claws curled to strangle my neck. I reached for my magic, but I had forgotten to open up the taps in my amulet after we landed, and was still recovering from the fight in the bakery. It was like trying to suck on a straw when all you had left in the cup was ice. Nothing came through. Instead, I caught the grip with the rim of my shield, then poked at his belly with the flat of my sword, slicing along the waist. Steel went into muscled flesh, but the creature didn't relent. It felt like stabbing cold mud. He shook the shield back and forth, nearly dislocating my shoulder, before rearing back with his right arm and punching the shield square in the center. The impact shook my bones and sent a shiver through my lungs. I tried to hack at his fingers, but before I could land the blow, he tossed the shield like a Frisbee.

I was still attached to the shield.

I spun foot to head and back again before coming to a sliding stop at the base of a broken statue. From this angle the knight looked less threatening, and more like he was going trick-or-treating with a gag candy basket. When I started laughing at that, I realized I must have taken a knock on the head.

"Come on, you've got to move," Ida said. She pulled me to a sitting position. There was a lot of blood streaming down her arm.

"You're hurt," I said blearily. She patted me on the shoulder, leaving bloody handprints on the steel. "Where's Chesa?"

"I don't know. And that thing is still out there." She tugged at my elbow, dragging me to my feet. "Great. Now . . ." Ida pressed my sword into my hand. "Hero stuff. Shoo."

"Need my shield," I mumbled.

"Your shield is wrecked. Couldn't stop a stiff breeze." She kicked at the rumpled scraps of my shield. "Going to have to make do with your sparkling personality."

"That's a good way to get dead. Besides..." I took a deep breath and felt at the reservoir of magic in my soul. There was a glimmering pool, shallow but ready to be tapped. "Check this out."

I scooped up the shield and opened the valve into my domain. A wave of light traveled through my body, burning away the dozen or so injuries I had sustained in my fight, then renewing my shield. The valkyrie's steel shimmered as it regrew. Ida whistled in appreciation.

"See? Magic ain't so bad." I tightened the enarme straps, shook out my wrist, and faced the darkness. "Now. What happened to big, bad, and bitey?"

Chesa's scream cut through the silence of the tomb. I ran toward it, my armor clattering loudly with each footfall. I went around a corner, just as a flarrow whistled into the ceiling, guttering harshly as it roared to life. In the sharp light, I could see Chesa kneeling at the base of a tomb with the vampire towering over her. She was trying to nock another arrow.

I barreled into the vampire, knocking it prone, though the force of the blow sent me reeling backward. Before I could recover, the vampire hopped to its feet and started toward me.

"Wait!" I shouted, dropping my sword to grab at the box stuffed in my belt. I pulled out the embossed box and cranked it open like a holy relic, holding it up to the vampire. "Stop! We're here to help!"

The vampire's eyes barely flickered to the dangling key before he charged me. I dropped key and box, bracing my shield with both hands. The impact sent me skidding backward. I came up hard against the wall. The vampire stepped over the fallen box and bore down on me.

"Idiot! Esther MacRae saved you and your kin! She sent us to warn you!" I threw my shield aside and tried to stand. "Will you just listen for a second, before Ida hears us?"

"I have heard all I need," the vampire growled. "Knight Watch killed my kin and scourged my bloodline. That she felt a pang of guilt at the end hardly redeems her genocide." He wrapped meaty fingers down the front of my breastplate and yanked me upright by the straps. "Why are you hunting us, small man?"

"Someone is setting you up," I said. "Making it look like the vampires are attacking again. You have to hide!"

"He's telling the truth," Chesa said from the side. "They're using machines to turn people into vampires. Tesla sent for us to help."

"We know of the scarabs. My brother was there when you arrived, looking into it." His voice was surprisingly urbane, given his bulk and the blood spattered across his shirt. My blood, at least in part. "Why should we trust you? If Tesla is behind this, it means—"

"Guys?" Ida's voice wavered from the other room. "I think you need to see this. There's a door."

The vampire growled deep in his chest. "The demesne. I must kill her, before she—"

"You're not killing anyone, and especially not Ida," I said, ignoring his challenging glare. "You have to trust us. We'll take care of this."

"Hm. We shall see." He dropped me. "We are watching you, knight. If you cross us, there will be cold blood in the halls of your domain."

Without another word, he bounded away. I waited until he disappeared before I picked up my sword and shield. Chesa retrieved the key and its box, handing it back to me.

"Pretty good, John. You didn't piss yourself," Chesa said with a smile.

"Much," I answered. "What do you think he meant? If Tesla is behind this, it means..."

"Don't know. Come on, before Ida gets suspicious."

Ida stood behind one of the tombs, apparently retrieving her torch. The device sputtered, throwing long shadows across the ceiling. We circled the tomb. She was deep in thought, examining a door hidden in the wall. She glanced up as we approached.

"What do you guys make of this?" she asked. "Some kind of secret entrance?"

I glanced nervously at Chesa, then fumbled for the key. "Look, we can explain everything. It's not..."

That's when I noticed the door was already open. Something had torn apart the lock, and the hinges were bent at a crooked angle. The door had been forced. Violently.

The secret of the vampires was already out, apparently.

CHAPTER NINETEEN

I stood there, staring dumbly at the broken door. It was made of stone, and would have fit smoothly into the surrounding wall if someone hadn't taken a hammer to the hinges. A brass plaque etched with the date 1066 covered the lock. The plaque had been peeled back like the corner of a cheap paperback, exposing the mechanism. The door hung open a couple inches. Air wafted through the gap, smelling like grave dirt and snuffed candles.

"What happened to the vampire?" Ida asked. "Did you kill it?"

"He ran away," I said. "Away from this door, I might add."

"Well, he'd already done the damage." She reached for the door. "Maybe I can still repair it. Or figure out what they—"

"Wait!" I grabbed her hand. There was a whole cabal of vampires hidden behind that door. Last thing I wanted to do was explain that to Ida. "We should wait for Evelyn."

"Speaking of whom . . ." Chesa craned her neck, looking around the chamber. "Where'd she get to?"

It took us several minutes to confirm, but Evelyn had completely disappeared. Other than a paw print burned into the floor of the room with the hidden door, there was no sign of either Lady Lumiere or her hellhounds. We met back at 1066 Rue de la Mort.

"That's weird," Ida said. "Maybe she went through here." She reached for the door, then looked at me. "You're not going to grab me again, are you?"

"No. But maybe it's better if I went first. We don't know what's through there."

"How chivalrous," she said. "But I'm a modern girl."

The door swung open, revealing a winding stone staircase descending into the earth. The steps were worn down by generations of feet, and a guttering torch hung just inside the door. Flickering light from below indicated further torches.

"Huh. This feels like an odd design for an aetheric dampener." Ida started forward, the blazing blue light from her torch held high. As soon as she crossed the threshold, the mechanical wonder in her hand dimmed and went out. She paused to shake it. The device came apart in her hands, sending pieces of clockwork bouncing loudly down the stairs. "What the Samantha Hill was that?"

"It's the Unreal," I said. "We've found another pocket of it. Which makes me think we should call for backup." I shot Chesa a meaningful look. "Ches, maybe you and Ida should go back to the entrance and try to get a message to the *Silverhawk*. I'll stay here and watch the door."

"I'm not sure that's safe. What if Evelyn went in there?" Chesa edged forward. "We should—"

"Ches!" I hissed, nodding vigorously at the clueless Ida, who was still shaking her broken torch. "Maybe you and Ida should GO? AWAY? So I can GUARD the DOOR?"

"Oh! Oh, yeah, right. Good call. Come on, Ida."

"Hm?" Ida looked up, a little baffled. "You know, I think this thing is broken."

The device in her hand had turned into a medieval torch, complete with pitch-soaked rags and gnarled wooden handle. A couple cogs were stuck to the pitch, and a stray electrical wire wrapped around the handle, but other than that it was straight out of the *Player's Handbook*.

Chesa took Ida by the hand and led her back toward the entrance of the crypts. As soon as they were gone, I pulled my own torch-and-tinder kit out of my satchel, sparked it up, then started down the stairs. A trail of sooty smoke plumed off my torch and flattened against the curved ceiling, following a line of blackened stone that spoke of generations of use, and lifetimes of torches. The stone stairs were butter-smooth beneath my feet. This place was old, the way ruins and mountain ranges were old.

The stairs curled down and down into the earth. Black iron sconces lined the walls every dozen yards or so, the flickering light from each one giving out just as I caught sight of the faint glimmer of the next torch. I lost count of their turning, and began to worry that I had missed another secret door when the sound of music reached my ears: piano, tinny and distant as it echoed off the stone walls and drifted up the spiral stairs. It felt out of place this far beneath the streets. I made a final turn, and came out onto a balcony overlooking a formal dining room, and the last refuge of the vampires.

It was a slaughterhouse. The smell of blood choked the air, rising from the dozen bodies that lay sprawled across the floor. Plush carpets ruined by pools of gore covered the floor. The furniture, what little of it wasn't already in splinters, looked like it had come out of a Victorian funeral home, ornate and macabre in equal measure. As I came into the room, the music hit a sour note, pausing for a long heartbeat before starting again. Sterling silver skull candelabras lay toppled across the shattered banquet table that ran the length of the room. A fire roared in the enormous hearth at the far end of the room. Both logs and bones crackled in the flames, sending thick black smoke billowing up the chimney. Oil portraits lined one long wall. The other, closest to me, was covered by a detailed, age-stained tapestry that seemed to depict a history of war, banquets, slaughter, and violence. A lot of red thread had been used.

The music came from a grand piano at the head of the table, offset from the fireplace by a giant bearskin rug. The body of a young woman lay akimbo in the center of the rug. Her blood turned the matted fur of the dead beast as slick as tar, and just as dark. A man sat at the piano, dressed in crisp white and startling red, his black hair slicked back from his face, revealing sharp features and long, pointed bat-like ears. As I paused on the balcony at the top of the final flight of stairs, I could see that his features were less human than I expected. He looked more like a wolf pressed into the shape of a man, all feral angles and snarling violence. Yet there was deep sadness in the music tapping out of the piano, teased out by his long, talon-tipped fingers. A dirge, as delicate as lace, as soft as smoke from a funeral pyre. I waited at the top of the stairs, almost afraid to disturb this strange and horrific moment.

The vampire ended my reverie. A note struck wrong, then another, and he smashed his fists into the keys. Ivory shattered under the blow, sending a dissonant chord crashing through the hall. I flinched back. He lifted his eyes to me, and they burned with amber light and ancient hatred.

"Have you come to finish her cursed work?" His voice was smooth as silk passing over a silver blade. He stood, and I recognized him as the vampire I had seen in the bakery. He loomed over the piano. "Well? Speak, child. Are you here to kill me?"

"What? No, why would I want to kill you?" I noticed something about the corpses strewn around the room. "These are vampires?"

"My family, my kith and kin, the only remaining sire of my bloodline, and the hope of my people." The vampire came around the piano. "And now they are dead. Surely, if you found your way through that door, you knew what you would find."

"Yeah, I just . . . I wasn't expecting this." I descended the stairs, stepping over pools of blood on the polished marble. It was only once I was on the ground floor that I noticed a series of heavy wooden doors partially hidden by the tapestry. Most had been broken open, their splintered frames hanging like loose teeth in the stone. "What happened here?"

"Who are you?" the vampire asked. His hand lay on a fencing rapier at his belt. It very much looked like the kind of weapon that could kill a knight. "We have not seen a mortal soul in a thousand years. Two in one night is more than curious."

"Sir John Rast, of Knight Watch," I said. "And you?"

"Jakub Everlasting, Earl of Darkhaven, and Sire of the Thousand Bright Moons." He surveyed the room. "Though they have passed from this earth, it would appear."

"Wait, a thousand years? Esther told me she helped set up this enclave. She's no spring chicken, but a millennium seems like a stretch."

"Ah, Esther MacRae." Jakub nodded. "So she has finally decided to betray our trust? Typical mortal perfidy. Such short lives, crammed with so much deceit and misery." He took his hand from the sword, but only to return to the piano and tap out a few sad notes. His earlier rage had destroyed most of the keys, and the only sound to come out was the discordant twang of broken strings. "To answer your question, our mythos is one of age. Time moves differently in our domain. Not so much that you'll return to a different world. Assuming you leave at all."

"Ah. Right." I took that as a threat, but was determined not to acknowledge it. "Something's going on in the Gestalt. Esther sent us to warn you, should things get dangerous."

"As you can see, your warning is too late." Another disjointed cacophony of notes from the piano. I began to wonder if my new friend was properly insane. "Go back to Esther and tell her that you have failed. As mortals always do."

The closest corpse was a young girl, dressed in crushed velvet, with a heavy necklace of silver chain looped around her throat. She stared sightlessly at the ceiling. There was a wound in her belly, and another on her exposed thigh. Beyond her was an elderly vampire, crook-backed and swathed in velvet robes. A trail of blood leaked from a narrow hole in the middle of his forehead. The rest of the bodies had similar wounds. Things that would certainly kill a mortal, but something about it sat wrong in my head.

"I don't understand," I said. "I thought you had to stake a vampire to kill it."

"They are not dead," the vampire said. "Merely empty. Their souls have been taken. Stolen by that vengeful bitch."

"What? Who?"

"Evelyn Lumiere, of course," Jakub said. "The scourge of the night."

"Evelyn did this?" I asked, incredulous. "How'd you survive?"

"My brother and I were away. At least, I assume he must also have escaped, as I don't see him here." Jakub closed his eyes, then shut the keyboard. "Alekzander will be frightened. I must find him, before he does something untoward."

"Big guy? Shoulders like Chicago?" I asked. "He's fine. Though I sent him running just before I came down here."

"I sincerely doubt that," Jakub said, rising. "My brother has not seen defeat in a thousand battles. He was not driven away from his home by a child in toy armor."

"Look," I said, ignoring his jab. "If you weren't here, how do you know Evelyn did all this? I've met her, and let me tell you, I doubt she was up for killing a whole room full of vampires."

"Pardon the expression, but it is in her blood." Jakub stood mournfully over the dead girl, his hands folded at his waist. "The Lumieres have been hunting my kin for generations. It is second nature to her."

"Generations? But I thought—"

"Hello? John?" Chesa's voice echoed down the staircase. "Ida and I are back, and we've brought electric friends."

"Tesla." I swore. "You need to get out of here. The Eccentrics can't know about you."

"And how are you going to explain all this?" Jakub asked.

"I'll think of something. Just . . . get out of here. Find your brother."

"Fine. But be warned, Sir John of Rast—"

"Yeah, yeah, if we betray you, there will be blood in the halls of my domain. Your brother mentioned that."

"Ah, so you truly have met Alekz." He smiled, an unsettling feral expression. "Think on what you have seen and what you have been told. There are stories even Tesla's science cannot fathom. The Lumieres are monsters."

"What does that even mean? She's a nice old lady."

"Nice old ladies do not keep company with hellhounds, Sir John." Jakub looked up at the sound of footsteps on the staircase. "We will talk, once this is finished."

A cloud of bats erupted from Jakub's chest, and he dissolved into their fluttering wings. With a screech they circled the room once, then spiraled up into the ceiling, to disappear among the rafters. The leathery flap of their wings faded into silence, echoing through stone corridors, until there was nothing.

"I sure hope not," I muttered.

Just then, Nikola Tesla, flanked by Ida, Adelaide, and The Good Doctor emerged from the staircase. They spread out on the balcony, staring at the carnage with wide eyes. Chesa followed timidly.

"Well," Nik said. "I hope you have a good explanation for this."

CHAPTER TWENTY

I stood there, surrounded by dead vampires, trying to come up with an excuse that didn't make me sound like an idiot, a traitor, or both. Moments passed. Tesla stared at me with the look of a man on the edge of technologically advanced violence.

"Well?" he asked finally.

"They were dead when I got here," I answered.

"Dead when you got here? Is that all you have to say? That they were dead when you got here?" He marched down the stairs, avoiding the same pools of blood that I had, gesturing to the surrounding bodies. "A room full of dead steampunks. My God, these people had families. And you just let the vampires—"

"These *are* the vampires, actually. Dead vampires." I pointed to the girl at my feet. "See? Fangs, pointy ears, general lack of skin tone. Vampires."

"What? What the . . . what?" Tesla stopped dead in his tracks. "But we killed all of the vampires!"

"Yeah. About that." I glanced at Chesa. The rest of Knight Watch gathered behind her, all pointedly looking anywhere but in my direction. "Esther spared a couple. I'd say about"—I did a quick count of the bodies—"six of them. No, eight. Jakub and his brother escaped."

"There are a couple more in the fireplace," Chesa pointed out.

"Right, so, ten. Let's call it an even dozen, just to be safe," I said. Tesla gaped at me. The rest of the Eccentrics weren't that far behind. They spread out through the coven, examining bodies and furnishings, poking their heads through the smashed doors that

149

lined the wall. I pressed on. "Though honestly we don't know how many they've created since then. I'd rather not speculate on—"

"Esther MacRae, on her own, just decided to betray our confidence and rescued a coven of bloodsuckers, then hid them? Inside the Gestalt?" Tesla was yelling by now, his face red and bulging with veins. "And then when we uncovered this fact, you came under the pretense of helping us, and somehow stumbled on that very cabal?"

"I had a key." I held up the display box Esther had given me. "Though clearly I didn't need it."

"We're done," Tesla snapped. "I'm dropping you off at the nearest faire. You can find your own way back to Mundane Actual. I don't care how you do it—ride a unicorn, hitchhike through the Middle Ages, join a group of wandering sketch artists. And when you get home, you tell Esther MacRae that the next time she contacts me, I'm going to drop a bomb on her jumped-up Medieval Times franchise so big—"

"Boss," Adelaide said sternly. I noticed that her arm was in a sling. Tesla whirled to face her, his mouth still working its way around the dimensions of this theoretical bomb. "Maybe take a look at this."

Adelaide gazed up at the tapestry. With all the blood and carnage in the room, plus the presence of a vampire, I hadn't given the artwork much of a look. The outside edges of the tapestry depicted your typical medieval scenes, tinged with gothic horror. Knights and peasants dying and killing by the sword. Crows with bloody beaks perched in dead trees, overlooking fields of corpses. Castles burning. Villages burning. Bodies burning.

Two figures dominated the center of the tapestry. On the right stood Jakub Everlasting, dressed in his characteristic white and crimson, though in the tapestry he wore enameled plate armor, trimmed in red, rather than a suit. He was reaching out to shake the hand of another man, whom I did not recognize. A fine Victorian gentleman in a gray evening coat and high-buttoned vest, with one foot resting comfortably on a skull. His only distinguishing feature was a scar on his right cheek that bisected his eye. He was also reaching out to shake Jakub's hand. In the space between them hung a clock with too many numerals. The air around the clock twisted like a heat mirage.

"I take it you recognize him?" I asked Tesla.

He nodded. "That is Claude Lumiere. I would recognize that scar anywhere. From his early experiments, before he earned a place in the Gestalt." Tesla grimaced. "What does it all mean?"

"It seems like the Lumieres were familiar with the vampires, at the very least. Why else would the bloodsuckers keep this tapestry around?" Adelaide asked. "Oh, look here."

She pointed at the image. Tucked behind his back, Claude Lumiere held a knife in his left hand. The point already dripped with black blood.

"What do you make of that?" I asked.

"The symbolism is apparent throughout the tapestry," Tembo said. He and the rest of Knight Watch gathered behind me. "A foot on the skull, conquering death. A hidden knife indicates betrayal. As for the clock . . ." He shrugged. "I have no idea."

"That's the scarab," Ida whispered. She moved close to the tapestry, producing a telescoping loupe from one of her many pockets. As soon as she extended the lens, it fell out and shattered on the floor.

"Looks like we're still in the Unreal," Tesla muttered. "Cassius stayed upstairs, just to be safe. Lady Adelaide, how is your arm faring?"

"Holding together, but only barely." I realized the sling was bound tightly to her clockwork arm. "Can we figure out what's going on and get out of here?"

"You can leave it to us, if you want," I said.

Tesla shook his head sharply. "You have betrayed us once. I'm keeping you close until this is resolved," he said. Then he pulled a table close to the tapestry and clambered up to get closer to the clock. Ida followed, leaning precariously against the wall. "Ida, my dear genius, you are correct. The threadwork is imprecise, but this definitely depicts the inner workings of the scarabs you retrieved from the bakery. What do you think it means?"

"I'm not sure, but maybe we can ask *her*?" Chesa knelt beside one of the dead vampires. It looked like a young woman, dressed in leather armor, lying on her side.

"None of us are necromancers, Ches. Unless . . ." I cocked a brow at Tembo. He shook his head. "No. So we'll have to stick with interviewing the living."

"Pay attention, John." She turned the vampire onto her face. There was a brass scarab clutched to the base of the vampire's neck, twitching slightly.

"Careful!" Ida hopped down from the table. "The last couple you smashed. Let's see if we can get this one intact."

"Double careful," I said, standing over Chesa. "That's a vampire you're reviving."

With Knight Watch clustered around one side of her, and the Eccentrics standing guard on the other, Ida bent over the scarab and began tinkering. She muttered a lot, trying various tools until she found one simple enough that the Unreal wouldn't interfere with its functionality. It took a few minutes, but she finally released the scarab from the dead vampire's neck.

Let me amend that. Formerly dead. Currently undead. However that works.

"There we go," Ida said, sitting up and proudly displaying the scarab. "Just a little scratching along the cowling, but we've got one fully functional, soul-sucking scarab. Now I just need to—"

"Death to mortal flesh!" the vampire shrieked, vaulting to her feet and grabbing Ida around the neck. She bounded off the table, onto the wall, and through the air with such grace I could hardly believe what I was seeing. Ida flapped behind her like a human flag. She finally came down on top of the hearth, perched like a gargoyle on the stone mantel. With one arm, she held our startled mechanic tight to her chest. With the other, the vampire pressed a silver dagger into Ida's neck.

"Squawk," Ida said through her lolling tongue. Her face was turning a worrying shade of purple, and her feet kicked weakly against the hearth. We rushed forward in a wave of steel and concerned expressions.

"Don't move!" the vampire shouted, shaking Ida for emphasis.

"Do the math, lady. Maybe *you* don't move," I said, drawing my sword. Gregory posed heroically next to me, and both Tembo and Chesa readied their attacks. The Eccentrics, robbed of their technological doodads, merely glowered.

"We don't actually need to threaten her," Adelaide said. "We just saved her life, after all."

"Ha! As though simpering mortals could save the life of Zofia Zinzadelle, queen of the night!"

"Zofia? Zinzadelle?" I asked.

"Yes. You have heard tale of my hunts, and tremble?"

"No. But it's a lot of Zees. Are you actually a vampire, or just a mundane who made the jump into the Unreal?" When she didn't immediately answer, I sighed. "Look, Zapf Dingbats, let our friend go. She saved your life. Without her, you'd still be twitching on the floor in a coma with that bug thing on your neck, sucking your soul into a little glass jar."

For a second, I thought she was going to tear Ida's head off, just to prove a point. But slowly she loosened her grip. Ida went from struggling to escape to scrambling to not fall the twenty feet to the stone floor. Tembo barked an arcane word, and purple light surrounded the frantic mechanic. She floated harmlessly to the floor.

"That was cool. Can you do that again, but up?" Ida asked.

"So I take it you're Knight Watch," Zapf said glumly. "And this is your vengeance."

"Yes to the former, no to the latter. We're here to help," I said.

"Maybe," Tesla interjected.

"No, we're definitely here to help." I sheathed my sword then extended my hand. "Come down here and we'll talk about it. Starting with how you know Claude Lumiere."

Just then, Bethany appeared out of the shadows of the ceiling. She dropped behind the vampire and struck. ZeeZeeZapf never saw it coming. Bee cludged her in the back of the head with a black sap. The vampire went limp, falling gracelessly off the hearth to tumble onto the bearskin rug with a meaty thump. We ran forward. Ida grimaced at the vampire's misshapen limbs and cracked skull.

"That's gonna leave a scar," she whispered.

"Bee!" I shouted in frustration. "You've got to stop doing that!"

"What?" Our rogue looked around the room. "I can't hear anything in shadow form. I'm guessing she was declaring our deaths and the endless reign of the nightbreed, right? Right?"

I shook my head, then toed the previously dead, briefly undead, and now questionably alive vampire.

"Well. I suppose it's a good thing that she's immortal."

Turns out immortality takes about twenty minutes to kick in. In the meantime, we searched the rest of the coven, arranging the bodies of the fallen vampires as neatly as we could against the wall. I explained what Jakub had said about their souls, that it was a different sort of death. There was nothing we could do for the bodies in the fire. The dozen or so rooms on the side were lavishly decorated, each with its own coffin. We did find several other exits from the main room, hidden in the ceiling or behind tapestries. One even branched off the chimney, though its iron door was too hot to open.

When ZeeZee came around, we poured her a glass of something viscous from one of the bottles behind the bar and Tembo cast Globe of Frost into a steel helm, which we then pressed over the knot on her head. She sat on the couch, glaring at the bodies of her family and sipping bloodwine from a pewter goblet.

And then she told us what happened.

Apparently the Lumieres had made contact with the vampires through Lady Lumiere's séances. Thinking he was dealing with spirits, Claude made promises in exchange for knowledge. And the knowledge that he sought was the secret to immortality.

"I think he fell into the wrong timeline," ZeeZee said. "He would have been better off in the Unreal. But his mind didn't work that way. He wanted to build a machine that would extend his life. We laughed. Then, one day, he stepped through the aether directly into Jakub's demesne. That got our attention."

She took a long drink, then sat back. "He made promises. Threats. Compromises. Jakub thought he could cure us, whatever that means. I never wanted to be cured. But here we are. When it became clear that Claude's intentions had nothing to do with helping us, and everything to do with his own power, Jakub cut off contact.

"You know what happened after that. The Lumieres came after us. Tried to force their way into our demesne. So we hit back."

"I can't believe the Lumieres would do that. Claude was a man of peace. Of Science!" Tesla said. "Your attack was completely unprovoked."

"And it wasn't just Lumieres who died at that party," Adelaide said. "Dozens of citizens of the Gestalt were slaughtered. Innocent men and women!"

"And how many survived?" ZeeZee asked.

"None," Tesla answered. "Only their daughter, Evelyn."

"So you have only Evelyn's word for what happened. But what if

I told you that Claude Lumiere was trying to open a portal into the Unreal? A powerful spell." She stood up and strolled to the hearth, where the bones of some of her kin still crackled in the flames. "A spell that required sacrifices to power it. Human sacrifices."

"What? That's preposterous!" Tesla shook his fist at ZeeZee. "Why are we supposed to believe you, an actual monster, over a woman I have fought beside for decades?"

In answer, she leaned against the hearth, gestured to the bones resting in the fire.

"Which of us is the monster? Truly?"

Tesla's face fell. Blinking, he looked around at the Eccentrics.

"I don't know what to think," he said. "I don't know who to believe."

"You don't have to believe me. Ask Claude, or Evelyn. The proof will be among her father's papers, or in that lab of his." She smiled at us. "Surely you've secured the lab?"

Tesla went white. He grabbed Ida. "Get upstairs and get the *Silverhawk* ready to fly. We need to get back to the Lumiere Estate as soon as possible."

Ida, obviously glad to be escaping the Unreal and getting back into the skies, scampered up the stairs.

"What I don't understand is how she overcame so many of you," I said. "She's not a very big lady. Sure, those hounds look rough, but—"

ZeeZee laughed. "Evelyn Lumiere is the archetype of the vampire slayer. Her father founded the class around her. Esther MacRae knows all about it. She helped him do it. Together she and Evelyn created the perfect domain, for one purpose. Slaying vampires."

"Gods. It's so hard to believe. Why would Esther not tell us?" Chesa asked.

"That woman has more secrets than you would believe, and more sins," Tesla said quietly. "Here's one more."

"Yes. But for all her power, Evelyn couldn't reach us. Esther saw to that. Tucked away in the Gestalt, Evelyn couldn't use her Slayer powers." The vampire shook her delicate head. "I still don't know how she managed to penetrate the veil of our obfuscations. It should have been beyond mortal ken."

"I think I do," I said. I grimaced at Chesa. "We brought the Unreal with us. She brought us here, just to get to you."

"So. Twice betrayed by mortals. I shouldn't be surprised." ZeeZee stood and rubbed her neck where it had broken in the fall. There was a thin purple line, but otherwise her flesh was unmarked. "Here is what I will tell you. The father had plans for his daughter. Plans that we disrupted when we interrupted his ritual. She blamed us for their death, as rightly she should. Her vengeance was terrible." She gestured to the room. "And now it is complete."

"Come with us. We could use your guidance in this fight," Tembo said.

"No. My father still lives, and my uncle. We will rebuild our world." Like Jakub before her, ZeeZee blurred in form and body. When she was finished, a sleek black cat perched on the hearth. "Without mortal help this time," that cat said. Then it leapt across the hearth and up the stairs, disappearing quickly.

"What was that about her father?" Tesla asked.

"I'll explain later," I said. "Let's get into the air. Before Evelyn can surprise us again."

CHAPTER TWENTY-ONE

We knew what we would find long before we got there. The plume of smoke cut a black line through the sky, visible for miles. Still, we pressed on, coming to a smooth landing on the gravel road in front of the Lumiere Estate.

Flames consumed the house. As we descended the stairs from the *Silverhawk*, I could hear glass shattering inside, and the groan of support timbers turning into embers. Clouds of cinders blossomed from the roof, and jets of flame twisted out of the gables, like devil eyes against the curling tar shingles. We stood in a semicircle in front of the gate, watching the conflagration grow.

"So much for searching the house," I said glumly.

"She must have known she was never coming back," Tesla said. "Burning her bridges, and any evidence that might have convicted her. Literally."

"Is there any hope of salvaging something?" Chesa asked. "You must have firefighting equipment on board."

"I'm not risking my crew in there," Skyhook answered. "No telling what sorts of surprises Evelyn left behind. All manner of nastiness in that lab."

"Honorious is right. It would appear Evelyn sabotaged her home to keep us from finding out what she was doing. You can bet that she prepared accordingly for our return and possible salvage operation." Tesla turned away from the blaze. "We can sift through the ashes later, but I doubt we'll find anything."

"It's not a complete loss," I said. "She brought a lot of stuff with her. Most of it is still on the ship."

"Oh, gods!" Skyhook exclaimed. "It could be riddled with bombs! Lads! Evacuate the cargo hold!"

"But our stuff—" I started, to no avail.

At their captain's signal, the team of Pinkertons streamed back on board. Moments later, every port and window cranked open, and piles of boxes, crates, folios, and gear tumbled down the side of the *Silverhawk* to land ingloriously on the gravel road. Including our kit, which flew so far it crashed into the cornfield across the way.

"Right. Greg, Bee, give me a hand retrieving that stuff," I said. "The rest of you, see if you can help out inside. Try to prevent the Pinkertons from evicting anything fragile."

"Little late for that," Chesa said, as a hutch of delicate china pinwheeled clamorously to the ground.

Tesla sighed. "They can be a bit too enthusiastic," he allowed. "Everyone on board as quickly as possible. If there are traps in that garbage, I want to be in the air before it detonates."

"We should go through the things Evelyn left behind, in case there are clues," Tembo said. "We need to make sense of why she would betray the Eccentrics' confidence so readily."

"I'm still not convinced she's behind this," Adelaide said. "I've known her my entire Gestalt-life. We've had tea together, hunted monsters side by side." She shrugged. "It doesn't feel likely."

"She was a mother to me," Cassius rumbled.

"Even mothers can go bad," I said. "But you're right. Once the *Silverhawk* is clear, we'll go through the remains." The armor stand, still holding my plate and chain, tipped out of the open cargo hatch to crash clamorously to the ground. "We're going to need to reclaim some of that stuff anyway."

"I'll get a broom," Ida said, skipping toward the *Silverhawk*.

It took the better part of an hour, but we found what we were looking for. I think Evelyn wanted us to find it. Why else would she have left it behind? It was like she was trying to explain herself to her former allies and friends. Still, Addie took it hard.

The evidence was contained in a single journal, written in Evelyn's crabbed handwriting, sprinkled through with citations to her father's notebooks and lab files, cross-referenced and dated in a cryptic classification system that made Dewey look like a paint-by-numbers coloring book. Since the lab, presumably with Claude Lumiere's notes still inside, was currently burning enthusiastically behind us, we would never see the materials referenced. It didn't matter.

Evelyn Lumiere had been raised to kill from a young age. Her parents had given her a very special kind of childhood, the sort of thing you might see in a montage at the beginning of a martial arts film. Weapon drills. Balance exercises. Fighting forms. An extensive codex of rules and regulations that formed her young body and mind into a weapon, with one purpose. To kill the living dead. To slay vampires.

It was as ZeeZee had implied. The Lumieres had founded the Vampire Slayer archetype in the Gestalt, with their daughter as the first student. It didn't seem to fit with their personas, but knowing what we did about their covert dealings with the undead, and their attempts to enter the Unreal, it made more sense.

What readily became apparent in her notes was that Evelyn knew nothing of those dealings. That night when the vampires burst through the veil, she was in her room, distracted from the ritual going on below. She heard the racket and came downstairs to carnage. In the pages of the notebook, she described descending the stairs to witness a vampire dressed in white and crimson (doubtlessly Jakub Everlasting) consume her mother, while four others fed on the tattered remains of her father. The rest of the guests lay dead, scattered about the ballroom like broken dolls. She went into a rage and, tapping into her years of training, drove the vampires back into their realm. Too young to pursue, it wasn't until Knight Watch, and Esther MacRae, got involved that she was able to follow through on her horrible revenge. She thought that task complete when she staked her mother, a decade later.

Evelyn was wrong.

Years later, as she went through her father's notes, she came across the *Story of the Night*, the same book that I had found among her things in her father's basement laboratory. It was no wonder she had distracted us from that discovery at the time. Through it, she learned of her father's dealings with the vampires, and his original plans for her training. She was meant to aid him steal the secret of immortality from the undead, and help Claude Lumiere achieve his dream of defeating death. The journal tipped into madness after that. Evelyn became obsessed with rescuing her parents, continuing on with Claude's research and Cecilia's spiritual experiments. Her mother was the first refugee from death, drawn back by the soul cage described in Claude's designs. With Cecilia's help, Evelyn was able to complete her father's experiments.

The result was the Immortality Scarab. With it, she could harness the power of death to bring life. By consuming the life essence of other creatures, Evelyn was able to strengthen her mother's hold on the mortal plane. And if they could find souls powerful enough, they might be able to rescue her father. But it would take truly ancient spirits to pierce death and empower the engine her father had created, not just to rescue him from death, but to gift him eternal life. Evelyn knew where to find such souls. Over the years she had figured out some vampires still lived, hidden from her by some trick of the Unreal.

"We led her right to them," I said, numb with shock. "And now she's off to bring her crazy dad back to life."

"Why is this our problem?" Addie asked. "Vampires truly are monsters, and Evelyn has always been kind to us. So she wants to reunite with her father. Let her, I say."

"You don't understand." Tesla tossed Claude's schematic onto the desk. "Such a ritual would destabilize the entire Gestalt. It would turn our timeline inside out, and consume it. The Unreal would spread through our world."

"It's not so bad," I said. "You'd get used to magic."

"It would not be your Unreal, but his." Tesla stabbed a finger at the schematic. "A nightmare realm conceived by a man who murdered a house full of dinner guests, who dealt with vampires, who turned his own daughter into a murderer. Just to appease his ego. Just so he, and he alone, could escape death."

"Ah. Well, when you put it that way . . ."

"Come. Burn all this. I want no trace of it left," Tesla said. He turned on his heel and marched toward the *Silverhawk*. "Claude Lumiere was my friend. But I did not know the darkness in his heart. I will not see it return to this world, or the next."

The raging inferno that had once been the Lumiere Estate faded into the distance. Both teams, in various states of undress, sat gloomily in the observation lounge, sipping period-appropriate drinks and staring into the middle distance. Eventually, I cleared my throat.

"It was the *Story of the Night*, wasn't it?" I asked. Tesla looked at me curiously. "The *Story of the Night*. I found it when we visited Evelyn's lab the first time through. Evelyn was pretty anxious to hide it away. I didn't think anything of it at the time, but there was something in there about a caged woman. That was all about Cecilia, wasn't it?"

"Caged woman?" Gregory asked. "Are you sure, Rast?"

"Well, caged dame. Same thing, right?"

"That book was in French, John," Chesa said. "Your French is terrible."

"Are you sure that's what it said, Sir John?" Tembo asked. "Caged Dame?"

"I . . . yeah, I think so. More or less."

"Cage d'âme," Tesla said patiently. "It means soul cage. It's a device for capturing the essence of a living being after they have died. Usually in the immediate aftermath, though in some cases it can be used to find and attract wandering spirits with unfinished business in the mortal world."

"Oh. Well." I shrugged. "I was close."

"That doesn't sound very steampunk," Bethany said. "Are you sure it's even part of the Gestalt?"

"An artifact of the spiritualism movement," Adelaide answered. "Séances and skeptics and all that."

"So it *did* have something to do with Cecilia Lumiere!" I said triumphantly. "She was into all that stuff, right? Is that how Evelyn summoned her ghost?"

"Why didn't I recognize this in the first place? It must be tied in with Claude's dealings with the vampires," Tesla said. "If he was trying to achieve immortality, and Evelyn continued his research, then the cage could be part of it."

"But what does all this have to do with the scarabs? The fragments we showed Evelyn weren't in the junk she left here, and they wouldn't have survived that fire," Adelaide said. "So the only remaining example is the one that was on Zofia. Speaking of which . . ."

The room turned to the corner, where Ida sat cross-legged on the floor, tinkering with the small brass contraption. It lay in carefully arranged pieces on the ground in front of her. Ida was dual-wielding sprocket wrenches, with a complicated pair of goggles pulled down over her eyes, the lenses twitching and telescoping as she muttered to herself.

"Find anything useful, Ida?" Tesla asked sweetly. When the mechanic didn't respond, he walked over and tapped her on her curly head. "Ida, dear? Are you with us?"

"Hm? Oh, yes. Sorry. Just a fascinating little bug." She pushed the goggles up onto her forehead, then sat there blinking for a few seconds while her eyes readjusted. "You're all so tiny!"

"Ida!" Tesla barked. "What have you learned about the scarab?"

"It's simple enough. I mean, mind-numbingly complex, and probably breaking a few laws of quantum, thermo-, and electro-dynamics. And I have a sneaking suspicion that it's got a little bit of the Unreal lurking in its gears. But, you know. Simple." Ida gestured at the pieces. "As you suspected, it absorbs souls and stores the extracted psychoactualization in these vials. What Evelyn does with it after that?" She shrugged. "You'd have to ask her."

"I would very much like to do that," Tesla said. "The trouble is finding her."

"I imagine that thing would show up on the Anomaly Actuator," I said. "If we wanted to take the time to head back to Mundane Actual and try to calibrate it."

"Landing the *Silverhawk* anywhere near HQ would cause catastrophic timeline instability, for both of us," Tembo said. "Mr. Tesla, how do the Eccentrics find and detect anomalies?"

"I invented an ingenious little device called the aethervox." Nik went to a cupboard tucked into a corner of the room and opened the doors. Something that looked very much like a television with the world's most complicated antenna lurked inside. "It serves both as a kind of mystical radar as well as a communication device. We have stations all over the world that broadcast and receive signals. With it, we're able to triangulate threats as well as communicate with other dwellers in the Gestalt. Better than that fool Edison and his telephone, don't you think?"

"Does it get cartoons?" Chesa asked. Nik blinked at her in confusion. She waved her hand dismissively. "Never mind. Just miss my Miyazaki."

"Could we use that to track these scarabs?" Tembo asked.

"There are hundreds of signals at any one time." Tesla flipped a few switches, and the screen lit up with amber dots. "With no clarity on what each one means. We would need to visit each anomaly individually to see if Evelyn and her scarabs were somehow involved."

"We could always split up to—"

"No!" I interrupted Addie before we could get too far down that route. "No splitting up, no leaving the healers behind, none of that!"

"It's nice to feel wanted," Matthew mused. "Makes a guy feel special, ya know?"

"I could calibrate the aethervox to a particular frequency," Ida said. "Given how strange these devices are, it might give us a signal we could use."

"Really?" Tesla asked. "Do you think that would work?"

"Better than wandering the skies, hoping to bump into her," Ida said. "Especially considering that Evelyn isn't a bird or something. You know, that you'd regularly expect to encounter in the sky."

"Right. Get started on that. I'll provide what technical assistance I can." Tesla turned to face the members of Knight Watch. "I'm going to have to confine the six of you to quarters while we do this. The less interference there is, the better chance we have of succeeding."

"Sounds great. I could use the rest," Chesa said, standing up and stretching. "It'll give us a chance to refill our magical batteries, too."

"I'm afraid I must insist on leaving those horrible amulet things switched off. At least until we have a signal," Tesla said.

"And I'd rather not crash the *Silverhawk*," Skyhook added. "Given your history of breaking my ship."

"Fine. But we're not going to be much use once we get there." I stood up, draining my goblet of warm mead. "Not without some time topping off."

"We will figure that out later. For now, to your rooms!" Tesla said, shooing us away.

Reluctantly, we retreated to our hay-choked cargo bay. The Pinkertons had come through during the earlier panic. Our things were all over the place, though they had added a new layer of insulating straw and a fresh supply of bedbugs. I went to my cot and started to unbuckle my armor. The stench coming off my linens was substantial, even for the fourteenth century.

"Do they have baths on this thing?" I asked. "All I need is a wooden tub and some soap. And about four hours with a wire brush."

"What you need is a dip in boiling lye, John." Chesa wrinkled her nose before disappearing into her cubicle. She and Bethany shared the far corner, though I had yet to see Bee rest. She was the kind of girl who didn't seem to sleep. Ah, to be that young again. "So what do you think about this soul cage thing?"

"Sounds familiar. Sounds like a lich, doesn't it?" I shouted over the top of the curtain dividing us. "Isn't that what they do with their souls? Put them in a cage?"

"Liches are distinctly not a steampunk archetype," Tembo said. "They're barely an Unreal archetype."

"It's in the *Monster Manual*, it's in the Unreal," Gregory said. "Except werewolves, for some reason."

"And vampires," I said. "Until recently." I hung my armor on its rack and sat on my cot. "Hasn't been easy. These things take forever to fill." I lifted the amulet Tembo had given me out from under my gambeson. The hammered iron was cold against my skin. "Not having access to the domain is rough. I feel like I'm starving to death. That last fight absolutely emptied me out, and I suspect it's going to be a while before I recover."

"Hopefully we've got a bit of a break, while they figure out that voxxie device," Chesa said. "Do you really think Lumiere is behind this whole thing?"

"Hard to argue with the facts," Bethany said. "Evelyn has the most to gain from building her own domain. She's trying to rescue her parents, or something along those lines. I get it. We all do crazy things for family."

"It's just . . . she didn't seem the evil mastermind type," I said. "We're putting a lot of faith in a vampire."

"At the very least, we need to find her and learn why she ran, and what she knows about this soul cage thing." I leaned back on the cot, stretching my sore back. "There's something both Evelyn and the vampire aren't telling us."

"Ain't that always the way?" Chesa called. I heard the shimmer of elven chain mail, and tried not to think about my ex-girlfriend, and what lay beneath that silvered armor. "Good night, everyone."

"Night!" echoed around the room. I nestled into my cot, and its aura of mildewing hay and filth, and tried to not feel too lonely.

Something immediately burrowed out of the straw and started nibbling on my shoulder.

"At least we've got each other, mattress-louse," I whispered, before drifting off to a deep and dreamless sleep.

CHAPTER TWENTY-TWO

Someone took an ice pick and drove it straight through my skull. It went in one ear, rooted around my brain stem, then exited my head out the other ear, no doubt trailing the glistening ichor of my formative memories, along with the brain meat responsible for my charming personality. At least, that's what it felt like.

I sat bolt upright in bed, kicking off the twisted gordian knot of my sweat-stained blanket in my rush to escape the ice-pick-wielding assassin. No, not an ice pick. An alarm. A very loud alarm dialed all the way to a thousand, blaring through the *Silverhawk*'s speaking-tube PA system. I clamped my hands over my ears and stumbled out of my cot. The floor lurched beneath me. I lurched with it, directly through the curtain partition and into the bulkhead beyond, dragging the makeshift wall down like an AT-AT winning the war on Hoth. I was alone. The rest of Knight Watch was elsewhere, though by the looks of things, they'd left their armor and gear behind.

"What the hell is going on?" I shouted, but the persistent hammering of the alarm crushed my words into dust. I kicked through the collapsed wall and found my gear. Slamming the helm onto my head cut out some of the cacophony. It would have to do. I scooped up my sword and shield, then charged out the door.

Pinkertons ran all over the place, checking gauges and yelling instructions at one another, their bushy mustaches twitching in distress. The *Silverhawk* swung wildly beneath us. I crashed against one bulkhead, then the other, trying to avoid cutting anyone open with my sword as I ran. I passed through the main library before sticking my head into the command deck. The place looked like an anthill in mid-collapse. Captain Skyhook stood on top of the command chair, weaving back and forth, a bottle in one hand. No one seemed to know what was going on. Finally, I braved the spiral staircase that led up to the observation deck. If the *Silverhawk* was going down, at least I'd have a good view.

That's where I found the rest of the team. They stood in a semicircle around the modified aethervox, hands clamped desperately to their ears, faces scrunched up in a range of emotions, from rage to disbelief to horror. The aethervox was set up next to the drinks cabinet, front open and parts scattered about, like a grandfather clock that had taken a shotgun blast at close range, and was now bleeding out. Ida stood in front of it, with her hands tucked neatly behind her back. She was wearing an elaborate piece of headgear, consisting of a pair of bulbous earphones attached by electric cable to telescopic goggles, which she had pushed up onto her forehead. The earmuffs were firmly in place, which explained why she alone did not seem bothered by the noise.

"... which will then alert me to the haunted radio signal," Ida said conversationally, pointing to the 'vox. "At which point—"

"I SAID TURN THE BLOODY THING OFF!" Tesla shouted at the top of his lungs. Ida frowned at him, then flipped a switch. The aural assault cut off mid-tone, sending a wave of relief through the team. Tesla pressed a quivering hand to his sternum. "Oh, thank God. I thought my brain was going to turn to jelly."

"You didn't have to yell," Ida said. She dropped the earphones off her head, settling them around her neck. "I can hear perfectly well in these."

"No, my dear, you can not," Tesla said, as he produced a handkerchief and began to mop the sweat from his brow. "Anyway. You were saying?"

"Well, if you'd been listening..." Ida groused. She turned back to the aethervox. "I've calibrated our 'vox to oscillate sympathetically with what I have come to call the Haunted Signal, corresponding to the tangle of protomundanity that forms around the scarabs when they extract psychoplasm. I theorize that the tangle persists even after the scarab has performed the extraction, like a kite string bumping along the ground behind a loose kite. At that point, the signal will trip an alarm." She reached for the switch. "Like so—"

"That won't be necessary," Tesla said, grabbing her firmly by the wrist. "Are you able to detect range and direction?"

"Should be able to." Ida gestured to the hazy amber screen at the top of the aethervox. "The trick is filtering out the noise. I've calibrated it to the appropriate psycholength, but if Evelyn has seeded other scarabs through the Gestalt, it might be tricky to pin down. Still, we should be able to determine a bearing and range."

"Grand. Excellent. Superior," Gregory said as he rubbed at his ears, grimacing. "Now. if you can just do something about the volume, we'll be all set up."

"Yes, yes, it's always something. Impossible to please," Ida said. She dropped the goggles down on her face, waiting until the eyepieces telescoped to their highest resolution before bending to work. "At least it works."

"So what now? We fly around until we find something?" Adelaide asked.

"Isn't that how it usually works?" I asked, drawing the attention of the rest of the team, who had apparently been too busy going deaf to notice my arrival. Adelaide glanced at me, then did a double take. Her face broke into a wide grin.

"Here to save the day, John?" she asked. Gregory smirked, while Chesa rested her face in the palm of her hand. At least the rest of the team was still fully occupied with the aethervox. I looked down.

"Ah," I said. "Forgot the pants. I'll just, uh . . . go get them."

"Hardly necessary," Addie said. "You know, the Spartans fought in the nude. I've always admired that commitment to form. Takes courage."

"Especially with the helm," Gregory said. "I think you have your priorities mixed up. I'd much rather get hit in the head than . . . you know."

"Despite his lack of preparation, we must applaud Sir John's reaction," Tembo said. "The next time that alarm goes off, we will be in hot pursuit within moments." He glared at the rest of the team. "Perhaps from now on we should all be prepared to act on a moment's notice."

"We can't sleep in our armor," Gregory said. "I don't care what the *Player's Handbook* says. That chain mail chafes." Then he nodded at my legs. "As you can plainly see."

"Turn around and show them what it does to your butt!" Bethany shouted.

"Last time I rush to your aid," I muttered as I hurried back down the stairs before they could needle me further. It wasn't like I was completely naked, though my smallcloth wasn't much. A furious blush ran down my face as I marched, shield low, back through the hallway. I was almost there when Gregory's heavy hand fell on my shoulder.

"I get it, Greg! I'm funny!" I shouted, batting his hand aside with my shield.

"Hey, hey, slow down. I'm trying to apologize." He was smartly dressed in his gambeson and tight leggings, looking as fresh as if he'd just stepped out of his domain. When I reared back with my pommel, he raised both hands in surrender. "Seriously, John, just listen."

"Make it quick."

"I just wanted to say I'm sorry. You know how the rest of the team gets, how sharp Chesa's tongue can be. I let it get out of hand." He glanced down at me. "At least you ran into danger. That's hero stuff."

"What? First Chesa tries to make nice, now you? Seriously, what are the two of you planning?" I leaned in, grabbing him by the collar of his immaculately embroidered tunic and pulling him closer. The smell of rosewater and pressed cloves wafted off the curls of his hair. "Whatever it is, I'm not falling for it!"

"Just being nice," he said sternly. He twisted out of my grip, straightening his tunic. "But if that's too much for you, then fine. See if I care."

He turned and marched down the hall, leaving me alone. The Pinkertons, who had been watching surreptitiously from the surrounding hallways, stared at me.

"What are you jokers looking at?" I snapped. They fell back to work, waggling their mustaches and chuffing quietly to themselves. I spun on my heel and marched, with as much dignity as I could muster, back to my quarters.

I had just reached the library when the alarm went off again. And, true to her word, Ida had done something about the volume.

She had made it considerably louder.

"Oh, for heaven's sake." I tried to fold my hand over my eyes, but my visor came down, pinching my thumb in the hinge. I disentangled myself with a yelp, then marched back toward the observation deck. "I think we got the point, Ida! Can we get her to issue those earmuffs for everyone? Because if this is going to continue, I need—"

Addie ran past me. Her face was serious. She didn't even slow down to mock my knobbly kneecaps or comment on my farmer's tan. Chesa and the rest of Knight Watch were right behind her.

"What's going on?" I shouted.

"Are you deaf, Rast? The alarm?" Chesa pushed me aside. She was stripping as she ran, discarding her princess dress at a full sprint. That was distracting, but I shook my head and focused on the task at hand.

"She found the signal?" I called after her.

"It found us!" she shouted as she disappeared around the corner.

"Okay, well, that's very exciting," I said, strolling back toward our quarters. First thing I did was open the tap into my domain. A bare trickle of magical energy leaked into my soul. I took a deep, cleansing breath. I figured I'd give Chesa time to change before I barged in on her. I reached the library sponson, with its floor-to-ceiling windows. "Not 'strip down in public' exciting, but who am I to judge?"

Something heavy came down on the roof of the library. Heavy enough to bank the *Silverhawk* in that direction. I stumbled against the bookshelves. Whatever had hit us thumped its way to the edge of the sponson. There were several other thuds around the airship, both distant and close, and the engines pitched into a frantic whine. A figure swung down from the top of the airship, bracing itself against the elaborate windows to peer into the library.

"Oh . . . Hel," I muttered.

A dead valkyrie clung to the side of the *Silverhawk*. Her skin was the dusty pale blue of the tomb, and her eyes were as black as inkpots. Her armor was emblazoned with skulls and bat wings, and when she smiled, the sharp points of her canines glittered in the light. With an armored fist, she shattered the glass of the observation window and swung into the library. Her clawed feet barely hit the ground before she drew a strange-looking sword. Its front edge was traditional steel, but the spine held a curling brass coil wrapped around a glass vial. As she wielded the weapon, the coil burst into electric life. Bolts of lightning slithered down the blade, arcing to the ground and tearing holes in the floor. I took a step back.

"You . . . are not . . . worthy!" The valkyrie's voice sounded like wind chimes in a hurricane. Cold fog wisped off the black steel of her armor. Even her wings were encased in bladed armor.

Speaking of steel, I was acutely aware that I was not wearing any armor, other than my helm. At least I had both sword and shield, though my magical well was nearly dry. My shield swung down to my arm, straps tightening against my forearm as I spun my sword once to loosen up my wrist.

"I've heard that before," I said. "Let's see if you're right, you emo bitch."

The valkyrie loped toward me. The blades on her boots tore holes in the teakwood floor, and the bladed feathers of her sharp wings dug gouges in the ceiling. I circled warily, shield in a solid guard, sword held high to either strike or parry. Her pale face watched me carefully. Shouts rose in other parts of the ship, and heavy impacts shuddered through the deck. I heard the boom of cannon fire, and felt the recoil shiver through the deck.

"You would have been happier with us," the valkyrie hummed. "Far happier than this flesh-cursed life. Look at us! We have ascended!"

"Solveig?" I asked. Solveig the Bashful was a Viking maiden, dead once in some distant battle, raised to the glory of Valhalla to await Ragnarok. Only she had waited too long, grown impatient, and tried to jump-start the end of the world. Knight Watch had put an end to it. "I thought you escaped?"

"Solveig's war is over. We have a new master now, bound in iron, forsaken of flesh," she drawled. "When he rises, you will know the taste of fear in your blood."

"I love that for you," I snapped, then twisted forward, slicing at the valkyrie's face with the tip of my blade. She ducked backward with preternatural speed, then lunged at my chest with her electrosword. I put the shield between us, sliding backward as the force of her blow shivered through my bones. Lightning arced through the Viking steel. It was fortunate for me that most Viking artifacts take Thor into consideration. I pushed her attack to the side, then desperately smashed down with the pommel of my uplifted blade, trying to catch her skull.

My hand slipped down the hilt, smacking into the shiny dome of her helm, losing the grip on my sword. The blade tumbled down her back to slide across the floor, finally coming to a stop just short of the gaping hole the valkyrie had torn in the window. Fortunately, I had struck her hard enough to daze her, apparently, because her inkpot eyes went wide, and her face twitched madly for a second. She didn't immediately eviscerate me, so I took a step forward and smashed her with the boss of my shield. The valkyrie slewed to the side, dropping her blade.

I leapt for her sword, rolling as I scooped it up. The handle felt like rubber under my gloved fingers, and there was a trigger. I pulled it, and a shock of electrical energy went up the blade.

"Holy cow, that's awesome," I said, then turned to face her. "Let's see how you like it!"

The valkyrie whirled on me. She grinned eagerly as we circled one another, the bright blue light from my stolen sword reflecting in the fathomless black of her eyes.

"Little mortal bites," she hummed. "I remember this about you. Sharper than you look. Solveig was soft on you."

"Too bad I was hard on her. Wait. I mean . . ." But that's when the valkyrie charged. Two ineffective swings of my stolen sword bounced harmlessly off her armored wings. I lost my grip on the trigger after the first strike, though a very satisfying crack of lightning shot through her body, outlining her skull before the sword fell silent. She howled, and then her claws were on my shield, wrinkling the edge and putting a dent just above my arm. I set my feet to brace for the charge, but the inertia of her metal bulk pushed me backward. I hammered away with the sword, but I couldn't get a clear swing around my own shield. Then I felt a sharp pain in the heel of my foot and looked down. A jagged shard of glass stuck out of my heel. It had come from the window. The broken window, gaping wide right at my feet. Beyond it, the open sky, and death.

I dropped the sword and grabbed the iron frame of the window.

"You forget, little man." The valkyrie's hot breath whistled through sharp teeth into my straining face. "Only one of us has wings."

My foot slid perilously closer to the jagged sill of the window. I dropped to one knee and pivoted a little, just enough to slide my other foot against the intact window frame. Shattered glass cut into my naked shin. The iron valkyrie pressed down on me. My spine bent backward. Even if she didn't force me out the window, at this rate she was going to break me in half.

"Give up, mortal," the valkyrie said with a sneer. "The Iron Lich will consume this world and remake it in his image. All will serve at the feet of his iron throne."

"Two things," I grunted. "First, didn't I already kill you once?"

The valkyrie answered with a sharp laugh and redoubled the pressure on my shield. The metal strained, and the wooden backing splintered.

I gritted my teeth and pushed back. "Fair answer. You've made your point. And second..."

With the last scrap of magic in my shield, I transformed it from a kite to a fist-sized buckler, then rolled to the side. The valkyrie, suddenly leaning against empty air, stumbled forward, straight out the shattered window.

I scrambled to my feet and ran to the window. Far below, the black speck of the valkyrie tumbled out of control. She finally recovered, wings folding out to catch the wind, turning her wild fall into a smooth corkscrew. Flapping madly, she started gaining altitude, turning in lazy circles toward the *Silverhawk*. She was coming back. I leaned against the broken window, panting.

"Second... Iron throne, Iron Lich... feels redundant."

CHAPTER TWENTY-THREE

"Rast, stop gawking out the window and put some pants on!" Chesa ran into the room in full battle dress, armored skirt and elven bow glinting in the flickering electric light. She took a quick look at the blood leaking from my shredded calves and stumbled to a stop. "I swear, every time I walk in on you, you're bleeding in a whole new way. What happened?"

"Old home week," I said. "One of the valhellions. Raised from the dead, I think, same bad attitude. I'll be fine. She said something about the Iron Lich."

"That's twice. We have to tell Tesla," she said.

"Yeah," I agreed. "And now we have a non-vampire source. Sounds like Lumiere's making a whole army of the dead."

"Well, go get your kit on. We can do the Scooby-Doo thing later. The rest of the team's already fighting. Addie's helping Gregory buckle his leggings in the back."

"I'll bet she is," I muttered, limping away from the window.

"Don't be a weirdo. Just get back there and get ready to fight."

"Some more. Fight some more." I gestured at the room. "I've *been* fighting."

"Ugh, whatever," Chesa said, then sprinted toward the front of the airship.

"I'm just saying, while the rest of you were putting your big kid clothes on, I was out here, buck naked, winning battles and taking names," I said to myself. "Actually, did I catch her name? There were two of them we killed, weren't there? Leddi? Vivaldi? No . . . Veldi?"

The *Silverhawk* shook and tilted wildly to the side. The crackle of gunfire echoed through the airship's claustrophobic hallways. I picked up the pace.

I left a trail of sticky, crimson footprints on the fancy carpeting that led to our containment cell. When I came through the hatch, Gregory and Adelaide were locked in a struggle with the knight's pants. He was in his chain-mail undercoat, which looked like a set of silver footie pajamas. Addie was behind him, both fists wrapped around leather straps that held the cuisses in place, yanking with all her might.

"If you would stop . . . moving! For just a second!" she shouted.

"You've caught the cuisses in my vambraces," Gregory said, jerking his elbow away from Addie's fists. "You're going to hogtie me!"

"Why in heaven's name is everything held together with straps and twine? Haven't you people heard of zippers?" She dropped the leather and bent to his ankles. The cuisses tumbled forward, falling off his thighs in a crash of metal. "Oh, piss. We're going to have to start over."

"There's no time," I said, limping in. "We've been boarded. Grab your sword and follow me."

"Listen, Rast, that's fine for you to—" Gregory's jaw dropped when he saw me.

"Is it really that bad?" I asked. Behind me, pools of blood seeped into the floorboards. "Yes, okay, I suppose it's bad. Have you seen the Saint? Or, science help me, the Doctor?"

"They're both in the infirmary, running triage." Addie glanced up, then joined Gregory in gaping at my wounds. "Holy cow, John. Did you walk across a field of broken glass?"

"That's exactly what I did. The valkyries didn't just knock politely at the front door, you know." Another round of crashing impacts shook the airship. I dropped onto my cot and started pulling on my leggings. Blood soaked into the cotton wadding immediately. It would have to do for a bandage until I could get some proper healing. "Greg, it's the valhellions. But they've somehow been raised from the dead, and the one I was tangling with mentioned someone called the Iron Lich." I looked at Adelaide. "That mean anything to you?"

"Doesn't sound familiar. What's a lich?" she asked. Gregory managed to get his chestpiece in place while she was distracted. Addie noticed, and started in on his shoulders.

"Depends on your rules system. Usually a necromancer who has

somehow trapped their soul in some kind of cage, to escape death."
I pulled on my greaves and started buckling together my spaulders.
In real life, this whole process takes around ten minutes, but Greg
and I were magical heroes. Convenient armor was just part of the
gig. "They're undead, they're powerful, and they're usually up to no
good. Did the Lumieres have anything like that going on?"

"Before we met the vampires, I would have said no." Addie
finished tying Greg together, then wiped her hands on her pant legs.
"Now? They're capable of anything."

"A great and foreboding evil," Gregory growled. He grabbed his
sword and held it against his heart, like a cleric casting Turn. "It is my
sworn duty to slay the servants of death, wherever I find them. I will
destroy this lich of iron!"

"Well, now you've screwed up the arms," Addie said. One metal
sleeve was buttoned up, but the other dangled from Greg's wrist like
a weird, misgrown wing. "Stop swearing oaths of vengeance for just
one second."

"You'll have to forgive him," I said. "Greg gets rambunctious
around apparitions of absolute evil."

"Yeah, that doesn't sound like our jurisdiction," Addie said. "Not
a lot of undead necromancers in the Victorian age."

"Not a lot of steam-powered robot men in the late 1800s, or
clockwork angels, or, for that matter, airships the size of yachts." I
threw my gorget around my throat, adjusted the fit, then kicked my
helm up into my hands. "Let's go smack some villains!"

"We have to find them first," Gregory said as he pulled on his final
gauntlet.

"Shouldn't be too hard." Addie stepped back, admiring her part in
the assembly of his armor. I noted three buckles out of place, and an
overtightening of the codpiece. "We're all stuck on the same airship.
Not like they have far to go."

The villains came to us. We exited the cargo bay and made our
way toward the front of the airship, weaving our way between packs
of Pinkerton agents in full retreat. Addie led the way, since neither
Greg nor I really knew the layout of the ship. We had spent too much
time confined to quarters to prevent things like selkies in the boiler
room. But looking around now, the situation was pretty grim.

"See, this is what Esther was talking about," I said. "The *Silverhawk* is awfully fragile for an HQ."

"We usually just fly away when things get rough," Addie said.

"Not so easy when you're being attacked by valkyries, is it?"

"I can see why you're so popular with your friends," she said. "You're a real gem of a conversationalist."

"I try." We came around a corner and found it packed with Pinkertons. "This looks promising."

Addie grunted, then unfolded her magical firearm into a short-barreled shotgun and held it like a prow in front of her, cutting through the traffic. "Clear the way!" she shouted. The Pinkertons pressed against the sides of the corridor, giving us just enough room to squeeze past.

"Should we be worried about falling out of the sky?" I called over the blaring alarms. The closer we got to the command deck, the louder they got.

"No!" Addie yelled over her shoulder.

"That's good."

"Because if we fall out of the sky, we'll all be dead, and there will be nothing left to worry about."

"Oh. Uh. Not so good."

"No," she agreed. She grabbed a limping Pinkerton by the arm. "Cooper! What's going on up there?"

"Some kind of Norwegian sky pirates, m'lady!" the man said. "The bridge is cut off, but Captain Honorius and Mr. Tesla are holding strong. There are incursions on the foredeck, the observation lounge, and the crew bar."

"Long as we hold the bridge, it should be okay. Where's the rest of the team?"

"Cassius and that magic man are at the bridge. The two medieval ladies . . ." He glanced at me and Gregory before swallowing hard. "They were last seen on the observation deck. Three of the Viking bitches are up there."

"Observation deck it is," I said. Greg nodded vigorously, but Addie grabbed me before I could make any progress.

"No offense, Rast, but there's nothing mission critical in Observation."

"My friends are pretty mission critical to me," I said.

"If the ship goes down, there'll be no saving them, no matter where they are. We need to get to the bridge."

"Damn your bridge!" Gregory shouted, much too loudly. "I will bleed and fight and die to save the lady Chesa!"

"And the rest of the team, big guy. Hold your exuberant horse." I turned to Addie. "Think about it. If the valhellions are pressing the observation deck, they must have some reason. This is not some random attack. They're after something."

"Perhaps it's you lot," the Pinkerton agent growled. "Nothing like this happened before you came aboard."

"And I never fought an undead valkyrie before today, either. We're all adding to our memory journals." I pushed him aside. "Come on, Addie. Let me and Greg storm the observation deck. You go to the bridge and see what you can find out."

She thought for a long moment, then shook her head. "No, can't risk it."

"Like hell," I said, and tried to move past her. She put a very heavy hand on my chest.

"Let me finish. I can't risk the two of you unattended in the *Silverhawk*. There's no telling what sort of protomundanity will manifest. I'll go with you." She cycled the chamber on her shotgun, then gestured down the corridor. "Lead the way, hero-man."

"Huzzah!" Gregory shouted, and charged down the hall, with Addie and the Pinkerton close behind.

"I think she was talking to me, man." I closed my visor and tightened the straps on my shield, then lumbered after them. "Anyway. Whatever. Huzzah."

We passed through the star . . . board? Port? The left-side sponson, which was set up as an open-air bar and lounge. I say "open-air" because the floor-to-ceiling bay windows had all been smashed out. Wind tore at us as we hobbled through, clinging to the inside wall like ants in a hurricane. When we reached the other side, Addie cycled the hatch and locked it, applying a pressure seal that made my ears pop.

"Much more of that and we're going to start running into some very mundane problems," she said.

"What do you mean?" Gregory asked.

"Air pressure. Drag. Lift. This thing doesn't exactly follow the rules of traditional physics. Those windows would never hold in a real pressurized cabin, not at this altitude. And every time reality is reminded of that, the Gestalt degrades."

"I get it," I said. "It's like eating processed food screws up the Unreal. We have to stick to a medieval diet or our powers degrade."

"Not to mention your colon." Addie looked nervously up at the ceiling. The lights flickered. "Point is, we need to solve this before the real world decides we're flying on nothing more than the power of imagination."

The next corridor was eerily quiet. The overhead electric lamps were out, and the only illumination was a dull red glow coming from a series of terminals at the end of the hall. Narrow doors lined the hallway, each sealed shut, with blinking white lights overhead. The far door was a heavy bulkhead hatch with a wheel lock and a small bulbous window.

"Doesn't look like they've been through here," I said as we crept down the darkened corridor. The adjoining rooms were sealed shut.

"Which is strange. They obviously breached the employee lounge. Where would they have gone?" Addie mused.

"What's in these rooms?" Gregory paused and pressed his face to the foggy glass of one of the staggered doors. "A greenhouse?"

"Crew housing. My room is over there." She nodded to one of the doors. "The room you're looking at belongs to Cassius. He has a thing for plants."

"Well, whatever they're doing, they—" I shut up as a shadow passed in front of the glass viewport at the end of the hallway. A metal wing blocked the light, then disappeared. Addie motioned us to stay still, then crept to the door and peered through. Her face fell.

"What?" I whispered as she crawled back to us. Instead of answering, she keyed the door to her room and waved us inside. It wasn't until the door was closed and locked that she spoke.

"Ten of those damned bird women in the mess. They've barricaded the exits and are loaded for bear. Some of them have guns."

"Valkyries with guns. I don't like that," I mused.

"How many of these bloody things are there?" Gregory asked.

"Well, we killed quite a few of them. Maybe they've been recruiting," I said.

"We can worry about the who of it later." Addie jerked her thumb back toward the mess. "Point is, we're not getting through that way."

"So how are we supposed to get to the observation deck?" I asked.

"I have an idea," she said after a moment. "Follow me."

Her idea was terrible. It was suicidal. It was exactly the kind of nonsense heroes are supposed to do. I hated it.

Gregory, on the other hand, was thrilled. That man never shies away from an opportunity to potentially do himself harm in the name of adventure. Weirdo.

We stood in the open door of the starboard cargo bay, about halfway up the length of the *Silverhawk*. The sounds of fighting echoed overhead, most likely from the observation deck. The floor thrummed with the steady thud of heavy cannon, fired from the belly turret under our feet. I hadn't even known the *Silverhawk* had external guns. Neither had the valhellions, apparently.

"You do realize they have wings, right?" I shouted over the tearing wind.

"That's the point, Rast! They'll never expect it!" she shouted back.

"Because it's stupid," I muttered to myself. "No one expects the stupid."

"Sorry?"

"Nothing!" I called back, plastering a smile on my face.

"We will strike at them from the air!" Gregory shouted, grinning like a maniac. "Hoist them by their own petard! The irony!"

"If they've breached Observation and the port sponson, they have no reason to be out here," Addie shouted at us. She was busily hooking up a climbing harness to my cuisses. The fit was tricky, and didn't inspire confidence. "All we need to do is crawl along the outside until we reach the observation deck without being seen."

"Are there handholds?" Gregory asked.

"Kind of. Have either of you ever been rappelling?"

"No," I said, just as Gregory gave an enthusiastic thumbs-up.

"Did a lot of free-climbing in high school. Good way to build up your core," he said.

"Good way to fall to your death," I answered.

"Well, it's like that," Addie said, testing the fit of her harness.

"Keep the cable taut and your legs straight. Lean out from the hull, like you're water skiing."

"Haven't done that, either," I said.

"Have you done anything outside?" Gregory asked, exasperated. "Rock climbing? Horseback riding? Swimming?"

"I read a lot of books," I said, leaning my head out the door. The wind deafened me, tugging me backward. "Won't the wind just knock us off?"

"Well, that's what the cable is for." She cinched the harness tight, then hooked it into a steel cable that led outside. "This is designed for maintenance crews, usually while we're docked. But I'm sure it'll hold."

"You're sure? Or you hope?" I asked.

"Yep," she said, then hooked her own harness to the cable and swung out into the wild blue sky. Gregory pounced after her, his metal legs flailing wildly for a moment before finding their grip. Neither of them tumbled off the side of the ship to their doom, so after a few deep breaths, I gripped the cable and followed Gregory out the hatch.

CHAPTER TWENTY-FOUR

The wind hit me like a hammer. The sheer force of it stole the air from my lungs and wrung the water from my eyes. My visor was open, and the gale forced its way past my ears, to whistle through my helm and into the dark places of my skull. It sounded like buzzsaws mating inside my ear canals.

It was loud enough that I couldn't hear my own screams, which meant Adelaide and Gregory couldn't hear them, which was fortunate because I was cranking out the shrieks like a litter of skittish cats on stage at a rocking chair competition. I made the mistake of looking down. We weren't that high up for an airship, but we were very high up for a man in plate armor, clinging to the side of the ship by a thin cable. We weren't even going that fast. The *Silverhawk* had drifted below the clouds at some point during the melee, and was bumbling through the air at a snail's pace. I could make out individual buildings below, set in a crowded grid that at first I mistook for suburban sprawl. But as I looked closer, I saw that I was looking at a fragment of the Gestalt superimposed over the mitochondrial swirl of cul-de-sacs, shopping malls, and the black snake of asphalt roads twisting through subdivisions. Distinctly Victorian buildings and the complicated superstructure of iron-wrought bridges, train tracks, and zeppelin towers bristled across the landscape. It looked like a fading photograph of Victorian London hung like a ghost over suburbia.

"What the hell is going on down there?" I muttered, straining to get a closer look. "It's like the world is flickering between reality and the Gestalt. Do you think—"

That's when I realized I was falling.

I didn't even feel the soft sole of my boot slip free of the *Silverhawk*'s metal flank, but suddenly I was sliding down the side of the airship, both legs straight out, my hands scrambling for purchase on its smooth skin. A gust of wind stuck my shield, strapped over my shoulder, and took to it like a sail. I pulled free from the airship and spun, end over end, to my doom. My vision became a pinwheel of sky and earth, with the bright metal flash of the *Silverhawk* in between.

Something yanked at my hips, cinching tight to my waist and strangling my thighs. I spun a final rotation, then swung hard and fast against the side of the airship. I struck with the hollow sound of a bell without its clapper, once, twice, bouncing loudly with each impact. Finally I came to rest. I dangled, facedown, from my harness. The world raced by overhead, getting steadily closer while I gaped at it, trying to drag breath into my lungs.

"Rast, you idiot." Addie's voice was surprisingly calm. She grabbed me by the belt and heaved. My feet scrambled against the *Silverhawk*, and I grappled with Addie's shoulders, nearly pulling her free. "The footholds! Use the footholds!"

"Come on, John. You're giving us a bad name!" Gregory shouted from his perch above me. The wind didn't seem to be bothering him at all.

Craning my neck, I saw a series of divots in the otherwise smooth surface of the airship's flank. Stretching my leg, I was able to poke one toe into the closest divot. Between that and Addie's irresistible leverage, I finally got into the correct vertical orientation. I clung to the guide wire like a man . . . well, like a man suspended off the side of a flying whale, with nothing holding him there other than the aforementioned wire.

"Have you got it?" Addie shouted at me. I nodded, and she released me.

"Wait, how can I hear you? How can I hear me?" I asked, startled. The wind had died down to a gentle roar.

"We're in the Gestalt bubble. It keeps fading in and out," Addie said. She nodded below us. I didn't dare look, not after my recent tumble. "Too many cars down there. Not enough imagination."

"Do you think that's the valkyries' doing?" Gregory asked.

"Don't know. But for now, the Gestalt is holding up here, which is giving us a reprieve from the wind. I say we take advantage of that," Addie said.

"I still don't understand how that works," I muttered.

"Kind of like how the Naglfr is open top, but none of us ever blow away," Gregory said. "Relax, Rast. It's really quite pleasant once you get used to it."

"I did ride a giant dog all the way to heaven once, I suppose," I said. The dog in question was Fenrir, while he was trying to catch the moon. With that in mind, I loosened my grip and relaxed. The ride really wasn't that bad. I looked around. "Are we slowing down?"

"Yeah. I don't like it." Satisfied that I wasn't going to hurtle off the side of the ship, Addie began climbing.

"Well, maybe we're landing?" I asked.

"Do you see a place to land?" She was already ten feet ahead of me, and climbing fast. I glanced down at the landscape, zipping past. Somehow the lower we got, the faster the ground seemed to be going. I'm sure there was science involved, but all I could think of at the moment is that we were definitely going too fast to land—at least, not in one piece. I tipped my head up to avoid looking at the cheese grater of trees and hills and rocks, then hurried after Addie, with Gregory close behind.

It was slow going. I focused entirely on getting one foot in front of the other, hands on the precarious cable, fighting the wind for every step. Even concentrating on my movement, it was increasingly clear that the *Silverhawk* was losing altitude. I was beginning to wonder if Honorius intended to put us down in one of these fields when I bumped into Addie. She had stopped in the middle of the *Silverhawk*, and was peering upward.

"What are—" I started, but she smothered my mouth with her hand. I followed her gaze upward.

One of the resurrected valkyries perched on the lip of the remnants of the observation deck. A pair of engines perched between her wings, flickering with bright blue electricity each time her feathers twitched. I couldn't see over the edge, but the iron framework of the great window was bent and twisted, bristling with shards of shattered glass. The sounds of fighting sang over the howling wind. The valkyrie carried a long spear, equipped with an electrical coil at the base of the tip, and was using it to poke at something that was out of my line of sight. With a screech that sounded like a boiler erupting, she charged forward, disappearing from view.

"We have to get up there," I said. The cable ran the length of the *Silverhawk*, but didn't lead up to the top. There were handholds, but nothing to secure yourself from falling. "Are we supposed to just free-climb this?"

"Hero stuff," Gregory answered, unclipping his belt.

Reluctantly, I followed suit and started the tenuous climb up to the lip of the observation deck. The winds held off long enough for us to reach the shattered ruin of the glass dome. Popping our heads over the edge, we were treated to a sight of absolute destruction. Bethany and Chesa stood back-to-back in the middle of a circle of five valkyries, armed with a variety of anachronistic weapons. Spears, tridents, and at least one steampunk chainsaw threatened the girls, all powered by weird electrical coils and vials of glowing green liquid. Chesa bled from several wounds, and the broken limbs of her bow lay at her feet, among scattered arrows. She twirled with her twin crescent daggers in her hands, dancing back and forth like a banshee.

Bethany fought with equal vigor, and a great deal more glee. Her face was smeared with blood, and she was grinning maniacally as she darted forward, swiping at any of the valkyries who got too close with the gleaming blades of her daggers. The valkyries circled warily, darting in when opportunity presented, and dodging back out before either Chesa or Bee could land a blow. Addie pulled us back down below the window.

"We've got to get in there," I said. "They need us."

"One second, hotshot," Addie said. "Did you see the guy by the 'vox?"

"What? No." I peeked back over the sill. There was a stooped figure beside the aethervox. The figure by the 'vox looked more like a pile of trashed furniture than anything, but now that I was looking directly at it, I could see it moving. "Who is that?"

"I don't know. But I'm guessing this whole thing is a distraction." Addie charged her shotgun, simultaneously transforming it into a weird, multi-barrel streetsweeper. "The two of you save your friends. I'm taking that guy down."

"Right. Greg, I'll draw their attention." I slammed down my visor and swung my shield off my shoulder. "You start picking them off one by—"

"VICTORY IN THE LIGHT!" Gregory d'Haute vaulted over the sill, waving his zweihander overhead. Adelaide clapped me on the shoulder and slid into the room, staying low to the ground and working her way around the perimeter toward the shadowy figure on the opposite side of the room.

I sighed. "Maybe wait for the tank?" I rolled awkwardly over the shattered frame of the glass dome and landed with a crunch among the broken glass. Chesa glanced in my direction. To my infinite joy, she actually smiled when she saw me.

My joy was short-lived. The closest two goth valkyries broke off from harassing Chesa and Bee to face us. Gregory, full of enthusiasm and an unreasonable faith in his sword, charged the first valkyrie. She caught his downward stroke with the crackling flat of her spearhead, then swept the shaft into his knee. Lightning arced down the length of Greg's two-handed blade, traveling through his armor with an audible crack. Greg went down in a tumble of steel and glistening curls. The second valkyrie was armed with a pair of wicked hand axes that contained spinning brass orbs behind the curves of their blades. She was just about to turn Gregory d'Haute into a selection of smaller Gregs when I bulled them both aside with my shield.

"I said! Wait!" Bright axeheads skittered off my shield, sending a shock through my shoulder and into my teeth. The smell of cooked meat drifted through the air. I slid to the side, straddling Greg and bringing my sword up in a wide swing that drove the valkyries back. "For the tank!"

"The ladies needed me," Greg spat as he rolled to his feet. The zweihander was nowhere to be seen. He drew the sharp length of his misericorde dagger. A gash of bright blood trickled down his forehead, and the tips of his hair were burned into crisps.

"They need both of us," I said. "We need each other."

He grimaced at me. Before the conversation could continue, we were both distracted by the imminent threat of death at the hands of the emo valkyries.

Axebitch charged at me, closing the distance before I could get my sword in a good guard. The sharp bit of her axes hooked the edge of my shield, dragging it down and exposing that half of my body to attack. Spears of static energy shot out from the whirling orbs in the haft of her blades, crawling through the mesh of my chain mail. I grimaced against the pain, then countered by thrusting my sword into her face. She disappeared from my field of vision, and a second later sharp pain jolted up from my lead knee. I ducked down, slamming the rim of my shield into her hand, then pushed up strong into her belly, shoving her back. I was so intent on this action that I didn't notice the two others, each armed with a long and wickedly barbed sword, circling around my back, not until they lunged at me.

In short order, I was fighting for my life, hacking in all directions, my shield constantly beset by ax and spear, while my armor rattled with multiple sword blows. The crack of electrical discharge and crashing metal filled the air. I managed to hook one of the berserker's axes with my hilt and toss it aside, but she simply took to punching me with that hand.

Gregory and Chesa and Bethany disappeared in a whirl of steel and shrieking valkyries, each fighting their own battle for survival. The math told me that at least I was doing my job, if three of the five were on me. That gave my friends a chance. Maybe if Chesa magically repaired her bow, or Gregory found his sword, we could turn the tide. All I had to do was hold out. Hold out, and keep fighting. So I did. It took a trickle of magic from my diminished reserves to keep going. I couldn't last forever.

I stumbled backward, until my legs came up against the hard sill of the broken dome. Once I was there, I was able to hold off my three attackers, fighting like a rat in a corner. Because I was. Except I forgot one thing, for the second time that day.

The valkyries had wings.

A shadow fell across my shoulders. I was just starting to get an inkling of the implications of that when heavy boots crashed into my shoulders. I went over like threshed wheat, sword tumbling free and shield flattening under my chest. I rolled over and got my shield up just in time to catch a heavy blow from a warhammer. The face of my shield dented inward, and the whole thing sang like a gong. My visor popped open, and I crabwalked backward, fighting the urge to drop my shield and run. The valkyrie who had ambushed me swung that warhammer like she was digging for gold. Her face was a twisted mask of hatred and rage, and her wings fluttered overhead, carrying her forward as I retreated.

An arrow slammed into the hammer valkyrie's shoulder, then another skittered off her arm. With a shriek, she kicked me in the face, then whirled to face this new assault. Gregory met her with a devastating swing of the zweihander, which he had apparently recovered, followed up by an uppercut with the big sword's thick pommel, a heavy blow that knocked her backward. I scrambled to my feet and drew my dagger, then fed a little magic into the shield to repair it and change its shape into something more practical in the close confines of the observation deck. Chesa stood on the shattered ruins of the drinks cabinet, magically repaired bow once again in hand, sending flights into the valkyries clustered around me. Each arrow flew true, puncturing wings and thumping into the joints between armor plates. I suspected that the repair of her shattered bow had tapped out her magical reserves, because she was sending mundane arrows into the enemy. I was looking around for my sword when an icy voice boomed through the air.

"That's enough of that, girls. Back to the nest."

The valkyries all backed away. Gregory and I closed ranks, joined by the bloody-faced Bethany, who seemed to have recovered the axes that I had knocked away from the valkyries, and was wielding them with grim determination. Warily, we watched the line of valkyries slowly part, revealing the speaker.

It was the figure who had been skulking near the aethervox. Its body was made up of the discarded spare parts from around the ship, all rusted disks and mismatched iron, shoved together into the rough approximation of a human being. Dull green light shone through between the parts, like sunlight streaming through the cracks in a door. The figure wore a tattered overcoat, and its face was nothing more than a couple nails hammered into a warped wooden board in the shape of eyes and a mouth. These features didn't move as the figure spoke. But the voice was familiar enough.

Cecilia Lumiere, in a much less charming form than when we'd last met.

"You've made such a mess of things, ladies. Hardly fitting. You may go," she said haughtily. "Leave these lovely boys to me."

"That wasn't the deal," one of the valkyries snarled. "Revenge! And—"

"As I summoned you, so I dismiss you. Go!" Her voice changed, echoing with power. The valkyries shied away from her, wilting like spring flowers at the first frost.

The valkyries fled. Dark shapes emerged from all over the *Silverhawk*, popping out of hatches and bursting through portholes, to flutter away into the sky. Cecilia watched them go with rusted, bent-nail eyes.

Cecilia turned back to us, warped head tilting to the side coquettishly.

"Well, now that that little unpleasantness is behind us, we can get acquainted." She took a step closer, trailing an arm made of bent copper tubing and bike chain across her clapboard hip. "It was so rude of Evelyn to tear us apart, don't you think? Just as we were getting . . . close?"

"I think I liked you better as a ghost," I said.

"I wasn't talking to you, child," she answered, then stepped closer to Gregory. "Tell me, brightlocks. Have you ever been with an older woman?"

Adelaide stepped from the shadows and laid the wide mouth of her shotgun against Cecilia's temple. She froze in place, immobile face still somehow registering surprise.

"He's not your type," she said, and pulled the trigger.

Wood and rusted iron flew across the room, along with the assorted springs and cogs that made up the rest of her skull. Cecilia's headless body fell to the ground, disassembling like a puzzle thrown in frustration against a wall. Clockwork gears and bent washers rolled across the floor, spinning like coins over the hardwood. The sound of the blast left my ears ringing, but even I could hear the rattling crash of several hundred pounds of mismatched steel gears shuffling against the floorboards.

In the wake of the construct's collapse, the horrific image of Cecilia Lumiere hung naked in the air. Glowing green skin pulled tight to her skeletal frame, tearing free in places to reveal desiccated organs and withered tendons. Her curly hair hung in rags from the peeling flesh of her skull. One eye socket yawned empty. Her teeth were crooked and broken, and the long, pale snake of her tongue flickered in the air. She shrieked in rage, then flew apart into a million sparking motes of burning dust.

"There, problem solved," Addie said. She spun her shotgun, working the lever to eject a casing and reload in one smooth motion. "No more creepy ghost construct."

"Um, guys?" Bethany was behind us, bent over the aethervox.

"That felt too easy," I said. "And how did she get onboard? That thing didn't have wings, did it?"

"Localized haunting," Chesa said. "Maybe the valkyries summoned her? Or maybe she—"

"Guys!" Bethany repeated. "Actual problem over here!"

Ida's modified aethervox lay open, its mind-boggling configuration of gears and levers running in reverse. The compass arm spun like a helicopter blade, and the amber screen had been replaced by a crackling void.

"That's a bit weird," I said, stepping closer. "Is it supposed to do that?"

"It looks a little . . ." Gregory started.

"Haunted," Chesa said.

"We don't do haunted in the Gestalt," Addie answered. "We're Lovecraft adjacent, but we keep his stuff in a little box, well away from the rest of the workings."

"Because?"

"It tends to break things," Addie whispered.

The screen cracked open, and a wave of black energy washed outward in a flash.

Just before it struck, I heard laughter echoing through the ship. Tinny and distant, coming through the speaking tubes, vibrating through the bulkheads, shaking the silverware and slithering through the chandeliers, like the ghost of a voice, cut free from its mortal form.

I threw an arm across my face. The wave of energy sizzled over me, tasting like static electricity in my mouth, prickling my skin, sending a vibration through my armor. I braced for the impact, magical or otherwise, that was sure to follow. It never came. After a moment, I lowered my shield and looked around.

"Well," I said. "That wasn't so bad."

"Just listen," Addie said. "We're screwed."

"What?" Gregory asked.

I strained my ears. It can be hard passing perception checks through a steel helm, but I didn't hear anything.

Greg agreed. "All I hear is silence."

"Exactly." Addie holstered her shotgun and ran for the stairs. "The engines are dead."

The floor fell out from under us. We dropped like a stone out of the sky, wind whistling through the broken windows of the observation deck, rising to a scream.

CHAPTER TWENTY-FIVE

The spiral staircase was not designed for use during a crash. I grabbed for the railing, pulling myself hand over hand down from the observation deck into the main corridors of the wounded *Silverhawk*. Demure alarms sounded with British-humor levels of understatement. "Emergency. Alert. Emergency. Impact Imminent," an automated woman's calm voice echoed through the ship. "Secure the kettle."

"Maybe better priorities!" I shouted as we tumbled down the stairs. Chesa moved effortlessly, hopping from step to step, her elven grace on full display. For me and Gregory, the fact that we were in full armor made it more a game of how hard we would fall. Adelaide stayed in front of us, landing on the carpeted main deck and taking off toward the bridge.

"Are there escape pods?" I asked as I ran after her. The airship veered hard to the right and began to corkscrew. It was like being on a Ferris wheel that had come unmoored and was taking a tour of the surrounding countryside. We slammed into first one side of the corridor, then the other, making our unsteady way forward, pinball-style.

"Ida said we wouldn't need them," Addie answered.

"Why not?"

"That's what I'm going to ask, as soon as I find her!" she said, bracing herself against the wall as we lurched once again. As her hand hit the wood paneling, Adelaide screamed in pain.

Her clockwork arm disintegrated, like a statue made of sand and dust in a strong breeze. The gears tumbled free of the mechanism, slipping like loose coins onto the floor to scatter down the hallway.

The larger structures, like the pistons that articulated her hand and elbow, collapsed in on themselves. The joint of her elbow and the bones of her fingers flew in all directions as the tension of their springs came unhinged. Addie grabbed at the stump of her arm as the final pieces of the mechanism slipped between the fingers of her flesh-and-blood hand.

"Are you alright?" I shouted.

"No!" she answered. The stump was raw and seeping blood. "I need the Doc!"

"It looks like you've lost your connection to the Gestalt," I said. "Last thing I'd want is that guy sticking needles in me without any magic behind it."

"Then a real doctor. Damn it!" She shook her fingers, dislodging the last bits of clockwork clinging to the bloody stump. "It stings like a bitch!"

"Let's head to the bridge," Chesa said, pulling us both forward. "If we fall out of the sky, that arm will be the least of our problems."

"Clear the way!" Ida barreled through us, a battering ram of brown curls and bespoke leather. "Need to get to the sponsons!"

"Ida!" Gregory grabbed at her, missing but slowing the engineer down enough to draw a sharp glare. "How are we going to land?"

"Manually operated mundane-integration collapsible airfoil package, port and starboard," she shouted. When we responded by blinking slowly, she slapped her hands together. "Wings, you idiots! We need to open the wings!"

"We have wings?" Addie asked, still dazed from the loss of her arm.

Ida stared open-mouthed at the gunslinger's bloody stump, then shook her head. "We're about to," Ida said, then pointed at Gregory. "Pretty boy! Go to the starboard sponson and wind the big red spring. The angry one, come with me!"

I turned to Chesa. "You get Adelaide to the bridge and see if you can find the Saint. She might need a miracle."

"Right. Be safe, John," Chesa said, squeezing my arm.

"Hey, falling out of the sky. Nothing I haven't done before."

Ida and I reached the shattered remains of the port sponson in short order. The horizon dipped in and out of view as the *Silverhawk* rocked back and forth. The tree line was getting close. In my head, I began to question the wisdom of standing next to a bunch of open windows during a crash. I said as much, in a jumble.

"I've already deployed the main sail," Ida said. "We're still falling, just not as fast. If we can get the wings out, we should be able to glide the rest of the way. Here it is!"

She threw aside the crushed remnants of a bookcase, revealing a train of wheels and pinions, all attached to a single large, red mainspring. A solitary latch held the spring in place. Ida grabbed the latch and pulled it free.

There was a brief whine of slithering steel. The primary wheel spun, clicked, then settled to a halt. We continued to fall.

"I take it that wasn't supposed to happen?" I asked.

"The spring must have lost tension somehow. All that time under pressure must have sapped it. Hm." Ida sat cross-legged in front of the contraption, tapping a small wrench against her cheek. "Neither wing will deploy until both release. Maybe if I had designed an escapement running a timer, so we could know when to wind it back up. I could even link it to a clock, maybe. Intriguing. I would have to redesign—"

"Ida!" I shouted. "Let's skip to the part where we make this one work."

"Oh, sure. Probably smart. Uh . . ." She tugged at the device with the wrench, eventually releasing a chain that was attached to the mainspring. "We'll have to deploy manually. Good thing I ran into you guys!" She handed me the chain. "Start pulling!"

I ran across the broken glass, following my own bloody footsteps toward the hallway. Or at least, I tried to, because after a foot or so the chain pulled tight. My feet slid against the floor. Like a good engineer, Ida monitored the situation from afar.

"You're going to have to go a lot faster than that," she called, leaning casually against the window. "The compartment doors haven't even opened yet. At this rate, you'll still be pulling when we're ten feet underground."

"We're pulling! Isn't there something you could be doing? Something useful?" I asked. "Something like—"

"Oh, releasing the chain. Right." Ida kicked something in the device. I flew across the room at full speed, to land in a jumble against the windows. "There we go!"

I looked up just in time to see the fruits of my labor. A door opened in the side of the airship, and a multi-sparred wing unfurled like a sail. It caught the wind, ribs straining to hold the billowing segments of the airfoil. The sudden drag pressed me hard against the floor. Shouts rose throughout the ship, accompanied by crashing plates and shattering glass. The *Silverhawk* veered upward, just feet above the grassy expanse of the ground. The wind of our passage flattened the grass in cylindrical whorls that widened in our wake. The wings creaked under the strain.

"You did it! You saved us!" I shouted, getting to my knees. "Way to go, Ida!"

"Thanks. You know, in retrospect I should have included a way to steer," she said thoughtfully. "That would have been helpful."

"Steer later! As long as we're not crashing now!"

"Well . . ." Ida pointed forward.

Barely visible through the curving front of the bay window, a shopping mall loomed in front of us. I had just registered the fact that we must be back in the Mundane when the signpost of a passing Mickey D's tore through our wing.

We pinwheeled to the ground like a broken kite. There was enough of the wing remaining to slow us down, but not enough to keep us aloft. The *Silverhawk* lurched to the left as we passed over the mall and into the parking lot beyond. I was just wondering what it would feel like to die of road rash when we reached the drainage pond on the other side of the lot. We hit the water like a wounded duck, sideways, and at great speed. That's all I remembered for a few minutes.

I came to with Ida sitting on my chest, poking at my face through my open visor. I sat up abruptly, throwing her into the water. Chesa stood in the doorway of the library, up to her knees in murky water.

"He's up," Ida said, standing quickly. "You might want to lose the armor. We're going to have to swim for it."

"John can't really swim," Chesa said. "It's okay. I think we've stopped sinking. We might be able to walk out."

"Is everyone else okay?" I muttered as I got to my feet. Water poured out of my armor. "Actually, am I okay?"

"You're fine. Nothing out of place," Ida said.

"All hands accounted for," Chesa said. "Addie's with Saint Matthew now. I'm not sure she's thrilled with his plans for her arm."

"She can file a protest with Esther later," I said, then trudged to the open window. "Let's get out of here."

The library sponson was flooded with about two feet of water. Books and broken furniture floated in a sea of muddy brown liquid that sloshed in through the open window. Bits of the wing bobbed on the surface, riding the wake that must have come from our crash landing.

We crawled out the broken window and over the shattered wing. The water didn't come higher than my armpits, though several inches of soft, mucky sediment coated the pond floor. After a bit, we reached the shallows, battering our way through a section of cattails before reaching dry ground. I looked back at our fallen bird.

Swarms of Pinkertons climbed over the exterior. The other wing had apparently folded over the top of the airship, and the agents were trying to get it cleared off. Tesla and Skyhook stood just above the bridge, hands on hips, watching the work. Tesla waved to us, then climbed back inside. I spotted Gregory and Tembo working their way toward us. Happily, Greg slipped and fell into the drink, coming up a few seconds later, sputtering.

"You really shouldn't be laughing," Chesa said. "How would you feel if that were you?"

"Like most days," I said. "You guys laugh at me a lot."

"Well, you're pretty funny. Just not in the ways you mean, sometimes."

Tesla reappeared, this time with a foldable canoe that he plopped into the water. He paddled past Gregory and Tembo, waving primly, before beaching his craft and climbing up to us.

"I'm glad to see you all survived. Very few injuries, thanks to Ida's ingenious wing...thing..." He looked back at the *Silverhawk*. "Honorius is heartbroken, obviously. But he'll get over it."

"Where's Bethany?" I asked.

"Still on board with Adelaide and the Saint. I think she's trying to keep them from killing each other," Tesla said. "He used marble, if you can believe it."

"For what?" Ida asked.

"Addie's arm! Looks like a real arm, but it's ivory. I don't think she likes it very much."

"Wait until she punches someone with it," Chesa said. "She'll come around."

"What exactly happened back there?" Tesla asked. "One second we were flying peacefully, holding off the sky pirates..."

"Valkryies," I said.

He shrugged and continued. "...and the next thing you know, we're falling out of the sky."

"It was the aethervox," Chesa said. She and I explained what we had seen, from the Cecilia construct to the portal opening in the screen and the black wave of energy. Tesla let out a low whistle.

"So she can possess makeshift bodies," Tesla said. "That's troubling."

"At first I assumed we were entering your stupid reality," Ida said, looking around. "But I don't see a lot of dragons roaming around."

"Uh, no. This is the real world. I can smell the processed grease from here." I squinted at the mall. There was a crowd forming in the parking lot. Tembo and Greg completed their exodus and slogged up the hill, dripping wet. "How are we going to explain this?"

"Leave it to mundanity," Chesa said. "It usually figures something out—weather balloon, or a fraternity prank. Something. The real question is how we get back into the Gestalt."

"Well, the *Silverhawk* is grounded. And that crowd is getting closer. Any of you have a portal to the Unreal nearby?" Tesla asked.

"I don't even know where we are," I said. "There's zero chance Esther's tracked us, is there?"

Tembo, wringing out his robes by hand, shook his head.

"Then we'll have to figure something out on our own," Chesa said. "We'll need to get our gear out of the ship at some point."

"The Pinkertons can retrieve it. No need to slog back and forth. We have lifeboats," Tesla said.

"What? You could have mentioned that," Gregory said, as a young catfish slipped gleaming from his shin guard. "Ugh, I'll never get the stink out."

"At least you've had a bath now," Ida said, wrinkling her nose.

True to Tesla's word, the cargo door on the *Silverhawk* creaked open, and a small dinghy launched from the interior. Matthew, Addie, and Bethany sat in the front, flanking the isolation chest, while a team of Pinkertons rowed them to shore. Once they beached, we helped drag the trunk through the reeds and onto dry ground.

"Addie! Your hand!" Chesa exclaimed.

"Yeah, yeah." The gunslinger's new marble left arm was smooth, with faint seams along her forearm, wrist, and the joints of her hand. As she worked to pull the containment chest out of the boat, her hand clicked like pebbles dropping into a glass jar. "I'll get used to it."

"Best I could do on short notice and little Brilliance," Matthew said. "Once we're done, I'm sure The Good Doctor can change it back."

"I retrieved the scarab." Bethany produced the metallic beetle from one of her many pockets, handing it to Ida. "Thought you might need it."

"I can probably reconstruct the tracking device," she said. "Just not in the middle of a parking lot. This place is so mundane it could run for president. We'll have to get as far away from here as possible. Get somewhere weird."

"Weird? In a shopping mall?" Chesa asked. "Sounds like your department, Rast."

"You mean that as an insult, but I assure you, it's the highest compliment you can possibly give me," I said. "I'll have us back into the Unreal in no time."

"If we're abandoning the *Silverhawk*, I'm going to need some supplies from my laboratory," Nik said. "And I'm sure Ida will as well."

"Nope." The young mechanic slapped the extensive toolbelt wrapped around her slim waist. "I've got everything I need right here."

"Well, then. I shall be back in a jiffy," Tesla said, guiding his canoe through the reeds.

"We should take the opportunity to tap our domains and retrieve our gear," Tembo said. "I suspect we will not be coming back this way."

"Gods willing." Gregory shook his soggy boot. The rest of us collected our magical items from the chest, while nervously watching the ever-growing crowd on the far side of the parking lot. After a few minutes, Tesla emerged from the *Silverhawk*, heavily burdened.

"Okay, John. What are we doing?" Chesa asked.

"I have what you might call a clever plan." I pointed to the shopping mall. "Follow me."

CHAPTER TWENTY-SIX

It was a long walk. Not by distance, don't get me wrong. I've learned to walk long distances in armor. That's the thing you don't get in your typical fantasy novels and games: the sheer boredom and physical strain of walking from place to place, carrying your entire life on your back, along with armor, weapons, and whatever you happened to loot during the last encounter. Trust me, I carry a lot less rope, ten-foot poles, caltrops, and months of rations in real life. That stuff's heavy.

No, I mean it was a long walk for reasons of emotional strain. There was a crowd of concerned mothers, bored teenagers, and unemployed bodybuilders loitering at the entrance to the mall, all drawn by our recent crash into their beloved drainage ditch. Their expressions were a mixture of horrified and confused, with a good deal of mistrust thrown in for good measure. The mundane world does not tolerate the weird. It didn't help that we looked about as ridiculous as heroes in the process of saving the world can possibly look. Half of us were dressed up like a high budget Actual Play troupe that had been living homeless in our costumes for the past three months. The rest of our little group looked like the extras from a failed reimagining of *The Nutty Professor*. Tesla wore the same electrical-generator-slash-traffic-light on his back that he had when we first met, with the addition of a pair of insulated gauntlets that covered his fists in coils of copper wire. Adelaide had once again adopted her look of cool detachment flavored with the promise of imminent violence. Ida looked the most normal, other than the telescoping goggles and collection of impossible tools.

The crowd gathered outside the shopping mall watched as we trudged the length of the parking lot in our sodden uniforms. It felt like the final fight scene between gangs of roaming cosplayers in a postapocalyptic movie.

"They're, uh, staring," Chesa said quietly.

"Well, we're worth staring at," I said. "How often do you think they see a silver whale fall out of the sky and disgorge a troupe of circus actors? This is high entertainment at"—I twisted to look at the sign—"the Mount Commons Grove Lake Mall and Entertainium Complex, presented by the Maxious Group. Rolls right off the tongue."

"So what's the plan here?" Addie asked. "Do we rush through, knock down a couple meddlers, then claim the moral high ground?"

"Um, no," I said. "We talk. Hopefully cleverly."

"A better question is what we're going to do once we're inside," Gregory asked. "I don't think they're going to have a portal into the Gestalt lurking in the food court."

"We're not going back to the Gestalt. At least, not immediately," I said.

"So what's the point of this?" Adelaide asked.

"We're going into someone's domain." I pulled my amulet out from under my cuirass and held it up. "I figure we can reverse the flow and use them to reach one of our domains. I'm just not sure whose, yet."

"What good does that do us?" she asked. "The Unreal is the exact opposite direction from where we want to be. The Lumieres are hiding in the Gestalt, remember?"

"Well, uh. Yeah, I know, I just figured it was a step forward."

"Well, it's not. It's a step back." Addie stopped walking. "I need a better plan if I'm going to risk walking into a place as mundane as a suburban mall. That could do irreparable damage to my mythos."

"Maybe we could reverse engineer the amulets and use them to access one of your domains?" I suggested. "The Eccentrics do have domains, right?"

"Yeah. Back there." Addie jerked a thumb at the wrecked *Silverhawk*. "I don't need an amulet to get there. I can swim."

"But obviously the *Silverhawk* has fallen out of the Gestalt, right? Otherwise, it wouldn't have crashed," I said.

Ida nodded. "Whatever those valkyries did to the aethervox, it knocked us straight into the mundane world. Unless I'm mistaken, none of our powers are working. Right?" She looked at Addie. The gunsmith sulked, but shook her head. "Right. So we're stuck in the real world until we find a way out."

"When I joined Knight Watch, I had to create my own domain. Discover it, basically. Maybe you guys could do the same thing?"

Ida cocked her head. "That never occurred to me," she said. "Odd. I mean, of course we could try. How did it work?"

"There's a magic door in Mundane Actual," I said. "Esther just . . . pushed me through?"

"Same," Chesa said. "Kind of rude. But after a minute I got where I needed to go."

"The amulets are based on the same magic as the door," Tembo said. "Limited transposition, keyed to nonmaterial teleportation of quintessential anima." Ida cocked an eyebrow at him. The big mage sighed. "Portals. They make portals."

"Oh, why didn't you just say that?" she asked. "No need for all the complicated words. If that's the case, I might be able to harness the power and get it to work for us." She took the amulet from me without letting me take it off my neck, dragging me close as she examined it. "I really don't know magic stuff. We'd have to get at least a little bit into the Unreal before I could try anything."

"Perfect. That's exactly what I was planning," I said, snatching the amulet out of her hand and standing up straight once again. "We just need to get into that mall."

"Because shopping malls are the most magical place in the world?" Chesa asked.

"Just trust me. And let me do the talking," I said. "We can agree I'm good at that."

The lead elements of the mob reached us while we were still approaching the mall. Lines of oversized SUVs channeled us into a single lane, making it easy for them to block our path. Two women, wearing what I can only assume were terminal levels of beige to distract their enemies and threaten their rivals, flanked a harried-looking security guard. At first I was pleased to note that the guard seemed to only be armed with a Taser. Then I remembered I was wearing metal armor, and was soaking wet.

"So what's all this about?" the guard asked, hitching his belt over his belly. "We don't want any funny business."

"Failed promotional stunt," I said. "For ... uh ..."

"For an amusement park," Chesa stepped in. "You might have heard about it. Over in ..." She glanced around. We hadn't really established where we were.

"Mount Grove ... Heights?" I ventured. The guard's forehead wrinkled.

"Don't know that I've heard anything about that," he said. The two mothers stared at us with pinched foreheads and pursed lips. "Could be where the skate park used to be?"

"No," Mother Thing One said. "We wrote a petition. That's going to be a farmer's market."

"Yes," Mother Thing Two said. "A petition. We write those." She poked me in the chest with her iron-hardened finger. "Often."

"Right, well. Early stages of development. As you can see"—I gestured to the *Silverhawk*—"we still have a lot of kinks to—"

"Kinks!" the Mother Things yelped together.

"I mean, problems. You know, not ... never mind. We still have a lot to work out." I pulled off my helm, resting it against my hip. "It's going to be a combination Ren faire, science museum, and ... library? Does that sound good?"

"I've heard things about libraries," the first mother said warily.

"That they're full of books?" I asked.

"Yes," she said, her worst fears confirmed.

"Will there be a skate park?" the other mother asked.

"No. No, of course not. Wouldn't want teenagers doing ... things."

"Lame," one of the attendant teenagers muttered, then shuffled off. It seemed that offending the vagrant child won us the affection of the Mother Things. At least, long enough to get past security.

"As long as there's no skating," One said.

"Nope. No skating. Now ..." I motioned toward the door. "If you don't mind? We need some oversized pretzels and a novelty hat. For research, of course."

The crowd parted. The security guard looked relieved to avoid some paperwork, and the rest were still just curious. But once we were inside, things calmed down.

"That was good," Chesa said. "As long as they don't go down to the *Silverhawk* and interrogate The Good Doctor."

"That might be amusing," I said. "At least the Pinkertons should be able to distract them. Mothers like men in suits and facial hair."

"So what now? We aren't actually getting pretzels, are we?" Gregory asked.

"I could use a pretzel," Ida said. "And they're consistent with our timeline. The bigger the better."

"We'll start with pretzels. But then we need to find a store." I walked up to the directory. Of course, what I wanted was at the far end of the mall. "That's a relief. A lot of these places closed down."

"What?" Chesa asked. "You're not taking us to another bookstore, are you?"

"Heavens, no. This is much, much nerdier." I marched off. "Follow me!"

The pretzels were unwieldy. There is a quantity of pretzel that is entirely appropriate, and then there are pretzels that defy logic and common sense: piping hot limbs twisting together, dripping with butter and chunks of salt the size and consistency of loose gravel. Those were the pretzels we had. Everyone seemed happy.

"I can't believe they let us carry our swords in here," Gregory said, carefully balancing his tissue-wrapped pretzel in one hand as he licked salt off his fingers. "I got arrested once for wearing my Ren faire cloak while I was Christmas shopping. Banned me from the mall for two years!"

"Arrested for being a nerd," Chesa said, rolling her eyes. "You and Rast have that in common."

"To be fair, I was arrested for public intoxication," I said. "I wasn't drunk. I was just practicing my Chaucer while I walked around in the park. Cops thought I was ripped to the gills."

"'Whan that Aprille with his shoures soote,'" Gregory declaimed. "'The drogthe of March hath perced to the roote.'"

"'And bathed every veyne in swich licour...'" I responded.

"Please stop. Both of you," Chesa mumbled into her hand. "People are staring."

"Let them," Gregory said. "I stopped caring what other people think about my hobbies a long time ago."

"Amen to that." I toasted him with the remnants of my pretzel, then shook the final bits of salt off my hands. "Let the mundanes be mundane. I have more interesting things to care about."

"Really, the two of you have more in common than you think," Chesa said, shaking her head.

"Us? The two of us?" Gregory asked. He and I looked at one another dubiously. "No, I don't think that's right."

"As far as the swords are concerned, the Mundane might be imposing its will," Tembo said. "Keeping them from really looking too closely at us."

"Then explain why no one has complained about my pistol," Ida said. I shrugged.

"Maybe we're just in the south," I answered. Then, looking up, I spied our destination. "Ah! Here we are! A refuge for the weary traveler at long last!"

The sign over the door read GROGNARD GAMES and was flanked by a shield bearing a twenty-sided die on one side, and a machine gun loaded with chain-fed six-siders on the other. The windows displayed stuffed dragons, plastic robots, and stacks upon stacks of board games arranged into a dungeon maze. Inside I could hear the alluring sound of shuffling cards and clattering dice.

Chesa skidded to a halt.

"No. No way. I am *not* going into a place like that. Never!"

"You're wearing a chain-mail battle dress and carrying arrows hewn from fresh saplings. Legolas himself would call you a bit of a tryhard, Ches." I put one arm around her shoulders. "No one's going to tell you about their D&D character. I promise."

"What is this place?" Addie asked, peering up at the sign. "Some kind of casino?"

"A casino of the imagination," I said. "Come on. I'll explain once we're inside."

Grognard was a pretty typical game store. Racks upon racks of plastic miniatures lined the walls, while standing shelves carried terrain, dice and dice accessories, and novelty items like plushie mimics and foam swords. The collectible card games were locked up behind the counter or under glass cases, their value calculated in multiples of monthly income. I had spent a lot of time in places like this, before I joined Knight Watch. I approached the gentleman behind the counter. He watched me with understandable trepidation. I'm sure this wasn't the first time a party of fully armed murder hobos had entered his store.

"Good sir," I said with a slight bow. "My party and I would like to make use of one of your gaming chambers, if such is available on short notice?"

"Uh . . ." He looked between us nervously, no doubt calculating the cost of potential damage to his walls, if we got too rambunctious with those swords. "It'll be fifty bucks deposit, ten dollars an hour."

"Are you kidding me?" I snapped, before swallowing my reaction. "I mean, yes, indubitably. A fair price for such a fine establishment. And we will need to rent supplies as well. The appropriate manuals, dice, character sheets . . . so forth."

"You don't have your own dice?"

"I'm afraid our current situation has left us bereft of many of the comforts of the modern gamer. Including dice." Again, a slight bow. He rolled his eyes.

"Yeah, okay. Hang on." He disappeared behind into the supply area behind the counter. The sounds of rummaging commenced.

"Rast, what are you doing? We don't have time for a game!" Chesa said.

"Patience, patience. Just play along."

"What's with all the bowing and the big words?" Adelaide asked. "Are you trying to impress him?"

"I'm trying to be awkward. I want him to think we're just a bunch of gamers looking to roll dice. Not the supercool hero dudes that we actually are."

"Oh, yeah. Definitely a mistake he would make," Chesa said. "We get mistaken for supercool dudes all the time out in the real world."

I would have continued this argument, but the shopkeep returned with a stack of books, pencils, grid paper, and a bag of mismatched dice.

"That'll be seventy-two dollars," he said, setting the books on the counter.

"Wait, you just said fifty."

"Plus the books. You can keep the dice, if you want. People leave them behind."

"Ooo . . . dice." Gregory pounced, pawing through the grocery bag.

"Right, whatever." I turned to Adelaide. "Pay the man."

"Me? Why do I have to pay for this?" she asked.

"Because . . ." I lowered my voice, which was pointless, because the guy was right there. "They don't have American Dollars where I come from. Remember?"

"I figured you were Canadian or something," the guy said. "That accent."

"Accent? What . . . never mind." I turned back to Addie. "You and Ida are the only ones with real money."

"I'm tapped out," she said. "The pretzel place took my money. Like, all of it. Antique silver quarters don't go as far as they used to."

"She's not kidding," Ida said, her cheeks sticky with butter and salt. She brandished her pretzel. "These were a nickel at the World's Fair."

"I deal only in the currency of genius," Tesla said, peering at the ceiling. "Your lighting arrangement, for example, is a travesty of the electrical arts."

"Hey!" the guy behind the counter said, pointing at Ida. "No outside food or drink!"

Ida growled at him, quickly stuffing the remainder of the pretzel into her mouth. Her cheeks bulged as she slowly chewed it up, glaring at him the entire time.

"Alright, so . . . what will you take that isn't money?" I asked. "We have a variety of useful items and services available, if you're interested."

"Okay, this is getting weird." The guy slid the books away from us, snatching the bag of dice from Greg's hands, then stepping back. "Go somewhere else."

"But we need the room! And the dice!" Greg pleaded.

"No, sorry. Not going to—"

"Hold on," Chesa said, sliding closer to the counter. "I know what guys like you want. What you really want."

The guy swallowed hard, looking her up and down.

"Yeah?"

"Yeah," she said with a smile.

CHAPTER TWENTY-SEVEN

My sword went over the counter, on a nice little mounting stand, between two posters of upcoming tournaments and a plastic dragon's head. The guy looked up at it gleefully.

"Gosh, thanks! That's perfect!" he said. "Enjoy your room. Three hours! Heck, a fourth hour on the house. And feel free to punch a hole in the wall, if you want."

"That's not how I expected that to go," I said sadly. Chesa patted me on the shoulder.

"Guys love swords. Let's not fool ourselves," she said. She pulled me away from the counter. I looked over my shoulder at my beloved blade.

"But I might need that," I said glumly.

"We'll get you a new one, sweetie," she said, stroking the top of my head. "Now where is this room?"

"Back here." Ida was already setting up terrain and the game-master screen. Greg dumped the dice in the middle of the table and started sorting through them. The rest of the team filed into the room. It was a tight fit with the six members of Knight Watch and the three Eccentrics, especially with Tesla in full electric-factory mode, and Gregory and I in armor. Adelaide stood just inside the door, arms folded across her chest.

"I still don't understand what we're doing here," Addie said. "Some kind of game?"

Chesa led me to the head of the table and sat me down, then went to the opposite side and helped Ida go through the books. "I've learned to trust John's plans. They usually sound stupid, but they get us where we need to go," Chesa said. She looked up at me and smiled. "He hasn't let us down yet."

"Not for lack of trying," Gregory muttered. There was a loud clanking sound under the table, and he looked sharply at Chesa. She made a face at him, and he shrugged. "But she's right. He usually gets us there, wherever there is."

"Sir John has an unusual way of doing things," Tembo said. "It serves him well in the Unreal. It never would have occurred to me to ride Fenris to Valhalla, or drive a Volvo through a dragon."

"What? He did that?" Addie asked incredulously. "And you still trust him?"

"It worked," Matthew said as he settled into one of the folding chairs, then leaned back and put his boots up on the card table. "That's all that matters."

"In this case, we're just trying to get into the Unreal, at least briefly." I moved the screen around a bit, then set my helm on the table and folded my hands. "We're going to use the game as a portal into Unreal. From there, one of you will need to create your own domain. That should let us reenter the Gestalt."

"So who's it going to be?" Greg asked, tumbling a handful of dice in his palm. "Addie?"

Adelaide thought for a long moment, then shook her head. "No, I think it needs to be Ida. She's the one who's going to put the scarab back together and get us a bead on the Lumieres. If any of us needs their power, it's her."

"I concur," Tesla said. "My Gestalt presence is already invested in the *Silverhawk*. I don't think I could create a new domain without corrupting that connection."

"I'm fine with that," Chesa said. Gregory nodded vigorously. Ida, however, hesitated.

"I'm not a fighter. Sure, I can find you Evelyn and her mother, but after that? You guys are going to be on your own."

"We'll figure that out when we get there," I said. "Now. If everyone would please sit down, we can get started."

"But . . . but . . . we don't have characters yet, or stats, or backstories," Greg said. "I'm thinking about playing a human paladin who—"

I raised my hand. "Rules bore me. This is a time for stories. So listen.

"You walk into a tavern. It's mostly empty, except for a bored-looking ogre behind the bar, cleaning glasses in his overly large hands, as well as a shadowy figure in the corner. You're tired, and hungry, and a little hungover from last night's battle, so you sit down. You're still waiting for the ogre to notice you when the figure in the corner rises."

"I roll initiative," Gregory said.

I hissed him to silence. The rest of the team crowded around the table, taking seats and shuffling papers. I ignored the distractions and leaned into the story.

"He comes over to you. It's a tall, thin man, with hair like a bramble patch, and the smell to match. He's wearing dirty old robes, and leans against a gnarled staff, without which he would probably topple over. When he gets to your table, he smiles, and you notice that he's missing about half his teeth, and half of those that remain are gold or silver. His breath smells like rat piss . . ."

"That's very specific," Ida whispers.

"Hush. The old man holds out his hand. In it, is a bright, golden key." I held out my hand, which sadly was empty. I changed my voice, doing my best swamp-hobo imitation. "You look like a group of healthy young adventurers. Could I interest you in . . . a particularly dangerous job? The treasures you'll find will make it more than worth—"

"I'm not giving him a bath," Chesa muttered. Ida laughed, while Addie looked at me like I had just sprouted wings.

"Okay, now I roll initiative," Greg said, clattering dice forcefully in his hand.

It took about half an hour, but eventually the walls of the room where we were playing faded out of focus. The party was arguing about the best way to cross a bridge which, obviously, would have been just to walk across it, but they had come up with a highly detailed and overly complex plan to scale the sides of the bridge, using twenty staves they had stolen from a passing farmer, eighty feet of silken rope, gathered from their starting equipment, and a sail they had made from their cloaks. The wizened wizard lay dead in the ogre's tavern, having been stabbed preemptively by Gregory. I had at least convinced them to search his body, which had given them enough information to start the journey to the necromancer's tower. The adventure was afoot!

To my great joy, none of them had tried to seduce any inanimate objects, nor had they adopted a random nonplayer character I had made up on the spot, nor were they scheming to corner the market on boiled potatoes. Chesa *was* carrying around a duck that she had rescued from the village pond, but other than that, things were going pretty normal. Normal, at least, for a group of gamers. It was a banner day in my career as a game master. Unfortunately, I had to ruin it all with actual adventure.

"Look, all we need to do is get the rope to the other side of the bridge, then we can tie a flying bowline around that tree over there," Gregory said. "Then we can walk across the rope bridge, thereby bypassing the obvious trap bridge that John has laid for us."

"We can't possibly get the rope that far," Ida said. "Terminal velocity on loose rope is something like fifteen meters per second per second, unless we tie it to something."

"Which is why we have the kite," Greg answered. "Speaking of which, John, you still haven't given me an answer on that wind direction question. Preferably with a map of prevailing winds, the relative humidity over the river, and—"

"Guys!" I said sharply. "Forget about the bridge for a second."

"Oh, you'd like that! Forget about the obvious trap." Greg folded his arms and leaned back in his chair. "This guy, trying to distract us from the ersatz bridge ploy. Ha!"

"Someone remind me why I play this game with you guys." Chesa sat with her head in her hands. "If it wasn't for this damned duck, I'd have left half an hour ago."

"Speaking of the duck," Ida said, perking up. "Does Malbert have any friends? Because I think I'd like a duck of my own. You know, if one is available."

"Guys!" I repeated. "Stop. Talking. About the duck. Or the bridge."

"Oh?" Greg sat forward, eager anticipation in his eyes. "Initiative?"

"No. Just . . ." I gestured away from the table. "Look around."

The room had faded away, replaced by dense fog and grassy dells. Thin light leaked through the murk, directionless and dim. Strange birds sang stranger songs in the distance. Only the table remained, slowly sinking into the sod under the weight of too many rulebooks. Gregory stood up, startled.

"It worked! Rast, you bloody genius, you did it!" He started gathering his gear, most of which he had tossed to the side as he became more engaged in the game. "I have to get back to the girls. There's no telling what sort of mischief—"

"Whoa now, Haute. That's not the plan," I said. "We're following Ida out into the mist. Not you."

"Yeah, but..." He peered longingly into the fog. His shoulders slumped. "Okay."

"How do I do this?" Ida asked. "Just start walking?"

"Take the amulets with you," Chesa said. "They're meant to be portals to our domains. Maybe the latent magic will help."

"Won't they just lead us to one of your domains, then?" Adelaide asked. She hadn't really participated in the game, beyond making snide comments under her breath, but now that we'd opened a portal into the Unreal, she looked really uncomfortable. "No offense, John, but I've heard stories about your forest of terrors. I want no part in it."

"Well, we're just going to have to find out." I motioned to the amulets, lying on the table in the middle of the dice pile. "Imagine your mythic self, and start walking. We'll stay here until you've established yourself, so we don't disrupt the creation of the domain. There should be an obvious path back, related to your mythic identity. For me, it was... well, falling out of the sky."

"What?!" Ida gasped.

"My domain is all about fear, and overcoming it," I said. "I'm sure yours will be much calmer. More mechanical."

"I followed a staircase growing out of a tree," Chesa answered. "Don't worry. The way forward will be obvious."

"And we're supposed to just wait here?" Tesla asked.

"We don't want to risk leading her astray," Chesa said. "It shouldn't take too long. And we have snacks."

Tentatively, Ida picked up the six amulets and clutched them to her chest. We watched as she walked out into the mists, disappearing soon after. It wasn't long before the mists faded, and the stained white walls of the gaming room reasserted themselves. Gregory visibly deflated.

"I'm going to want that back," Gregory said. "Unless we're taking a detour to our own domains, I'm dangerously low on magic power."

"Don't worry, Greg. I'm sure she'll be back soon," I said. "And we can get on with finding and defeating this Iron Lich character. In the meantime..." I nodded to the table. "Initiative?"

"I thought we were just crossing the bridge?" he asked.

"Well." I smiled wickedly. "You can certainly try."

CHAPTER TWENTY-EIGHT

The bridge golem was busy taking Gregory apart one limb at a time when Ida returned. The party had gotten halfway through their plan to foil my dastardly trap when one of them slipped and set foot on the bridge. From there it was just a matter of initiative rolls, failed saving throws, and a lot of damage dice.

Fortunately for the team, the ceiling tiles of the room we were actually in collapsed as a cylinder of steel smashed through them, crushing a life-sized cutout of Galadriel and sending bits of foam insulation spraying across the room. Dust and debris floated in the air, coating everything in a fine layer of white, chalky powder. Coughing, I ran to the door and barricaded it with a fallen bookcase of complicated German board games before the owner of the store came to investigate the disturbance.

"What the hell is that?" Chesa swore, waving her hand in front of her face.

"I'm guessing Ida found her domain," I said. A second later, the door thumped open an inch, revealing the store owner's panicked face. I put my shoulder into the door. "See if you can get it open."

The cylinder appeared to be a single piece of seamless steel. It extended up into the ceiling, and had embedded itself a couple inches into the floor, like a pillar of gleaming metal. Tesla, Tembo, and Chesa ran their hands over the surface while Greg, Addie, and I fought off the increasingly frantic efforts of the store owner. Bethany was filling her pockets with dice, while Tembo stared curiously up at the hole in the ceiling through which the cylinder had come. Eventually, Chesa gave up and started banging on the pillar. After a minute of that, a glowing line formed on the surface, traveling like a burning fuse in the shape of a hatch.

"Stand back," Addie called. "Ida has a thing for explosive bolts."

Fortunately, Ida had settled on a more practical solution. Once the blackened edge of the hatch was revealed, the door slid open, revealing a narrow chamber about the size of a coffin, with an opening at the top. The sharp sound of rushing air filled the room.

"Are . . . are we supposed to get in there?" Chesa asked.

"Well, we're going to have to do something," I said. The owner had deputized several other patrons, and together they were straining our skills as an immovable object. "Like . . . quickish."

"Where others fear, heroes lead!" Gregory declared. He lunged toward the tube, fitting his wide shoulders into the chamber. His oiled hair stood on end as the rushing wind pulled at him. After a second of sitting there with his eyes squeezed tight, he peeked around. "Is there a lever or—"

Just then, a translucent tube with a rubber gasket around its lip descended from the opening at the top of the coffin. It settled over Greg's shoulders with a thump. His eyes bugged out as the skin of his face *smeared* upward. His muffled screams disappeared a second later, when he was sucked wholesale up into the tube at incredible speed.

"Well," I said. "Who's next?"

"I'm going to wring that little nerd's neck when I get up there," Adelaide said. She folded herself into the tube, squeezing her eyes and mouth shut. The glass tube returned and took her with it. The rest of the team followed in short order, with Matthew laughing hysterically as the tube consumed him, leaving only Chesa.

I looked at her impatiently. "You're up." The door banged open behind me, upsetting a large pile of games and pulling the hinges out of the drywall.

"You'll be okay?"

"Sure. Maybe hand me my shield before you go?"

Chesa sifted through the wreckage on the floor until she found my helm and my shield. She also pocketed a handful of dice. I cleared my throat.

"Anachronism, Ches. Leave the twenties. You can probably keep a couple of the sixes, if you're dead set on it."

"You're no fun," she said. With a sigh, she tossed the offending dice on the table, then handed me my shield. Then she pressed my helm down on my head, twisting it until my face popped into view. "Be careful, John."

"I think I can handle a room full of gamers," I said with a wink.

She smiled at me, then got into the Horrifying Tube of Sucking and disappeared.

I tightened the enarme straps of my shield against my forearm. There was no magic left in the shield, just steel, and with my amulet gone I was left with mundane skill. I seriously doubted the store owner and his cabal of gamers would try to do me any harm. Still, it helps to be prepared. Right after they gave a strong heave against the door, I released my grip on the handle and backed quickly away. A second later they struck again, this time piling through the unsecured door and landing in a pile on the floor.

"What have you done to my room?" the owner exclaimed, jumping to his feet. He was covered in the fine white dust that was still falling from the ceiling. The rest of his squad lay there, staring mutely at the destruction Ida had wrought. "You're going to have to pay for this! Where . . . where did the rest of them go?"

"That's really hard to explain," I said. "So I won't try. No chance I can have my sword back?"

He answered by screaming incoherently and scrambling across the shattered remnants of the table.

With a sigh of regret, I backed into the pillar, holding my shield tight to my chest and waited for the vacuum to pull me out. The owner was just lunging for me when the tube dropped over my shoulders, and the howl of a thousand hurricanes filled my ears.

I would have liked it better if the tube had been *straight*, or at least smooth. But for some reason, that horror ride was filled with bends, kinks, ribs, grates, significant decreases in width, and the constant, endless screaming. My screaming, of course, but also the high-pitched shriek of whatever hell-machine was providing the suction. I bounced through corners and around bends like a pinball before landing, head down, in a padded chamber. It was pitch black. At least the screaming stopped. The hell-machine's, of course. I kept at it for a couple heartbeats. I lay there, head bent at an awkward angle, arms pinned to my sides, legs curled against the tube. Waiting.

"Hello?" I called out. "Am I in the right reality?"

Eventually, the doors opened and I was pried free by Gregory's perfumed hands.

"We heard you coming a mile away," he said with a smile. "Rattling around like a musket ball, you were."

"There's a handle on the inside, Rast," Ida said. She stood at the controls to the world's most complicated pipe organ, throwing stops and pedaling key-changes. "They're trying to open the valve. I'm going to have to exit without the appropriate protocols."

"Last thing you want is that crew finding their way in here," I said. "Speaking of which . . ." I looked around. "Where *is* here, exactly?"

The room was the physical embodiment of *Machina Mundi* writ large. Gregory and I stood on a platform at the center of an enormous clockwork mechanism, surrounded by vast wheels and coil springs, inset with smaller cogs that ran their own trains of springs, escapements, and timing shafts, echoing in mechanical precision into the far distance, like a constellation of clocks seen from the inside out. For all the machinery, it was incredibly quiet. Only the faint ticking of the escapement and the gentle click of brass teeth sliding together disturbed the silence. Even the platform where we were standing was part of the mechanism. Its edge was lined with cogs, synching seamlessly with the surrounding clockwork.

"I'm thinking about calling it Clockwork Prime," Ida said, throwing more switches, then hauling on a lever taller than your average bear. The terrible howling whine that I had simply taken as background noise cut out, and the metal coffin folded shut and retracted into the ceiling. "What do you think? Too pretentious?"

"It's apt," I said, looking around. "But where do you live? There's no bed, no kitchen . . . nowhere to sit down and rest."

"Yes, well . . ." Ida turned to face me, and for the first time since I'd entered the domain, I actually looked at her. "That's not really a problem for me."

Ida's face and hands were entirely mechanical. Her brown curls, while still out of control and lustrous, were now coil springs and segmented tubing. Tiny clocks regulated the movement of her irises, and when she moved tiny wisps of steam puffed out of her back. As she made an adjustment to the console in front of her, the tip of her finger irised open and a small, articulated screwdriver emerged, pecking delicately at the keyboard before retreating into the digit. Her leather pants and oversized tool belt were fabricated from articulated aluminum, buffed to a mirrorlike sheen.

"Oh. Wow," I said.

"Yeah. I'm adjusting to it. You can get the jokes out of the way, if you'd like."

"No, no. No need for jokes," I said quickly. "Just not what I was expecting."

"I think it suits you," Gregory said. "Do you think you'll be like this all the time now, or only in the domain? Not that it isn't lovely, just . . . wondering."

"My data set on that inquiry is incomplete. Queueing . . . queueing . . ." She stood ramrod straight and began rocking back and forth. "Beep! Boop!"

"Uh . . ." Gregory and I exchanged nervous looks.

"Relax, you idiots," Ida said, loosening up. "I'm just playing with you. Come on. The others are waiting down below."

A door irised open in the middle of the platform, revealing an open shaft that was quickly filled with a second platform from below. This one at least had a handrail. Ida opened a gate in the handrail and ushered us through. A small console on a pedestal rose from the floor at Ida's gesture. Her hand melted into the console, cogs and pistons disassembling and integrating with the face of the control panel. I tried not to stare. With a hiss of steam, we began to descend through the darkness. The lightless shaft smelled like motor oil and hot metal.

"So, the rest of the team is already here somewhere?" I asked, averting my eyes.

"Yes. Time works strangely in this place. They came through about an hour ago."

"I should have mentioned that. Domain-time and real-world time run at different rates. I'm sure you could calculate a conversion rate, if you really—"

"I have already begun work on the time matrix," Ida interrupted. "It would really help if you could carry watches with you next time you go through. I've created a prototype that monitors time flow, heart rate, and . . ." Her voice trailed off as she realized our complete lack of interest. "Please proceed with your explanation."

"Right. Uh. Point is that time will run slower here. Gives you a chance to recuperate, or refuel, and whatever it is you do in that body." Another awkward glance at Gregory. "Wait, Greg, you went through the portal before Chesa. Did you somehow arrive after?"

"He did not. But he insisted on waiting until you arrived," Ida said. "In fact, he was getting quite anxious about your well-being." She turned clock-face eyes in my direction. "He was trying to convince me to send him back through, in case you needed saving."

"Let's not exaggerate," Gregory said with a snort. "I was more concerned he would screw up and let that mob through the portal."

"Mm," Ida said, and made no further comment.

"Nice of you to care, Greg," I said, clapping the big man on the shoulder. "But you should know by now that I'm the one who pulls your ass out of the fire, and not the other way around."

"Statistically and in my experience, you both require emergency assistance on a frequent and almost ridiculous basis," Ida said. "But that's just my . . . admittedly precise . . . observation."

We both snorted and guffawed and generally pretended she was wrong. I was still mulling an appropriate response when the elevator reached its destination. We descended through the ceiling of a large room that would have been spacious if not for all the clockwork.

The interior of Clockwork Prime was a slithering mass of gears and pistons, glistening with oil and the clattering syncopation of eternal engines counting time. The floor appeared to be a series of room-sized cogs, very slowly grinding together, their facings and relative positions changing with each bone-shuddering tick. There were walls and doors, but they existed only as approximations of the real thing: dream-like memories of regular human habitation, rather than faithful or practical reproductions thereof.

Chesa and Adelaide waited in a miniature sitting room, the chaise longue and divan slightly too small to be comfortable. Tesla was fully engaged examining a gearwork orrery at the center of the room, while the rest of Knight Watch relaxed beside a series of horse-sized pistons that pumped soundlessly along the far wall. As we descended from the ceiling, they jumped to their feet. Chesa's boot caught on the edge of a coffee table, overturning it. Ida glared at her with singular precision.

"You're back! Or here!" Chesa said. "We were starting to worry."

"She was worried. I was resigned to your death," Addie said. "Try to be more punctual in the future, will you, Rast? For our sake, at least."

"Sorry to be an inconvenience." The elevator reached the floor, integrating smoothly into the clockwork ballet. The handrails hissed open with a puff of steam. I was just starting to disembark when Ida rushed past me.

"Those are really only meant for decoration," she said sharply, brushing by Chesa to return the coffee table to its original position. She stepped back, considered the table, then made a slight adjustment. "Please leave the furniture alone."

"Right. Sorry," Chesa said, then turned to me. "So. Everything okay?"

"He's fine," Gregory said, a little more dismissively than was necessary. "I was about to rush to his rescue when he finally decided to turn up."

"Just a reminder that I have no control over the time flow in this place," I said. "I left right after you did. It's not my fault Ida dreamed a clock within a clock outside of time."

"Enough chatter," Ida said. "We need to find where Evelyn Lumiere went."

She crossed to another room in the rotating schema of walls, ignoring the heavy crash of gears as she stepped from cog to cog. The rest of the team joined us, though Tesla kept getting distracted by the machinery. We had to take turns pulling him away from examining the various wheels and dynamos that made up Ida's domain.

"Have you gotten a bead on the scarab's signal?" I asked, stepping carefully over to the next room. There was a wall rotating toward us, and Addie had to rush before it cut us off from the rest of the area. The rest of the team waited until the door opened again.

"Still processing. We seem to be working with three separate entities at this stage. Evelyn, who as near as I can tell is tied to the Unreal through her archetype as the original Vampire Slayer. Cecilia Lumiere, acting as some kind of poltergeist or medium for higher powers. And this Iron Lich character, who could be Evelyn, or her father, or some unknown third entity that has yet to reveal itself. In fact, I have a theory . . ." Ida said, then fell silent. This room looked suspiciously like the bridge of the *Silverhawk*, though instead of a bay of windows, there were smoky glass enclosures, populated by blinking lights drifting through thick fog. Ida went to one of the control panels and started pulling levers, adjusting knobs, and generally fiddling around.

When she didn't continue her sentence, I prompted her. "And what is the theory?"

"Oh. Well, usually people stop paying attention when I start in on the theories. They just want the answer, as quickly and simply as possible. And I don't have the answer." She looked over her shoulder as Tesla, lagging behind the rest of us, finally made the leap to this space. "Do you want brief or complete?"

"Let's go with brief," Addie said warily.

"Very well. I believe that this Iron Lich figure is Claude Lumiere, resurrected by his daughter in an attempt to bring her family back together."

"What? Why would she do that?" Addie asked.

"Heavens if I know. Families are nothing but trouble. My mother was very insistent on sending me to college, when I had a perfectly good library and plenty of notebooks at home. But no, that wasn't—"

"Ida?" I said. "The lich?"

"Oh, yes. The lich. Well, considering she seems to have raised her mother from the dead and constrained her in that cage, I hypothesize that Evelyn was working on a similar solution for her father. Hence, the Iron Lich."

"It's also possible that this Iron Lich contraption was Claude's intention from the very beginning," Tembo said. "Zofia spoke of dealings with the Lumieres, and the father's plans for immortality."

"If that's the case, why wait this long?" I asked. "Surely she could have enacted her father's plan shortly after his death."

"Perhaps Evelyn didn't know about it," Tesla said. "She was zealous in her pogrom against the vampires. Though when I knew her, she killed them in a more traditional manner."

"Including her mother, if I remember correctly," Bethany said. "Seems kinda weird, if your plan is to just resurrect them later on."

"Claude Lumiere did not survive the attack, and Cecilia was turned by seeming accident," Tesla said. "Though if your pet vampire is to be believed, the Lumieres were responsible for the slaughter, in their effort to complete the ritual that the vampires interrupted."

"That's a big if," Addie said, crossing her arms. "I don't trust that bloodsucker any farther than I can throw her."

"Two point four meters," Ida said. "On average."

We all looked at her in confusion.

"The average distance a human can throw another human of equal weight and size. That makes some assumptions about grip, harness, passivity, and preparation time of—"

"Evelyn did say she had been reading her father's journals," I interrupted, cocking my head, trying to scrape the inside of my skull for a memory. "Maybe she figured out what they were trying to do, and decided to replicate it?"

"Are we sure she wasn't just trying to finish her crusade against the vampires?" Chesa asked. "She did a pretty thorough job of it."

"Doesn't explain the scarabs, or the clockwork valkyries, or even the original attack on the bakery," Addie said.

"We'll have to ask her." Ida threw another switch, and the fog in one of the glass cases began to clear. It resolved into an image, blurry at first, but quickly growing much sharper.

It was Evelyn Lumiere, accompanied by her two hounds, rushing down what appeared to be a boardwalk. The ocean crashed in the background, and the sky was the color of burnished pewter, churning with the opening stanzas of a tremendous storm.

"How are we seeing this?" Chesa asked.

"Science," Ida said simply, then adjusted another knob. The image jumped forward, then came into much sharper focus. "Do you see what I see?"

There was something on Evelyn's back. Though she was old and somewhat frail, she seemed to be lugging an enormous metal tube over her shoulder. It appeared to contain a series of glass orbs, each one filled with a glowing, greenish liquid. Steam hissed from the end of the tube, regulated by a series of dials and gauges.

"What is that?" I asked.

"We won't know for certain until we catch up to her," Ida started. "But . . ."

"If I had my guess," Adelaide said, stepping in, "those are the souls of the vampires."

CHAPTER TWENTY-NINE

Clockwork Prime, it turned out, was a kind of airship. Not surprising, considering Ida's origin story and the practicalities of her Gestalt image, but it felt weird to be in a domain that was capable of flight in the mundane world. Especially when it felt like we weren't moving at all. At least, not forward. We were certainly moving in circles. Constantly. Every time I looked up, the rooms had shifted and the walls had changed, and the clockwork under our feet just kept on ticking forward and around and back. It was enough . . . enough to . . .

"John, you're not looking so great," Chesa said.

"Motion sick," I said, pressing my eyes closed. That only made it worse. "Is there somewhere in this domain that isn't spinning constantly?"

"The Spindle. But I don't think you'd like it up there," Ida said.

"I'm willing to give it a try. Where is it?" I asked, standing up woozily.

"At the top. Overlooking the vast emptiness of Probability Space. Oh, which is spinning around us, so maybe that wouldn't help," Ida said. I sat back down. "Don't worry. We're almost close enough to connect to reality once again. The part of reality where Evelyn is, that is."

"And what are we supposed to do once we get there?" Gregory asked. "Last time I checked, you took our amulets to open the door to this place. We're out of magic."

"Oh. Forgot about those." Ida clattered some keys, then threw a lever. Pedestals emerged from the floor beside each of the members of Knight Watch, holding our amulets on crushed velvet cushions. "There you go."

Gratefully, I looped the cold steel shield around my neck and dropped it down the front of my gambeson. I was about to tap into my domain when alarm bells started going off. Ida glanced over at me.

"Reminder that we're deep in Gestalt space. Please keep your timelines in the upright and locked position until you've disembarked."

"Right. Sorry," I said. Chesa glared at me. "We'll just be in low-power mode when we get there. Hopefully we can distract her while our reserves fill."

"We still have armor, and our swords are sharp," Gregory answered. "I'm willing to take that risk."

"At least you still have a sword. Mine's sitting on a wall in some game store." I pressed my hands against my face, fighting down the rising tide of bile in my throat. "I can't believe we've come this far, and now we don't have the means to fight."

"It was never about our domains, John. They help, but the will to fight, the reason to get up and get after the darkness when all hope is lost . . . that comes from someplace else." Greg pulled me to my feet and tapped me on the chest. "That comes from in here."

"I'm already nauseous," I said, sitting back down. "Let's not make it any worse."

"He's right, John. You were fighting sword and shield for years before Knight Watch stepped in. And you didn't have any of your cool magical powers when you faced off against Kracek, did you?" Chesa asked. "I don't love the idea of going in there without elven magic. But we can't give up now."

"Fine. Fine, whatever, you've made your point." I sat up a little straighter. "We'll go in naked. Well, not naked. Just mundane. I wish I had a sword, that's all. Any sword."

"That can be arranged," Ida said. "I won't be joining you, obviously. Not in my present condition. But I have a fully functioning workshop here in the Prime. I'm certain I can fabricate a functional blade for Sir John. Do you have a schematic?"

"Sharp thing, about yay long?" I held out my hands and squinted. "The pointier the better."

"Yes," Ida said. "I can do pointy."

✤ ✤ ✤

"Okay, that's *too* pointy."

The monstrosity that arose from Ida's auto-forge was a mandelbrot set of scything blades, centered around a basket hilt the size of my head. The whole thing was five feet in diameter, and must have weighed sixty pounds. I wasn't sure I could even hold it without skewering myself on one of its many points.

"I put in the parameters you described," Ida said, frustration in her voice. "It's not my fault that you ordered something vague. You'll have to be more precise."

"He wants a simple arming sword," Greg said. "Overall length about three feet, two and a half feet of that in the blade, the rest in hilt, guard, and pommel. Double edged, steel, handle wrapped in leather, bone guard, heavy iron or steel in the pommel. Under three pounds in weight. Unless you want something lighter, Rast? How's your arm strength?"

"It's fine," I snapped. "And the guard needs to be steel. I know that's atypical, but I catch a lot of blades with the hilt, and I don't want that breaking off."

"Better. Thank you. Not everything needs to be a poem." Ida punched the numbers into the auto-forge's console and stood back. After a few moments, a gleaming splinter of bright steel emerged from the device. "Acceptable?" Ida asked.

I took it in hand and gave a few practice swings. "Yeah, this is good. Good balance." We had set up a series of target dummies on the far side of the room. I went over and sliced the arm and head off one of the quintains, then stepped back. "Nice and sharp. I like it!"

"Does anyone else need anything?" Ida asked. She looked pointedly at me. "A toothbrush, for example?"

"About a thousand arrows, and the quivers to carry them," Chesa said. "Not literally!" she added, when Ida started punching in the numbers. "I'm just used to an endless magical supply. How about... sixty? Does that seem right?"

"I'm good to go," Gregory answered. "Steel and courage. That's all I need."

"The Saint and I are nothing without our magic. We'll hang back until we can establish a solid connection with our domains," Tembo said. "And I believe Lady Bethany carries enough knives for a handful of Scotsmen."

"Three and a half Scotsmen," Bee said, balancing a spinning dagger on her fingertip.

"One more thing," I said. "Can I have the scarab?"

"I was hoping to add it to my collection," Ida said reluctantly. "Why do you want it?"

"If Evelyn is using them to power her cursed contraption, I want to study it. Maybe I can figure out a way to stop them."

"That feels unlikely," Ida said. But she produced the brass beetle from a compartment and handed it over. "Just . . . try to not break it."

"Then let's get to it." Addie stepped onto the elevator.

The metal coffin tube ride was no more enjoyable on the way out than it had been on the way in. If anything, it was worse, because Ida insisted that we start the journey upside down, so that we came out right side up. I didn't argue. Anything to get off this constantly spinning carousel of gears and pistons.

We emerged in the middle of a spinning carousel of gears and pistons. I thought I'd taken a wrong turn somewhere and arrived where I had started, but as I stepped out of the vacuum tube, I spied Adelaide crouching behind a crudely painted horse. Mechanical organ music clamored overhead, and flashing bulbs blinked overhead. Everything was painted in gaudy reds and yellows and golds. I smelled the strong scent of saltwater in the air. The movement of the platform put me off my balance, and I stumbled to one side, ramming shoulder-first into the side of a wooden sleigh painted the color of sea-foam.

Chesa came out of the tube right behind me. She squinted at the lights distastefully. The look on her face reminded me of our first date, down at the . . .

"Amusement park?" I said out loud. "Why are we in an amusement park?"

"It's just the one carousel, on a boardwalk. I think Ida's portal kicked it into overdrive. Contact with the Gestalt will do that to machines sometimes," Addie said. "Just hang on. It'll pass."

The rest of the team joined us a second later. The vacuum tube was somehow connected to the center pole and crown bearing of the carousel. As soon as the portal closed and lifted out of view, the lights on the carousel snapped off, and the music dwindled into eerie silence. Slowly, the carousel creaked to a halt. In the relative darkness and quiet, the painted horses and jumping gazelles looked haunted. With Tesla and Adelaide in tow, Knight Watch was up to eight members. Way more than was customary. We were in a warehouse full of abandoned carnival rides. Dusty sheets covered most of them, but every so often a painted clown's head or rusted dragon boat stuck out of the canvas. Our carousel sat at the center of the operation, its covering torn and twisted by the machine's sudden and unexpected activation. Now that the machine had fallen silent, I could hear seagulls in the distance, and the crash of waves against a shore.

"This feels really Mundane," I said. "Or straight-up haunted. Take your pick."

"Ida did the best she could. Evelyn has to be around here somewhere, sneaking through the Gestalt," Addie said. She brought her shotgun to her shoulder, sweeping the warehouse floor. "But I don't think she's right here."

"We saw her on a boardwalk. Let's see what we can see." I stepped off the carousel and through the graveyard of forgotten amusements. "Chesa, do your elven ears hear anything?"

"Still working on filling my magic, would rather not tap it yet," she said.

"Right. Magic." I opened the tap in my amulet, letting magical energy trickle into my soul. It would be a while before I could do anything tricky, but it felt good to be more than mundane. I saw the same relief on the faces of the rest of Knight Watch.

The sliding door at the end of the warehouse was cracked open. Now that the carousel was off, it was our only source of light.

"Did anyone bring a torch?" Chesa asked.

"Left it in my bag," I said. "Along with fifty pounds of jerky and three hundred feet of rope. So I guess that was a mistake." We stumbled through the warehouse, occasionally bumping into covered rides and sending plumes of dust into the air. By the time we reached the door, we were coughing, bruised in shin and pride, and generally ready to be outside. I put my shoulder into the sliding door and shoved. The door rumbled open on rusting casters and rattling chains. Muted gray light poured inside, along with a stiff breeze, heavy with salt. "At least the door wasn't locked."

We stepped outside into a light drizzle that was falling from a low sky. The boardwalk extended in both directions, one side lined with weather-beaten warehouses locked tight with rusting chains, the other side looking out onto a short span of filthy beach, and the ocean beyond. Waves crashed every few seconds off the pebbled shore, sending salt spray over the warped planks of the boardwalk, mingling with the cold rain. Two seconds in the open, and I was already soaked to the core. In the fog and rain, it was impossible to see more than a dozen yards in either direction. The only sounds were the waves, and the lonely song of seagulls, pinwheeling through the clouds overhead.

"Well, this is dreary as cold mud," I said. "Where are we? New Jersey?"

"I think this is Atlantis," Adelaide said quietly. "I thought it sank long ago."

"Atlantis? Like, the mystical island nation from Odysseus?" I asked.

"It was Plato," Tembo said. "But this does not feel like the Republic to me."

"It was a failed attempt at consolidating the Gestalt into a single, stable entity. Kind of a permanent delusion," Tesla said. "It was Claude's greatest ambition. It would have attracted people from all over the world, and let them dream out loud."

"So like Disneyland, or Harajuku," I said. "What happened?"

"The Lumieres were the driving force behind it. After what happened to them, the project faltered," Tesla said sadly. "Evelyn claimed it sank into the ocean."

"If her father was planning something greater, this is where he would have hidden it," Adelaide said, grimacing. "Hidden from the world, yours and ours, tucked deep into the Gestalt like a bomb waiting to go off."

"I thought Claude simply wanted to build a permanent steampunk Utopia," Tesla said. "It seems his ambitions were more diabolical than I imagined."

"Kind of weird that they made it look like a giant boardwalk," Chesa said. "Are you sure this isn't Atlantic City or something?"

Just then, the clouds parted long enough for us to catch a glimpse of the farther ocean. There was something large and metal among the waves, its spine ridged like a boar, with a glass eye the size of a city block. The waves crashed against it, but it didn't move. I only had a second's view of it, but I got the impression of immense size and weight. Gregory gave a low whistle.

"Definitely not Atlantic City," he said.

"Yeah. That's the *Kraken*, the Lumieres' personal submersible. Which means Evelyn is definitely around here somewhere," Addie said. "The question is, where?"

"I think I know." I pointed to the left, along the length of the boardwalk.

Even through the fog and rain, the lights shone bright as lightning. Whatever they were illuminating was cloaked by the murk, but it was tall. At the base of the tower, a whole village's worth of blinking lights and flashing pillars spread out into the ocean. In the silence that hung between crashing waves, we could hear music.

Carnival music, slightly dissonant, twisted by distance and echo into a cruel mockery of circus laughter and amusement park levity.

"Haunted amusement park!" Bethany said enthusiastically, pulling her hood over her head to shield against the rain. "Let's go!"

CHAPTER THIRTY

The closer we got to the park, the more haunted our surroundings became. Ghostly figures circled the tower of lights, giving off their own ephemeral glow. The sound of music rose, and the dissonance got worse. It was traditional carnival music, but played slower, and in a lower key. Some of the notes dragged out much too long, and others were broken into a jumble of fragmented echoes that disappeared into the roar of the surf. The park itself was built on an enormous pier that extended out into the storm-tossed waters. The bright lights of the park reflected off the low-hanging clouds in a motley of greens, reds, and sun-golden yellows, blinking and flashing and rolling in waves of bright ribbons of color that turned the dark pewter sky into a cheerful tapestry. That didn't stop the rain, of course.

We reached the entrance to the park. A weathered archway led inside, framed with flickering light bulbs and painted in gaudy pinks and greens. The sign over the archway advertised "Electr-O-World" and the O in the center was a gaping mouth, complete with teeth and a dangling tonsil. I came up short, staring at the all-consuming vowel.

"That's hardly comforting," I said. "Electr-O-World. How are all these machines still running after all this time?"

"Gestalt," Adelaide said. "The entire island was built on Gestalt power, and with Gestalt logic. It's amazing what you can do with science."

"Well, it's seen better days," Chesa said. "Half the stalls look empty, and the rest are pretty beaten up."

"You forget that most of the steampunk world thinks this place

233

was destroyed," Adelaide said. "It's surviving on the strength of belief of the Lumieres. Most of whom are dead."

"Were dead," I corrected. "So what do we make of that?" I pointed at the tower of light at the center of the park. It looked like a cross between the Eiffel Tower and an unlit Christmas tree. Three large horizontal arms ran the length of the central spire, each one capped with a brass sphere. The lights that had first drawn my attention through the fog were simply running lights that traced the edges of the tower. Glass-and-steel platforms stretched up the length of the structure, but other than the flickering bulbs of the running lights, the tower was dark.

"Le Tour d'Elysee. Tower of Heaven, more or less. It was the central attraction. The wonders of electricity, created by Claude Lumiere. I didn't think much of it," Tesla said with a sniff. "Bit gaudy for my tastes."

"Evelyn's journal mentioned an Immortality Engine that her father was designing," I said. "Seems like a pretty obvious place for it."

"I reviewed the plans for that tower, and oversaw part of its construction," Tesla answered. "Nothing about it seemed unusual to me."

"And yet before today, you would have counted Claude Lumiere among your closest friends," Tembo pointed out. "I think it warrants investigation."

"Good enough for me," I said.

"I'm with John. Lightning Tower," Chesa said.

"As much as I don't like the idea of being close to something like that while wearing metal armor"—Gregory shrugged—"looming tower of electric death seems like a good start."

"Anything that claims to be the tower of Heaven but looks like a ruined carnival ride is right up my alley," Saint Matthew said. "Maybe they'll have angels!"

"I sincerely hope not," I muttered as I passed beneath the archway that led into the park. The rest of the team followed close behind in a vee formation.

Unfortunately, traveling to the tower was easier declared than executed. Like most tourist traps, Electr-O-World was a maze. The proprietors wanted you to get lost, they wanted to draw you from one finely tuned money extraction stall to the next, without actually going anywhere. The iron tower at the center was the obvious destination for most visitors, but the surrounding amusements and vendors were the source of all the profit. The longer they could keep you from your destination, the more money they made.

"Glad to see that hasn't changed in a hundred years," I muttered.

"What was that?" Chesa asked.

"Oh. The maze of amusement. It's like casinos. You can't just walk from one end of those things to the other. You have to wind your way past a thousand flashing displays and slot machines just to find the bathroom."

"Haven't spent a lot of time in the casinos," Adelaide said.

"Really? You seem the type," I said, raising my eyebrows. "Steamboats and cardsharps, the whole thing."

"Let's focus on the task at hand, Rast," Chesa said.

"Right, right. Task at hand. Which appears to be"—I looked around at the labyrinth of glowing signs, boarded up vendors, and shuttered rides—"getting lost in a haunted amusement park."

"There is more to it than that," Tembo said. He was walking at the center of our loose mob of adventurers, but now he looked around curiously. "I wish we had sketched our route a little more clearly."

"Worried about getting lost?" Gregory asked.

"No. Worried that we might be walking through a giant summoning rune," he said. He raised his staff in front of him and began an incantation. The spell wrapped around the dark wood of the staff like coiled lightning. Wind fluttered through his robes, matching the beating rain of the storm overhead. Slowly he rose into the air, until the sandaled soles of his feet hovered just over our heads. I made a point of not looking up. "Yes," Tembo said, looking around. "The stalls, the pathways, the amusements . . . They are very intentionally laid out. Not to distract. To invoke."

"What does that mean?" Addie asked as Tembo floated gently back to the ground.

"It means that this entire park is part of Lumiere's Immortality Engine." Tembo dispersed the remaining magical aura with a flick of his hand, sending sparks showering through the rain. "And once the incantation begins, a ritual this size will be very difficult to halt. If not impossible."

"All the more reason to hurry," I said.

The lane ended in a courtyard, centered around a mechanical orrery, similar to the one at the center of Ida's domain. A statue capped the central spire that acted as an axis for the rotating planets. The planets were depicted by verdigris-stained brass spheres that ran on cogwheel tracks. The display was silent, though the engines looked to be in good working order. I was still examining the engines when the statue at the top moved.

It was Evelyn Lumiere, wearing close-fit plate armor over a dancer's gown, with an open-faced helm and bandoliers looped across her chest, stuffed with wooden stakes. I called a halt, then lifted my visor.

"We found your little science project, Ms. Lumiere," I said.

"It took you long enough," she said with a smile. She looked twenty years younger. I noticed a pair of hoses protruding from either side of her neck, leading to a device on her back. Perhaps she had been sampling her father's cooking. "So, what now? Have you come to stop the evil witch?"

"Something like that," Gregory said. He ran a thumb along the crosspiece of his zweihander, eager to fight.

"I don't understand all this, Evelyn!" Tesla pushed his way past us. The coiled gauntlets of his generator were tucked away behind him. He extended his hands, pleading. "After all these years, why would you turn on us like this?"

"Turn on you? Hardly. It was you who betrayed me. Betrayed my father!" Evelyn hopped agilely from the spire down onto the mechanical sun, dancing down its length to land on the amber face of Mercury. "You and Esther MacRae could have saved him at any time. Instead, you used me to destroy the one hope for rescuing him."

"Neither of us knew he was in league with the vampires. And, frankly, I'm not sure that would have improved our disposition in the matter." Tesla took another step forward. "This can end, Evelyn. No one has to die."

"The people I care about are already dead." Evelyn leapt from Mercury to an out-of-orbit Earth. "But I'm going to save them. And nothing you can do will stop that."

"Very well." Tesla threw his arms forward. The gauntlets folded out, latching on at biceps and elbow before clamping onto his wrists.

Brilliant electricity coursed through the coils, underlighting his face with blue light. "We will settle this your way."

"About time," Gregory muttered, striding forward.

"Careful," Tembo said. "You saw what she did to those vampires."

"Good news." I lowered my visor and joined Gregory. "We're not vampires."

"That's fine," Evelyn called down. With a whirl, she drew a pair of steel stakes and assumed a fighting stance. "I'm sure the skills will translate."

Before I could move any closer, Evelyn leapt from the metal surface of the Earth, skipped off the rotating silver of the Moon, and vaulted over our front line. Tesla let out a startled cry as she flew overhead. Chesa, made of sterner stuff, sent two arrows flying toward the slayer. Evelyn dashed those aside with her metallic stakes, redirecting them toward me and Gregory. I caught them both on my shield.

Evelyn came down between Chesa and Tembo. She landed in a blur of slashing stakes and striking boots. Tembo's staff flew from his hands, then a sweeping kick took his legs out from under him. Evelyn was just about to drive a stake through his heart when Addie's pistol boomed. The shot struck the slayer in the shoulder, spinning her off the mage and through the air. Evelyn kept up the motion, landing only long enough to jump high up into the rings of Saturn. She perched on the golden disc to glare down at us.

"Addie, my dear. I think that tea is off," she snarled.

"I was going to ghost you anyway," Adelaide said. With a spin, her revolver changed to a lever-action rifle, which she cocked and sighted at Evelyn. "Literally."

The muzzle jumped, but Evelyn was already gone. Dancing from orb to orb, she disappeared behind the sun's mass. Addie followed her with shot after shot, sending sparks off Saturn, Mercury, and finally old Sol itself. When Evelyn dropped behind the golden orb, Addie swore and collapsed her rifle into a shotgun.

"She's a fast one," she muttered. "Going to have to get creative."

"Faster than I remember," Tesla said. "Though it has been some time since I saw her in action."

"What's that thing on her back?" I asked.

"No idea," Addie answered. "We can check once she's dead."

"Chickens before they hatch, dearie." Evelyn appeared out of the shadows of a broken ride to our rear. She vaulted over us, landing in a squat in our path. The streak of blood on Evelyn's shoulder from Addie's shot was smeared over pale flesh. The veins of her neck and across her forehead were dark and throbbing. She was healing at an astounding rate. "Though you may find death has little dominion over me."

Gregory yelled and barreled toward her, zweihander drawn back to swing. Evelyn sneered at him, then leapt high in the air. She kicked him once in the chest, a second time in the face, then danced down the length of his blade to charge me. I stopped gaping long enough to assume a guard. One of her stakes crashed against my shield before she skipped back into the shadows and disappeared.

"I've seen those kinds of moves before!" I shouted. "Chesa! Flarrows nocked!"

"I can't hit her," she answered. "The old crone's too fast!"

"You're not going to have to. Trust me. Back to back, everyone!"

We formed a circle and faced outward toward the darkness. The rain pounded down on us, and the only light was the dim glow from a couple of the surrounding amusements, and the tall spire of ghostly illumination of the Tour d'Elysee.

Evelyn sprang from beneath the billowing sheets of a mothballed park ride, silent as she zipped across the boardwalk, straight at me. I barely got my shield up before she barreled into me. One stake glanced off the Viking steel, but the other slammed into Gregory beside me. He gasped as it punctured his shoulder, dimpling the steel and drawing blood. I was just whirling to face this new attack when Chesa found her mark.

The first flarrow went wide, but the second thumped into Evelyn's armored chest. Designed to provide precise illumination in any condition rather than to pierce steel, the flarrow stuck to the curved front of the slayer's breastplate before bursting into brilliant light. I was momentarily blinded by the sunburst.

Shrieking, the slayer backpedaled away from our little circle. I watched as her skin seared and the veins of her face turned a deep black under her pale flesh. Plumes of noxious smoke curled out from under her armor. Her limbs twitched like a pinned beetle. She dropped her stakes and batted ineffectually at the shaft in her chest, fingers blistering each time they brushed the glowing arrow. Finally, she knocked it free. The flarrow clattered to the ground, still burning. Evelyn was nothing more than a shadow as she leapt out of the circle of its illumination, leaving behind a trail of smoke and ash.

"Well. That was dramatic," I said.

"What just happened?" Gregory asked. The rest of the team was staring at the circle of light, and the cinders that were still drifting to the ground in Evelyn's wake.

"I think she's been supping at the table of her enemy," I said. "Using the juice from the vampires' souls to power her abilities. Maybe that's part of why she's losing her mind."

"Or perhaps it is merely a sign of her madness," Tembo said. "Either way, good thinking, Lady Chesa."

"That was John's idea," she said. "I'm just the messenger."

"I suspect that was only enough to drive her off for a bit. She'll be back," I said with a shrug. "Let's get to the tower toot sweet. If we can stop the ritual before she recovers, it might not matter."

Just then, a single stroke of lightning, as wide as the sky and bright as the sun, struck the Electr-O-Tower. With a groan, the three rotating arms of the generator started to spin. With each rotation, bolts of energy arced between the brass spheres at their ends, building in power until they started grounding into the park itself. With each crackling stroke, the arms spun faster and faster, until the sound of their passage was a thunderous roar. Overhead, the storm began to rotate in conjunction with the generators. The lights in the park flickered out as lightning reached out of the ground to dance across the iron trestles of the tower, as though the structure was drawing all the power into itself.

"Or not," I said, and started to run.

CHAPTER THIRTY-ONE

We approached the tower in a loose skirmish line, sweeping down the littered avenue of the boardwalk four across and two deep. Gregory and I took center, flanked on the left by Addie and the right by Nik Tesla, his gauntlets crackling up a storm. I would have preferred some distance from the inventor, given my armor and the casual way he was throwing out static. Chesa, Tembo, and Saint Matthew followed behind. Bethany had disappeared into the shadows as soon as we started moving, though there was an occasional flicker of steel and silk out of the corner of my eye. There was a groundswell of Unreal power seeping into the world around us, or maybe our amulets were finally finding their pace, because I could feel the magic coursing through my system. With the main lights of the amusement park extinguished, and the low clouds of the overhanging storm smothering the sky, we advanced in near absolute darkness. Only the Electr-O-Tower provided any illumination, and the ghastly green glow drifting from its flanks didn't do much to light the way.

Now that we were closer, I could see that the Tour d'Elysee was a much more complicated structure than I first imagined. From a distance it looked like a cross between the Eiffel Tower and a Van de Graaff generator. As we approached, I gazed up at a madman's collection of high gothic archways, gargoyles, and arcane symbols worked into the twisting latticework of the main tower. Bundles of thick cable and brass tubing burrowed through the tower like vines dangling from a dying tree. It was as if the steel tower had grown up through the middle of a medieval cathedral, tearing the building apart as it rose into the sky. The main entrance gaped open. If there were once doors, they had been removed long ago. About halfway up the length of the tower, the three arms of the generator tore through the air. The strings of electric bulbs that hung down the outside of the tower oscillated in the wind washing off the rotating arms. The bulbs themselves were shattered, but their filaments glowed with ethereal light.

"Good place for a boss fight," I said. "Or a glorious death."

"Think positive, John," Gregory said. "Why not both?"

We passed into the shadow of the Tower of Heaven, as Tesla had called it. The interior looked like a haunted house crossed with grand Parisian architecture. A steel-and-glass barrel ceiling ran the length of the space, with marble stairs that branched off the main space, leading to lower hallways. The superstructure of the steel tower glittered through the glass dome overhead. At the center of the pavilion was a wide dais, held aloft by a collection of marble figures that struggled under the weight of the platform. The arched entrance to the pavilion was crowned with a verdigris-covered brass monument, backlit with the same ghostly green light that had replaced the electric bulbs running the height of the tower. The statue depicted a robed woman holding a laurel aloft, flanked by four resplendent horses. They appeared to be trampling an old man with a scythe. I paused and gazed up at it.

"Well, that's the fanciest thing I've seen since we got here," I said. "What do you think it is?"

"Pretty girls and their horses, doing a violence," Gregory said. "Who knows? This place looks familiar."

"Yeah? You've been to a lot of haunted towers?" Chesa asked.

"No, but in my senior year of high school I went to Paris with the French class," he said. "I wasn't taking French, of course, but I was able to talk my way onto the trip."

I rolled my eyes hard enough to get dizzy.

"Of course you did," I said.

"This place looks just like the Palace thing. The big one. Next to the small one."

"The Grand Palais?" I asked. I had never been to Paris, obviously, but I harbored dreams. "I suppose it kind of does. Which means this . . ."

"That is the victory of Immortality over Time." The voice echoed off the marble and glass, reverberating as it traveled.

A clockwork sarcophagus rose from the center dais of the pavilion, an orchestra of iron, bone, and marble. It looked like a pipe organ with all the machinery exposed. As the sarcophagus rose, plumes of steam and darker gasses rolled out of it. At the center of this hodgepodge of pipes, gears, tubes, and wheels was the Iron Lich, embedded in a niche in the machinery. His body was a collection of polished iron, like the parts of an elaborate statue dissected and then held together by shafts of metal or, in some places, weathered bone. Clockwork glimmered in the construct's joints, mingling with exposed bone and translucent conduits that throbbed with dark purple light. Exhaust pipes, spewing thick, noxious smoke rose from the shoulders like the decapitated wings of a fallen angel. The creature's head was an iron cage, in which was suspended a bleached human skull, held in place by a collection of hinged pistons and clockwork gears.

The sarcophagus lurched to a stop. A collection of pipes detached from the immobilized body of the lich, each one releasing with a hiss of steam and foul liquids. Once it was released, the construct took a heavy step out of its tomb. His foot came down on the marble floor with a heavy crash. The Iron Lich stretched, like a man waking from a long sleep, shaking off flakes of rust and cascading sheets of debris. Then he turned to face us.

"Appropriate, don't you think?" he boomed.

"What have you done, Claude?" Tesla asked. "What have you become?"

"Immortal. Or nearly so, thanks to my dear girl," the lich boomed. "I have made a miraculous recovery, with the brilliance of my science. And no thanks to you, I might add."

"There are borders I will not cross in my research," Nik said. "Something you should have learned."

"Science is no place for cowards. Now, let's end this. I have work to do." The monstrosity that had once been Claude Lumiere held out one mechanical arm. A door dilated open in the floor, and a staff rose out of the ground. It was classic undead stuff, straight out of the props department of an eighties horror flick. The body of the staff was made of mismatched metal pipes, sprouting tubes and wires that crawled along the length like burrowing vines. The whole contraption was crowned by a winged skull with glowing, iridescent eyes. Claude pointed the staff at Tesla dramatically. "I will crush you like the mortal bugs you are."

"Look, I'm no mad genius super scientist trapped in a body of his own creation, but last time I did math, we outnumbered you," I said.

"For now." The Lich nodded toward us. "Ladies? See to our guests."

"With pleasure." Evelyn whirled out of the shadows, landing with a thump in front of her resurrected father. Her face was scarred along one side, and the charred gap in her chest told the damage the sun-bright arrow had wrought. But she looked fit to fight.

"You're going to just feed her to us? Your own daughter?" I asked. "Or did she not tell you we already beat her just now?"

"I warned her of the bloodsucker's weakness," Claude said dismissively. "She has seen the truth of her father's guidance."

"I've had some upgrades," she snarled, then sprinted toward me.

A pair of metal wings unfurled behind her as she ran. Like a whip, a stroke of lightning traveled from her shoulders to the tips of her wings, forking outward in jagged lines of bright white light, finally grounding in the surrounding iron framework of the Palais. As she ran, the electricity traveled with her, dancing from wing to ground in a flickering strike that stitched a line of soot into the marble. The air hummed with the sound of constant electrical discharge.

"She just got lightning wings somehow?" I asked. "Seriously?"

"SCIENCE!" the Iron Lich boomed, striking the floor with his staff.

I was made sharply aware of my metal underwear. Beside me, Gregory swallowed so hard I thought his throat was going to detach from his spine. I took a step back and bumped into Adelaide.

"Mind if I step in?" she asked.

"Be my guest," I said.

The crack of gunfire was impressive. Evelyn twisted to the side, catching the bullets in the protective corona of her lightning field. Molten lead sprayed across the floor, hissing as it hit the marble. She continued to bear down on us.

"Huh. Well." Addie slapped her rifle back into place into something larger. "Worth a try."

"Let a professional scientist handle this." Tesla raised his coiled gauntlets, bumping his knuckles together with the crack of electrical discharge.

Evelyn screamed as she closed. Lightning sprouted from her wings. Tesla met it with a cloud of static discharge. Forks of blue-white electricity tangled in the air between them. The grounds on Tesla's generator clacked open, feeding current through his insulated boots and into the ground. Wave after wave of high voltage force washed off the pair as they wrestled in the middle of the pavilion.

I took another step back.

"I'm staying away from that," I said. Adelaide nodded numbly as the air sizzled and cracked. The smell of burning oxygen, fried hair, and hot metal filled the air.

"Come now," Cecilia purred as she descended from the ceiling. Her wispy form was wreathed in green light. "Don't be shy. We've only just gotten started."

"I feel like I can manage the insubstantial ghost woman," I said. "Saint, you want a crack at this?"

"I'm just here for the heals, man," Matthew said, holding up his hands. "Little enough Brilliance to go around. And I get the feeling we're going to need all of it."

"Show some faith," I said.

He laughed. "You're a trip, man. Faith. That's good."

"They're just trying to distract us," Chesa said. "Go for the lich. We'll take care of the girls."

"I'm afraid I can't allow that," Cecilia said. She raised her translucent arms overhead, twirling her hands together, as though she were gathering yarn.

In the distance, the sound of torquing metal and groaning wood rose above the howl of the storm. Black shapes whirled past the glass ceiling, like leaves in autumn, but the size of cars.

"What have you done, Rast?" Gregory asked.

"Me? Nothing! I just made fun of her, just a little bit. This isn't my—"

A dozen panes of the ceiling shattered, spraying the interior of the Faux Palais with splintered glass that fell like diamonds to the marble floor. Misshapen metal plates, some small, some as tall as a man, flew into the room. They fell on Cecilia as though she was a magnet, forming first a box, then a larger, more familiar shape. The sound of their impact was like buildings falling. I covered my head and ducked, afraid of losing my head to one of the scything steel plates. When the noise died down, I stood and stared at what Cecilia had become.

"Is that ... a tank?" Gregory asked.

"British Mark V, unless I miss my guess," Tembo said. When we all turned to stare at him, he shrugged. "I had my hobbies as a boy. She's replaced the sponson cannon with Vickers light machine guns, though. A clever choice, considering her opponent."

"Us?" Gregory asked.

"Well, yes. A pair of knights on foot, and a collection of frankly unarmored fools." Tembo gestured at Knight Watch. "We're hardly equipped to handle such a weapon."

"Good thing guns don't work on us," I said, squaring up to the still-immobile tank.

"Mundane firearms, no," Tembo said. "Haunted steampunk machine guns, driven by the ghost of a spiritualist?" He shrugged.

"Well, then what do you suggest we do?"

"Defeat it quickly," he said. "Instead of yammering on about it."

A gout of greenish-black smoke erupted from the back of the Mark-Cecilia. The tank didn't have a turret, and its long, rectangular body was unwieldy on the marble floor. But as Tembo had pointed out, mounted in each side sponson was a nasty-looking machine gun. Bright green light pierced every crack in the armor, and poured out of the half dozen vision ports on all sides of the vehicle. The clamorous engine fired up, and Mark-Cecilia rumbled toward us. The machine guns twitched, as the woman inside tried to get a handle on her new body. The barrels eventually pointed at me.

"Everyone behind me!" I shouted. "I've got this!"

I grounded my shield just as the rattle of gunfire burst from the haunted tank. Pouring magical energy into the bulwark, I expanded it and thickened the steel. A deafening clatter came from the other side, as a seemingly endless stream of bullets slammed into me. The impact sent jolts down my arms and into my bones, but the barrier held. Closer and closer she rolled, the treads tearing at the marble as she bore down on my position. My shield was so heavy that I couldn't move. The steel dimpled and began to glow red hot.

"John, we have to move!" Chesa shouted. "She'll run us down."

She and Adelaide both crouched behind me. Gregory was to one side. I had no idea what had happened to the rest of the team.

"You go! Fall back and then scatter," I shouted back. The drumming staccato of the hail of gunfire nearly drowned out both our voices. "I'll hold her attention."

"How do you plan on doing that?" Gregory asked.

"I'm a tank, too, aren't I? I'll think of something."

With another burst of magical energy, I expanded the size of the shield even more to the sides, giving them room to maneuver. Chesa and Addie went first, carefully creeping backward, trying to stay out of Mark-Cecilia's line of fire. After a few seconds, Greg gave me a sharp nod, then followed. The shield wavered as he retreated, but I buckled down and held it in place.

When they were far enough back, Chesa and Addie leapt clear of the enfilade. Ches did something elven and strange, twisting the light. It made me dizzy, but apparently the spirit in the tank didn't notice them go. That left me. The clanking of her treads on the marble was getting awfully close. I could feel the rumble of steel through the floor, and taste the necrotic smoke boiling out of her engine. Time to do something clever.

The closer Mark-Cecilia got, the wider apart the impact of her shots became. If you know anything about First World War tanks, you're not surprised by this. The sponson guns can't target anything closer than a dozen feet, because after that the body of the tank is in the way of their shots. Cecilia noticed, of course. For a second, I was worried she was going to back up. Instead, the hammering of her Vickers died out, and her engines roared into high gear.

She was just going to run me over. Perfect.

I drew all the energy back into my soul. The shield returned to its natural shape, a round Viking targe, much the worse for wear from all the machine-gunning, but still intact. The front of the tank loomed over me. She was coming fast, green light playing over my face as she charged. I grabbed the front glacis plate, heaving myself onto the sloping nose of the vehicle just before it ran me down. There was a view port, but I figured Cecilia wasn't really using it. Sure enough, there was a shriek from inside the crew compartment, and she slammed on the brakes. Thankfully, inertia is still a thing in the Gestalt.

The Mark-Cecilia slid across the marble floor, sponson machine guns cranking up and down as she tried to get a bead on me. Chesa and Addie watched from cover, horrified expressions on their faces as I clambered onto the top of the tank. I jammed my dagger into one of the dozens of revolver ports to help me hang on.

"What now, insect? Are you going to stab me to death?" Cecilia demanded, her voice echoing through the hollow interior of the tank.

"Not exactly," I said, producing the Immortality Scarab Ida had given me. I hadn't had any time to study it, what with the haunted amusement park, the murderous vampire slayer turned lightning angel, and the ghost tank, but there was one thing I knew about the device.

It sucked spirits. Hard.

I slapped the scarab onto the top hatch of the Mark-Cecilia and turned it on. The little bugger's sharp claws burrowed into the steel like they were butter, digging in like a tick. The twin vials on the back started to pump, their pistons cycling madly. At first, nothing happened. Then a trickle of green light dripped into the vials.

Cecilia shrieked once again. Both Vickers opened fire, spraying lead indiscriminately across the Faux Palais. Even the Iron Lich dove for cover as the tank spun in circles, both guns blazing, engine roaring, soul screaming in protest. I wasn't sure it would kill Cecilia, but it obviously bothered her. All I had to do was hang on for dear life.

It didn't take long. About thirty seconds after I had applied the scarab, Cecilia abandoned ship. The plates of the Mark V collapsed in on themselves, reverting back to the random pile of junk and debris they had been before Cecilia gave them life and purpose and form. The Vickers fell silent, then dissolved into base parts, filthy with rust and coagulated grease. The tread flew apart, and the whole vehicle settled in on itself. Cecilia's spirit shot through the roof of the tank, shrieking as she fluttered around the ceiling, like a firefly in a jar.

Eventually she landed next to the construct of her husband.

One down. Two to go.

CHAPTER THIRTY-TWO

Cecilia Lumiere was much reduced. The thin visage of her face floated over a mere sketch of feminine grace. The edges of her body hung frayed in the air. Her light flickered, and nearly went out.

Scooping the scarab off the pile of junk that the Mark V had become, I held it overhead like the skull of a vanquished god.

"Looking for this?" I shouted.

"Kill them!" Cecilia shrieked. Her voice had lost much of its volume, but none of its hatred. Claude nodded.

"I shall, my dear. Have no fear. But first... You have given so much." He turned to the bare glimmer of Cecilia's soul, then swept his staff in her direction. The mouth on the bat-winged skull creaked open. "I'm afraid I must ask for the rest."

Cecilia's eyes went wide as she was sucked into the staff. Her form disintegrated into a frantic cloud of glowing light, desperately trying to hang on to the physical realm. The sound of her passing was like glass shattering. When she was gone, the lich's eyes flashed green for a brief moment. Slamming the staff onto the ground, Claude Lumiere tilted his head to the sky and laughed.

On the far side of the room, Evelyn Lumiere threw Tesla to the ground. Their battle had been going on in the background of all this. The ceiling and floor were charred from lightning strikes, and the air around them hung with smoke and the tang of electrical discharge. But not even the eighth manifestation of Nikola Tesla was a match for Evelyn Lumiere in single combat. Nik lay in a heap at the slayer's feet. But her attention was entirely on the Iron Lich.

"What have you done?" she shrieked. The Iron Lich turned

casually in her direction. A dusting of motes, the protoplasmic remnants of his wife, floated around his shoulders. Her stakes clattered to the ground. "You killed her!"

"Cecilia knew the risks when she began this endeavor. She understood the sacrifices that would be asked of her," he said, taking a step in her direction. "Of both of you."

"You abandoned her to die! The vampires would have never gotten her if you hadn't locked me away. I'm the one who saved her from their curse," Evelyn said, stalking toward him. "I'm the one who brought her back. Not you!"

"And an admirable job you have done. But the time for recriminations is over, my dear girl. Without the skills I gave you, and the knowledge I left behind, you would be lying dead in the ground. You should be thanking me for your power, not threatening me with it."

"You never gave me a choice," Evelyn said coolly. "But I'm making one now."

She drew the sword she had taken from the valkyries, its clockwork and electrical coil spine whirring with aetheric life. Lightning coursed along the length of her wings and through her body, turning her eyes into bright spears of light. I felt a thrill of hope as she leapt into the air, sword held high, toward the abomination of her father.

"I don't have time for this," Claude said casually, then pointed the staff at Evelyn.

A bolt of lightning, as green as emerald and bright as the sun, traveled from Evelyn's heart to the tip of the lich's gruesome staff. For a brief second, the corrupted outline of Evelyn's skeleton, much changed by magic and perverse science, shone through her flesh like wood in the midst of a bonfire. Then she was gone, and plumes of green-and-black energy swirled through the air to collect in the gaping mouth of Lumiere's staff. Of the vampire slayer, there was nothing left—neither ash nor bone nor glimmer of flesh. She never even had time to scream.

"A pity," Lumiere said quietly. "You give them everything, and what thanks do you get?"

"You bloody monster," Tesla said, slowly pushing his way up onto his feet. "That was your daughter. Your family!"

"Family is nothing after death," he answered. "Trust me, I've been there. She wouldn't have lasted much longer, consumed by her own hatred, and the desire for revenge. If I hadn't given her a trail to follow, both of them would have been trapped in the space between living and dying. Seething for eternity. I loved them more than that." He stopped about thirty feet away. "At least this way, they got a chance to act out their fantasies of vengeance before their hatred snuffed them out. And now they may rest."

"You almost sound merciful," Tesla said. He limped to where I and the rest of Knight Watch stood in stunned silence. "What happened to you, Claude?"

"I died. It happens to everyone, eventually. I simply wasn't willing to let things go just yet. I had plans that had not quite come to fruition." He crossed his arms, resting them on the outstretched wings of his skull staff. "Fortunately, my lovely daughter was the curious sort. She did just enough to bring me back, but not enough to bind me."

"Her mistake," I said. "So what's your plan? Are you going to come along quietly, or do we have to force the issue?"

"I never could get used to Americans. So direct. So crude." Claude stood up straight, collecting the staff in both hands. "You will have your answer, monsieur. When I am ready to give it."

"I'm afraid we really can't wait." I lowered my visor and fell into a guard position, pushing past Tesla. The rest of the team followed suit.

"Afraid? Not yet," Claude purred. "But you will be."

For a lumbering automaton of steel and bones, Lumiere moved with unexpected speed. He crossed the thirty feet between us in two strides, his feet skating across the marble as though it were ice. He swung the staff at me with a backhanded motion. I caught the blow on my shield, but there was enough strength in it to stagger me to the right. I tried to swing at him, but he was already past me, barreling into Tesla. The leader of the Eccentrics saw him coming, though, and dodged handily out of the way. There was a brief crack of electricity, and the air hummed with power. I thought we were about to witness a boss fight, but Lumiere kept going.

Right at Saint Matthew.

"He's going for the healer!" I shouted. The Saint was still harassing Gregory in the back line, menacing him with prayers and foul-smelling poultices. Gregory had the damaged pauldron off, and his naked arm was streaked with blood. As the Iron Lich thundered toward them, Gregory looked up in shock. He waved Matthew away, then took up his sword and prepared to take the charge.

The lich thrust at Gregory with his staff. For all his undead celerity and gentlemanly behavior, Claude Lumiere had never dueled with sword and shield. He was depending on brute force and the unnatural constitution of his monstrous unflesh to win the fight. Unfortunately for him, Knight Watch spends all our time battling such things.

Gregory easily took the thrust with the forte of his blade, then used the inertia from Lumiere's charge to send the lich stumbling to the side. He followed up by swinging his zweihander in a wide, overhead arc that would have decapitated a mortal. The blade clanged off the iron cage around Lumiere's skull, throwing sparks and bending wire.

Lumiere snarled, battering at Gregory's chest with the center of his staff. There was enough strength in the blow to knock the paladin back, but he recovered quickly, slamming pommel and hilt into Lumiere's hands before thrusting the point of his sword at the lich's face. Lumiere retreated, but only far enough to give himself room to swing the staff. He caught Gregory's lead foot at the ankle, sweeping him off-balance. Greg stumbled, recovered, and set up a guard for the expected counterswing. But Lumiere didn't press the attack. The lich simply reached out and laid one finger on Gregory's exposed forehead. It opened him up to a wicked riposte, which Gregory gladly took, driving steel into Lumiere's belly. But it was already too late.

A flash of emerald lightning passed up Lumiere's arm, traveling from Gregory's forehead up into the lich's chest. Lumiere seemed to swell, as though his lifeless lungs were taking a deep, cleansing breath. Gregory's eyes went wide. He crumpled to the ground.

Chesa and I both yelled out in shock. Matthew, ignoring the threat of the lich still looming over Gregory, rushed forward. Addie, Tesla, and the rest of the team were still processing what they saw.

Starting from his forehead and traveling across his face and down his arm, a wave of withering corruption consumed our paladin. His skin went dry and wrinkled. His eyes clouded. His hair, once lustrous, hung like dull rags on his head. The armor was suddenly too large for his shriveled body, and too heavy for his withered strength. He fell in a heap of disheveled steel. The sword slipped from spotted hands knotted by arthritis.

I was already moving to his side. Chesa screamed, but all I could hear was the blood hammering in my head as I charged the lich. Lumiere was still turned away, his attention fully on the Saint. I bulled into the lich's hip, putting shield and sword into the back of his leg. He flopped forward gracelessly. I straddled Gregory's fallen form, glaring down at the Iron Lich.

"Greg! Greg, babe, are you okay?" Chesa knelt at my feet, turning Gregory over on his back, feeling at his neck for a pulse. "Can you hear me?"

"My . . . knees hurt," Gregory whispered. "And my . . . my everything else."

"We'll get you some Aspercreme and a nice Darjeeling, big guy," I said. "Get him out of here, Ches."

Working together, Chesa and Matthew dragged him out of harm's way. The Iron Lich clambered gracelessly to his feet. He dusted off his collar, then cocked his head at me. Bethany and Tesla flanked me, their weapons ready.

"Anxious to die, are you? Fair enough. As your friend will soon discover, there are fates much worse than death." He lifted his staff high overhead. The winged skull's piercing eyes began to glow.

The report of a gunshot echoed through the Palais, and the tiny skull exploded in a cloud of bone dust and broken gears. A plume of protoplasmic energy jetted out of the top of the staff, like the flame of an oxyacetylene torch.

Adelaide cycled the chamber on her sniper rifle, ejecting a shell the length of my hand. The telescoping lens on top of the rifle whirred loudly as she took aim again.

Lumiere howled in frustration. The lich grasped the staff in both hands and twisted, cranking some sort of gauge closed, until the flame eventually sputtered and died. He whirled on Addie.

"This will not go well for you, Lady Adelaide! The Lumieres remember their grudges."

"I'll get over it," she said without looking up, thumbing the cylinder closed. But before she could fire, Lumiere threw a bolt of lightning in her direction, spoiling her shot.

The lich roared and charged toward her. I intercepted him with a blow to the back of the head. He backhanded me, a casual strike that I deflected with my shield.

"You keep forgetting that I'm here and, frankly, I find that a little insulting," I said.

"It is meant to be insulting," Lumiere answered. "Now get out of my way."

"Don't think I will." I slid more directly into his path and banged my sword against my shield. "This is what I do. Annoy villains."

"You have a gift for it, I'll grant you that." He lunged at me, swinging the broken staff wildly. I deflected the main strike, turned his feint into a clean riposte, then kicked at his supporting leg. It was like kicking a light pole. The shock went all the way up to my knee, numbing my leg. I limped back, but he pressed the attack with the staff. I was desperately fending that off when he dropped the staff and grabbed my head with his open hand.

"Let's see how brave you are after this," he snarled.

There was a flash of green light, and then a sensation like having your skeleton pulled out of your body by the teeth. I could feel the necromantic magic coursing through my blood, plucking at my vital organs.

"Unhand him, fiend!" Tesla's voice, followed by a bolt of brilliant white light. Fire arced through my flesh, and all my muscles seized up. But Lumiere dropped me.

I collapsed to my knees and clawed at my helmet. The steel was hot to the touch as I fumbled it off my head. Maybe that thin layer of steel plate and leather and chain saved me, or maybe I was already an old man at heart, and the lich's magic was baffled by my bitter, cynical soul. But once I got the helm off, I could see that my hands were in one piece. I hurt, but not as badly as Gregory looked. I turned the helm over in my hands. There was a handprint burned into the face, throbbing with necrotic light. I whistled.

"That was close." My throat was dry. I got to my feet and looked around.

Tesla and Lumiere were squaring off. Chesa had her bow in hand, but no arrow, and was looking between me and Gregory with growing concern. Adelaide had finished with her rifle, and was taking aim at the lich. Gregory, his hair white and the skin pulled tight across his skull, was in the care of the Saint.

"John, are you alright?" Chesa asked.

"I've felt worse. How do I look?"

"Like a cocky version of *Revenge of the Nerds*, minus the glasses," she said. "So pretty much normal." She glanced at me again, then smiled. "Your hair's gone white."

"Wait, what?" I tried to pull my locks down where I could see them. A couple strands came loose in my fingers. They were as white as snow. "Ah, heck! I look like Anderson Cooper!"

"It suits you," she said. "Considering the alternative."

"Yeah. Right." I glanced at Gregory uncomfortably. "I'm sure he'll be fine, Ches."

"You've gone far enough, Claude," Tesla said, interrupting our little conversation. "This ends now."

"You don't know what you're doing, Nikola. It took so long to get here. I have sacrificed so much." He took an uneven step toward Tesla. Apparently whatever Nik had done to get Lumiere to drop me had done some damage. "Think of the possibilities. Think what we could accomplish—"

"I've heard enough of your excuses, Claude. I am a man of science, not . . ." Tesla gestured dismissively at the Iron Lich. "Not whatever it is that you've become. An abomination!"

"Very well," Lumiere growled. "You have made your choice. Now I must make mine!"

The Iron Lich charged forward, arms outstretched, hands grasping for Nikola. Addie fired first, two shots that ricocheted off the lich's metal body before a third struck his skull, cracking the bone. By then he was too close to Nik to risk a shot, and Addie's gun fell silent. Tesla backpedaled, but the lich was too fast, too large, and too determined for Nik to escape. At the last second, Tesla cracked his knuckles together, opening the circuit on the generator.

Lightning filled the air.

The first stroke limned the Iron Lich in golden light, shining through the cracks in his skin and outlining his skull in a corona of fire. Still he stumbled on, and so Tesla fired a second bolt into his metal body, and a third. By now, Lumiere was slowing down. Tesla dodged out of reach of those soul-sucking hands, but kept his finger on the trigger. Bolt after bolt arced from Tesla's gauntlets into the

Iron Lich. With each bone-jarring crack of electrical discharge, he slowed down. Until, finally, he stopped and sank to his knees.

"You were brilliant, Claude! A genius beyond your time!" Another bolt, and Lumiere spasmed. Tesla was furious, his eyes lined with tears, his face twisted in a mask of rage. "You could have been anything! The greatest of us! Your name could have lived in the halls of ether for all eternity." *Crack! Shiver!* Lumiere slumped forward. Steam wafted off the glowing plates of his body. His skull, suspended in its cage of iron, smoldered. "But you threw it all away. For what? For what, Claude! Tell me!"

Out of the corner of my eye, the slightest movement caught my attention. The remnants of Cecilia's tank were melting. No, no melting. Metal shuffled off the Vickers, dissolving into curls of rust and corroded copper. What remained was a hillock of moss and broken gravestones, out of place in the marble expanse of the Palais. I looked around wildly. The columns were dissolving into the rough bark of willow trees. Fog pressed against the paned ceiling, pouring through the broken windows to crawl along the floor like a predator. Even the air, heavy with electrical discharge and gunpowder, shifted into the deep funk of the grave.

Something was happening.

"Nik, wait!" I shouted. "I think—"

"Then you must take your secrets to the grave!" Tesla said. He clasped his hands together over his head, and a final, terrible stroke of lightning shot from the generator on his back. It pierced the Iron Lich through and through. Jagged bolts of electricity grounded into the floor, traveling through his hands and knees, dancing along his metal spine, until they flew out into the tower itself. The lattice frame of the glass ceiling turned into a net of glowing light.

High above us, the spinning generator arms glowed bright, then dissolved into a ring of glittering stars. Around us, the world changed.

Huddled on the ground at Tesla's feet, the Iron Lich began to laugh.

CHAPTER THIRTY-THREE

"Hey, he's already done that. The lightning, and the ominous chuckle." I pointed at Lumiere with my sword. "Is he allowed to do that twice?"

"Shut up, Rast," the three of them said at once. Tesla watched Lumiere's crumpled form, while Chesa and Adelaide kept their weapons pointed at the lich's caged skull.

"What's so damned amusing, Claude?" Nik asked.

"Oh, Nik. So many things." The lich got deliberately to his feet, taking the time to dust off his shoulders as he stood, as Tesla backed up carefully. "Every time I think I have failed, there you are, to pick me up again. First with the plans for Atlantis, then the vampires, and now this. It's so kind."

"What do you mean? What are you on about?" Tesla demanded.

"I couldn't have built this place without you, my dear Tesla." Lumiere gestured grandly to the replica Palais, and the triple generator arms rotating overhead. "Your contributions to the science of wireless transmission were an invaluable asset to my research into soul transferral. And if you weren't so focused on the generators and cabling and your foolish projectors, you might have looked at the true purpose of the design. The entire community was dazzled by your electric lights. As if such frippery could truly change the world."

"In his defense, electricity is pretty amaz—" I shut up at their collective angry glare.

"Meanwhile," Lumiere continued, once my rapt silence was assured, "I was free to carry on with my experiments, right under your nose."

"Until the vampires killed your whole family," Addie said. "Real pity."

"It was!" Lumiere said gleefully. "I really thought that was going to be the end of my whole plan. They must have caught wind of what I was up to, and didn't want to share immortality with a mere mortal. I'm not sure. You'd have to ask . . . Oh wait, you can't, because they're all dead. Killed by our dear friends the Society of Eccentrics, along with Knight Watch."

"You're right, of course," Tesla said. "I was a fool. I counted you as a friend, Claude. I trusted you, admired you, even sought to help you. That blinded me. But I have seen the schematic for this place. My eyes are open. And I can't let you carry through with it."

"Why? Because it will destroy your precious Gestalt? Look around, Nikola. The Gestalt is dying on its own. Gone are the days of heady science and brash adventure. How often do you get new recruits?" Lumiere sneered, an impressive feat for a skull without lips suspended in an iron cage. "I'm saving you from oblivion, you fool!"

A strong wind blew through the Palais, carrying a familiar scent. You might have smelled it once or twice over the course of your life, snatched from mountain peaks, or in the deep valleys of the world, far from the corrupting influence of modernity. The Unreal, shining through the thin tapestry of your life, revealing something beyond, something more. Something magical. I took a deep breath and smiled. Then I realized what was happening.

"We need to get the two of you out of here. Immediately!" I grabbed Addie by the shoulder and pulled her away from the remains of her rifle. She pushed me away, but as she did, the rifle came apart. It was like a tree limb, rotten from the inside out, tearing free in the slightest breeze. It just disintegrated in a shower of mismatched parts. She stared at the stump of a trigger guard, clutched in her ivory hand.

"What . . . what . . . is happening?" she muttered.

"It's the Unreal. Your Gestalt is collapsing. Grab Tesla and run." I pushed her toward the door. "We'll take care of this."

"We can't just leave you here," Tesla said. "There's—"

Some critical component in his generator gave way. Like a teakettle boiling over, a cloud of sparks and scalding water erupted from his back. The explosion threw Tesla to the ground and sent a plume of steam high into the air. I threw my shield over Addie, protecting us both from the debris cloud. Once it was past, I ran to Tesla's side.

"Perhaps . . . a strategic retreat is in order," he mumbled. The back half of his suit was blown off down to the knickers, and his skin was raw with blisters. I helped him to his feet, then handed him over to Addie.

"Just get out of here. We'll be fine. This is why you got us involved. None of you are any good in the Unreal," I said. "Call Ida. She'll get you out of here. Greg! You're going with them!"

"I shall not forsake my oath to protect the weak and stand against the darkness." Old Greg rattled to his feet and, with much grunting and moaning, drew his zweihander. He held it high on quivering limbs. "Such is the path of the knight! I must—"

He collapsed into a pile of arthritis and steel. We winced in sympathy.

"It's okay, big guy. The Saint will set you right after this is all over. Matthew? Get him out of here."

"On our way," he said, hooking an arm under Greg's elbow and dragging him off the ground. "Oof. You're heavy for an old man."

"Are you sure you can manage without us?" Addie asked.

"We'll figure it out," I said. "Chesa, you ready?"

"As ready as I can be," Chesa said. "Lumiere is getting away."

"What? I thought he was going to kill us first?" I asked, looking around.

Sure enough, the Iron Lich was limping back to the platform from which he had originally risen. Thick black smoke poured out of the sarcophagus, covering the gallery and rolling in noxious clouds across the floor. He had reached the perimeter of the smoke, and was making good time to the coffin.

"We have to stop him," I said. "The rest of you get out of here. Chesa, with me!"

"Okay, bossy," she said, following as I ran forward. Lumiere looked at us over his shoulder, then picked up the pace.

"You're not getting away this time, Bonebro!" I shouted. My armor clattered around me, so I couldn't hear his response, but I was pretty sure he was running scared.

I was wrong.

As I reached the leading edge of the pool of smoke, my eyes and lungs started to burn. Tendrils of smoke clung to my legs as I ran, building up like vines creeping up to my knees. I coughed, and something deep in my chest pulled free. I wrenched my visor open and skidded to a halt.

"Too . . . much . . . smoke," I gasped. Chesa came to a stop outside the smoke. She pulled her cloak over her mouth as the murk roiled closer. "Get back!"

"You know, I was worried about you at first," Lumiere said as he strode toward me. "Sir John of Rast. Dragonslayer. Savior of Valhalla. When Tesla finally figured out what was going on and reached out to Knight Watch, it gave me pause." I tried to square up to him, but a coughing fit racked my body, and I went down to my knees. He glared down at me, hands on hips. "It seems like my concerns were unwarranted."

"You're a bastard, and a creep, and your face looks like someone dropped your head into a vat of acid," I said through gritted teeth. "And I'm not done with you yet."

I scrambled for my sword, bringing it up in an arcing slice toward his guts. He deflected the blow with his shin, then drove his knee into my face. I went down onto my back. The smoke rolled over me in choking waves. I coughed so hard it felt like my ribs were going to break. When I tried to roll away, Lumiere put a foot onto my left shoulder, pinning me in place.

"Oh, but I think you *are* done," he said, then began to grind his heel into my bones. The steel of my armor groaned as he torqued the plates open, and I could feel the joint straining to stay in its socket. I shouted in pain. He laughed. "I'm done playing with children who think they are heroes. Without your magic, you're nothing but a boy in fancy clothes."

He released me, casually kicking me in the face once again as I tried to get up. By the time my vision cleared, he was disappearing into the plume of smoke that rose from the open tomb in the center of the Palais. I rubbed my jaw and watched him go. The smoke receded, until it clustered around the platform. Chesa ran to my side.

"John, are you alright?" she asked. "I lost sight of you both in the smoke, and thought he might have taken you with him. What happened?"

"He reminded me who I am," I said, struggling to my feet. My face throbbed in pain, my shoulder was screaming, and my pride whimpered like a dog that had been whipped. "The guy who gives up." I looked up at the plume of black smoke. It was climbing to the ceiling, like a geyser. Or a tower. "I really hate that guy."

"John, I hate to say this, but I think we have to get help," Chesa said. "It's just the two of us, and you're pretty beat up. We need to get you to the Doc, get Greg back to his zealot self. Maybe find a way to get the rest of the team over here." She looked up at the tower of smoke. "You and I can't do this alone. We're both tapped out of our domain power, and without our magic—"

"Exactly. Without our magic." I fished my sword off the marble and slid it back into the scabbard, then hitched my shield over my shoulder. "So we get our magic back."

"What? John, that's impossible. We're surrounded by the Gestalt. That was the whole point of the amulets. Mine's open full, but it's not refilling me fast enough. Without a portal to our domains, we're trapped," she said emphatically. "Cut off from our mythos."

"So we find a way back," I said. "A new portal. We make one."

"Well, unless you see any magical doors to the elven forests around here, I've got nothing," she said. "And I don't know what the particular path is to your domain, but I'm guessing it has nothing to do with an amusement park off the Jersey shore."

"You might be surprised. Lots of ways to be scared, Ches. Only one way to be a hero," I said with a smile. "And that's not giving up."

CHAPTER THIRTY-FOUR

"John, I think you've been hit in the noggin a couple times too often." Chesa followed about ten feet behind me as I marched toward the tower of smoke.

"What are you talking about, Ches?" I asked over my shoulder. "I've always made bad decisions."

"No, I mean, literally. That hat doesn't fit as good as it used to."

"What? Oh." I pried the clip free and pulled my helm off. The throbbing in my skull eased slightly. "Ah. Much better."

"But the decision thing, too. What's your plan here?" she asked.

"I'm afraid that if I told you it'd just ruin the surprise." I tossed the bassinet aside and ran my gauntleted fingers through my hair. The side of my head was sticky with blood, and sensitive to the touch. I resolved to not get hit there again.

"Is that a clever way of saying that you're making it up as you go along?"

"Ches! You besmirch my . . . something. Intellect?" I grinned wickedly. "Have some faith. I really do have a plan. Lumiere's a lich. I've read the *Monster Manual*. If I can press him, I'm pretty sure I can get him to open a portal to my domain by mistake."

"That's a lot of ifs," Chesa said.

"Well, it's the best we have." I reached the border of the smoke plume. A column of dark clouds roiled high up toward the barrel ceiling, easily twenty feet across, so thick that it was impossible to see even an inch into the murk. Though the surface of the cloud churned and stirred, the overall column appeared stationary. Other than the clank of my steel boots on the marble, and the delicate tapping of Chesa's battle slippers, there was no other sound. I craned my neck to look up the length of the billowing tower. "Okay, Claude Lightpole. What you got going on here?"

"Careful, John. That stuff's noxious," Chesa warned.

"Oh, I remember. That's a lesson I have thoroughly learned. In fact..." I cocked my head, thinking back to Lumiere's laboratory in Evelyn's basement. "Huh. I wonder if it really is that obvious."

"If what's that obvious?"

"The lesson. Tell Tembo he was always my favorite," I said, then plunged forward.

A cacophony of sound struck me, a wave of hammering and clattering and bone-deep crashing that nearly deafened me. A couple feet in front of me, a wrought iron spiral staircase was corkscrewing out of the ground in fits and starts, each jerk upward accompanied by a shuddering thump. Counterweights on long chains dropped down the center of the staircase, driving whatever engine was lifting the contraption into the air. It was breathtakingly loud. I looked behind me.

The cloud of smoke was just that...a smoke screen, and not even a real one. Pure illusion. I could see Chesa mincing about on the other side, probably trying to decide if she should follow me in or go back for the rest of the team. I reached through the faux cloud and grabbed her by the arm, dragging her through. She had the decency to shriek.

"I'd say keep it down, but I doubt anyone can hear us in the middle of all that," I yelled over the tumult.

"How did you know it was fake?" she yelled back.

"Remember Lumiere's lab? The maze, and all the mechanical rats? He thinks like a scientist, and he's training us to react the way he wants. Poison cloud, then an illusion to hide this tower. The mist itself probably dissipated shortly after he started. That's why he was so anxious to get away, rather than wait around and finish us off. He had to get inside before the facade took hold."

"Seems awfully elaborate. How'd he know someone would be here to chase him?"

"Good question. Not sure. In fact—" Just then, the tower stopped moving and locked in place. Its mechanisms fell silent. My last couple syllables were still at a full shout, and the words echoed through the empty Palais. I lowered my voice. "Hm. Well, he probably knows we're here now."

There was movement at the top of the iron staircase. The whole structure creaked back and forth. Glittering light flashed, then the groan of rusted metal.

"He's opening the windows," Chesa said. She had backed all the way to the illusion cloud to get a better view of the top of the tower. "There's like a skylight or something."

"We better start climbing," I said.

Chesa drew and fired her bow in a heartbeat, barely taking the time to aim. Overhead, glass shattered, and Lumiere's eerie voice barked out in surprise. Chesa smiled, then trotted past me.

"That'll keep his head down for a little while. Might slow him up a bit," she said. "Hurry up!"

"I thought you didn't have any of that elf magic left?" I asked as I labored after her. Running in plate armor, while possible, was taxing. And I'd done a lot of running recently.

"I was a good shot long before I was an elf princess," she said. "Just like you were a smart hand with that sword before you knew the first thing about Knight Watch."

"I mean . . . a couple tournament wins isn't exactly Lancelot," I said, blushing furiously. "But, yeah, I guess I know a thing or two about hewing in twain."

"Save the charm for the lich," she said, taking the stairs two at a time. "And your breath for the climb!"

"Right, right," I muttered.

We fell into an easy rhythm. Every couple turns of the spiral staircase there was a platform with pulleys and spent chains of weights. Chesa had to wait for me at each one. The first few landings, she leaned out from the tower to scan the ceiling with her bow drawn. After a while, she gave up on that.

"He's gone through the skylight," she said. "I've lost sight of him."

"Mm-hm," I gasped.

"What do you make of all this? The pulleys and stuff."

"Mechanical . . . advantage . . ." I paused to catch my breath and lean against one of the windlasses. "All this is probably under tension, waiting to be triggered."

"But why did it work?" she asked. "I thought we were in the Unreal."

"Pulleys ain't rocket science," I answered. "Otherwise crossbows wouldn't work. Looks like he knew the rules. Planned ahead."

"Went medieval, rather than steampunk. I get it." She rapped me on the chest with her knuckles. "Let's go, Iron Man. We're not even halfway up."

It felt like an eternity before we reached the top, and when we did, I promptly collapsed against the rails. The empty sarcophagus rose from the center of the floor on an iron plinth in the middle of the platform, along with a slice of the marble floor. It rested about four feet below an open skylight. I couldn't see beyond the ceiling from where I sat, and lacked the motivation to stand up and examine it. What I could see was the engine that had lifted the tower into the air. Enormous gears in the flooring, and chains as thick as my thigh, drove the tower. Four nozzles sprouted around the sarcophagus, attached to some kind of tanks and a pair of bellows that hooked into the main chain drive. I studied all of this from a seated position, while Chesa stalked around the skylight.

"Timed," I said, thumping the tanks. "Once he triggered the sarcophagus, he was on the clock. When the cloud came out, he had to move or get left behind."

"Or he could climb the stairs, like we did," Chesa said.

"I don't recommend that. Especially after you've just returned from the grave."

"So what was the purpose of the staff? Of"—she shivered uncomfortably—"absorbing his wife and daughter like that?"

"Tech grounded in the Gestalt, maybe. But once the souls were captured, the energy could transfer." I started to get up, but the weight of my armor kept me pinned in place. "Enough! If I'm doing this, it's naked."

"Hard pass," Chesa said. "You can't fight without your armor."

"In point of fact, I can fight perfectly well without my armor. I just can't take a hit. But that's sort of the point of tournament fighting. I'll just pretend I'm dueling the Tatertot again." Our previous nemesis, Herr Totenshreck, had had a sword that killed at a touch. I lifted my arms in the air. "Come on, give me a hand getting out of this trash can."

Chesa rolled her eyes, but several acrobatic minutes later left me stripped down to my dressing jacket, leggings, and coat of chain. I shook the feeling back into my legs and hopped up and down a couple times to adjust the lay of the coat.

"So much better," I said with a sigh. "I'm beginning to think knight is a mug's class. You and Bee have the right idea. Agility all the way."

"Let me know how you feel after the first hit." Chesa looked me up and down. "You kind of look like a kid wearing his favorite King Arthur footie pajamas."

"Man, I would have killed for King Arthur footie pajamas." I buckled on my sword belt and shield. "Okay. Let's do this hero thing."

A small set of stairs led up to the plinth where the sarcophagus rested, and a section of iron rungs folded down from the open skylight. I clambered out into the cutting wind and driving rain. Lightning flashed in the graying distance, followed by thunder that rattled the iron frame of the tower. My woolen undercoat soaked through in a heartbeat. Chesa followed close behind, though her elven armor seemed to wick the rain like a duck.

Elves, man. They get all the cool stuff.

There was no immediate sight of the Iron Lich. We were standing on a circular catwalk that ran along the base of a towering round joint that served as the base for the iron-framed generator arms. Now that we were in the Unreal, the arms had taken on an ephemeral quality. Still metal, but the orbs at their tips looked like crystal spheres, and instead of electricity they left a trail of stars in their wake. The stars expanded outward like waves against the cloudy sky. I peered at them curiously.

"Are those faces?" I asked, pointing. Chesa squinted through the rain.

"You might be right. What is this thing?"

"A soul cage," I said. "Making those ghosts, I'm guessing. Man, this Lumiere guy is grim."

"Speaking of . . . Where'd he go?" Chesa shouted over the storm.

"Up, I'm guessing. Unless he grew wings and flew away." I trotted along the catwalk until I found a staircase leading into the wheel joint. "This way!"

Once we were beneath the main structure, we were briefly

sheltered from the storm. The metal on metal grinding of the bearings briefly drowned out the wind and beating rain. It was like standing under a cement truck full of metal balls. The center of the joint was hollow, like a pipe, with a ladder leading straight up the middle. The ladder was anchored at top and bottom, but couldn't touch the sides of the tunnel because the machines that drove the arms whizzed just inches away. There didn't seem to be any other exits. I checked the straps on my shield, then prepared to climb. Chesa pulled me back.

"What?" I shouted over the din of the bearings.

"Rain's ruined my bowstring." Her voice was barely a whisper, though I could see she was putting her full lungs into it. "Supposed to be magic, but between the Gestalt and the Mundane..." She shrugged.

"Can you fix it?" I asked. She shook her head.

"Going to have to replace."

I craned my neck to look up the length of the ladder. It was hard to tell, but it seemed like the space beyond was sheltered from the elements.

"Do it. Then catch up." I started up the ladder. She grabbed me again.

"Be careful," she said.

"Aren't I always?" I said.

She smirked, then slapped my butt and turned her attention to the bow.

Crawling up the wheel joint was like passing through a tornado. The spinning walls of the passageway howled past me, barely inches from my knuckles as they clutched the iron rungs of the ladder. Each time the brass spheres at the ends of the arms sparked, the air of the passage filled with static electricity. The first time it happened, I almost let go of the ladder, I was so shocked, both literally and figuratively. And the noise... the sound of grinding ball bearings and rumbling steel arms, the thump of voltage passing through the tower, the bone-shaking hum of the generators revolving... by the time I reached the top of the tower, I was numb from brain to bones. I just wanted to get out.

Scrambling past the anchor at the top of the joint, there was about ten feet of solid steel before I got to the end of the passage. I paused on the last rung and looked down. There, far below, I could make out the tiny form of Chesa starting her ascent. I hooked my arms around the top of the ladder, shook some feeling back into my hands, then poked my head up and over the lip of the passage.

We were close to the top of the Tour d'Elysee. Atlantis spread out in all directions, a gray and black landscape, static against the churning whitecaps of the open ocean. On the far horizon I could see the shoreline, glowing like a cloud of distant fireflies. A storm-battered tarp spread over the platform to keep the rain off, but several tears in the fabric had already formed, and rivulets of water poured through. The platform itself was an uneven mashup of pipes and catwalks spread over thrumming engines and spinning gears. It was a great place to fall to your death. You wouldn't even have to fall that far. The teeth of hungry gears churned mere feet away, ready to bite.

At the far end of the platform stood the twisted abomination of Claude Lumiere. He busied himself with a pylon that protruded from the floor. He fit a glass vial into a cavity in the pylon, then twisted a dial. The pylon retracted into the floor, locking into place with an audible sigh. When he was gone, Lumiere strolled to the edge of the platform and gazed out over the gray roofs of Atlantis. As I clambered out of the shaft, the mists that surrounded us began to clear, giving me a view across the ocean, to the glowing horizon of the city beyond. At first, I thought he was just admiring the scenery.

That's when I noticed that the shore wasn't glowing with electric light, or even the flicker of gas lamps. I could make out steel trestle towers, and grand halls, the collected delusion of the Gestalt all gathered in one place. Zeppelins traced patterns in the sky and, even from this distance, I could see clockwork wagons and the marble domes of an ancient Paris, brought back to life by the power of imagination.

And it was burning.

CHAPTER THIRTY-FIVE

My boot scraped across the steel grating of the walkway. Claude Lumiere turned to face me with casual disinterest. Behind him, the otherworldly flames of the distant dream city burned against the sky, throwing his silhouette into sharp contrast. When he saw me, Lumiere cocked his head to one side.

"You are just as persistent as they warned me you would be," he said. His voice sounded like sandpaper on bone. "The valkyries, those demons you sent back to hell, even the noble old dragon, they spoke of you with much hatred. I thought it misplaced, but"—he shrugged—"you seem worthy of it."

"I try to piss off the worst sort of people." I set my feet and drew my sword. "And you are absolutely the worst sort of person."

"You don't have to die here, you know," Lumiere said. "This isn't even your world. It's no one's world. A false place, full of faux people."

"None of the Eccentrics strike me as fake. Ida's the purest nerd I've ever met, and Adelaide has more life in her trigger finger than you have in your entire body. Literally. Even The Good Doctor is a real person, somewhere under that mask," I said, stalking toward him. "You're the only one that rings false. A lich in a steampunk costume. An abomination, pretending to be a miracle."

"Clever words. Come, join me in this conquest. I can give you something your costume kingdom can never offer." He held out a hand toward me. "Immortality, in the heart of a true realm of magic and power."

"You should have made that offer before Evelyn tried to kill my friends, or the valkyries crashed the *Silverhawk*. Or, heck, before you turned Greg into the Quaker Oats guy." I swung my shield down from my shoulder, firming the straps against my forearm. "That's three strikes. I'm here to collect."

"Worth a try." He held his empty hand out to the side. There was a crack of lightning, and the gnarled length of his skull-wing staff appeared. "Don't say I didn't offer something like mercy. Which is more than you deserve."

He came at me like a street thug, swinging his ridiculous staff with both hands in a wide, sweeping arc. I ducked down, letting my shield deflect the opening blow, then chopped at his leg. Lumiere hissed and fell back. I pressed the advantage, hacking at wrist and shoulder before slamming my shield against his chest, forcing him even farther back. My sword wasn't doing much against the brass and iron of his body, but it was clear Lumiere didn't like it. I was starting to feel pretty good.

"You know, I have a question. Where'd you get the whole lich schtick from?" I asked. Lumiere punched at me with his iron gauntlet. I ducked aside, smacked him on the inside of the arm with my shield, then hacked down at his shoulder as his arm flew wide. He stumbled back. "I've met your daughter. You died a long time ago. Gygax hadn't even rolled initiative yet."

"Do you honestly care?" He caught my next swing with the body of his staff, twisted my arm down, then took a swipe at my head. I gave ground. He used the space to gather himself. "Or are you simply looking for an excuse to talk?"

"Bit of the former, bit of the latter," I said, adjusting my positioning. Lumiere had drawn me toward the edge, and I didn't want to slip and plunge to my death. "I would say that I'm trying to get under your skin, but you don't have any."

"Your confidence is admirable. It will serve you well in Hades." A quick thrust of his staff tested my shield, and when I tried to chop down at him, I was surprised to find his hand wrapped around my wrist. "Lucy likes an ego."

"Why am I not shocked that your devil is a woman." I tried to twist my hand out of his grip, but he shrugged off my effort with steel fingers. "How very French."

"I heard that," Chesa said, finally emerging from the middle of the platform. She drew an arrow to her cheek. "Drop my ex, or I'm going to fill you full of holes."

"Ineffectual whelp! You dare to threaten a living god?" Lumiere boomed.

"'Living god'? Man, I really wouldn't go that far." With a grunt I finally freed my wrist. "You're more like a haunted mannequin. I hate to think what's going on under your belt."

"Fools!" Lumiere tried to backhand me, but I pedaled clear, catching his clumsy strike on my shield. Steel gonged like a bell. "Do you understand where you are? Do you understand what I can do?"

As soon as I was out of the way, Chesa let loose with a quick volley of arrows. The first flight glimmered with magical light, and struck with a heavy thud on the lich's metallic carapace. That clearly stunned him, but then the rest of the arrows clattered harmlessly off his armored hide. Chesa grimaced as she reloaded.

"Your magic fades, even as mine grows." He threw his hand in Chesa's direction. A pair of icy blue bolts shot out of his palm to race at her. She tumbled out of the way. Where they struck, the bolts left a patch of glimmering frost. Lumiere laughed. "Where is your science now, Nikola? Where is your power?"

"Don't get cocky," I spat, charging forward to catch his wrist with the steel rim of my shield. His arm snapped back. "That's my job."

Rather than answering, Lumiere gave an iron-lunged roar, smashing at me with his open hand. I brought my lingering magic to bear, creating an invisible shield around the hilt of my sword. It held for only a second, flickering blue and red before it collapsed like a soap bubble in a hurricane. The lich's fist went into my belly, doubling me up. I stumbled backward. Chesa sprinted toward us, dropping her bow and drawing the twin crescent blades. Lumiere spared her only a glance.

"Ches, wait, he's—"

When she got close enough, Ches leapt into the air, blades drawn back to strike, legs arching forward, a grim expression creasing her face. Lumiere caught her with one iron fist around the neck. She jerked to a stop in midair, flopping like a doll at the end of the lich's arm.

A wave of power surged through Lumiere. It pulsed through

Chesa's limp body. She twitched, her arms going rigid, eyes and lips straining back, as though every muscle in her body was firing at once. She tried to scream, but the only sound was a strangled rattle.

He dropped her. Chesa fell to the ground, stiff as a board, eyes wide open and staring at me.

"—death to touch," I finished.

"Not death. She will live, for now." He stalked toward me imperiously. "To watch your end. To see you fail. After that ... I may have need of a queen.

"Here you are, at the end. Alone. A pity they left you here to fail." I kept backing up, and he kept following me. "I would like to see Tesla's face when this engine fulfills its purpose, and my soul is sealed to this body, and this domain. We are at the beginning of something wonderful, you and I. I would have loved an audience."

My back came up against the railing. Behind me there was nothing but the open sky, and a deadly drop. I glanced over my shoulder, then swallowed and set my shield. No turning back now. When I looked back, he was grinning hideously, as though he was feeding on my terror. It was a healthy feast, I assure you.

"Nowhere else to run, Sir John. What are you going to do?"

"I have one question," I said. "Before you kill me."

"Why not?" he assented. "What would you know before I extinguish your pitiful life?"

"Is that important?" I asked, pointing over his shoulder.

Bethany crouched next to the pylon. In the time it had taken him to drive me across the platform, she had pried open the panel and lifted the metal tube from its couch. As we watched, she slipped the glass vial from its niche. When she saw us looking at her, Bee smiled and lifted the glowing green tube over her head.

"Don't want me to drop it, do you?" she asked.

"DON'T!" Lumiere and I shouted simultaneously. When Bee gave me a funny look, I continued. "Souls, Bee! We're going to need those!"

She scowled at me, but instead of smashing the vial to the ground, she slipped it into her haversack and gave Lumiere a jaunty salute. "Be seeing you, Boney!"

As soon as the vial left the pylon, the mists closed in around us, and the constellation of stars emanating from the spinning generators flickered and went out. Though I could see flickers of flames through the cloudbank, the shoreline disappeared.

"Gah!" Lumiere whirled away from me, chasing after Bethany with his staff outstretched.

Before she got halfway to the ladder down, he sent a bolt of blue light after her. She dodged two of them, shifting into the shadows to stutter-jump across the platform. But her third jump failed, and she was left sprinting for the exit in a very mundane manner. The lich slashed at the air, and a portal opened in front of him. He disappeared, to reappear at the top of the ladder. Bee skidded to a halt before she slid into him.

He reached toward her with a finger that glowed with necromantic power. "Two queens are better than one!"

"You're not my type!" She spun blades out of her cloak, throwing half a dozen with the flick of her wrist. They bounced harmlessly off his metal body, but distracted him enough for her to run back toward me. "What's the next step in this plan of yours, John?"

"Persist," I said as I marched past her.

"I'm out of magic!" she shouted.

"Then improvise!" I answered. The lich charged toward me, glowing hand outstretched. "You're going to have to go through me, Lightpole!"

"Through all of us," Tembo said as he and the Saint clambered out of the ladder shaft. Lumiere glanced at them dismissively, until a gesture from Tembo's hand jerked the vial out of Bethany's satchel, drawing it to the big mage's open palm. Lumiere swung at it, but Matthew struck him with the bristled flange of his mace.

"You have a weapon?" I asked, incredulous.

"It's mostly decorative," Matthew said. "It's supposed to have this censer thing in the middle, but I always forget to light it. Pretty cool effect, really, and in the right light it—"

"Enough!" Lumiere shouted. He lifted his staff overhead. Green lighting coursed along the metal spars of the tower, joined by bolts of flickering light from the surrounding storm. "All Flesh Dies!"

Slamming the staff into the ground, Lumiere conjured a wave of coruscating black energy that washed across the platform. Matthew was the closest, and the first to fall.

The Saint's face turned as white as bleached bones. The mace tumbled from his quivering fingers to bounce off the floor. It was quickly joined by his trembling form. The wave washed over him, turning him the color of mist about to melt before the sun. Tembo was next. There was a flicker of the mage's other form, the massive elephantine giant that stalked Tembo's domain, but as the spell hit him, Tembo crumpled. Thankfully, only his arm went over the edge of the edge of the shaft, to dangle limply against the ladder's iron rungs. The vial rolled from his twitching fingers, to rest against the twisted mask of Tembo's horrified face.

Bethany tried to outrun it, but without her magic, she was little more than quick. Not quick enough to outpace the inevitability of death, and all the terror it contained. Her bright face turned the color of ash, and tears filled her eyes as she fell. All she could do was whimper as she bounced off the floor.

The wave rushed forward, straight at me. This was it. This was the moment, sink or swim, fall or fly. I ground my heels into the platform and braced myself.

It was so much worse than I was expecting. Pure terror gripped me. My legs went limp, and an endless chasm opened in my heart. My soul, my flesh, everything I knew and cared about, fell into that vast and bottomless pit of despair, to be swallowed whole by hopelessness. I felt my knees hit the platform, and the sword slip from my numb fingers. In my head, I was back at the most hopeless moments in my life. The rejection that had plagued me through my youth, the mockery of a hundred bullies, the dismissive glare of my mother and the cold indifference of a father who knew more about sports than his own son. Burying my first dog, and my second, then my grandmother, and a close friend whose drunk brother sent them both over an embankment before I was old enough to understand such a loss. The realization that this is what waited for all of us. Loneliness at the moment of death, and the empty grave. My blood turned to ice, my lungs emptied in a long, jagged sob, and my heart froze in place. Fear held me in place.

Lumiere strolled casually to Tembo's limp body and, stooping, picked up the pulsing green soul vial. He gave the big mage a desultory kick, then returned to the pylon. I could have sworn he was humming to himself.

But fear is nothing but the knife you hold against your own neck.

My life had been ruled by fear. It had crushed me, ruined me, driven me to darkness. Until, one day, I chose to face those fears. The day I joined Knight Watch. The day I became the only kind of hero I understood.

The man who falls down, and stands back up. Fear knocked me down.

I stood back up.

CHAPTER THIRTY-SIX

The long, deep tendrils of fear slowly fell loose from my soul. The emptiness in my chest, like the prickly hollow heart of a geode, gradually filled with new blood, and new hope. Hope, and something more. With a ragged grin that split my face like a bloody wound, I stood and faced the Iron Lich.

"There's something you should know about me," I said. "Fear is nothing to me. Fear feeds me. Fear drives me."

Lumiere whirled around, more surprised than afraid. He gave my shivering form a perfunctory glance, then checked the rest of Knight Watch. When he saw that the others remained in their fear-induced comas, the Iron Lich visibly relaxed.

"You would have been better off staying down," he said. "There's no shame in it. Your friends have the right idea."

Paralysis stiffened my legs, but I dragged them forward, lurching toward the lich. He watched me for a couple halting steps, then finished with the vial. It clicked securely into place, but the pylon refused to lower into the floor. Bee must have broken something. Frustrated, Lumiere summoned his staff anew. The bolt of lightning that brought it to his hand wasn't as bright, and the crack of thunder barely shattered my consciousness. Of course, that might have been the blood hammering in my head, or the staccato detonation of adrenaline turning my heart into a snare drum. I leaned down to pick up my sword, and nearly toppled forward. Was going to have to take this slow while my body recovered.

Besides, I needed to give my domain time to take effect. The hollow place in my bones, aching for magical energy, was slowly filling. But I wasn't there yet.

"Aren't you curious how I managed it?" I asked. "Your greatest power, an aura of supernatural fear, and I brushed it off like water off wax."

"Ah, I'm sort of new to this undead wizard role. But I like it. All this time I spent tinkering with engines and poring through schematics. All the pointless math! When I could have just pointed and—" Lumiere swept his staff toward me. "Boom!"

A clap of thunder rolled out from Lumiere's gnarled staff. The platform shook as a wave of power traveled toward me. I got the shield up just as it reached me. The force emptied my lungs and squeezed down on my head. It forced me back. I skidded backward, chain boots throwing sparks off the metal floor, but somehow I managed to stay upright. When I lowered the shield, Lumiere was still strolling toward me.

"I'm glad you're finally seeing the appeal," I said, spitting blood. "Let me show you some of my tricks."

Rushing toward him, I gathered magic into my stride, drawing in the inertia of a battering ram. My boots shook the ground. Even his bleached bone face managed to register shock as I barreled into him with my shield.

The impact sent him flying. Staff and lich went in opposite directions. Lumiere landed in a heap at the base of the pylon. The staff skittered to the shaft at the center of the platform. I rushed toward it.

"I'm guessing this is pretty important to your whole Evil Mage motif," I said, and kicked the staff into the open shaft. It spun twice, banged off the ladder, then got caught in the spinning jaws of the open gears and exploded. "Oh, man. That must suck for you."

"Impudent fool! My power is greater than mere trinkets." He stood. "I don't know how you overcame my curse, but your parlor tricks will do you no good against the full strength of this tower!"

"I tried to explain it, but you were yammering on about how much you hated math." I stalked toward him, sword and shield held carelessly at my side. "My domain is fear. It's literally the thing that connects me to my mythic self." To prove my point, I summoned the armor that was lying discarded at the bottom of the ladder. Helm and pauldrons, spaulders, gauntlets . . . the whole kit appeared, first as barely sketched lines of light, and then as steel and leather and brass.

The armor settled comfortably on my shoulders. "You had to open the door. But once it was open, I was home."

"It will take more than one brave knight to defeat me," the lich growled. He pressed his palms together, then spoke a shattered word. Light flared between his fingers. As he pulled his hands apart, a blade of shadow and silver formed between them. Gripping the blade in his right hand, Lumiere waved at me dismissively. "Come and die, mortal!"

"I'm getting there, hang on." The ache in my legs and heart was calming down. The armor trick, while impressive, drained a lot of my power. The mists beyond the railing were starting to clear again, and the shoreline flared into bright relief. Dark wings flashed through the corner of my vision. Even with the pylon disabled, the Tour d'Elysee was drawing the lich's domain into the Gestalt. I had to hurry. "Okay. Let's do this."

Lumiere lunged at me, chopping down with the mystical blade. The leading edge of his weapon was pale silvery blue, the color of the moon reflecting off a still pond. It was as sharp as a cold wind, though, despite its insubstantial form. I caught the swing with my buckler, but his edge bit into the steel, digging a gouge down the face of the boss. I stabbed from behind the safety of cover and was rewarded with a shriek of pain. But Lumiere's sword was light, and he was fast. The pressure on my shield disappeared just as something bright and hard hit my forehead, dimpling steel and knocking my visor off its hinges. I stumbled back, and he pressed.

"Death is inevitable. It can be merciful, or it can be cruel," Lumiere said, sending wide, slicing cuts arcing at me. "I have chosen cruelty for you."

"Thanks," I stammered. "But I'll have to pass."

I caught his next strike with the hilt of my sword. The eldritch blade cut into the brass of the guard, and I twisted. It wasn't enough to disarm him, but Lumiere twisted awkwardly to maintain his grip. Setting my shield against his chest, I knocked him off balance. He managed to hook his free arm around my legs as he went down, taking me tumbling with him to the floor. We both sprawled, scrambling over each other to get up.

One icy hand closed around my ankle. I looked down to see that Lumiere was gathering power into his fingers, chanting some profane dirge under his breath. I put my knee into his chin, clapping his mouth shut, then stomped down once, twice, a third time. Bone cracked under my boot, and a satisfying green light poured out. Lumiere shrieked and let me go. I rolled to my feet. My shield was gone, but Chesa's pair of sickle blades lay nearby. I picked them up and gave them a twirl.

The lich rose. A glimmering crack ran the length of his face, bisecting one eye and leaking a sickly, green glow. He held one hand to the side of his head. When he finally looked up at me, I laughed.

"Immortality ain't all it's cracked up to be, is it?" I asked. "Get it? Cracked? Because your face is—"

With a scream that rattled the very steel of the tower, Claude Lumiere threw himself at me. I swung one sickle blade at him, while catching his fist in the curved belly of the other. He ignored both, letting the elven steel cut deep gouges in his unflesh as he barreled into my chest. My breastplate wrinkled, and I rolled back with the force of the blow. He clawed at my face and neck. Blood poured out of jagged cuts along my cheeks. I forced both blades between us, then poured a little bit of my shielding magic into them. It was enough to drive him back, but just as quickly as he retreated, the hulking mass of the Iron Lich rebounded. Pearlescent light danced off the face of my makeshift shield as he battered at me with both fists. Each blow drove me back, one step, three, until I was skidding and stumbling backward.

"You! Are an annoying! Little! Shit!" He punctuated each of these pronouncements with a double-fisted crash. My bones turned to jelly under the assault. Chesa's blades shattered, and I was left grappling with the undead wizard with my bare hands and the desperation of the living when faced with certain death. Eventually he got past my defenses and landed an open-palm strike on my head. My helm flew off, and my skull rang like a bell. I spun around, dizzily fleeing, stumbling, weaving across the open platform like a drunk man. I eventually came down against the pylon. Using it to steady myself, I turned to face the Iron Lich.

"Have you considered a career in marketing?" I asked through blood-spattered teeth. "You make one helluva pitch."

"Joking until the end," Lumiere said. He stalked toward me, chest thrown forward, balled fists straining at his waist. "I would admire that, if I didn't hate you so much."

"I do what I can." I dragged myself upright, resting my cheek against the cool glass of the soul vial. "Sorry, folks. Desperate times."

Before the lich could move, I drew my dagger and slammed the heavy brass pommel into the vial. It took two strong blows, but finally a crack formed along the top. With a sharp hiss, souls began to escape the container.

The shriek came from behind me. I didn't expect that. But there was a thunder of leathery wings, and then I was thrown roughly aside. I hit the deck and bounced, then rolled over to face the lich. There was someone else on the platform. Huddled over the still leaking pylon, the crimson-and-white form of Jakub Everlasting had his back turned to me. There was a flash of light as he pressed his hand against the glass. The hissing stopped. I was still working my way to my feet when the vampire whirled on me.

"Zoria was right. We never should have trusted you!" he yelled. "My kith are in there! I can hear them screaming, deep in the bowels of that glass. You could have destroyed them once and for all!"

"You're a work of art, Sir John," Lumiere purred. "Making enemies at every step of your path. What were you thinking?"

"That someone might want to have a word with you," I said. "I think the three of you have some unfinished business."

"Three of us?" Lumiere cocked his skull at me in confusion. "What—"

A section of metal girder tore free from the floor and flew across the platform. It smashed into Lumiere, throwing him backward. More bits of torquing metal bent up, wrapping themselves around Lumiere's arms and legs. With each thrashing blow, more and more of the tower turned against their master.

"Hello, my dear." Cecilia's flickering green figure, clothed only in scraps of diaphanous cloth that stretched tight over her emaciated body, floated over her husband. "I have a few questions about where you think this relationship might be going."

"Bitch!" Lumiere howled. He threw the snaring metal away, but each discarded panel or pipe was quickly replaced with two more. The tower groaned as the furious poltergeist tore it apart.

"You should be going." It was Evelyn who spoke this time. In the afterlife, she was a young girl, small boned with gawky, outsized joints, and a face like a doll. She carried a bloody stake in one hand.

"Our hold on this world is slipping. But we will finish this before we go."

"I'll take the assist." The rest of Knight Watch was slowly coming to their senses, shaking off the paralyzing fear that had gripped them. "Couldn't have done it without you. Though, to be fair, you're kind of the cause of all this."

"Your work is not done," Evelyn whispered. Her figure was fading fast, and her voice was a bare tickle in the back of my brain. "Where we first met. Hidden. You must . . ." She disappeared, flickered back into view, then disappeared again. Only the voice remained. "Destroy it, or this means nothing."

"What? What do you mean? Your house?" I racked my brains. "That place is ashes and dirt, lady. What are you talking about?"

"Among the clouds . . . quickly . . ." She cut off with a sharp gasp, then there was a ghostly whistle, high pitched, cutting through the air like lightning.

Red eyes appeared in the shadows. The hellhounds bounded out of cinder-curling gates, their scaly backs rippling with muscle as they ran at Lumiere, slavering jaws gaping wide. Lumiere saw them coming, and had the decency to scream in terror.

"I've got it!" I shouted. Jakub stared at me in confusion. I grabbed Tembo, pulling him upright. He was unsteady on his feet, but I shook him hard. "Tem! We need a portal!"

"Yes, it would appear that retreat is in order," he said dreamily and began to cast. "I can get us back to shore, and then—"

"No," I said, grabbing his hand. "We're going somewhere else."

CHAPTER THIRTY-SEVEN

The smell of freshly baked bread wafted through the portal in the moments before we stepped through. The bakery looked different in the light. An orderly queue of patrons waited their turn at the counter, while pairs of faux-Parisians sipped complicated coffees and nibbled delicate baked goods at a collection of tables that lined the street. We came out on the sidewalk across the street, Tembo leading the way with his dimension-altering staff. Bee and I set up a perimeter, then signaled the all clear. Saint Matthew and Chesa were the last ones through the portal before it closed.

"Are you sure about this?" Chesa asked.

"One hundred percent," I answered, though my actual certainty hovered around the seventy percent mark. "Evelyn said the cage was in the sky, where we first met."

"So that would be her house, right?" Chesa looked around the street uncertainly. "Shouldn't we be there?"

"My first thought, too. But, first of all, that place burned down. Secondly, Evelyn told me that was wrong."

"And you're trusting her?" Bee asked. "The lady who tried to kill us? That's what you're going with?"

"I am," I said. "The soul cage is here. I'm sure of it."

"That's some big Grace energy," Matthew said, patting his belly. "I love it. Hope it doesn't get us all killed. Do I smell donuts?"

"I thought the tower was the soul cage," Chesa said. We were crossing the street, much to the startled concern of the café dwellers at their tables. "Lumiere kept going on and on about it."

"Yes. I mean, partially. That's where he kept most of his soul, and

285

where he used the souls that Evelyn had gathered to complete his transformation into the Iron Lich." We reached the curb in front of the bakery. The patrons outside scattered, abandoning their steaming cups of coffee and their croissants mid-nibble. The commotion was drawing the attention of the folks inside. "But we're all forgetting the central concept of a lich. You can't just kill them."

"Because they've got their soul on backup," Chesa said. "How did I miss that?"

"We've had a lot going on." I stopped in front of the door. Inside, Pierre came out of the kitchens with a look of confusion on his face. When he spotted us through the window, he dropped his tray of madeleines and began running in tiny circles. "Trust me on this. I can explain later."

"I'm in," Bethany said.

"You bet," Matthew answered. The others smiled or nodded, preparing their weapons. Chesa was the last to respond.

"Okay, John. I trust you."

"Right." I drew my sword, then shouldered my way through the door. The tiny bell tinkled as I entered the patisserie. The crowd, still waiting in line, stared at us in disbelief.

"Apologies, folks," I said. "This is about to get weird."

One of the things that marked me in my pre-Knight Watch life was that technology tended to break around me. It was inconvenient at times. My car was always breaking down, my phone dropped calls and occasionally turned into a deck of cards, computers bricked in my presence. Light bulbs dimmed and flickered as I passed. But once I assumed the mantle of the Unreal, it became a much bigger deal. Not only could I ruin technology by my presence, but I had to actively avoid artifacts of the modern world to maintain my mythic identity and powers. That meant a lot of boiled meat, and no books that hadn't been copied by hand, usually with illuminations in the margins. As the Eccentrics found out, even the Gestalt was vulnerable to my presence. And when you get a whole group of technology-averse cosplayers in the same room, the effect can be dangerous.

If those cosplayers start manifesting magical powers, it's only a matter of time before the Unreal takes over. As these lovely faux-Parisians were about to find out.

Folding the enarme straps firmly around my wrist, I transformed my shield from targe into wall shield, then planted it into the black-and-white tiles of the floor with a crash. Patrons scurried away, cursing in French and English and Martian. With a twirl of my sword, I invoked a barrier of shimmering light that spread out from my shield in either direction, then washed forward like a wave, upsetting tables and driving the remaining bakery-goers against the far wall.

Pierre emerged from behind the counter, armed with a rolling pin.

"Non! Ce n'est pas bien! Vous devez tous partir! Immediatement! Je ne vais pas—"

"Okay, okay, you're kind of straining Mademoiselle Couturier's lessons, Pete!" I shouted over the general din of confusion and outrage. "This will only take a second. Everyone, do a trick!"

Tembo started the ball rolling. Literally. He produced a marble-sized orb of swirling light in his palm. When he blew on it, it rolled across the floor, getting larger and larger until it struck the far wall, exploding into a cacophony of colored streamers, confetti, and tooting horns. I gave him an odd look.

"Birthday trick," he said with a shrug. "I figured it was better than fireball, given the circumstances."

"Unusual restraint from the mage," Bee said. She hopped over the shimmer barrier of my shield, then started jumping from shadow to shadow, her form rippling into insubstantiality with each leap. The sound of her passage was like satin tearing.

"Come on," I said, turning to the others. "It's going to take everyone."

The rest of the team got involved. Saint Matthew glowed brighter and brighter, until the light coming off of him was like lightning in the shape of a soccer dad. Chesa's bow twanged like a harp as she sent flights of arrows into progressively smaller targets, bouncing arrows off walls and glassware. The small group of Gestalt citizens huddled in the back of the shop was properly freaked out by now. Pierre squatted under one of the tables, hands over his head, shivering. The effort was quickly depleting my magical reserves. I could feel the power draining from my bones like sand running out of a broken clock.

The change happened suddenly. A fog bank rolled down the street outside, obscuring the surrounding buildings. In the gloom, streetlamps turned on, devolving from electricity to gas to torches in a matter of heartbeats. The baked goods filling the display cases boiled and seethed, delicate pastries frothing into inchoate masses, croissants curling in on themselves like pill bugs, until nothing remained but pancakes. Stacks and stacks of doughy, damp, flavorless pancakes.

"Oh, thank Heaven," Matthew said. He cut his light, then leaned over and rested his hands on his thighs. A puff of golden mist came out of his mouth when he spoke. "I don't think I could have kept that up much longer."

"I'm pretty sure you've given me a suntan on that side of my body," Bee said, peeling back the collar of her leather armor. There was a sharp line of lobster-red skin next to pale white. "Ugh."

Pierre cried out in distress. The diminutive baker threw himself at the nearest case, pulling open the top and sinking his hands into a messy stack of pancakes. Bringing the dough to his mouth, he licked the top of one of the cakes, then burst into tears.

"Why, monsieur? Why would you do this? C'est un crime contre le pain!"

"I'm sorry for your pain, Pierre. But this had to be done," I said, then looked up at the ceiling. "There. Do you see it?"

Last time we were here, the ceiling had caught my attention. It was a beautiful painting, comparable to the Sistine Chapel or the video scoreboard at the Cowboys' stadium in Arlington. Rosy-cheeked cherubs frolicked around gilt roses, and a sky of impossible clouds embraced a pair of figures at the center. There was a robed woman, holding a silver laurel over her head. She was standing on an iron platform, under which a crowd of skeletons was slowly being crushed.

"Immortality conquering Death," Tembo said. "Like in the Palais."

"It's different in the Gestalt. Something about apples and barely clothed nymphs. But once you get into the Unreal..." I nodded, looking around. "We're going to need a ladder or something."

"My apologies to the proprietor," Tembo said, then sent a bolt of lightning into the ceiling. The crack and shatter of plaster and plasma deafened me. Chunks of ceiling cascaded down, along with dust, lathing, and flakes of gilt. Chesa and Bee both sheltered under my shield, which I had reflexively lifted overhead as Tembo gestured upward.

Once the dust settled, we were left staring at the debris. It was not all plaster and wood. An iron cage lay in the middle of the floor. The bars were etched with runes, and capped with brass and other alchemical elements. There was no door in the cage. But inside, bound in copper wire, was a tiny doll, with button eyes, a scrap of real hair, and a disturbing resemblance to tanned human skin. A bright red line dimpled the doll's face, cutting across one of the eyes.

"Well, that's disturbing," I said. Bethany leaned down and poked at the doll through the bars with her dagger.

"So, what, we're supposed to destroy this somehow?" she asked.

"Seems like it." I gave the cage a desultory kick. "Tem, can you get that thing open? Metal to mud, or something?"

"My reservoirs are empty, Sir John," Tembo said. "As I suspect is true for most of us. We will need to find a mundane solution to the problem."

"I could pick the lock, if there was one," Bethany said. "There's not even a door."

"Right. Brute force." I stood up, dusting my hands together. "Let's see if there's a hammer in the back. Or a pry bar. We should be able to—"

The little brass bell on the door tinkled again. The Iron Lich stepped into the bakery. He looked rough. Deep gouges covered his once pristine carapace, and the crack I'd put in his skull had spread to his jaw, leaving his mouth hanging loose on one side. His left leg looked like a candle that had been left out in the sun for too long, and every time he moved there was a loud clattering sound deep in his chest. But he was carrying a length of iron trestle that was sticky with blood, and he looked ready to use it. The few remaining customers screamed in terror and ran through the kitchens. Even Pierre, still mourning the loss of his croissants, had the presence of mind to flee.

"Unhand the doll," Lumiere growled. "And then everyone gets hurt."

"I think you've got that backward?" I said, putting myself between the team and the lich. "Aren't you supposed to offer to spare us if we hand you your weird, creepy soul-doll thing?"

"My offer stands," he said, then tried to take my head off with the iron beam.

I tripped as I backpedaled out of range of the swing. He limped forward, dragging the twisted remnant of his left leg behind him. Lifting the beam in both hands, he prepared to smash my face into the back of my skull.

Best I could do was scramble closer so I was inside his reach. The cudgel came down, smashing plaster and cracking the floor even worse. Both his elbows went into my shoulders. At least it spared my noggin, but I was forced to sit back down hard and fast. Tembo gestured toward the lich, and there was a flicker of light around his fingers, but nothing materialized. The big mage was still shaking his hand when Lumiere kicked me to the side.

"Don't let him get the cage!" I shouted as I rolled against the display case. Bee obliged, vaulting over a broken table to scoop up the doll and its container. Lumiere roared and threw his beam at her like a javelin. It missed her, but the resulting explosion of plaster and paneling sliced her up pretty bad. She hit the ground hard, and the cage bounced away. Chesa went for it, but Lumiere grabbed her by her braids and tossed her against the wall.

"You think you can come into my world and do whatever you want?" Lumiere's booming voice echoed through the bakery like a land mine. "You have ruined my family, my plans, and now my soul." His steel fingers closed on the cage. Holding it up, he smashed Tembo in the face, then backhanded Matthew. Both went down. "The only way out of this is death. For all of you!"

"Pass!" I shouted. He rotated slowly toward me, the now bloody cage overhead. "You're going to have to give me that doll, Claude. Before I get serious."

He looked slowly around the bakery. The rest of the team was down. The room was in ruins. The civilians were gone. There was nothing but destruction and waste.

"Serious how? Seriously funny?" he asked.

"Worse." I kicked my sword into my hand, gripping it in both hands as I took the best guard I could without a shield. "Seriously swordy."

"That's the dumbest thing I've ever—"

I charged forward, shuffling my feet through the wreckage to keep from tripping. Startled, Lumiere swung at me with the cage, but his footing was terrible and he overextended, stumbling slightly to his left. The tip of my sword rattled between the bars, piercing the doll inside. Lumiere gasped, grabbing at his chest. I didn't wait, driving the sword all the way forward until my hilt cracked against the iron cage. Then I rotated on my right foot, driving my shoulder into his chest with the full weight of my body. Which, admittedly, isn't that much, but it was enough to get him to drop the cage.

Lumiere grabbed at me as I pushed away from him. Whatever pain he felt was masked by the sheer terror in his voice. "Wait, I can save you!" he shouted as I ran past the counter. "Immortality! Think of it! No end to life!"

"I'd rather die a hero than live a monster." I hit the kitchen door at a full sprint. Just as I'd hoped, the whole patisserie had descended into the Unreal. A broad hearth burned where the stoves used to be, with a roaring fire in its heart. I skidded to a halt and launched the cage off my sword and into the flames.

Lumiere's soul burned like a flare. Spears of hot white flame jetted out of the doll's head and hands, and then the whole effigy burst open. A fiery heart of pure white light roared, flickering into green and coruscating waves of blue and black. The iron cage melted like wax, sealing the blacked outline of the doll into the floor of the hearth. Behind me, Lumiere's shrieks filled the world.

The Iron Lich burned from the inside out. The light erupted between his joints. Flames licked the metal plates of his chest, and crawled between the gaps in his hand. The crack in his skull bubbled with molten iron, which fell in hissing, spattering drops to the ground. He went to his knees, falling apart even as he reached toward me, hands clenching as though he meant to strangle me with his last breath. But there was no breath. Claude Lumiere was long dead. This mockery of a life drained out of him, burning away in a plume of noxious smoke and the screams of a man who clung to life so hard he crushed everything in it that might have mattered.

He toppled forward and came apart. Inside that frame of iron and bone and ivory, there was nothing that looked like a man. Only ashes, and the brittle machinery of science.

CHAPTER THIRTY-EIGHT

Jakub stared at me like I was an unloved cat, returning a previously buried mouse, complete with maggots. We were sitting in a quiet café on the outskirts of Paris. Actual Paris, not the faux version that bubbled throughout the Gestalt, or the gothic landscape that meant so much to the Unreal. Tesla had managed to deliver the invitation and arrange the meeting. I didn't ask how.

The lord of the vampires sat primly on his chair, hands folded in his lap. To a mundane viewer, he might look like an overdressed banker, or an almost-familiar actor, or maybe just a goth on graduation day. Judging by the few disinterested glances that we drew, no one else saw his pointed teeth, or the thornlike tips of his claws, or the feral set of his eyes. The mundane world was doing a good job of covering up the monster, at least for now. As long as he didn't try to tear my head off and bathe in my vital fluids.

"Thanks for showing up," I said. "I wasn't sure Nik was going to be able to find you."

"Ever since you gave them our address, the Eccentrics have been dropping by like a mob of angry peasants," he answered. "We have found other accommodations, but Zofia haunts the old place."

"So what happened at the tower?" I asked, taking a sip of my coffee. A spike of pain went through the back of my throat, deep into my skull. "SO. SWEET," I gasped.

"It turns out, Claude Lumiere was more than a match for us. Hardly surprising, given his hand in the creation of the Slayer archetype. But humiliating, nonetheless." He took the coffee cup from my shaking hand, then carefully poured the contents into a nearby plant. "I take it you fared better."

"Every Achilles has his heel. There was a lot more Vodun in his mythos than I expected, to be honest. But we got it done. And your family? ZeeZee? Aleks?"

"Zoria is well. Alekzander is watching from across the street. He is looking for an excuse to come over here and pummel you."

I glanced out the window and saw the hulking vampire, trying to appear innocuous behind the pages of a copy of *Le Monde*. "I'm sorry you've been driven from your home," I said carefully. The next part was delicate. "Were you able to save the others?"

"You know very well that I wasn't," Jakub said stiffly. "The bodies, certainly, but Lumiere's machine—"

"Great!" I rummaged around in my haversack, then produced a wooden rack of a dozen glass vials. Viscous green liquid filled each one. "I think we got them all."

"What is this supposed to be?" he asked primly.

"The souls. I figured you'd want them back. Tembo extracted them from the primary concoction. We're working on parsing out the rest, but there are so many." I sat back in my chair, reaching for the cup before remembering that it was empty. "Anyway. I hope you're able to do something with them."

Jakub looked fragile. He reached out for the rack and picked it up, his taloned hands clicking against the glass. His hand shook a little.

"You aren't going to cry, are you?" I asked.

"There is no water in my body," he said simply. "Thank you. I did not know what to expect from this meeting, after so many years, and such ... violence ... between our people."

"That was different people. And as we've both learned, the Lumieres manufactured most of that drama." My skin was beginning to crawl with all the mundanity, even in ancient and blessed Paris. I folded my napkin on the table and stood up. "Good luck. We won't be bothering you. And if you ever need anything, you know where to find us."

Jakub stood suddenly and, to my great terror, hugged me. I wasn't wearing my armor, because even for Paris that seemed a little extreme, so the strength of his grip crushed the air out of my lungs and made my bones creak. I coughed for mercy into his ear. When he released me, he took a step back.

"You have my thanks, Sir John of Rast," he said solemnly.

"Nothing to it." I left him there with his family, feeling pretty good about myself.

Hopefully, nothing terrible would come from releasing vampires back into the world. Right?

Right?